CATCHING DARK

Caroline Henry Series Book 2

DB Jacobson

The characters and events portrayed in this book are fictitious. Any similarity to real persons, living or dead, is coincidental and not intended by the author.

ISBN-13: 9781736299531
ISBN-10: 1477123456

Cover design by: DB Jacobson
Library of Congress Control Number: 2018675309
Printed in the United States of America

To my boys and their endless inspiration to keep going.

CONTENTS

Chapter 1

February 14

"I had a dream I killed someone."

Nina Williams, my psychologist, was just settling into her chair. She adjusted her skirt under her thigh, and gave me a curt smile, "more nocturnal crime-fighting?"

No, it really happened, it's just easier to describe my propensity to get myself involved in the underworld of seedy characters as dreams to Nina.

I spent my ample time and acquired skills to investigate cold cases, rape, murder, and, in general, violence against women. In an unofficial capacity of course; however, I did produce results that eluded the authorities. All anonymously. To the outside world, I'm just a short woman, barely passing 5'2" with red hair and a small successful business in Pasadena.

This particular "dream" all happened unconventionally. I normally get my cases through my sister, Lauren, a social worker at Cedar Sinai dealing with domestic violence and rape survivors. This particular time, it fell in my lap. Or maybe, more accurately, it skidded across the road to avoid a peacock.

In my little town of Glendora, there is a wild flock of peacocks that roam the streets. I had taken my nephews, Lauren's two boys, to watch them peck across town. We had just met with the male peacock, a full plume of blue and green tail feathers on full display when a woman swerved onto the curb to avoid said peacock. The flock scattered and she looked harried and confused. I made sure she was okay and took the boy's home. Of course, they were disappointed that they did not get more time watching the peacocks, so I promised to get them their favorite treat, donuts.

I saw the woman, again, behind me in line to get donuts. As I was walking back with my nephew's sugary treats, I noticed a nail was sticking out of her tire. I waited to tell her about it. God forbid I ignore it and she ended up plastered on the side of the 210 freeway. I gave her my mechanics info, let her drop my name, and continued on my merry way.

An hour later, I saw her again, this time at the park I had taken my nephews so my sister and her husband could have some *alone time*. She recognized me immediately, thanked me, and started peppering questions at me. I don't know whether it was the insane determined look in her eye or her pathetic attempts to look casual about the questions, or maybe it was because I had nothing else to do, but I decided to help her. She was looking for her missing friend and thought maybe he was hiding out at one of the sparring clubs within the LA area. I am familiar with the sparring clubs, as I have continued my education in self-defense. It took several days for her to even tell me her missing friend's name, Tadashi Becken. Beck, as my new friend Chris, called him.

Looking for Beck was like trying to make sense out of a labyrinth. I had acquired my research skills when I married a military policeman, John Henry, who specialized in cybersecurity. He taught me how to procure information in a nontraditional, possibly nonlegal, way. He taught me how to investigate cold cases in a way that allowed me to ghost in the background undetected. He taught me everything I needed to know, and then he died. I was devastated but leaned into my skills to cope with the loss. I honed these skills after countless solved cold cases. I used my sharp expertise to find Beck.

Only Beck was not missing; he was hiding from some very dangerous people. He was involved in a large human trafficking ring. At the time, I was convinced he was perpetuating the ring's success. It was a few chance encounters for him to introduce himself to me. I kept our brief meetings a secret from Chris after I got the sense from Beck that he did not *want*

Chris to look for him. I even provided a safe place for him to sleep and have a night off of the lam.

From the moment I knew he was good; I knew I was in trouble. He was attractive and capable. I had not wanted a man the way that I wanted Beck to want me since my husband had perished. Beck was a danger to my own self-preservation, and he was indifferent to me. I still cringe when I think about kissing him and him not reciprocating.

After a misadventure into Beck's home, which ended up getting Chris taken as ransom for Beck, it left me in a tough spot. I couldn't leave her fate in the hands of trafficking gangsters, but I also unwillingly cared for the man they wanted in exchange for her and did not want anything to happen to him either. I followed her abductors hoping to remove her from their care with limited involvement. I called Chris's fiancé, a LAPD detective, and had him trace the GPS of the phone for back-up. I also called Beck, knowing he would need to know that Chris was in danger.

All hell broke loose when Beck showed up. I ended up dropping from the rafters to disarm Jose Garcia, a gangster kingpin. A fight ensued. The fight included me stabbing Jose Garcia in the leg, leaving him to bleed out. We rescued 6 trafficking victims and Chris that night. Beck fell back into the shadows before police secured the property. It was my guilt about not feeling guilty from killing Garcia that led me to my "dream" emanation.

I smiled up at Nina, "yeah, nocturnal crime-fighting." I nodded in agreement. "When I woke up, I did not feel bad about killing him. Shouldn't I feel some kind of remorse even if I just dreamed it?" I pinched the pad of my thumb's palm.

"Do you believe your actions were justifiable?" Nina was looking down at me, over the top of her reading glasses.

Abso-fucking-lutely, he was going to kill me if I had not killed him. He had the advantage. He had thrown me to the ground, standing over me preparing to send a fatal blow to my head. Add this to the fact that he was trafficking women, peddling drugs, and all-around a terrible human being. "Yes."

"Perhaps you feel like you should feel remorseful because of your past." She was leaning forward twirling her readers between her fingers.

"What past?" I was confused. She narrowed her eyes at me and sat her glasses down on the table next to her.

"Perhaps you feel like you should feel guilty because you have not processed the traumas of your childhood."

I shook my head, "That still does not make sense. Why should I feel guilty about my childhood?" I was beginning to feel obstinate, a little pissy.

"You survived trauma where others did not." She took a sip of her coffee and continued, "You vowed to protect your family at the tender age of fourteen. I feel you may be harboring guilt for not being able to protect Lauren."

Well, that opened up pandora's box.

Lauren and I were are friends and sisters, she is a year and a half older. We had been through hell together and lived to talk about it. We all internalize trauma differently. Lauren forgave and continued to live a life of happy ignorance. I doubt she forgot; she just did not want her past to poison her future. It was her mantra that she had shared with me countless times. I held onto the rage in the quiet recesses of my mind, never fully trusting, never fully allowing myself to be vulnerable.

We were a part of six kids: Lyle James, Lauren Nicole, me, Thomas Corbin, Annie Ruth, and Jennifer Lynn Taylor. If my mom was not pregnant, she was drunk. Before she finally held onto her sobriety, she could be classified as a functional alcoholic. From the outside, she looked sober. However, we always knew when mom was on a bender. She would lock herself away in her room, only coming out when we were at school. We would find her passed out on the couch, sitting up, covered in her own vomit. I guess she was cognizant enough to know that if she was going to get shit-faced, it was best to not drown in her puke.

Outside of her benders, she was sweet and caring. She would read us a story every night before bed. Fresh cookies would greet us when we got home from school. Clean house, hot dinners, folded laundry were the norm, when she was on the wagon. Unfortunately, she only stayed on the wagon for about a week at a time.

Our dad was a long-haul trucker. He suffered from bipolar disorder. We never knew who we would get when he would come home, Jeckle or Hyde.

Some weekends, he would be the best dad. Trips to amusement parks, ice cream for breakfast, he would entertain and play with us for hours. His highs were so high. But his lows consisted of beating our mom to a bloody pulp. If he knocked her out before his anger had abated, he would take turns beating Lyle, Lauren, or me.

Lyle was the oldest. I characterize Lyle in two ways, pre-concussion and post-concussion. Pre-concussion Lyle was the best brother. He would help Lauren and I with the other siblings while dad was away, and mom was indisposed. When I was eleven, Lyle had experienced a severe concussion from a football accident. After that, his personality changed. He was no longer the caring doting brother that assisted in the parental duties that we split between the siblings.

When my dad was away, Lyle was evil. I would wake up to Lyle holding a knife to my throat. When mom had locked herself away, and Lauren and I had tucked Annie, Thomas, and Jennifer to bed, Lyle would attack us. Once, he zip-tied our hands to each other and took turns kicking us and punching us until we passed out. He was careful to avoid the face. A fat lip could potentially tip dad off. Dad made it clear, if anyone was going to be the punisher, it would be him.

When Thomas turned 12, I was only thirteen, Lyle started beating him too. Only as an adult did I find out Lyle told Thomas he would kill me if he ever told anyone. I was tipped off to his beatings when I saw Thomas limping and cradling his ribs after a night Lyle had not shown up to beat me and Lauren.

The next night, Lyle did not come for me again. I heard him abusing Thomas. I could not stop my feet from running to stop the abuse. That was the night I learned all about water-boarding. It was not physically painful, but it was terrifying. I was only grateful that I was taking the abuse and saving Thomas and Lauren from the torture.

After that, I started to provoke Lyle on purpose. I would take the beatings, so Lauren and Thomas were safe. If dad was home and he caught me provoking, both Lyle and I would suffer to the rhythm of a swinging leather belt. The pain of his punishment was worth keeping my siblings safe from torture. Lauren was too kind to deserve to be hurt the way Lyle brought pain to us. Thomas was too young and scared to deserve the torture. I knew I could handle the pain and torture. I had always been braver than my size suggested, and my red-haired genetics made my pain tolerance higher than average. I would let Lyle torture me physically while my brain disassociated. I hated my brother, I hated the pain, I hated that his compulsion to hurt me brought him joy. But I gladly sacrificed myself to protect my family.

Lyle died in the car accident that also took my father's life. Annie and I survived the wreck. Annie never forgave me. We never truly got along. She always believed I was the troublemaker, the bossy one that forced her to do her home-work and brush her hair.

Annie thought my dad and Lyle hung the moon. She

was too young to fully understand that dad was beating the shit out of us. She was too young for Lyle to start abusing her. Lauren and I worked hard to shield Thomas, Annie, and Jennifer for as long as possible. Thomas was older and caught on quickly when Lauren and I would force him to bed early when dad was home. Annie and Jennifer were none the wiser. Annie only saw the beautiful side of both dad and Lyle. She saw the man who would treat us to ice cream and a brother who would push her swing at the park. Annie blamed me for the car accident. Which in truth, I may have been to blame.

The day before my dad was to arrive home after being gone for two weeks, Lyle savagely tortured me. He zip-tied me to a chair and made superficial cuts on my upper leg. If I so much as whimpered, he would smack me across the face. That night he told me that he was tired of me protecting Annie. Panic took over me and I promised myself that I would not let Annie be near Lyle.

When my dad got home, it was the good dad that showed up. He offered to take us to get ice cream. Jennifer was taking a nap, Lauren and Thomas declined. Annie and Lyle were heading to the car when I rushed after them. Annie was annoyed that I was going to ruin her fun. She only saw me provoking Lyle with no knowledge of the whys. She thought I was the troublemaker, always moody and making everyone miserable. "Why are you even coming, you can't even eat ice cream!"

I couldn't eat ice cream. I was not quite lactose intolerant, but full fat dairy made my stomach cramp, and I would writhe in pain for hours. But I had to go, I had to protect her from Lyle.

I will never forget the sneer on Lyle's face when he saw me pulling open the car door. Annie sat next to me pouting. Lyle pulled the vanity mirror down from the front seat, knowing I could see him, and he could see me. He mouthed the words, "I'm going to kill her tonight." Rage, panic, and desperation filled my body. I swung my left foot up to kick Lyle in the arm that was resting on the center armrest hoping it was enough to provoke him to leave her alone. My foot missed and I kicked my dad in the arm. He swung around and punched me hard in the face. He knocked me out.

I woke up at the hospital. When dad turned around to punch me, he had veered into oncoming traffic. Lyle was not wearing his seat belt and was thrown twenty feet. Dad died on impact. Annie suffered a gash on her forehead, that she covers with bangs to this day. Because I was limp from being knocked out and belted up, I only suffered from a mild concussion and whiplash.

Lauren told me about dad and Lyle's fate, "whatever happened, happened. It was meant to be, nothing would have stopped fate." To this day, I believe Lauren lives by her own words. She does not let things bother her, she just trusts that things will work themselves out; that we suffer for a reason; and that no matter how obscure and unimportant it may seem initially, something good will come of it.

Thomas was almost indifferent, almost catatonic after the accident. Then he picked up life and would not talk about it. Jennifer was too young to fully understand everything.

Mom was worse than before. For the first year, she did not emerge from her room except at mealtimes and to use the bathroom. She was always drunk or crying, or drunk crying. Lauren and I had shed our abusers, so we happily split the household duties. Lauren had just turned 16, so she would get the groceries, and she would cook. I would clean and help with Thomas, Annie, and Jennifer. While Lauren cleaned up dinner, I was in charge of homework and baths.

Lauren, Thomas, and I had all gotten jobs to help with the bills. It's amazing how much water six people use. At the beginning of every school year, we would pool our resources and buy school supplies. Life went on like that until Lauren graduated and left to go to the University of North Carolina. She was accepted on a full academic scholarship.

She was happy to experience college life. It was liberating to only have to take care of herself. I think she felt guilty leaving me with all the responsibilities, but I did not mind. I had long established myself as the protector of everyone. At that point in my life, I had been protecting my siblings for the majority of my childhood.

After the accident, I signed up for free karate classes at the YMCA. I vowed I would never allow someone to hurt me or my family again. I loved learning skills and continued to mature in my self-defense knowledge. I took any course from standard self-defense to Jiu-Jitsu, to bow fighting. I even took capoeira. I took my vow seriously, but I failed.

In the middle of spring break in Lauren's freshman year of college, she came home unexpectedly. I thought she was surprising us, but something was wrong. The light that normally showed in her eyes was dim. She slept in my double bed with me for three days crying herself to sleep before she let me know what happened.

She had gone to Florida with her newest girlfriends. They were staying at the beach house of one of her dorm's suitemates. They went out to bars, dancing, and living life recklessly. The third night out she remembered getting to the club, but she woke up in an alley. Her underwear was missing, she was bleeding from her knees and hands. She went to the emergency room to have her worst fears confirmed. She had been raped and left brutalized. She had tested positive for Rohypnol. The rapist had used a condom, but she still had to endure the agonizing wait to see if he had infected her with anything else besides shame.

She finished the semester and transferred to Clemson to be closer to home. She switched her major from political science to social work. After that, we never lived more than 50 miles apart. I graduated high school and joined her at Clemson. I went to school through the summer, took extra courses to graduate with a double degree. One in business, one in criminal justice. Lauren took an extra year after she lost college credit hours due to her switching schools and majors, so we graduated together. She continued her education to get her doctorate in psychology to become a social worker psychologist.

She even found a way to follow me to California. I had met John Henry while at a coffee shop. He was attending Citadel in his senior year, while I was in my freshman year at Clemson. He was polite and respectful, and so handsome; brown hair, hazel eyes, toned tan arms. I was smitten. After he graduated from Citadel, he joined the army, became an MP (military police), and was eventually stationed in Southern California. I loved it compared to Charleston. Gone were the muggy nights and mosquitoes large enough to bite off your toe. We were married and life was blissful. When he was discharged from the military, we stayed in Southern California and made a home for ourselves in a little suburb in LA. He became a volunteer firefighter and we lived off his trust until my business began to pay for our life.

Lauren was soon to follow when amazingly her, new at the time, husband had accepted a job in LA working for Ernst and Young as a business auditor. Lauren accepted a job at Cedars Sinai as a social worker. She knew how awful life could be as a domestic abuse and rape survivor and wanted to be there to help women where no one helped her. John and I were happily married for almost ten years before he died in one of Southern California's largest forest fires.

"Do you mean when we were beaten, or when she was raped?" I was feeling flushed with anger. Stupid ginger blood and sensitive flushing responses.

"All of the above. Do you feel guilty for not protecting her?"

I thought about it, "Of course I feel guilty. Why wouldn't I?"

"I feel that you should not feel guilty about that. You were young, you had no control over what your brother or father were doing. Additionally, you were still in high school and a different state when she was raped. I feel your guilt, once again, is misplaced." She steepled her hands and stared directly in my eyes.

I stared back and threw my hands in the air, "What should I feel guilty about then, Nina?" My tone was a little cagier than I wanted it to be. Nina did not seem to mind. She simpered at me.

"Do you feel guilty about the accident that took your father and brother's life?"

I let out a sigh of exasperation. What kind of question was that? Of course, I felt guilty that my actions killed two people. I shook my head and rubbed my eyes trying to collect my thoughts. "Yeah, probably."

"Do you feel guilty because you feel like you may have caused the accident? Or do you feel guilty for surviving?"

I furrowed my brow and scowled at the carpet. At that moment, I was not sure where my guilt was truly placed. While my actions did kill two people, there was limited negative impact to my life after their demise. I was practically unscathed, as a matter of fact, I came out of it in a better situation then I was in before. She looked thoughtful at me, giving me a minute to contemplate.

"Which is it?" She finally asked.

"Both I guess, or maybe none." I snorted, "Grief is a bitch, huh?"

She lifted her cheek slightly as if fighting off a smile or maybe a look of sympathy. "Grief can be complicated."

Yeah, it is complicated. It is difficult to process feeling relieved that they are gone but missing them as well. It's hard to separate the good and the bad. "I'm glad they are gone, and I feel guilty about being glad."

I looked up to the clock, desperate for it to be 4pm and the session would be over, "It looks like my time is up." I stood up slowly and made my way to the door.

"You're a good person Caroline. Don't let guilt change that." Nina placed her readers to the end of her nose as I walked out of the door.

Chapter 2

February 16

"Auntie Ro, mama wants to talk to you."

"Lennon?" When I answered my phone, I was expecting Lauren to answer back since I got the call from her. However, it was my four-year-old nephew, Lennon, on the other end.

"Is something wrong with mama?" I kept my tone light and placating; I was talking to a four-year-old after all.

"No, mama's busy with Taylor. He went poopoo on the floor and mama is cleaning it up." Taylor is my two-year-old nephew who is potty training and, apparently, not successfully.

"How did you call me Len?" I had just realized that said four-year-old had called me on his own volition.

"I told the phone to call you." Kids and technology: they were taught about it at the same time they were saying their first words.

"How can I help you, bud?" I was sitting outside my Pasadena condo that I use as an office. I had just refilled the pantry and the closets. I tried to keep a decent number of long-shelf-life items in case I had to hide out in my secret hiding place for a few days. After my condo was used to house a few rescued trafficking victims, my pantry and closet were listing dangerously low.

"Mama said she needed you to come here." His tone was so matter of fact like it was obvious and superfluous for him to even answer such a ridiculous question.

"I'm afraid I'm a little too far away to help with the poopoo Len." God help me, I may be only 18 miles away, but I was not dealing with that shit, literally.

"Hello?" Lauren had taken the phone from Lennon. I could hear the swooshing of noises as it exchanged hands.

"Hey Lo."

"Ro? What's up?"

"Your phone called me; you tell me." I smiled to myself. The life of a mom with two kids is tough, literally juggling toddlers while maintaining a perfect house, I shuddered at the thought. I had already raised my siblings; I was good for now.

"Did you call Auntie Ro?" I could hear Lennon's muffled response.

"Sorry about that, but I did need to talk to you." She continued talking to me this time, always multitasking.

"What's up?" I turned my Prius on and waited for my phone to sync up. Hands-free talking was a must if you wanted to make it home without a $200 ticket.

"Mom is leaving Monday, and you have not spent any time with her since she got here a week ago!" Speaking of guilt, Lauren knew how to spread it on thick.

"I've been busy." My tone was slightly petulant. I *had* been busy, if you consider tracking down a missing man, saving a friend that was being held hostage, and saving six traffic victims, busy. Which, I do. Though, I had completed most of those tasks before she came back to town, but honestly, I had been busy with other things. And it was not like I had not seen her in the past month, she had been in town one month prior. My mother was retired and flew to California almost every month and stayed for a week each time.

"Uh huh." She did not seem convinced. I did not tell her about my evening activities. Not that I couldn't trust her, I did not want her to worry about me. "Listen, we are having dinner here tonight. I already told mom you would be here, so you can't back out."

I rolled my head to face the ceiling of my car and closed my eyes. It was not that I did not love my mother, but she drove me crazy. My primary reason for considering going over to Lauren's house for dinner was because I knew it was something that she really wanted.

I sighed, "Okay, what time?"

I could hear the smile in her voice, "Be here tonight at 6pm and bring watermelon. Lennon and Taylor have been on a huge watermelon kick, we ran out last night."

I ended the call and changed course to Vons. Fortunately, watermelon was on special and on huge displays as soon as I walked in. My visit was short. I grabbed a few essentials and left.

When I got home, the house seemed quiet, lonely. I put away the food and changed my clothes into my workout gear. I headed down to the local Krav Maga studio to take a quick class before dinner, so I could work off any pre-emptive frustration from an evening with my mother.

Krav Maga is like military street fighting. It had combined so many of the concepts of self-defense I learned in my youth and showed me a way to efficiently use force to protect myself and others. I had dedicated years to the practice, and when John was alive, he was pushing for me to continue through my Dan levels within the black belt. It seemed pointless after he died to keep pushing myself, especially since my skills were more than enough for me to protect myself.

Nathan Sanchez was there teaching a group of young kids the basic beginner lessons. He was a Krav Maga instructor part-time. He also owned a pool cleaning company. I had initially met him when I was frustrated about my pool's algae problem.

After John died, I took over the pool maintenance. I called Nathan's company in desperation, as I try to swim most nights, and swimming in a swamp is not ideal. Turns out a fig from my neighbor's tree had fallen in and was stuck in the lines. After a sizable bill later, I signed up for a maintenance plan and my pool has been perfect ever since.

It was two weeks after the fig incident that I happened to be at the Krav Maga studio at the same time as Nathan. We talked a little and he asked me on a date. He was cute, tan from being outside all day, and kind. The date was nice, not necessarily cerebrally stimulating, but he made me laugh. We started, as the kids say, hooking up. It was casual. I was not interested in anything permanent. I assumed we were on the same page. I nodded over to him and proceeded to my class.

Sixty minutes later, I was drenched in sweat and high on endorphins. I went home, took a quick shower, and headed over to Laurens, watermelon in tow. I had to take some steadying breaths before going in, my mom made me crazy sometimes. She never addressed her issues with us. I may not have gone through a twelve-step program, but I am pretty sure apologizing to those you had hurt is on the list.

"Hi honey, you look so good!" My mom was holding me at an arm's length smiling, finally pulling me into a tight hug. The watermelon found its way onto the entry table.

"You do too, mom." She did, she looked happy and sober. My mom is a beautiful woman with blonde wavy hair. Age had started to show itself as it crept around her eyes and smile lines, but she was still stunning. She is taller than me, slimmer, built more like a waif.

"Let's eat, I'm starving!" She rubbed my arms up and down for a second and released me.

"Auntie Ro!" Lennon and Taylor were running to me and yelling. Both caught me around the legs in an embrace. I picked up Taylor and patted Lennon on the head. "Taylor, I heard you pooped on the floor today." Taylor started giggling, Lennon answered for him.

"You know he did, I already told you! It smelled very bad, Auntie Ro!" I set Taylor down and gave Lennon a proper hug, "I bet it did."

"Good, you're here! Help me chop that up." Lauren pointed to the watermelon and walked into her kitchen. "Sorry boys, your mom needs me."

I set the watermelon down on the counter and grabbed a cutting board. Lauren handed me a large sharp knife. I could hear the boys squealing in delight as my mom chased them around the room.

"How was your day?" I asked Lauren as I began sawing into the melon.

Lauren scrunched her face, "It was okay."

Juice was making its way from the melon and onto the counter. I looked back at Lauren, "Something happened at work?" I guessed.

She gave me a tight smile and shrugged, "What else is new, right?"

She only acted like this when someone was *really* brutalized. "Do you want to talk about it?" I asked hoping for a distraction, a case to solve, a criminal to pay his debts to society.

"Not right now, not while," she waved her hands around, "the kids are up."

I understood and pocketed this conversation for later. She never discussed the brutality of her cases in front of the innocent ears of my nephews.

"Burgers are ready. Hey Ro!" David Kemp, Lauren's husband walked in and kissed her on the cheek. He grabbed a beer from the fridge, popped it, and took a deep drink. "Want one?" He tipped his beer in my direction. "I'd love one!"

"Okay, David will bring you one outside. Mom wants

to eat on the patio. Grab that bowl for the watermelon, will you?" Lauren nodded over to the appropriate serving dish and carried her platter of food outside.

Mom and the boys were chasing each other around with water guns. Squealing in delight, their shirts were damp. Water was dripping from their hair.

"Okay boys let's put those down. It's time to eat." She turned to mom, "Thanks for distracting them so we could finish getting the food ready."

"Of course, honey, what are grandmas for?" She aimed one more stream of water at each boy and turned laughing towards the table.

Dinner was good, the boys were excited about the watermelon. The sun set as the twinkling lights, that covered the patio, flickered on. Lauren got up to put the boys to bed.

"Have you spoken to your brother or sisters recently?" Mom had pushed her plate away and was sipping on her seltzer water. I really wanted another beer, but after David and I finished ours we switched to lemonade to not tempt mom.

I set my lemonade down, "Yeah, Thomas is meeting me in Iceland in a few months. We are going to drive around the island for about ten days." Thomas Corbin is my younger brother. After childhood, he became a doctor. He joined Doctors Without Borders and had been traveling for the better part of five years. I think he did not like to stay in one place for too long. Maybe it was because the idea of "home" did not carry the same weight for him as it did to society. Or maybe because "home" meant a place of abuse. When I hung out with Thomas, we did not talk about our childhood. We planned adventures together.

He is one of my best friends. I never had to go into detail about what was wrong when I was feeling sullen, he always knew when something was bothering me. He could have been in the jungles of Haiti and call me when I was feeling particularly alone. It was like the weird twin phenomenon without the identical genes.

"Why would you go there? Ain't it cold there? Baby, you don't do well in the cold." My mother's Southern drawl stretched words in her slower cadence.

I forced a smile, "I've been to Iceland before mom. It is absolutely beautiful, and Thomas and I are going to chase the Northern Lights at night, hike waterfalls and glaciers during the day. We are really looking forward to it!"

She waved a hand at me as if to shoo the conversation along. "What about Annie or Jennifer?"

"Not recently, but Lauren told me Annie made principal at work. So, I am sure she is just busy." Annie was an architect at Gensler in Atlanta. She had been working her butt off to become a principal. Not that she told me any of this. She kept our relationship cool and distant. I was not going to force myself on her, she was justifiably, in her mind, angry with me. Lauren kept me up to date with Annie. They talk about once every two weeks. Despite her anger towards me, I still cared about her. I would call her, but after dozens of my calls rolling to voicemail, I had gotten the hint.

"How's Jennifer doing?"

Jennifer was a married kindergarten teacher. Her husband was successful doing something with real estate in Charleston. I had never truly gotten to know Kevin; he was always too busy with work. Jennifer and her husband, Kevin Stewart, bought a house with a guest house. They convinced mom to move in with them. After a few arguments, mom obliged.

"Pregnant!" Mom practically was bouncing out of her chair with excitement to tell me.

"That's great, I'm happy for her. I'll call her soon and

tell her myself." My relationship with Jennifer was fine. I was sad that she had not called to tell me her good news. At least I thought our relationship was fine.

"Oh, don't tell her I told you! I'm just too excited. My only grandbabies live a million miles away. Now I will have one in my own backyard!" Or *you're* in *their* backyard. I controlled my face as the snide comment slid through my head.

"What did I miss?" Lauren was back from putting the boys to bed.

"Jennifer is pregnant." I directed my comment to Lauren.

"Oh, I know, she told me a week ago." The look I gave Lauren was closer to WTF?

She quickly responded, "It's not my news to share." And she pointed her chin at mom. "Besides, it is very early in the pregnancy. She only told me because I when she got the call from her doctor confirming."

"Well, it is past my bedtime! My flight leaves early tomorrow, and I still need to pack!" I hugged my mom as she kissed my forehead. "Don't be a stranger, baby girl." And she gracefully walked into the house and disappeared to the guest room.

I turned back to Lauren, "Well that was almost painless."

She rolled her eyes, "You are so dramatic, Ro!"

I smiled back, "I know!" I took another sip of lemonade as I heard David crack a beer in the kitchen.

"Alright Lo, tell me about your client that has you so down."

She fidgeted, "You know me too well." She stuck her lower lip out and flipped her blonde hair over her shoulder with a sigh. She was not only stressed; she was worried about her client.

I nodded, “That I do, what’s going on?”

“Fifteen-year-old girl was brought in today after she fainted in school. Turns out she is pregnant.”

I nodded, “That sucks.”

She snorted, “That’s not even the worst part.” Now we are getting somewhere. I think I shifted myself forward.

“She is about twenty weeks pregnant, it’s a boy, and she has pre-e.”

“Oh shit.” Pre-eclampsia, a possible fatal hypertension disorder during pregnancy. I only knew about it because Lauren feared she had it when she was pregnant with Lennon.

“I haven’t even gotten to the bad part.” She took a breath, I held mine in anticipation.

“She does not know who the father is. Claims that she was a virgin, that she has never even kissed a boy with tongue.” I guess a virgin mother would not be a first, but the last time it did cause quite a religious uproar.

“Is she telling the truth?” It was not out of the realm for a fifteen-year-old to lie about her promiscuity.

“Her parents believe she is. She seemed confused and emphatic that she was not lying.”

Curious, “Yeah but even if she were raped, she would have a time reference where she lost time. She would be in physical pain after the fact. There would be immediate signs after the trauma.”

“That’s just it, Ro. Her timetable is not reliable. She has narcolepsy. She is *always* losing time.”

“But there are drugs to combat that!” I began to say, but Lauren interrupted again.

“Yep, legal amphetamines, highly regulated.” She nodded.

"Was she taking her meds?" Curiouser.

"Her older brother sold a two-week supply to his friends a few months ago. She did not want to tell her parents and get him in trouble. She had to wait two weeks before she could refill. She tried to stay awake with caffeine, but it did not work." This was getting interesting.

"What about the physical markers of rape. If she were a virgin, she would have had pelvic pain, bleeding, something to tip her off."

Lauren shook her head, "Nope, she has been taking horseback riding lessons. She moved to bareback lessons around the same time." I drew in a deep breath and cursed silently. I had only ridden a horse a few times as a child, but even with a saddle, I was sore for a few days. I could not imagine the pressure on one's pelvic floor while learning the new style of riding.

"Can she recall any lapses in time that confused her? Any time she was away from home?" I felt like I was grasping at straws.

"Three times, in that two-week time frame. Once while at work, she is a barista at Java in Burbank. The second time was after hiking at Griffith Park. She had stopped to eat; she had brought a packed lunch and a blanket. The third time was at school in the library."

Hmmm. So, three possible opportunities to investigate.

"What actions have been taken so far?" What I *really* meant was, how much leg work have the cops put into this. I was already going through the silent list of things to work through to help find the young girl her justice.

"OB did an amnio to get the paternity DNA results. Police are trying to rule out the father and brother first." Gross, but I understood the necessary nature of the test. Abuse typically happens by people you know the best.

"What else are the authorities doing?"

"They are getting warrants to collect DNA from all the male workers from both Java and her high school."

"Anything else?" Come on Lauren be my font of information I know that you are!

"We did a tox screen, she tested positive for ketamine."

"Shit! Recreational or do they think it was a part of the attack?"

"She denied recreational use, so we can assume it was a part of the attack."

I took a deep breath. Okay, so I had three places to investigate, endless computers to hack, and a person with access to ketamine to find.

"Well, Lauren, it sounds like they are doing everything they can." I tried to ease her mind.

She pinched her face, but smoothed it out as she said, "You know what? You are right! Every time I tell you about one of my clients, the authorities find the guys and make an arrest. You're like a good luck charm!"

If I were drinking, I probably would have choked. It's not good luck, it's tirelessly finding the right person so they could pay. I put my hands in the air, "What can I say, I'm good at tipping the karmic scales!"

I left shortly after our conversation ended. I went home, pulled out an empty composition book, and began writing down everything Lauren told me. I left the hacking into her work account and the countless other computers for tomorrow. I was mentally exhausted from the day's conversations. I was physically exhausted from having my sleep interrupted for the past two nights. I crawled into bed at 11pm, pulled the covers over my head, and fell asleep immediately.

Chapter 3

February 17

The light buzzing of my cell phone next to my hand woke me up. It was 2am. My main alarm was not tripped, my backup alarm notified me of someone else's presence in my home. The primary alarm has badges on the windows and a flag in front of my house. It deters the dumb criminals that want to smash and grab, rape, and maim. The secondary alarm is not advertised on every available surface. It's a series of pin cameras interconnected and relayed to my phone. If there is movement, I know about it.

My intruder was not harmless, but he was not here to steal anything or harm me either. This was the third visit from him in as many nights. I knew all about him. My intruder, Tadashi Becken, Beck. Apparently, dropping twenty feet to incapacitate a gangster then stabbing said gangster in the leg leaves a lasting impression. I was not sure why he kept coming to visit me in the wee hours of the day.

I scrolled through my phone and watched my intruder pass through the kitchen and go into my study. I suppose now was as good a time as any to greet him. I rolled under my bed and slid the trap door aside.

My late husband and I added two trap doors that were connected under the house with a small tunnel. We also included two different secret passages. Playing games and solving mysteries was foreplay and we used the whole house to engage. On the practical side, if there was a true home invasion, I had a safe area to hide or escape depending on the situation.

The first night my intruder stopped in, I slid into my bedroom trap door and waited inside silently. After he left, I crawled back into bed, but my nerves were too heightened for sleep. I desperately wanted to go into the kitchen, where he had made a kettle of tea, and ask him why the hell he had disappeared from my life for weeks.

I had been hopeful after we saved the trafficking victims together that he would at least be interested in being friends. He knew where I lived and even knew about my secret office in Pasadena. My office is actually a condo owned by my alias, where I conduct my investigations. He knew all about my second life, and when we parted ways after saving the girls, I was hoping he was interested in *both* of my lives. I stayed hidden because I was still too mad and embarrassed about his indifference to our unrequited kiss.

It may seem ridiculous to be mad about a simple unreciprocated kiss, but to me it was not a simple kiss. After John died, I closed myself off from people and intimacy. And while, yes, I was banging my pool boy, Nathan, I never let him kiss me. That simple act seemed far more intimate than full penetration for five minutes. I had not kissed someone on the lips in nearly three years before I braved the courage and allowed my unexplainable desire to override my rational brain. I *wanted* to kiss Beck and feel his lips on mine. It was a feeling that I had given up on. When he blinked numbly at me after the fact, I thought I would die from embarrassment.

The second time he stopped in, was much like the first. He did not take anything. He did not venture towards the bedroom. He just pursued the house like any curious guest. It was almost as if he were daring me to find him like he wanted me to confront him. Maybe I was being dramatic, perhaps he just wanted to talk to me. I stayed rooted to my safe haven in bed. I watched his progress, unable to move and ask him what he wanted.

Perhaps it was latent anger from his rejection. Perhaps it was the idea that I knew he knew I was watching his progress through my home. He knew all about the various cameras I had set up between my house and my condo. I had shown him the application where all my surveillance was stored as a way for him to understand that my condo was a safe place for him to rest and stay hidden from the likes of Jose Garcia. Perhaps I kept myself from running to his side because I wanted him to feel the weight of rejection by ignoring his presence in my home for two days straight.

Two days of worry and anxiety had passed, and I was determined for tonight to be different. Now, I was truly curious what had prompted him to drive the thirty miles to my home in the middle of the night for the third night in a row.

I gathered my courage and I traveled down the tunnel that spit me out in the hall adjacent to my study. I kept tabs on my intruder through my cell phone. I slid the trap door aside and eased myself out. Light as a feather on my toes I stepped into the study and leaned into the doorway casual and cool.

"Hello, Beck." I had spoken clearly, not loud, but enough to break the silence.

He barely looked up from a composition book he was reading. One eyebrow raised as he replaced the composition book to soldier next to 100 other composition books. His light brown hair had streaks of gold and was pulled back in a top knot. His eyes were silver and shaped like almonds. His body was muscular but not bulky and he stood just over 6 feet tall. He was an intoxicating mix of Japanese and Norwegian. His face was handsome with sharp features. My research all pointed to him being a sort of assassin, but that is hardly the correct term. Perhaps modern-day ninja. He was also a chef, which was *intriguing.*

"Are you not wondering why I am here?" His tone was light and amused.

"I wondered that three days ago." I walked over to where he was standing. "What can I help you with?" I said with an indifferent expression on my face. I hoped I appeared to be cool and calm. I mentally sighed. He looked good. His jeans were just tight enough along the hips and thighs to be very aware of his musculature and *size*. His cotton shirt hugged his pecs. I clasped my hands behind my back to keep myself from touching him.

"You have interesting hobbies, Caroline." He motioned to the composition books filled with solved cold cases. I internally winced. There was nothing like a sexy man seeing that your nighttime endeavors mostly included solitary activities that took up ample time.

"This coming from a man that has been wandering around my house for the past three nights?" I gave him a sardonic smile.

"I was curious about you." He pulled another composition book down. I fought the embarrassed cringe I could feel forming. He had just grabbed a composition book of a case that took me months of sleepless nights to solve. I did not want him to read through my unfiltered and sleep deprived thoughts while I looked on. I definitely did not want him to get to the part in my investigation where my brain snapped, and I wrote a poem about how much I wanted to catch the man that was raping women with cucumbers in the alleys of USC campus. I believe it went something like: Roses are red, violets are blue, when I find you, I'll stick my own cucumber into you, causing you pain every time you poo. *Ugh, I was embarrassing.* I did catch the rapist, but I did not have a cucumber on me at the time.

"Can I interest you in some tea?" I asked as I pulled the volume out of his hand and placed it back on my shelf. He answered with his eyebrows as one quirked up.

I silently walked to my kitchen, turned the light on, and grabbed a kettle. I flipped my gas stove on and filled the kettle with water before turning back to Beck. I leaned my elbows onto the granite island and looked up to him from my lashes. The granite was cold against my skin, I stifled a shiver. I let my long red hair fan out across my shoulders.

"Do you not have further inquiries as to why I am here?" He stood on the opposite side of the island with his hands behind his back.

I shrugged, "I have plenty of questions, but..." I crinkled my nose, "You don't really answer my queries, so I have to rely on my assumptions." I turned away from him to not betray the look of disappointment I could feel spread across my face.

"And why do you assume I am here?" His deep voice continued.

I shrugged again, "I can deduce that you are not here to hurt me or steal from me. You know as well as I do that, I will simply take it back." I turned to look at him with a half-smile.

"Besides, you are too good to hurt me." I turned around to the cabinet to retrieve two teacups. I did not want to see his expression as I said the last part. I was hoping that I was passively negating his previous comments about being a monster.

I felt his eyes watching every movement. I realized that my sleeping attire may not be completely appropriate for tea with a ninja. Oh well, it's what he gets for intruding into my private domain in the middle of the night.

I turned back and filled the teacups brimming with hot chamomile tea. I bit my lip; it was not as if my sleeping attire was much different from when I kissed him while sharing a pull-out sofa with him. I was practically throwing myself at him then, and he did nothing but question my actions. I doubted the ample butt cheek that curved out of my boy shorts truly impressed him, and even though my tank top was see-through, he seemed as uninterested as he was weeks prior... not that I was bitter. At least, I hoped he did not realize that I was a smidge bitter about the whole thing.

"It only seemed fair that I returned the favor. You were

at my house, and you did not take anything *physical* from me." His silver eyes burned into me. I wonder if he realized I copied his hard drive. I was very careful to leave no trace of my intrusion on his computer. Although it is entirely possible, he has a camera in his bedroom. My mind began to wonder what kind of footage such a camera could have acquired with a sexy ninja assassin as its owner. I brought myself back into the moment, daydreaming is not advisable when confronting an uninvited guest in your home.

"Am I making you uncomfortable, Beck?" I waved to my attire, hoping to draw attention to it. I am not self-conscious about my body. I run 6 miles every morning, swim laps most evenings, and take some form of self-defense 5 days a week. My muscles are lean and hard. If I were to flex, you could see definition, but I did not look overly muscled otherwise. I watched his eyes quickly drink me in. It was almost satisfying.

"This is your domicile, Caroline, far be it for me to dictate how you dress." His eyes looked like he was amused by my question.

I nodded and sipped my tea.

"Why *are* you here?" I asked quietly.

A smile tickled his eyes but did not make it to his mouth. "You intrigue me, Caroline."

I scoffed, but he further explained himself. "You went out of your way to help Chris, a practical stranger. You help a lot of strangers and never let them know that you are seeking out justice on their behalf, so you are kind and selfless. You are petite, but you seem to be undisturbed that your size could disable you in a fight, so you are brave. You are beautiful, but you do not take a man. Not to mention, exceedingly smart and *very* good with computers." He returned my sardonic smile. I swallowed. Yep, that confirmed he knew I copied his hard drive. I changed the subject away from my hacking into his personal life and got to the crux as to why I thought he was at my house.

"Okay, thank you. Can I tell you why I think you are here?" He actually smiled and shook his head as if I was unbelievable. To be honest, I could not believe that I was coming off as cool as I thought I was. He had just called me beautiful, and I did not blush. It might have been a first for me.

"You are intrigued by me, but I feel like you mostly want to fight me." It seemed like a practical thing to believe. We had fought side by side, and at one point he did look impressed by my above average skills.

One brow moved the smallest amount. "You don't want to hurt me; you just want to see what I can do. Like I said before, you are too good to hurt me. But sparring with me... It's your foreplay." I heard hope in my tone and felt the blush spreading up my chest. I did not want to sound hopeful when mentioning foreplay to a man like him.

"Why do you think this?" His head cocked to one side. I sprung on the counter and used his shoulders to launch myself behind him. I wrapped my arms around his neck while my legs were draped firmly around his waist. He chuckled. I compressed my arms in a submissive hold around his throat and released a moment later. My thighs squeezed across his hips; my calves felt a large distinct bulge. I bit my lip.

He slowly pulled me around and sat my bottom on the counter, my legs still around his waist. The granite felt cold against my butt. He placed his palm on my collarbone and rubbed his thumb in light circles. I stifled a shiver.

"Is it my foreplay or yours?" He let his hand drop to between my breasts, his thumb gliding back and forth on my nipple. I bit my lip and narrowed my eyes fighting the urge to moan and arch back.

It's not like I haven't had sex since my husband's passing. I had a one-night stand in Ireland about seven months after John died. There was also Nathan, said pool boy. He was handsome, kind, but average in every other way. I fought the urge to look down at Beck's hips, when my calves wrapped around his waist, his bulge definitely did not feel *average*.

Sex with Nathan was more about pressure release than a physical connection. Sometimes it was too quick for me to have much pressure released, not that I told him that. Sometimes it was just about wanting to be desired. If Nathan told me it was over, I would probably shrug and allow him closure. Nathan did not know me. He had no idea that my evenings consisted of crime scene photos and deep dives into others' personal lives. He did not know my sordid childhood in detail. He knew me as a pretty face that sparred with him. But Nathan never gave me that feeling that starts as a slow-burning fire in the base of your loins... not like Beck did. I grit my teeth. I should not think about that. Beck did not want me, not like that.

I pulled his hand away from my chest with both of mine and looked at his palm. If I were to believe in palmistry, then he would have a long life. His heart line started and stopped. There was a large gap that proceeded past his lifeline. I could interpret that he had love in his life for his formative years but was alone for a long time. Whenever he does find love, it will be until he dies. I suppose it is a good thing I do not believe in palmistry. He was far too attractive to allow only one love in his life.

I dropped his hand and slid off the counter. My hips pressed against his thighs, his lips nearly touching my forehead. He stood very still as I slid to the side and walked back to my bedroom.

"If you are still here in two hours, you can join me for my run."

I heard him softly chuckle as I looped into my bedroom.

I crawled into my bed and pulled my phone out to watch his progress. He finished his tea while looking through my pantry. He washed the cups and the kettle before stepping into my bathroom. I assume he was leaving through my window there. The bathrooms are the only places I do not have cameras. That would just be creepy. I am a vigilante, not a voyeur. Sleep eluded me; my nerves never fully relaxed.

I still suffer from insomnia, most days I do not get more than 3 hours of sleep. On a very good day, I got six hours, but my intruder had woken me up again. Perhaps it was not fair to call him my intruder, but it was the emotionless moniker that kept me from reliving his rejection in cringing detail.

I replayed the encounter in my head. Beck was a type of mysterious sexy that made my stomach clench, but he was a no-go. His life had been as tragic as mine, but where I forced myself to live in society, he became a ghost living in the periphery. Yes, he had a good job at an up-and-coming restaurant. He was the head chef, and I had tried his food once. His restaurant, Banjo, was too far away for me to frequent, but the food was good enough to consider it. He kept everyone at an arm's length and breaking into my house was tantamount to flirting. I did not want to want him.

I think I came off cool and indifferent. It was a façade I have been working on for decades. Manny tells me I act like I have ice water running through my veins. I smiled when I realized he never did tell me why he was at my house. Not really.

Did Beck say he was curious about me?

I guess I should be flattered. It is a rare occasion when someone is curious about me. When I am in public I work hard to blend. My copper hair is a memorable trait. In my personal life with my sister and nephews, I allow my red hair down. When I am working a case, I hide my hair beneath a light brown page-boy wig. I typically don brown contact lenses, and neutral clothing.

Over the years I have created a second life under the name Leslie Mixon. She is completely fictitious, but she owns a condo in Pasadena, a new BMW, and works as an independent contractor and investor and partial owner of my business, Infinity Apothecary. Perhaps it was extreme paranoia that led me to create Leslie, but so far paranoia was working to keep me safe.

The condo is a handy place to change identities if needed. I use it as a depressurization chamber of sorts. Leslie will go into the condo after a night of surveillance and I leave to head to my home in Glendora. The condo was also the place Beck felt comfortable hiding trafficking victims he had rescued. It was *that* night when I realized wanting Beck... hurt.

What does *curious* even mean to a guy like Beck? I don't want to flatter myself in thinking he was interested in me in *that* way. I mean, I doubt he is thinking about my sexual prowess. He had perused enough of my composition books to know my nightly activities had little sex in them. No, maybe my instincts were right, he was curious about my physical abilities. When we rescued Chris, he saw me drop twenty feet on the head of a kingpin. He saw me kick, punch, flip, and finally stab a sex trafficking kingpin and come out unscathed. I feel it is safe to assume women my size do not typically opt for fighting above their weight class. He saw me do all this and we saved six women before they could disappear into the seedy world of human trafficking.

Of course, he could be curious about my investigation skills. He was reading my composition books which contain case notes, theories, evidence, and actions. They are all thorough, logical, and solved. They are my mementos from cases that I poured weeks into solving. Most things do not beat the high of realizing your hunches are right and the bad guy can't make their getaway. Most of my cases are rape victims, the most under-reported crime.

Lauren unknowingly gives me cases to work. Day after day she talks to victims who just want the problem to go away and won't report it. My frustration and drive to help the victims came from the fact that even they did report it there was a high likelihood that nothing would happen. If a stranger attacked them and there were no witnesses, the case fizzles out before it can get started. Then there are the women that don't want to report it to the police at all. The hospital is obligated to report it, but without the key witness, i.e., the victim, the case dies out. Even DNA samples that hospitals scan only find past offenders or people that have submitted their DNA to online analysis sites or by court order. But let's be honest here, if you were a serial rapist you are not going to fill out an online profile that practically gives the police your full confession. But I will. I work the case. I find the rapist, creatively collect their DNA, and submit a profile that leads the police to an arrest. I am perfectly fine with allowing others to take credit. Notoriety would hinder me in finding the truth for the victims.

I was restless in sleep until I gave up at 4am. I flipped the TV on and watched the news.

> "Another woman disappeared yesterday. Lisa Henderson was gardening in the front yard of her Yorba Linda home. Video surveillance from her home camera and her neighbor's camera confirm she was in her yard when she disappeared. Unfortunately, no video exists of the abduction. Police are asking the public for help in finding Mrs. Henderson. She is the third disappearance in fourteen days. Bobbi King and Flora Sanchez are still missing. Please call the hotline below if you have any further information."

I pulled my composition book out from my nightstand. I noted the time, day, name, city, and the police department in charge. Three women in two weeks. No rhyme or reason for the abductions. All were done in broad daylight just out of reach of a camera and all were women - that is where the similarities ended. King lives in Culver City and Sanchez lives in Riverside. In Los Angeles standards that is practically in another state. All varying ethnicities, ages, and even affluence. The victims seemed like they were taken on impulse, but too many coincidences made me doubt it was all left to bad luck for the victims.

In today's world, everyone is being monitored 24/7. Phones, TVs, computers all data mine, all listen for keywords then record your conversations unknowingly. Doorbells transmit entryway images for all the world to see. Baby monitors can be hacked so a stranger could watch an anonymous baby sleep. Hell, even innocent video conference calls could be watched from a business's competition anonymously.

The fact that all the women were abducted without the tiniest shred of evidence as to who took them gave me chills. Whoever was doing this was well organized, methodical, and had probably been planning for weeks. I would venture the guess that he or she was also good enough at technology to see the neighborhood surveillance images and find blind spots or create them.

I set my composition book down and rubbed my eyes. I stood up and began stretching for my run. Twenty minutes of yoga later I was warmed and limber. I set out of my front door and began my routine.

I enjoy running not only for its health benefits but also for the mental clarity it provides me. The abductions were worrisome. I wanted to clear my head to allow an idea of who or how these women were being taken. No ransoms, no evidence, just gone. I also needed to prioritize my hacking schedule for Lauren's client.

I looked around my yard hopeful to see Beck's figure approach me. By mile one I was paranoid he was planning on attacking mid run. By mile two I convinced myself I was crazy to think he would attack me. By mile five I was disappointed that he did not show. By mile six I was resolved in knowing that Beck was not worth my time and I should stop thinking about him. Why did I even care whether or not I saw him again?

I got home and warmed up my overnight oats. I read the newspaper while I ate in silence. Nothing new about the abducted women just repeated information from 4am. I finished and washed my bowl thoroughly. It is not like I am a neat freak, but dried oatmeal is like concrete on my stoneware. I showered and padded over to my closet. I selected a plum shift dress with leopard print heels for work. I looked edgy, perfect for my hipster clientele.

I own a small business, Infinity Apothecary, on a trendy street in Pasadena. I carry high-end skincare and locally made high-quality goods like knit sweaters and blankets and La Mere. I also carry a large section of vegan-friendly, animal cruelty-free, clean products like moisturizers, and makeup. It's a growing market and has increased my business by 40% over the last year. My clientele ranges from teens with their parent's credit card to socialites to fit and active octogenarians.

I employ six associates. I pay well over the state's minimum wage and commission on top. I provide health insurance, vacation, and sick days to all my employees. Their loyalty has been their thank you. My turnover rate is incredibly low. I had only lost one associate and it was due to her moving to Colorado for her husband's job. I love Infinity and my staff makes my life easier.

Chapter 4

February 17

"Hey, Boss lady!" Manny greeted me with a smile, "Love the shoes, girl," and he purred at me. Oh, Manny! Manny Valdez is my sales manager. He is as cute as a button with blonde streaked hair, green eyes, and a personality that made men swoon. Of course, he was the total package and gay, another no go. Not that I would ever consider him like that. He was too valuable to Infinity and my sanity. We had worked together long enough that I knew we had mutual love and respect for each other. Working with Manny was always a pleasure. He's bright, charismatic, funny, but knew when to be professional. The whole staff adores Manny.

Monday mornings are reserved for management meetings. Manny goes over the sales numbers from the previous week and notes things that are selling. My operations manager, Rani Patel, goes over inventory results, logistics, and payroll. If Manny is the heart of my little operation, Rani is the brain. She is a short, thin Indian woman around 40 years old. She grew up in San Diego but does not have the carefree surfer-boy mentality. Her sense of humor is dry, sarcastic, and a little quirky. Not all the staff understand her, but they respect her. Our Monday meetings typically last an hour, Manny and Rani munch on donuts I bring from Donut Man, a legendary donut establishment in Glendora, while we lay out the success of Infinity.

Following my first meeting of the day, I typically meet with local artisans looking for a place to sell their goods. I don't get to spend nearly as much time with the customers as I used to. As our business began to boom my hours increased. I went from working 5 days a week, 8 hours a day to 7 days a week 11-12 hours a day. I had Rani do the math and we figured we could actually hire people to take over the selling. I cut back immediately to ten-hour days 5 days a week. After John died, I cut back again. Now I work 4 days a week, ten hours a day.

After five hours of meetings, I took a break to enjoy a quiet lunch at my favorite outdoor restaurant. The food is all farm to table and the ambiance is perfect to enjoy on a sunny California day. I ate my sandwich and started up my laptop. I pulled my composition book out, taking notes as I went. I needed to get Lauren's case started, but my mind kept drifting to other things. Missing women, missing Beck, then back to a narcoleptic pregnant teen.

I signed into Lauren's work computer, using her credentials I happened across. Okay, I was sneaking around her office and found a post-it with her password written on it. Sloppy. Finding the client's file was easy. Her name is Rebecca Hamilton, age 15. I copied down her social security number, her work address, her school information. I checked out her social media profiles, writing down anything that could be important. I set up an alert for when her paternity test would have results. The case could solve itself, but I did not want to be caught off guard if it did not.

After I had a good sense of who she was, her hobbies, her dreams, I moved on. First, I hacked into Java's HR site. It was easy enough to get the entire roster of baristas and managers at that location. I pulled up schedules from sixteen weeks ago, taking into account the two-week time frame she lost as well as the fact that twenty weeks pregnant does not equate to the attack taking place twenty weeks prior. I noted the names of anyone who overlapped her shift. I started there.

I followed the same process with her high school. In the end, I had 23 men's personal lives I needed to hack. I was not sure which avenue to take. Would I look for disturbing images to verify their inclination for rape fantasy? Or do I hack each individual's Amazon accounts looking for ketamine purchase? Although, ketamine can be purchased in other places.

I looked at my watch, it was time to get back to Infinity.

The rest of my workday continued without incidence. Manny's sales were on fire, so business was good. I was leaving right as Brooke Lawson was showing up. Brooke is a sixty-year-old hippie with wavy white hair. Well, she was a hippie in the 70s, she went straight-laced in the 80s and 90s. Now she was a happy, free-spirited, grandma of three. She worked three evenings a week, so she could "keep her social skills honed."

"How are your grandkids, Brooke?" She had taken last week off to "go on an adventure" with her daughter and grandchildren, ten, eight, and six years old.

Brooke gushed, "Oh Caroline, it was magic! We took the kids to Dale's yurt in Arizona. We lived off the land, told ghost stories at night by the fire. We did not want to come back, but Willow needed to get back to work." She added with a pout. "Lived off the land" meant eating the variety of fruit and vegetables that Dale grows in his Arizona greenhouse, next to said yurt.

Dale was Brooke's husband of forty years. They got married while barefoot on the beach and with a flower wreath around her head. I had seen the pictures of her wedding when she asked for my help to load said wedding pictures onto her social media profile. Willow was their love child. She is more corporate, less free-spirited; she is an accountant. All three of her children attend private schools in Pasadena. Willow only takes part in one yurt trip a year, reserving the rest of her vacation days to soak up the sun in kid-friendly hotels in exotic locales. If Brooke had her way, they would all live in the yurt full time. She has been very vocal about the overrated tent being off the grid.

It collects rainwater and has a connection to a local stream in case of drought. It boasts solar panels for power, a composting toilet, and an outdoor bathtub where you can "bathe under the stars." I'm sure it's lovely, but I could see Willow's hesitation about living off the grid with three still-growing children and aloof parents.

"I'm so pleased to hear that everyone enjoyed their re-connection with nature." I said to Brooke as I gave her a hug and turned to leave.

"Caroline?"

"Yes, Jessica?" Jessica Lincoln was my youngest member of the staff. She joined us when she turned 18 and had been working while attending UCLA. She is the quintessential California blonde bombshell surfer chick. Her hair goes to her waist, golden blonde. She surfs most weekends and volunteers at animal shelters. She has a big heart and an even bigger smile. I always thought of Jessica as a little sister. Occasionally she would ask for boy advice, but she stayed remarkably professional considering her age.

"My birthday is coming up." Her smile was a little bit timid.

"Okay. Just let me know when it is, so I can make sure you are off."

"It's my twenty-first birthday." Gosh, has it already been three years since she started?

"Okay. I'll make sure you get the day after off too." I winked at her and went to grab my bag.

"No, it's not that. Well, yes, I still would like you to make those accommodations. But I was wondering if you wanted to come."

I was a little taken back. "Sure, just let me know when and where." It's not that I do not get invited to after-work drinks, but it had been a while since I had been invited to a twenty-first birthday party.

I bid Jessica and Brooke goodbye and made my way back home with a million other people traveling East on the 210 freeway. To be honest, the only time I stay on the freeway for my entire commute is if it is in the wee hours of the morning. All the rest of the day, it's a safe bet you'll want to commit Hari Kari from the slowpoke playing Candy Crush on their phone instead of maintaining a consistent speed.

I stopped into my normal Monday evening Jiu-Jitsu spot for an hour of vigorous sparring. It may be the biggest highlight of my day when I see some machista underestimating my size, and he ends up on his back. There is always the initial shock, whistles, and the inevitable rematch.

Home was quiet and empty. I missed the days when John would greet me with a smile and a case file to work through. I would open the file like it was a present on Christmas Day, giddy and excited for my favorite game to play. He would lay out the evidence one piece at a time, in the same order that it was found. He would present each interview in the same order. If I made the wrong assumption, I would get a verbal hand-slap. If I was onto something, he would smile his crinkly smile. He had a deep-set dimple, giving his smile a crooked, but adorable look. His hazel eyes would squint when he was really smiling. I miss him.

After he died, I took my own version of a walk-about. I traveled the world for six months. I stopped by to visit Thomas. He was working on Africa's Gold Coast. Work survived without me. Lauren had a harder time. She was worried that I would never come back, but I did.

I sautéed broccoli with chicken breast and served it with brown rice for dinner. I opened up my laptop to start the "review" process into possible suspects. I worked quietly for a few hours before deciding to end the day with a late-night swim. Water calms me down. When I swim at night, I find it easier to fall asleep. Sleep to an insomniac is always elusive, but once you find something that works—it's ritual.

After the fig incident, I planted mature hedges that boasted fast dense growth. My pool was now surrounded on three sides with a 20' evergreen wall. It was too thick to see through, and it hid the five-foot concrete block wall that originally separated the properties. It was completely secluded from my neighbors visually. It was privacy that I preferred.

The pool light illuminated the water like a blue-green gem glowing in the night. I stripped bare and began swimming laps, vigorously at first to warm my body up. After ten minutes I slowed my pace down for another twenty minutes. In the last twenty minutes, I switched to my kickboard, keeping my head above the surface. I was a few minutes away from finishing when I felt the water shift, waves were coming from the wrong direction. I swam quickly around to see Beck sitting at the far end of the pool, legs resting knee-deep in the water.

His face looked serene as he looked towards the sky. It was a velvety blue-black, the moon was full, and you could make out the pinpricks of Jupiter and Saturn twinkling.

"You scared the shit out of me, Beck!" I hissed. My heart was racing again from the adrenaline of an unannounced visitor. I could feel my pulse burning at my ears and my hands were shaking. I was not mad at his appearance. I was exhilarated. I secretly cursed myself for betraying my promised nonchalance towards the man that kept eluding me. Well, eluding me emotionally, physically he kept showing up when I least expected him.

He dropped his gaze down to me. His silver eyes glowed and reflected the blue-green water. The lights cast his face in sharp relief, emphasizing his facial structure. His was jaw squared, with strong cheekbones. His nose was straight and narrow, his lips were plump and dark. His arms were bracing him against the pool's edge, they looked chiseled in marble.

God, he is a gorgeous man.

"I did not mean to startle you, Caroline." His tone was light and clear.

I swam over to him, using my kickboard to hide my naked chest. "It's fine, I was not expecting you." Especially after he stood me up for the morning run, "What are you doing here?" I was five feet away from him, standing straight, but still covered in water up to my neck. The kickboard pushed against my chest, my chin resting on the top of its foam.

He turned his gaze back up to the sky, perhaps to give me privacy, or maybe he just was not interested. "I want to get to know you." He said finally as if he were talking to the sky. I followed his gaze to make sure he was not talking to someone else, a bird maybe. I did not want to be hopeful that he wanted to get to know me because he was interested in being more than an occasional friend. Too many rebuffs had dampened that hope. The fact that he was not even trying to see my naked body, all but solidified my reservations that he wanted to get to *know* me, know me... like in the Biblical terms.

When I saw no other audience, I think I snorted, "What can I tell you, you have not already figured out by snooping around my house?"

Still looking up, he smiled, "Just because I know what you do, does not mean I understand why you do it." Fair point. I investigate enough people to see their habits but have no context or motivation behind what makes them tend to their actions.

Maybe I was testing his will power, maybe I was seeing if he was interested in me (or confirmation that he was not), whatever my motivation I stepped forward, pushing the board aside. I walked until I was one foot away from his legs still sitting in the water at the pool's edge. I was fully exposed from the belly button up. "Can you hand me that towel?" I pointed to the folded object sitting on the chair almost directly behind him.

He directed his gaze to where I pointed, and I walked up the stairs towards him. He stood up to meet me at the stairs. Though I was completely naked, his eyes never left mine, never strayed down one iota. I dried my face and arms, but wrapped the towel around my waist, leaving my chest exposed. I guess I was curious as to how far I could push him. Still not the tiniest glance, "Okay. Make yourself at home. I need to shower. We can talk when I am done."

Well, that hurt the old ego. Clearly, he was not interested in me. I tried to not allow myself to be offended. I mean, I understand I am not everyone's cup of tea. Boys were pretty ruthless in middle and high school to confirm that not everyone likes a redhead. I was sixteen when a particular dipshit in my gym class told me why people called me ginger, "You're like a gingerbread cookie, you look human, but have no soul." I punched him in the mouth and was expelled for three days. Another twit from high school reminded me, "I've never met a pretty red-head, and you're in the category of people I have met." I did not punch her. I did not want to be expelled again, I just went home and cried.

I turned the water on and waited for it to heat up. I stared at myself in the mirror, being critical of every inch. I am comfortable with my body; I work very hard to keep it toned. My boobs were a decent size considering my limited body fat. I still had hips, like an athletic hourglass. My butt was nice, perky, and round. I was told I had a big butt in high school, I hated it at the time. But now, I like it. I stared at my heart-shaped face next. Light freckles covered my small button nose and lightly feathered across my cheek's apples. My lips were broad and full, my lower lip slightly larger, out of proportion to my upper lip. My eyes were crystal blue. I stared at myself until the mirror fogged up. I thought I looked fine. Better than fine, but he did not betray the tiniest glance down to my goods. He could be gay. Or he could just not be interested in me. Why does he only have one category? If he did not look at my boobs, he's gay? I scoffed at my own short-sightedness. I stepped into the shower.

I did not realize how cold I had gotten, the water burned at my skin until I finally matched its temperature. I considered just staying in the shower, allowing myself to drown in my own self-pity of Beck not being interested. But I did not want to waste the water. Southern California is in a perpetual drought. Volunteer waterboarding while wasting precious resources was a bad move environmentally. I got out of the shower and wrapped myself in my white terrycloth robe. I finger-combed my hair allowing my waves to dry naturally. I shrugged again in the mirror as I walked out of the bedroom. If he was not interested while I was buck naked, it honestly did not matter what I looked like.

Beck was sitting at the kitchen island. He had made a kettle of tea. He was reading my composition book with Rebecca Hamilton's info. He looked up when he saw me approach. I think he looked relieved that I was dressed. I mean, letting someone down is awkward for all parties involved. It is particularly difficult if one party, me, won't take a hint. He poured me a cup and pushed the teacup towards me. I picked it up and went to the opposite side of the island. I wanted to get my space so I would not be tempted to embarrass myself by touching him again.

"Ok, Beck, what can I answer for you?" I looked at him through my lashes as I took a deep drink. This was not my tea. It was delicious, but not the tea I have ever purchased. I looked at the cup confused, pulling it away from my mouth.

"It's my own assortment." He answered my quiet puzzlement before I had said a word.

"It's really good. What brand is it?" I took another sip and set my cup down.

"It's not a brand, I make it." Of course, he makes his own

tea assortment. He probably dried the leaves and ground the spices, that combined with that face and body. I shook my head to clear the smutty thoughts.

I nodded casually and stared at him, waiting for his questions. We sat in silence and drank our tea. He looked content, maybe a little bored. My brain was going back and forth between *this is weird* and *maybe he does like me and is nervous.*

I finally broke the silence after there were only dregs left in my teacup. "So?"

"Why do you do it?" He was staring at me. His eyes were hypnotizing like a cobra dancing to music.

I shook my head to break the connection, "Can you be more specific?" I hope I sounded calm and indifferent. I was trying to mirror his vibe, but it is hard to duplicate a perfectly handsome, calm, cool, collected ninja assassin at a witty match of verbal sparring. I had a hard enough time keeping my tongue in my mouth and my head out of the gutter.

He moved to the other side of the island, taking the seat next to mine. I remained where I was, fighting every urge in my body to not turn towards him. He was close, I could feel his body heat grazing my arm.

"Why do you investigate these rapes and violence against women?" All things considered; it was the easiest question he could have asked me. He was already in on my secret, so that cat was out of the proverbial bag. I kept my eyes forward and shrugged. I let my finger trace the lip of the teacup, "Why not?"

From the corner of my concentrating eyes, I saw him lift his hand in my direction. His fingertips were gentle on my chin, he slowly directed my gaze at him.

"Why did you do that?" I asked, not that I minded with the physical contact. It just felt intimate and considering his determination not to sneak a peek at my girls, the action seemed weird.

His eye contact was back, more intense than before.

"I want to see your eyes when you talk to me." His deep voice was low but clear.

"Why does that matter?" My voice was barely above a whisper.

"It's easier to tell when someone is being sincere." I nodded like I understood what he was implying and turned my gaze away from his. Of course, he is using my eyes as little lie detectors. It was probably some crazy interrogation tactic he learned along the way. He gently pulled my chin back and rested his palm against my cheek. His thumb rested just below my lips. It was warm and made my stomach do flips and bursts in fire like Barnum and Bailey's finest. I wanted to kiss him, wanted it bad. I settled for biting my lip. I was not going to fall victim to another unrequited kiss.

"And I like looking at your face." He said as he rubbed my lower lip with his thumb, freeing it from my teeth. I think I was holding my breath to keep from gasping.

"Oh." I fought the blush I felt forming.

His eyes were smoking with emotions that seemed unclear to me. I was still trying to figure out what "I like looking at your face" means. Maybe it was a part of the interrogation tactic. Like him complimenting me sets a baseline of a response. Although he could want to kiss me. No, that's not it either, I mean, I like looking at Mickey Mouse's face, but that does not mean I want to kiss it. He leaned forward. Shit, maybe he was going to kiss me! I licked my lips in anticipation.

"Why violent crimes against women?" He asked low and clear again. *No get back to the face comment, I need more information on what the heck that even means.*

"I guess I want to get justice for people that can't get it themselves." He nodded and leaned a little closer, his eye contact was intense like he was staring into my soul. It was hard to not look away. Maybe he *was* playing a game. The more questions I answered the closer he would get until we were desecrating the counter. I could definitely play *that* game. Then again, he could be trying to get a better look at my pupil responsiveness.

"I do not understand why, though. What prompted you?" He asked with a furrowed brow.

I furrowed my brow back in response. "Do you not believe the altruism to seek justice is enough? Please do not tell me that you underestimated my intent for good." I said quietly. I was purposefully being evasive. I did not want to discuss my abusive childhood or my sister's rape with a man that I hardly knew.

He brought his other hand to cup my other cheek. *Hell yes! This was starting to bend towards more kiss kiss then tell tell.*

I saw my phone light up on the counter, someone had just sent me a text message. I stayed present in the conversation. I mean, I didn't really have a choice, his palms were firmly securing my cheeks.

"I do not underestimate you, as much as you underestimate yourself. And I know you are a good person. I knew that the moment you helped me hide the girls away and bathed them. Even in the brief time you had left to have dinner with Chris, the girls felt the calm you brought them to leave." He smiled softly at me. "But I am not naive enough to believe that something did not happen that made you want to seek other's justice."

A smile still played around his lips, but he continued with his intense staring contest. I almost rebutted that I did not underestimate myself, but I did not want to interfere with this game if it was in fact a game. "What prompted you to start investigating these crimes?" He repeated again, clearly seeing right through my evasive comment. His voice was barely above a whisper, lips one inch from mine. I parted my lips and leaned in to close the gap.

"Caroline?" Someone was knocking on my door. Beck dropped his hands and leaned away. I scrambled to my phone to check if I could see who just messed up my game of chicken. It was Nathan. He had just sent a text saying he was heading over. I did not remember calling or inviting him over. I looked longingly over to Beck's retreating figure. He nodded to me as he shut the patio door behind him. I stood rooted to the spot until Nathan rang the doorbell. Sheesh, a little impatient tonight.

I opened the front door, slightly annoyed, very revved up.

"Hey, gorgeous," Nathan pushed his way in, kissing me on the cheek. It felt wet, I wiped it away.

"I don't remember inviting you over." I tried to keep the accusation out of my voice. It's not like he knew he had just interrupted something that I was convinced would be mind-boggling.

"I decided to surprise you!" He held up a bottle of wine. It was white wine; I hate white wine. He had already made his way into my kitchen and was looking for the wine key. I followed in after him and opened the correct drawer and handed him the tool. I refrained from stabbing him with the spiral end, reminding myself that he had no clue that the man of my literal dreams just left. He popped the cork and poured himself a glass. "Want some?" He took a sip.

"No, I was about to go to bed, I have to work early in the morning."

"I'll make it quick then." He gulped down his glass and walked over to me, untying my robe. It did feel good to feel attractive. It felt good for someone to appreciate my body and not ignore it. Did I wish it was Beck taking such interest in my body so much so that he would untie my robe? Absolutely, but as it was, I figured if I was not going to physically have sex with Beck, doesn't mean I couldn't *pretend* Nathan was Beck. He leaned in and kissed my neck; I moaned and arched my body into his.

It was enough to get the boy at full attention. I kissed him back deeply, imagining his tongue was Becks. It was the first time that I had kissed Nathan on the mouth. My Beck fantasy had overruled my rational sense to keep my lips to myself. I wrapped my legs around Nathan's waist pulling him into me. He carried me to the bedroom and placed me on the bed. Tonight, I was working through my Beck fantasy. Nathan hovered over me as I pushed him aside, taking control. I rode on top, forcing his hands to caress my nipples. I arched my back and grabbed his free hand forcing it to rub me in soft circles. I arched further back, bracing my arms behind me. Two minutes later Nathan was done. I was not. Funny, for some reason I thought my fantasy Beck could somehow make Nathan last longer.

"That was great." Nathan kissed my forehead as he pulled his pants back on. "Well, I know you were about to go to bed, so I would hate to keep you." Right, sure, minute man. Bang and bail. I needed to do something about him. Like a poorly trained dog, you don't know how awfully unsocialized they are until you start shopping around. I did not want to train him. I wanted to take him back and demand a refund, but then again, can you get a refund from a stray?

I heard him leave and played out the rest of my Beck fantasy, ending in convulsing waves.

Chapter 5

February 18-20

I woke up feeling well-rested and at ease. I checked the clock, 5:30am, got about six hours of sleep. I stretched as I walked into the kitchen to warm up the kettle for my morning tea. I flipped the tv on to the news while the water warmed.

> "Police discovered the remains of Bobbi King early this morning. She was found less than a mile from where she had first disappeared fifteen days ago, at a nearby park. Police believe King was held at another facility and her abductor had moved her remains postmortem. We are waiting on autopsy reports to determine the cause of death. Police are still looking into the disappearances of Flora Sanchez and Lisa Henderson. Sanchez has been missing for ten days and Henderson was reported missing and assumed abducted yesterday. If you have any information that may help with the investigation, police are urging you to call the following hotline."

I flipped my computer open and began to extract information. The autopsy was scheduled to be completed in a few days. The preliminary report showed older defensive wounds, most likely from the initial attack. Her remains were laid out spread eagle, in the same clothes she was wearing when she was abducted. Her hair was fanned out. The person who found her thought she was sleeping. When the police removed her body from the scene, they found a long cut from her sternum to her pelvis. This psychopath had sliced her open, performed exploratory surgery on her. I swallowed back bile.

I turned off the tv and shut my computer, disgusted. I tried to clear my mind through my morning yoga and run, but the image of the crime scene photos kept drifting back into my head. Work was the same, busy. Manny and Rani were in a deep discussion about the news of Bobbi King. I left early unable to fully concentrate on anything past the haunting images from the Bobbi King report. As I was leaving, Manny gave me a sealed envelope. It was an invitation to Jessica's twenty-first birthday party at the end of the week in Arcadia. It was at a new trendy bar.

"You're coming, right?" Manny asked.

"Yeah, I told Jessica I would. I am sure I will be the oldest person there, but I'll make do."

Manny laughed, "You and me both, but I am glad you are coming out. The whole staff will be there. It will be good for them to see you let loose."

When I got home, I delved deeper into the life of Bobbi King. I tried to retrace her steps in the last few days of her life before her abduction. Nothing out of the usual. I watched countless security footage looking for anything suspicious when something appeared twice. I thought I was on to something when I saw a white Prius driving up her street and then again at the grocery store, she had shopped on the day she was abducted. It could be something, except Southern Californians love white vehicles. It's too hot for any other color. With long commutes and traffic that will go from a twenty-minute drive into a two-hour drive, fuel-efficient cars were the preferred mode of transportation. None of the footage got a clear view of the car and the license plate was not visible in the grocery store footage. The residential footage was better, but it appeared mud was caked on the plate obscuring everything but the expiration date.

Frustrated, I switched gears and started looking into the Rebecca Hamilton suspects. DNA results concluded that I was looking for a Caucasian. It further narrowed down my results to 15. I watched endless hours of security footage from Java, trying to find when she fell asleep. It was problematic because she fell asleep in the breakroom which was located off camera in Java's back room. It was difficult to deduce when she "lost time" because I could only gather when she took her nap based on when she was off camera, but clocked in.

A day and a half later I had ruled all my suspects out, an hour after that, so did the police because the DNA did not match any of the male employees at Java or from her high school. I was frustrated to be back at square one, and I was disappointed I had not heard a single word from Beck since Nathan stopped in. He had made the comment about me "not taking a man" I did not want to correct him that I had a booty-call, but based on his hasty departure, he was now fully aware.

I did not want to be disappointed; I mean Beck thought I was interesting but that does not equate to wanting a relationship with me. Wait, did I even want a relationship? If I was being honest with myself, it did not matter what I wanted in this instance. All the information I had acquired regarding Beck was insanely limited, but not one piece of it showed he had had any form of sexual relationship with anyone. Not one dirty picture on his computer, not one sext on his phone (I hacked into his cell phone account, sue me, I was curious). He was either celibate or hooked up with random women he picked up at bars. It was possible, but not likely.

He was not the type to just let any random woman into his life. It's also possible he was dating someone from his work, and she doesn't know he has a cell phone. It's a weird thing to hide, but he was a weird guy. Intense, sexy, but weird. The thought of him dating someone made me feel angry. Not because she could be a waitress, line cook, or bartender. I was angry because he had shown preference to someone that was not me. Then the realization hit me, I was jealous of a person that might not even exist. I just fabricated an entire relationship and was mad at him for not telling me. I need to get my head examined. No, that appointment was not for another few days. What I needed was to see him. Well, I wanted to see him. I needed to figure out who had drugged and impregnated a 15-year-old girl. *Head back in the game!* I made up my mind.

"Banjo! Richard speaking." Banjo was the restaurant that Beck worked at. It was a mix of Asian BBQ with American BBQ. It was rustic but delicious and growing in popularity every day.

"Hi Richard, is Beck working?" I tried to keep my tone casual and sweet.

"Beck, you mean the chef the LA Times just voted 'up and comer in the area'? Yep, that Beck is here, alright." Richard had a thick Southern accent. Being from Charleston I was pretty good at figuring out which part of the south he had hailed; my guess was Southern Alabama.

"Sweetheart, can I ask who is callin'?" Oh, southern men and their propensity to give pet names to unknown women. I hung up before I felt the need to actually answer. What would I say anyway? *Oh, no, I don't actually want to talk with him, I just want to see if he is occupied so I can sneak into his house and try to see if he has a girlfriend.* Ha, what is wrong with me?

Temporary insanity, apparently, because I was already pulling out of my driveway to head West towards his loft. I was lucky to have just missed traffic. I pulled onto his street within 35 minutes. I parked and scaled the fire escapes like I had done the first time I broke in. Well, not broke in, simply entered without his permission. Four stories up and I slid through the open window into his bedroom.

His bed was low on a platform, the flooring was polished concrete, but the fifteen-foot ceiling was paneled in light wood. It gave the room a light, airy, and Scandinavian feel. His bed was made with crisp corners on his gray duvet, pillows lined up flat two stacked on each side. There was a pair of small side tables in light wood with clean lines and a modern dresser in a slightly darker wood tone, but still streamlined. The whole bedroom was not matchy-matchy but was comfortable, lived in. It was the aesthetic that Ikea was trying to create, but none of his furniture appeared to have come from flat packaging, rather it looked built from scratch.

I walked over and opened the first nightstand. Nothing of significance to me; a small collection of photos, aged around the edges. A Japanese woman holding a baby, looking at it with a smile only a mother has for her newborn baby; the same woman with a toddler sitting on her lap, the toddler was handsome with gold hair, his eyes were light and almond-shaped; the same woman slightly older, staring out of a window. I put the photos back. I assume that was Beck's mother, and possibly him in the photos. Next to the photos were a set of postcards all written in Japanese, they too looked aged around the edges. The other nightstand was empty. I guess the Gideons had not made it here yet.

I walked out into the living room. The far wall was completely covered in windows. The space was light and bright. His low sectional sofa was also gray, a white and black patterned rug separated the living space into its own area. There was a series of oak stained bookcases that lined one wall. The opposite wall had a long console table and a large painting of crashing waves. I padded over to the bookcase to see what reading stimulated his mind. One shelf contained leather-bound classics. Another shelf was a series of Japanese books also bound in leather. Another shelf held different folk tales from Norway, they were aged with yellow, the pages were brittle. The last shelf I looked at had more modern books, one on meditation, one on mindfulness, I picked up an unmarked yellow book and flipped it to its front, Tantric Practices. My stomach quivered as I replaced the volume. Interesting read if he was actually celibate.

I walked over to the console table. It had three cabinet doors and a small shelf. I pulled open the first door. It was filled with old records, I thumbed through the volumes. I was surprised to find several Beatles albums. I stood up and looked at the top of the console table, I saw a small break in the wood and realized it was not a table, it was an old record player console. I slid the top aside to see an old but well-preserved record player. I pulled out the Beatles album and began to listen. I was brought back to my youth.

After the accident, Lauren and I had a practically worry-free existence. Yes, our mother was catatonic, but we were free to live our lives without fear of being abused. We found a Beatles album in the basement with an old record player. We would play happy tunes and dance and laugh. I smiled at the memory and turned the volume low so I could still enjoy it without disrupting the neighbors. I walked over to the kitchen and opened the cabinets. It was a unique assortment of Asian labels and Norwegian foods. The fridge was full of fresh greens and fruits. I grabbed an apple, grabbed Tantric Practices, and sat on the sofa. Flipping through the volume while listening to the low crooning of "Yesterday", I felt comfortable. I did not feel like I had intruded into Beck's domain. I felt like I belonged. Maybe that was why I did not leave after I found no evidence of another woman in his life. Or maybe I just wanted to see him with the roles reversed, me intruding into his life.

I heard the soft metallic click of the front door lock sliding aside. I concentrated on the volume, acting indifferent and casual. It was amazingly difficult to look casual while thumbing through illustrated porn. I heard him close the door and hesitate for a fraction of a second. I flipped the page and took another bite of the apple.

"Do you want something more substantial to eat?" He did not seem surprised. He sounded expectant as if he was continuing a conversation. I looked over to the kitchen and gave him half a smile. I stood up and replaced the volume back on the bookshelf. Walked over to the bin and tossed the apple core.

One eyebrow perked up as I stopped in front of him, "are you not surprised by my presence?" I looked up to him through my lashes.

"When you did not show up at the restaurant, I figured you would come here." Always pragmatic and rational. I should not have been surprised, I called, left breadcrumbs, and he had highly deductive reasoning.

"Not a lot of people calling you at work?"

He pulled some fish out of the bag and began preparing silently. He tossed spinach and white beans into a skillet with oil and garlic. The whole kitchen began to smell intoxicating. "I think you have deduced that I do not have people coming into my house at all hours of the night."

Did I hear a twinge of jealousy or was I projecting guilt? Perhaps in the dark recesses of my brain I only hoped he was jealous. It would imply he liked me enough to be jealous. I shook my head and the thoughts of my hope he was jealous away.

"How would I know that?" I asked innocently. He placed the fish in the pan and waited for the sizzling sear to die down.

"Do you?" I think his silence was making me anxious, or maybe I was hungry and not acting rationally. Either way, my question came out a little desperate, a little whiny. Not the composed, almost indifferent conversation I was hoping for. He flipped the fish, another sizzle as he added cherry tomatoes to the pan.

"Do I what?" He was pushing the tomatoes around the pan, they burst into the sautéed spinach and garlic.

"Do you have anybody?" The words came out like an uncontrollable dirge. Why should I even care if he did? He saw Nathan, deduced what he was there for. Why would I care if he has the same arrangement?

"Who was your late-night visitor?" If he was pretending to be uninterested, he was aces at it. He almost sounded bored.

"A stray I picked up a few months ago." There was the slightest lift of a single eyebrow followed by pulling his face back to neutral and plated the fish, spinach, and beans. He passed the plate over to me, "eat."

I took a seat opposite of him, he stood and ate, still not looking at me. Where was all the intense eye contact from the other night? Maybe he *was* jealous. Or maybe he was under the impression that I am unavailable, and he wanted me to be. I allowed myself a few seconds of excitement over the notion, then I realized it was not likely based on the evidence, i.e., his mannerisms toward me while I was naked as a blue jay. We sat in silence until our meals were finished. He grabbed my plate and placed them in the sink, he turned around and finally looked at my face.

"Do you have a lot of strays you picked up?" He asked finally. I was almost offended that he was shaming me, but his tone seemed lighter and more amused.

"Just two strays that show up late at night, both I have not seen in a few days." The smallest hint of a smile reached his eyes but did not matriculate to his mouth. "We did not finish our conversation the other night. I was making myself available in case any *question* pops up." I was trying to sound suggestive, he still looked bored.

"I think I got all my answers." His expression was soft, but his silvery eyes looked smokey. I took a few tentative steps towards him, stopping directly in front of him. "Are you sure there is nothing else you wanted to ask me?" I stepped forward again. Now I had to look up at him. He followed me with his eyes and was now adjusting his gaze to meet my close proximity.

He reached out to stroke my cheek and let his hand rest

on the side of my neck, "is there something *you* want to ask *me*, Caroline?"

Yeah, something like, do you want to make out?

I smiled back tentatively and started to reach my hand to touch his face. I really wanted to feel his lips. They looked firm, slightly purply-pink.

BING!

The noise startled me, then I realized it was a notification on my phone. The autopsy results for Bobbi King were in. I dropped my hand and backed away, "Can I borrow your laptop?"

He nodded once and left me alone in the kitchen. I should feel embarrassed right? Wasn't I just throwing myself at him, and then backed out? I walked over to the sofa; he handed his laptop over to me. He walked back into the kitchen. I could hear water running, I assume he was cleaning up.

I opened up the report and read it in silence. I don't know how long I sat staring at the screen, but I assume my expression was a mix between, 'I'm going to be sick', and horrified.

"Is there something wrong?" Beck was standing in front of me, looking almost concerned.

"Bobbi King." My voice was a warbled whisper.

"What about her?" His voice was quiet but clear.

"He tortured her." I shook my head horrified at the last days of Bobbi King's life. I slowly closed the computer, unable to stand to see the photographs and diagrams of Bobbi King's extensive abuse she endured any longer. I rubbed my eyes and allowed my palms to cup my cheeks while I stared at the concrete floor and summarized what I had just read.

"He bound and starved her, there was nothing in the stomach or bowels, they were completely empty. She had deep cuts around her hands and legs where the bindings cut into her." I winced and dropped my hands away from my cheeks. I looked up into his silver eyes. "They think he raped her repeatedly the day before she was killed, no semen, just tears in her vaginal wall. He strangled her; it appears with his hands. After she died, he opened her up. He drained her blood. It appears he bleached the intestines and her uterus appeared scrubbed clean." I swallowed at the lump that had formed. I turned my eyes away from Beck's intense stare.

"They think she was killed within 12 hours of when she was found." At some point a tear escaped my eye. I wiped it away quickly.

He kneeled down to be level with my face, but he did not touch me, "What information have you acquired?"

I gave him the rundown on all the avenues I had gone down. At one point he looked impressed, but he pulled his expression back to neutral.

"I basically have nothing, and I did not even come here for the Bobbi King case. I need help with something else." This time his expression did change. He looked thoughtful as if he was considering helping me even though he did not know what I was going to ask.

"Start from the beginning. Who is the new case? And what do you want to ask of me?"

I launched into Rebecca Hamilton's case. I told him about the pregnancy, the narcolepsy, the gaps in time missing, and finally, the paternity test that had no match.

"So, you see, the only other loss of time happened at Griffith Park. I need to recreate it. I need to take a nap in the park, and I need you to watch and see if anyone tries anything. She had ketamine in her system, so someone saw her sleeping and drugged her. He somehow removed her from the picnic area without anyone watching and..." I let the statement hang.

"You believe the person who did this was a stranger?" He looked skeptical; one brow was arched.

I threw my hands in the air, "I don't know, it's possible someone followed her there, like a customer from work. But the ketamine, the secluded area, it feels premeditated. Like whoever did this has done it before. It is possible that Rebecca was just a product of bad luck and timing to fall asleep within the grasp of a rapist." He nodded, I continued. "I'm assuming if that were the case, the predator would be repeating his behavior with home-field advantage. He has not been caught yet, and honestly if Rebecca had not gotten pregnant, no one would be the wiser." I was pacing now. Beck had replaced my spot on the sofa. He was watching me like a tiger stalking its prey, eyebrows low above his eyes.

"When do you want to do this?" He asked finally.

I looked at the clock, it was 2pm. When Rebecca went it was 3pm, she was there for two hours.

"Now?" I was flexing my hands in little fists waiting for his reply. I was bracing for his rejection again. I held my breath.

"Shall I pack a picnic?" His smile looked sardonic. Shock that he was willing to give up his afternoon to help me spread across my face. I took a few quick steps towards him as if I was going to hug him in my relief, but I stopped myself before I did. My brain was quick to falter my steps and preserve the dignity of not allowing another rejection.

He narrowed his eyes at my faltered steps as I bit my lip and took a step towards the door. "Thank you. Yes, we should bring some water, it's about a twenty-minute walk to the area where she fell asleep."

The drive was pleasant. He avoided the highways, stuck to surface streets. We pulled into the park. The Hollywood sign and observatory loomed in the distance. Beck had changed from his chef garb to joggers. He pulled his shirt off and pulled a backpack over his shoulders. His stomach and pecs were perfect. His eight pack of abs was chiseled in definition. Each ab was slightly off center from the next. His pecs were defined and strong. He had light veining and a v-cut that disappeared into the waist of his joggers. His muscles looked more defined than the last time I had seen him without his shirt on. I turned my body away from him before I let my mind wander further. I led the hike.

It was a beautiful day, 80 degrees, blue sky, slight wind that was refreshing as the hike steepened. He stayed 5 feet back, we did not exchange a single word. When I got to the spot where Rebecca frequented, I laid out a blanket and nodded to him. He disappeared behind a copse of trees. I closed my eyes and focused on my surroundings. The breeze would occasionally tickle hair across my cheek. I flipped to my stomach with my head on my arms. I let the sun soak into my back and legs. I fought hard to not fall asleep, so I let my mind wander to at least appear to be asleep.

I thought about Bobbi King and worried about Flora Sanchez's fate. Wherever Flora and Lisa were, surely, he was starving them. Would someone find them before it was too late? Would I find them? I thought about the white Prius and how I could check Flora and Lisa's footage to see if I could spot one in the background of any of the footage.

The sun was setting, it went from being bright yellow to orange. I felt the air pressure around me change and I snuck a glance. Beck was lounging next to me. He was on his back, leaning on his elbows watching the sunset, he looked like a model in a cologne ad. I admired him for a second, then the realization of our mission crept back in, "What are you doing?" I hissed at him.

He chuckled, it sent a thrill through me, "You have been here for two hours, no one is here, we are completely alone." I turned my body to my side to face him. Ugh, why couldn't he be wearing a shirt? Now I just wanted to slide my fingers up and down the planes of his perfect abdomen. He was more tempting than I wanted to admit.

"Oh," was all I managed to say.

He turned to look at me, "Beautiful." I wanted to say, *who, me?* And bat my lashes. He turned back to the sunset and nodded. I followed his gaze. It was a spectacular display of orange, red, and pinks. We watched the amazing painting of nature in silence, "We better get going before it gets too dark, that's when the real crazies come out."

He gave me a half-smile and nodded in agreement. He pulled a shirt from the backpack and stuffed the blanket in its place. He shrugged his top on and led the way back to the car. The view from behind was pretty good. His butt muscles were perky and round. He did not skip leg day when he worked out. God, I need to get my mind out of the gutter.

When we got back to his loft, he did not invite me up. I was disappointed, but I reminded myself that one, I had hijacked his afternoon, and two, he was clearly not interested in me like that. I made my way east thinking hard about today's developments.

I decided that on the subject of Rebecca Hamilton I needed to spread the possibilities of who attacked her out. It was no one with direct contact with her. It could be a regular at Java, it could be a boy at school. It was someone that knew she was narcoleptic and not on her meds. Close to her but not obvious. The boys at her high school were a possibility, but horny teenage boys can just ask horny teenage girls for ass. It felt unlikely that something this well thought out and organized could come from a group of males whose amygdala had not fully formed. I needed to review her social life more closely.

In regard to Flora Sanchez and Lisa Henderson, I needed to recheck the footage. Perhaps if I found something, I would send an anonymous tip about the car. I also wanted to answer the nagging questions; how were the three women related? Or maybe more broadly, how is it possible that the three victims could have a common visitor? I thought of my dad, a long-haul trucker. But this was not long haul, it was all local. Maybe a delivery service or a company that trucks goods. It had its possibilities.

I got home, jotted down the possibilities, and stripped down for a quick swim. After today I needed to relax. Nathan called. I ignored it. I knew I was putting off the inevitable, but I was occupied trying to now solve a murder AND find a rapist. My plate was too full for the "It's not you, it's me" speech.

I swam my laps thinking of potential businesses that could distribute their goods all over southern California. It had to be a small enough company where they only had one or two delivery drivers. Small farms and bakeries were the top of my hit list. They could potentially deliver to the local grocery stores. Maybe he saw each woman at the store and thought she was too irresistible and took her after stalking her. Weirder things have happened.

I finished my laps and laid out all the possibilities. I looked for local farms, bakeries, and the like, trying to match them with local stores. Nathan called again. Ignore. I moved my operation to the bedroom and continued until past midnight. My eyes started to burn as I finally shut my laptop. I needed to sleep and get my head back together.

Chapter 6

February 21

Bobbi King's image haunted my dreams. I felt compelled to find her justice. She died in an awful way and I owed it to Flora and Lisa to redouble my efforts. My eyes burned as I tried to open them. I made a pot of tea and turned the news on while eating my oatmeal.

> "Kelly Parker, from Dana Point, has been reported as missing. Parker was at the beach when she disappeared, and her belongings were abandoned on a beach blanket. Coast guard has been sweeping the waters to see if she fell into the ocean or if she was pulled in from a riptide. Police are also concerned that her disappearance has similarities to the disappearance of Bobbi King, Flora Sanchez, and Lisa Henderson. Bobbi King's remains were found three days ago. If anyone has any information regarding Kelly Parker's whereabouts, please contact this number below."

Shit. Another one, possibly. She could have drowned, awful, but possible. If she did not drown and she is another victim, the sad reality is, there is now more evidence that would point to the culprit. First thing first, rule out drowning. I loaded her social media to see if she at any point mentioned her ability to swim, enjoy it even. What her beach habits were; did she go in; or just enjoy the sounds and breeze. Her bathing suits did not appear conducive for doing anything but looking pretty. They were small with intricate patterns and rhinestones. I checked her background. She is a fitness instructor, got her start as teaching water aerobics to senior citizens, now teaches HIIT to celebutants. I doubted greatly a water aerobics instructor could not swim. Surely, she would also know to swim parallel with the coast until the tide released you. Another victim.

I stretched and ran to let my head mull over the new information. An hour later I pulled out my research matrix and added Dana Point into the new area for delivery companies like furniture, farm, and bakeries. I came up with one company that has a small delivery staff of two. They serve areas from Dana Point to Riverside, Pan Bakery located in Covina, fit my criteria. They had two delivery drivers that dropped off at all the Whole Foods, Gentry Jackson and Paolo Guitierrez.

It was not a perfect match because Flora had been abducted from a Vons. People are extremely loyal about where they get their groceries. Habits are a hard thing to break and the ritual of grocery shopping is practically religious. Only a few instances in life would prompt anyone to change their shopping habits: they moved; they married; they graduated; they had a baby. To my knowledge, Flora had done none of those things in the past five years.

Four hours later I had ruled out Paolo. He had been on medical leave for the past two weeks for a slipped disc. That meant Gentry was completing all the runs. Okay, I have a suspect. He did not own a white Prius, but that was grasping at straws. Gentry lived in West Covina, perfect. I slid on my hat and headed over to my condo in Pasadena. An hour later Leslie Mixon emerged. I clicked the fob to the black BMW. It was hot, but the leathery smell was satisfying. I entered Gentry's address into the GPS and headed over to West Covina. I drove by his house; It was small in a neighborhood built in the 1950s. All were a single story with small yards surrounded by white metal fences, each in their own degree of rust and decay. Gentry's house was average with an average amount of rust. No car parked in the driveway. The garage was slightly lifted with a lattice gate across the bottom. Hmm, he must have dogs.

I looped around and headed to an adjacent street that had a decent view of his house. I would at least be able to see when he got home. I adjusted my light brown page boy wig and pushed my glasses up. The windows were tinted enough that you would have to cup your hands and press your face against the window to see me. The brown contacts were drying to my eyes, but overall, I was deep in disguise to find a killer, an itchy eye is nothing compared to the torture those women were going through. An hour later, Gentry pulled into his driveway. He had a newer black pickup truck. He shuffled into his house and turned the kitchen light on. My research suggested that he was working from 5am to 5pm because of Paolo's injury. It did not exactly give a lot of time for planning, abducting, and disemboweling but twelve hours a day is still a lot of time.

I slid out of the BMW. I was dressed in dark gray running shorts, a black top, and gray sneakers. I pretended to be on my evening jog. The sun was hot and low in the sky. I reached his driveway and pretended to tie my shoe. I slipped a GPS tracker under his hitch. I stood up and looped back around the block towards the BMW. Satisfied with my little jaunt, I headed back to Pasadena and shed Leslie Mixon's persona and headed into a sparring club in Pasadena.

It felt good to use my muscles, all the adrenaline of possibly catching a killer or rapist had me on edge. I always felt jittery when I was close to a suspect. Or like a wind-up toy whose spinner is broken. It was a good release. I headed home for a nice shower and congratulatory beer perhaps. I nixed the beer when I thought of Gentry deciding to visit his victims at midnight. I needed to be on my A-game.

Nathan was parked in my driveway. *Take a hint buddy.* I mentally sighed, I was being a bitch. He did not understand that I changed the rules. He still has no clue about Beck. Not that there is anything going on with Beck, but still. I was not being fair to him. I knew it, but sometimes when things get to a point of more trouble than they are worth, it's much easier to ghost the problem than wasting the energy trying to fix it. I rolled down my window, "what's up Nathan?"

"Nothing, just wanted to talk." He nodded to the garage. I opened it, and pulled in. He took the opened garage door as his own opportunity and walked in with me. He followed me into the house through the mud room. I walked into the kitchen and filled a glass of water.

"Can I get you anything to drink?" Damn those Southern hospitality manners, they come through even when you are trying to be off-putting.

"Beer if you have one." I opened the fridge and popped the top, handing him one. The beer looked good. Maybe I should reconsider the beer, but I was nuts deep in an investigation and if Gentry left, I needed to be able to follow him at a moment's notice. He took a deep swig. It looked good. Damn him.

"Who's Beck?" Nathan asked while thumbing the side of the beer bottle.

I controlled my face to seem confused, but mostly I was thinking: *Did Beck confront Nathan after his short visit? Did Nathan see Beck? Oh God, why do I even feel guilty. I owe nothing to either of these guys.*

I remained calm and indifferent, "I don't know who you are talking about." I took a sip of water to rehydrate my mouth that had gone dry from the stress of confrontation that my anxiety imagined I was about to have with Nathan. He grinned at me and took another swig. I watched condensation slip down the bottle. If I had wanted a beer before, it was nothing compared to wanting it now. I was staring at the cat that ate the canary. He coolly grinned at me and nodded. Apparently, I was not convincing enough in my denial.

"So, you normally moan other guys' names when fucking someone else?" He did not look mad, he looked amused. I on the other hand was speechless and trying not to projectile spit water at him. Apparently, I was a little louder with my fantasy than I intended. I shrugged and shook my head. *Well, this is awkward.*

"You can date other guys; we are not exclusive." He shrugged. *Not exclusive? We were not anything to be exclusive about! And the exclusive comment coming from him? Ha! He bangs more single moms and desperate housewives than anyone else I had met.* I stayed silent and indifferent, my RBF in place.

"We never had the official talk anyway." He set his beer down. He raised his hand to stroke my cheek. Maybe it was guilt that kept me rooted in place, maybe it was just sheer embarrassment over moaning Beck's name. "Sorry I rushed out of here the other night. When you said another guy's name, it kind of freaked me out. I left without finishing you off. Thought I would stop by and correct that." *Ugh, now? Nuts deep in an investigation. I don't need to be nuts deep in anything else.*

I decided I was just going to ignore the whole saying-a-different-name-during-sex fiasco and focus on the proposition.

"Tonight, is not a good night. I am working on something for my sister and I am pretty tired from all the work I have been doing."

He looked thoughtful, "Is he coming over tonight?" His eyes looked a little hurt. Maybe I was just imagining it. Wouldn't be the first time I had imagined someone caring more than they did. I mentally winced, *get a grip.*

I shook my head, "No one is coming over tonight, and I am not dating anyone, including you."

If he did not look hurt before, he did now. *Crap on a cracker.* I was not imagining it at all. I hurt his feelings with that last one.

"Listen, I like our arrangement. I just thought I would tell you, if you wanted more, I'd be willing to make some sacrifices." He said.

Sacrifices? Ha! Does that mean he would sacrifice his

two other side pieces? I doubted that greatly. Nathan was a bachelor, kind of a player. He had offers all the time. Women really do have a pool boy fantasy. Add that to the fact that he teaches children self-defense and is in pretty good shape... We have always been honest about what this was. Perhaps he is changing the rules because he thinks someone else might want me. I felt a little smug then annoyed that he wanted me all to himself. I did not want him all to myself. I didn't really want him at all. He was a stray cat that I fed and kept coming back. I should stop feeding into this, but when you stop feeding cats, I am pretty sure they yowl loudly for the neighbors to hear. I don't know how that would actually happen. He is not the boombox on the shoulder type professing his love for all the world to hear. Hmm, he is the type to show up randomly and take his chances, but if he showed again while Beck was here... I grimaced at the thought.

"I'd hate for you to sacrifice anything on my account." I worked hard not to add a sarcastic emphasis on "sacrifice", but I don't think I was completely successful. I smiled sweetly to hide my grimace that was surely percolating onto my face.

"Okay, I can see you are into this Beck guy. I'm just saying if he's not all you think he is I can make myself available." He winked at the end. Ugh, this guy had sex on his mind 24/7, but what guy doesn't? I mean... probably Beck. How many times would I have to throw myself at him, literally and figuratively, before stopping? I try not to be an optimist; I am a realist. I have seen the harsh reality of the world. I have seen the dregs of society at their most guttural instincts. My brain is a realist, my hormones and my heart are optimists to their squishy ends. My brain normally wins out, and it will again.

"Once again, I am not 'into' anyone. I appreciate your offer, but I need to get to bed." I mean, I didn't want to be "into" Beck. I had spent a lot of one-on-one time with Beck in close proximity and not once had he moved in for the proverbial kill. My brain kept chanting; he is not into you. My heart and hormones kept telling my brain to shut up and wait.

Nathan wagged his eyebrows at me, “I can join you in the bed.” It took a lot of willpower not to punch him in the face. I am sure he was trying to be charming, but at this point in the quagmire of my brain and heart, I let my guttural instinct reign supreme. And she is a bullet spitting bitch. She is a hitter and biter.

I pushed him towards the door, “Goodnight, Nathan.” I think my brain and heart simultaneously sighed. Punching a man that wants to bed me, in the face would essentially close the door to everyone that wanted to bed me. My realistic brain reminded me of the nice pressure release that Nathan provided. My heart reminded me it was better than nothing.

I walked back into the kitchen to sit down and check the GPS tracker on Gentry’s truck.

“Are all your strays that persistent in staying after they have been dismissed?” Beck was sitting at the counter, drinking from my glass of water. I stuttered to a stop. How much had he heard? I cringed, not one bit of that conversation was meant to be overheard. My heart smiled; my brain cursed.

“Apparently they are.” There you go, cool as a cucumber.

He actually laughed; my stomach burst into butterflies.

“Okay, I’ll go.” He stood up to leave. My heart stopped beating and my brain screamed pressure release.

“No stay, you do not live close, and you clearly wanted to talk to me about something.” I took a seat opposite him and reclaimed my glass of water. It seemed strangely intimate that he drank from my glass. I took a sip. He watched; a smile lifted one corner of his mouth. *What does that smile mean?*

“Your friend has some interesting theories.” He leaned forward, narrowing his eyes but maintaining the intense eye contact that I had come to expect.

I scoffed, "how much did you hear?" I was praying he had only heard the last part, where I denied everything. On second thought, do I want him to think I am not into him? I did not actually know what I wanted.

"Enough to be confused."

Shit. The likelihood that he had heard everything was pretty high. I mean, it would be pretty confusing to hear that someone moaned your name during sex, then denied being into you, while a third party was insisting that you were in fact into them.

I waved a dismissive hand trying to look blasé. "Don't listen to a word Nathan said. He has a pretty one-track mind."

"It wasn't what Nathan, that's his name?" He tilted to head as if to confirm his answer before he continued, "It's not what he said that confused me."

"Oh," it was not elegant, but I did not know what else to say. I did not want to tell him that I fantasized about him or god forbid that I was, in fact, into him. I pulled open my laptop for something to do. I mean, I had plenty to do aside from this conversation that felt a little like a tightrope walk. I glanced up from my work, he was staring at me. His face looked neutral.

"Do you have any more questions for me?" I needed to break the silence. My hormones were hoping for something along the lines of favorite positions.

"Several." He stood up and walked to the cabinet and poured himself his own glass of water. Where were my manners when I actually wanted to be cordial?

"I'm an open book, Beck. Ask away." I continued typing. I had locked into Gentry's GPS and synced it to my phone for easy tracking.

"What are you working on?" He sat back down, but this time he was in the seat next to me. His body was turned towards me, but he was looking at the computer screen.

"I'm tracking a suspect from the Bobbi King crime." I began pulling up my matrix to show him.

"Is that why you were in West Covina?"

I stopped typing. I think my jaw dropped and I stopped breathing. "Were you following me?" My voice was low but clear. I was not sure if I was pissed at him or at myself for not realizing that someone was following me.

He narrowed his eyes and titled his head before responding. "Not intentionally. You passed me going the other direction. I was coming up to see if you had any thoughts on the newest abduction." A tendril of hair had fallen across my face, he pushed in behind my ear.

I thought about how lucky that little hair was and refocused on the conversation, "you could have called."

He smiled, lifted one eyebrow, "is it not customary to wait until someone has given you their number before calling uninvited?"

"You come here uninvited all the time, isn't that uncustomary?" I had turned my head to face him. I was smiling, almost flirting. My heart responded by beating a little faster.

"Your phone number is unlisted; your address is not." Hmm, it's a practical reason, I mean if you ignore the multiple B&Es.

"Or maybe you just wanted to see me." I turned back to my computer. I did not want to see his reaction in case he was going to blow me off again. He just chuckled; it was thrilling.

"Do you want me to want to see you?" His voice was seductively low. My breath hitched.

"I do not know if that question is pertinent to the current investigation." I chanced a glance at him. He had a half-smile, and he shook his head.

"Who is Leslie Mixon?"

I narrowed my eyes to him. He knew all about my alias, in fact he knew about several of them. He had stayed in my condo and I watched him look through my closet full of disguises and wigs. He smiled with one side of his mouth before amending his question.

"Maybe the better question is, why did you make up Leslie Mixon?"

I heard my teeth click together. He wanted to know why I started separating my life from real and investigations. It was a leading question that involved too many details about wanting to protect Lauren. I looked back at him, trying to mask my shock. I was hopeful that I just looked confused. He reached up and cradled my chin and pulled it to face him. Man, I like this game, but these questions are harder to answer than the ones before.

"Leslie is a business partner." His eyes narrowed, detecting my lie. Maybe he was just watching my pupil dilation. *This is not a seductive tactic; it's a lie detector.*

I sighed and bit my lip again. "Leslie is my alter ego for when I am going out and tagging suspects. I use her identity and condo as a decompression chamber. If someone follows her, they stop at the condo. But apparently, there is a flaw in my system because you followed me while I was Leslie Mixon. So, tell me, what area do I need to clean up so I can keep Leslie's identity separate from mine?"

He chuckled, "No, the disguise is very good, and had I not seen your closet of disguises…" He leaned forward in his seat and licked his lips. "I am an expert in the art of blending in and deception. I highly doubt anyone except me would be able to make out that it was you." It was a relief, but it did not answer my question.

"Yes, you stayed well-hidden for weeks while the

bounty on your life was active. Where did you stay exactly?" I was leaning in, like a reverse of our little game, but apparently, I was too aggressive, or I was making an ass of myself assuming he wanted to kiss me because as soon as I leaned in, he dropped his hand and turned his body away. *Well, it looks like I blew it again.* I knew it was a lie detector tactic.

"You still have not answered two of my questions." Now I was confused because the only question I had straight up ignored was the "want me to want you" question.

"Which are?" I tried not to fidget, but I was basically waiting for him to ask if I liked him. I had no idea how to answer that. Do I tell him the truth and risk him blowing me off? Or lie when he actually likes me? Or tell the truth and hope for the best that he actually likes me?

"What prompted you to investigate these crimes?" He pointed to my laptop. I screwed my face up trying to remember when he had asked me, "I asked you the last time I was here, you were unable to answer then. I am hoping tonight will be different." Oh shit. That was when Nathan stopped by and Beck slipped out the back.

"Oh." I felt relieved that it was not an embarrassing question about a stupid crush. It was just a question regarding my abusive childhood, my sister's rape, and my husband's lessons on how to investigate. No big deal. I rolled my mental eyes.

"It's a long story." He nodded, prompting me to go on, "I have all night." Damn, was that a proposition?

"I guess the short answer is, someone attacked my sister and I vowed to get justice where she did not."

He nodded, "What's the long answer?" He had turned his body towards mine again. I took another sip of water. "That requires a change in venue and attire," I pulled my shirt, that was still damp from sparring earlier in the evening, away from my body. He nodded in understanding.

"I'm going to take a shower, give me a minute." He nodded again. *Or you could join me.*

"What?"

"What?" Shit, did I say that out loud? I briskly walked out of the kitchen and to my bedroom before my blush could burn my ears off. The shower was cold but refreshing, I was *almost* not thinking about him joining me as I turned the water off. I dried off, pulled on a tank with matching boy shorts, and headed back out to the kitchen. It was empty. I looked around; I think I had started to frown at missing out on time with Beck when I heard him move in the living room.

He was sitting on the sofa leaning back, reading a book from my shelf. Touché.

I sat down, facing him, sitting with my back to the armrest. "So, the long version."

Chapter 7

February 22

I gave Beck the Reader's Digest version of my childhood, skipping over the truly gruesome parts and the survivor's guilt and PTSD that I still suffer from. He did not interrupt. He would occasionally wince when I would slip and share something brutal. I felt like I talked for hours. Maybe I did because I did not remember stopping or going to sleep. When I woke up at 4:30am to my phone alerting me that Gentry was on the move, I was in my bed. I wondered vaguely if Beck had carried me to my room after I fell asleep while talking to him.

I was in too much of a hurry to feel embarrassed for being a bad host. I had to get going. I needed to set up another GPS on Gentry's delivery truck. I was shocked when I saw Beck sleeping on my couch. He looked beautiful, but I pulled myself silently out of my house and slid into my car. Fortunately, Gentry's work was halfway between his house and mine. I sped over just in time to see him getting out of his black truck. The delivery vehicle was idling, and someone was just finishing up the load. Ten minutes later, Gentry pulled out and went to his first drop off. I pretended to drop my keys and attached the tracker to the front bumper. I was back at my house by 5:30am. Beck was no longer sleeping on the couch. I was mad at myself; I could have woken him up. Surely, he would have joined me. I looked around for a few minutes, but Beck was gone. I was too frustrated with myself for not leaving a note or waking him. I felt like I had lost time with the one person's time I craved. I pushed open my bedroom door, and hastily got dressed for my morning run.

I was just getting my stride when the feeling of being watched started to tickle my senses. Before 6am, no one but an occasional dog walker was usually awake on the quiet streets of Glendora. I convinced myself I was being paranoid. Just because I had just followed a guy around does not mean someone was doing the same to me. I increased my speed just in case. I was just rounding the corner of the Mason's house when someone launched at me from behind a car parked against the curb.

He hit my stomach with his shoulder mid-stride, like a linebacker going in for a tackle. I used the momentum of our fall together to twist us in the air, putting myself in the position on top. I sat on my would-be perpetrator's chest and reared back to perform a head butt to knock him out. As I pulled my head back though, the sprinkler pivoted and caught me directly in the face, disorienting me from my self-defense prose.

"Jesus, Ro, after all this time, I still can't get the drop on you."

I blinked the water out of my eyes, "Thomas?" Thomas Corbin, my younger brother. I had not seen him in months. His curly light brown hair was just above his shoulders. His stubble was almost to beard status, but it was him alright.

"Yeah, big sister, now get off me, you weigh a ton!" I ignored the weight comment.

"What. The. Hell. Are you doing here? I thought you were in Haiti." I pulled myself to my feet and held my hand out to help him up. He gladly pulled and wiped the wet grass off his back. I swatted at the mud on my knees. And punched his arm to release the latent adrenaline.

"Came to surprise you!" He rubbed his chest where I had landed on him, but he seemed to be fine.

"By surprise do you mean, you tried to attack me? I could have killed you!" I was staring at him in disbelief. One, for the fact that he would try anything so foolish, and two, because he was here, not a million miles away helping hurricane victims. He was here in the flesh, and he was a sight for sore eyes.

He did his classic full body laugh that normally ended with him slapping his knees until his fits of laughter subsided, "Kill me?" He laughed harder. "Tiny thing like you? You could not kill me, Ro!" He took a deep breath to calm his laughter, "Besides, the minute you would have realized it was me, you would have stopped yourself." He coughed a few times and sidled to the sidewalk.

"I *did* stop myself when I saw it was you. But if that sprinkler had not hit me in the face, you would have a ridiculous bruise on your forehead to explain to Lauren." Lauren hated violence and would have been disgusted by even our pretend fighting.

"Oh well!" Thomas smiled down at me, "I figured I would join you for your little run. Try to keep up, slowpoke!" His smile turned into a chiding joker's grin and he took off running.

Thomas and I had run cross country together in high school. He was always faster than me, but since his five-year stint with Doctors without Borders, I doubted he kept up with his cardio as much as I had. I let him run ahead of me. I kept my pace, waiting for him to tucker himself out. After a mile, I was passing him by. I worked hard not to sneer as elapsed him. He kept a decent pace. He only finished about twenty feet behind me.

"You are out of shape baby bro!"

He was bending at the waist with his hand on one knee and was pressing on his side with the other hand. He silently nodded with a grimace. "It's hard to find time to run when you are saving lives." He huffed between words. I rolled my eyes.

"Where are your bags?" Thomas always stayed at my

house when the wind blew him in from whatever foreign country he was breaking from. He pointed his thumb behind him at a dark sedan rental, still nursing his side.

We walked over together as he dug the keys out of his pocket and pulled out one large duffle bag and one smaller black bag, I assume, his medicine kit. He followed me in the house and went to the guest room that John and I had dubbed 'Thomas's room'. No one else would come to visit. My mom and Jennifer would always opt to stay with Lauren. Annie had never been to visit, but she was very busy with her career, and the fact that she hated me, kept her on the other ocean.

"You just missed mom." I was chopping up chicken into strips and placing them into a salad for lunch. We had spent the morning in our own quarters. When we got back from the run, Thomas retired to his room. He was probably napping after a six-mile run his legs were no longer used to making. I had been checking Gentry's tracker and spiraling my investigation out for the Rebecca Hamilton case. Nothing concrete in either investigation.

He was munching on a carrot stick, "Nah, I stopped in Charleston first. Annie drove up, hung out for a few days." He shrugged; he knew my relationship with Annie was strained. I snagged a crouton and crunched.

"They didn't know." Thomas had stopped crunching and was looking at me with a pained expression.

I was confused, "Didn't know what?" I popped another crouton in my mouth and crunched loudly.

He watched the movement for a second and waited for the loud crunching to stop, "Didn't know about dad and Lyle." I forced myself to swallow the unchewed bits. It tore at my throat with its sharp edges, I winced. In hindsight I am not sure if it was the bleeding esophagus or his comment that made me wince.

"I don't want to talk about that." I said quickly.

He graciously changed the subject. He was always able to read my emotional climate. Lauren may be my best friend, but there were times that I thought Thomas could read my mind. Or maybe he was just more in tune with my mood swings because he had them too. We bantered on about dumb trivial things like the weather and how loud Lauren's house is when the boys are awake. I was trying to process what he meant by "they didn't know" and its ramifications to my strained relationships. It was safe to assume he was referring to the abuse, but I did not want to think about that. I was also trying to squash the thoughts because I did not want to relive the pain. I wanted to make dumb jokes with my brother and enjoy his company.

"Hey, listen, my coworker is having a party tonight. She is turning twenty-one and wants me to go. Any interest in accompanying me?" Our salads were long gone, and we were sitting on the sofa. He was watching tv and I was watching the computer. Still nothing out of the ordinary.

"She's a little young for me, don't you think?" Gross. I knew my brother had a way with the ladies. He was a handsome, single doctor. He definitely did not need my help getting a date, and I would never set him up with one of my employees. I threw a cushion at him. He caught it and placed it under his head, settling into the couch further. He looked tired. I guess living in third world conditions while trying to save children from mosquito-borne illnesses can really wear you out.

"Nah, I promised Lauren I would have dinner at her house. I think she was expecting you to be there too. You should probably call her and let her know you are not coming." He yawned and rubbed his eyes.

I was positive Lauren had not mentioned anything about dinner at her house, but then again, she also neglected to mention that Thomas was going to be in town. I called her to let her down. Apparently, she was convinced I would not have plans so a last-minute invite would not have been a big deal. I tried not to be offended. As it stood, I had always adjusted my plans to accommodate hers. She was disappointed but she almost sounded relieved that I was trying to have a real social life.

I tossed Thomas a spare key to the house as he was leaving and went to get ready. I stared at my closet for a while trying to figure out what would be appropriate. I was in my thirties heading out to celebrate someone's twenty-first. Had I been ten years younger, I would have opted for something slinky and pink. Slinky and pink did not exist in my wardrobe. My wardrobe consisted of workout clothes and business attire for vendor and staff meetings.

I ended up with a pair of skinny jeans that stopped at the ankle and a turquoise silk blouse that hung slightly off one shoulder. I selected gold cage heels to set off the look. I guess I was dressed age-appropriate, but professional enough that it did not invite gossip about my attire from my co-workers.

When I got to the new trendy bar, Ice, I saw it was fairly busy with an overflowing patio. Parking was limited to street parking only, so I ended about a block away. I parked under a streetlight, but there was a small stretch of street where the lamp had burned out. I checked my purse for my taser and proceeded with caution through the dark spot. I chided myself for being so paranoid and shook it off as I walked into Ice.

"You came!" Jessica was pulling me into a hug and squealing into my ear. She pulled me to the corner where she had thankfully secured a table for six, though eight people were squeezed around it. I opted for a spot between Rani and Manny. Jessica was back at the bar flirting with some guy. I noticed her shirt read, *Birthday Girl!* She was clearly scoring free drinks. Oh, to be young and blonde and beautiful. Rani must have been thinking around the same lines.

"How many free drinks do you think she will score tonight?"

Manny answered, "That little kitten is drinking for free!" He purred at both of us. Brooke looked over to us to see what we were laughing at. She followed our vision's path and smiled, "She has the whole world by her little finger!"

"Yeah, but if we play our cards right, she will hook us up too." Tempest was nursing her own cocktail.

Tempest George and Lydia Ming were sitting opposite of me. Both had been with Infinity for over four years. Tempest is a black trans woman and absolutely, astonishingly beautiful. I hired Tempest when society considered her a man. Even then, she was beautiful, but she was shy and uncomfortable in her flawless skin. Becoming the person, she felt like on the inside, made her confidence increase exponentially. She was no longer meek, she was vivacious.

Her makeup and clothes were always flawless, everything about her was beautiful and perfect. She could crook her finger and guys would line up to get her a drink. She is funny and real. So, it was ironic that she, of all people at our table, was looking for free drink castoffs. The customers loved her and in general, she kept me in stitches.

Lydia Ming was an aspiring actress. She was tall and thin with more sarcasm than me and Rani combined, which is a lot of sarcasm. Lydia and Tempest could have a full conversation just by moving their eyebrows - I had seen it happen before.

Jessica walked up to our table followed by a tray of shots. "That guy wanted to make sure we rang my birthday in right!" She pointed her thumb behind her and started passing the shots around. Tempest raised her eyebrows at Lydia, and we all understood the mood. Apparently, we *had* played our cards right, because the free drinks kept showing up at the table. Rani and I, the oldest of the bunch, shrugged at each other and tossed the shot back. It was sweet and smooth. I would call it dangerously good because three more of those and I would be on my ass, but I decided to stick to seltzer with a twist of lemon for the rest of the night. It's a sneaky enough drink to make it appear like I was imbibing. Rani stuck with her coke, not even trying to appear as if she were drinking anything other than her soda.

We ended the evening when Jessica tottered over and tried to sit on my lap. As amusing as it was for the whole table and bar, Manny and I decided together that we needed to get Jessica safely back home.

"I'll take her home." Manny had to yell in my ear. The bar was pretty popular and as the evening wore on it was packed and loud.

"Are you sure?" I yelled back. He nodded. "She doesn't live far from me." I looked around; the rest of our crew was coming to the same conclusion. It was time to go. We all got up and gathered our things. Jessica's arms were slung around Manny's waist. Several guys who had bought her shots were staring daggers at him, but he was more concerned about keeping Jessica from puking on him to care about their malevolent glares. It was quiet outside, and we were able to talk with each other at a normal range.

We were in a small circle with Jessica hanging on Manny, falling asleep on his shoulder.

"I'll take sleeping beauty here. Tempest and Lydia, can you guys walk together? Rani and Caroline?" Manny was speaking to what was left of the group. He was breaking us up into walking buddies. He was always so considerate and kind. Tempest and Lydia nodded and were already digging for their keys. Rani turned to me, "You do not need to walk me to my car, Caroline. I am a forty-year-old woman, I am not what the guys are looking for."

Manny cut her off, "Rani, there has been a rash of muggings in the area and it is just plain dumb of you to object. Caroline does not mind!" He turned to me and stared at me as if daring to say otherwise.

"Come on Rani, where are you parked?" I tugged at her hand. Manny seemed satisfied and we all parted ways.

"Jessica seemed to have fun tonight." I was trying to change the subject as Rani shambled next to me.

"Caroline, Manny is not looking, you don't have to walk me to my car. I am not helpless!" She stopped moving and crossed her arms. I raised an eyebrow at her, "Rani, Manny is right, there have been a few muggings and I would hate it if I let you go on your own from here and you were attacked." I tried to lay the guilt on thick, but she saw right through it.

"I'm an old woman, with no purse, and no curves. I doubt the bogeyman will attack someone that looks like a lost boy!" Images of Peter Pan's grungy sidekicks popped into my mind, I shivered at the thought.

"You do not look like a lost boy, more like Ticker Bell." I tried to joke, she scoffed but relaxed a bit. "Jessica is going to puke in Manny's car." Rani smiled to herself as the puking seemed like a good punishment for his insistence on her escort. I laughed. "Didn't he just get his car detailed?"

Rani smiled and nodded, "Have you ever tried to get the stink of bile from your upholstery?"

"Have you?" I stared back in surprise, Rani was not the type to let loose and vomit in her car. She was too much of a control neat freak, which was probably why she was fighting so hard to walk down a deserted street by herself around midnight. "I am forty, not a prude, Caroline. I have lived a life that existed before spreadsheets and inventory control. Believe it or not, I have *even* stayed out past curfew." She cupped her hands on either side of her cheeks as if in shock.

I chuckled and nodded. "Okay, smart ass." She grinned back at me with her eyes narrowed, emphasizing her sarcastic intent.

"That is my car right there." She pointed to her SUV parked under a streetlight. "I think I can make it the rest of the way." She further narrowed her eyes and set her jaw as her grin melted away, but I did not argue.

"It was fun Rani, drive safe!" I stayed where I was and watched her get into her car. I turned around to make my way back to my Prius. Rani had parked two blocks from Ice, in the opposite direction of where I parked. I walked the three blocks with my head on a swivel. When I saw my car about 100 feet away, I calmed down and started feeling around my purse for my keys.

"Give me your purse or I'll slit your throat." A man hissed in my ear. He was holding me from behind, a knife was pointed at my throat. I tried not to panic. I grabbed his arm that was wielding the weapon. I braced myself and with all my body weight threw myself headfirst down, forcing my attacker to lurch forward and flip on his back. The knife was knocked out of his hand, but in the fury of movements, it fell down and grazed into my left thigh. I scurried to grab the knife before he was able to regain his footing. I kicked him hard in the knee and when he went back down, I kicked him in the face. He crumpled to the ground like a rag doll. Shaking from the near attack, I reached down and took out his wallet. I snapped a picture of his drivers' license and with the blade in my hand, relieved him of a chunk of hair. I ran to my car, weapon still in hand.

I was about a mile away from Ice when I stopped to toss the knife in a rogue trash can. The adrenaline had died down and my leg was hurting. I looked down. The knife had cut my thigh on its descent down. I thought it had just grazed my jeans, which made me mad enough. But my leg was bleeding a pretty steady flow. I looked at the gash. It would require stitches. I cursed at the inconvenience and opened my glove box. I kept about two feet of duct tape wrapped around an old gift card in there in case of emergencies. Duct tape can literally do anything. In this case, I was going to use it as a bandage. I ripped my jeans further; they were already ruined. I ground my teeth with annoyance. They were my favorite jeans, they actually fit, and the fade was just right. I tore even amounts allowing me to fully access the wound. I pulled out a length of duct tape and patted it in place. It was not perfect, but it would have to do.

I called the police to tip them off about the mugger's identity. They insisted I come in to file a report but considering I had done more damage than he had, I declined. By decline, I mean I said something along the lines of, "Either take his information and thank me for giving you this shithead's identity or go fly a kite." I hung up before I could be further interrogated. Apparently, being tired and bleeding made me a little crankier than my normal demeanor.

I needed to go to the ER. I knew this cut was going to require stitches, but I did not want unnecessary questions from well-meaning social workers. I grinned at my realization that I had a doctor at my disposal for at least a few more days.

I limped into my kitchen from the garage. Thomas was sprawled out on the couch drinking beer and eating chips, "Late night sis, I was starting to worry." He did not look up, just crunched another chip and flipped the channel.

"Thomas?" There must have been something in my tone because he jerked his head around. His eyes were wide, "What the fuck happened?" He had a full view of my ripped bloody jeans.

"Someone tried to mug me." I chuckled, "You should see the other guy." He was already moving towards me. He did not laugh at my joke. I thought I had delivered the line perfectly.

"You need to go to the hospital, Ro!"

I shook my head, "It's a flesh wound, but it will need stitches." He did not look amused.

"I can't operate here, Ro! It's not sterile, you could get sick!"

I started laughing, "I'm pretty sure a few stitches are not surgery, and" I looked around, "what's the difference in practicing medicine in my house than another country? Did you think I would forget about the time you had to perform surgery in a freaking mud pit?"

He had been in Madagascar after a massive cyclone had ripped through the island. The flooding was devastating. There was no solid ground to operate. He ended up sinking ten inches into the muddy ground while suturing a child's chest shut.

He growled but left and went to his room to grab his medicine bag. He recognized the lost cause of arguing with me. I took the opportunity to shimmy out of my torn jeans and throw on a pair of running shorts. I am not modest but sitting in my underwear while my brother stitched up my thigh would be weird. He met me in the kitchen. He had already grabbed the vodka I stored in the freezer and was wiping the island counter down.

"Sit up here, it's the best lighting in the house." I followed his direction and sat on the granite counter. It was cold and still wet. "Nice touch with the duct tape." His eyes were focused and slowly peeling the duct tape back. I would like to say that it was painless, but it was not. Apparently just because the leg hairs were light and more peach fuzz than anything else, they still hurt to be ripped out by the roots.

He smeared the brown-orange liquid over my cut and

shook his head at it. "It's deep here, almost to the muscle. I will need to do an internal stitch there and probably another seven stitches to close it up. But you are right, it's a flesh wound."

He was quiet for a minute while he gathered the appropriate tools, "How did it happen?"

I gave him the play by play. He rolled his eyes at me for hanging up on the police, but he stayed silent through the rest. "I only have a local but based on your genetic predisposition against painkillers it will only take the edge off." The wives' tale about redheads needing more painkillers than the average person held true for me. We discovered this when I was ten. I was getting a tooth pulled that was too stubborn to come out on its own, and the dentist ended up tripling the normal Novocain dosage before I was numb enough to pull.

"Slight pinch." I watched him shoot a few spots with his needle and placed it back on the counter. He would occasionally poke at the skin and ask if I could feel it. I still could. After five minutes, he shrugged and started.

I let out a gust of air when he pulled the thread through the internal stitch. My eyes popped slightly, "Sorry." He murmured but was concentrating on his small sewing techniques. After particularly painful threading, he stopped to allow me to catch my breath.

He looked thoughtfully at me and set the needle and thread down on the sterile napkin.

"They didn'tt know, Ro. They did not have a clue what Lyle and dad did to you, to us."

I narrowed my eyes and fought to control my anger, "I do not want to talk about this, Thomas!"

He cut me off, "Well, I don't want to be sewing up my sister in the middle of the night because she is too stubborn to go to the ER, but here I am. And since I am sewing your leg up, and you are stuck here. You are going to listen. I know you don't want to talk about it, but you are going to listen."

I fought against my instincts to close my ears and hum. I did not want to risk him leaving me with finishing up my gaping leg. My sewing skills were enough to get a button back on a shirt but patching up my leg would be rookie work and would leave a nasty scar. I stared back at him with narrow eyes and flared nostrils. He smiled tightly, clearly seeing my acceptance that I was stuck if I wanted his help and continued.

"Annie was talking shit about you. You know, like she always does." I did not know that for sure. I just assumed she did. She was pretty spiteful about me to my face; behind my back, it was probably pure vitriol.

"I told her she did not know what she was talking about. She was a bit stubborn, like you, but she listened. I did not tell her all the details, but I told her that Lyle was a psychopath, and you were spending your nights keeping him from us. I told her that Lyle only got me a few times, but Lauren told me that it was almost nightly for you." He took a deep breath and continued sewing. "Mom was pretty upset, Annie was in denial, Jennifer said it made sense." Another tug.

"Why did you kick Lyle that day? The day of the accident." Thomas was done with the stitches and was working on getting a bandage in place. I sighed and told him about Lyle's threat. He nodded silently, "Thought it must be something like that. Annie asked, but I did not know." He was backing away from the island, pulling his tools back into his bag. I sat up and swung my legs off the counter.

"Give Annie some time, it was a lot to process. I think she will come around though."

I did not know what else to say, I just sighed and relaxed my face, "Thanks for the stitches, Thomas."

His eyebrows raised slightly, "Take it easy for a few days. No full bore running at least."

I laughed, "Yeah, you might finally be able to keep up."

Chapter 8

February 24

Thomas stayed for the weekend. We stayed up late, drank beer. My leg had healed enough for me to beat him in the morning runs again. Lennon and Taylor used him as a jungle gym. It was good wholesome family fun I didn't realize that I missed.

Nathan stopped by once, had a beer with Thomas, but left before it was too late in the evening. He lingered on the front stoop of my house while giving me *the look* that meant he really wanted a quickie. I made him settle for a kiss on the cheek, it was pretty lackluster. I did not hear from Beck once.

Thomas was a good distraction during the day, but at night I was constantly thinking about not wanting to miss Beck. My mind kept flashing to when I shared the bed with him, and he held me all night. It made my plight to be content that he was not in my life, that much more difficult, remembering the solace I felt as he held me. I did not want to want him, but my nightly solitude desperately wanted him to hold me again.

I had some time to follow up on a few leads in Rebecca Hamilton's case. It led me to looking at friends of friends. I convinced myself that her narcolepsy would be something that friends would gossip about.

Gentry followed his schedule every day. Only once did he vary his routine to visit his mom in Glendale. I even went into his home while he was in Corona making a delivery. I was right, he had dogs. Fortunately, they were more of the lazy, good boys that could be easily swayed with dog treats and head pats. Nothing in his home stood out. Even his internet surfing was run of the mill hetero tendencies. I was chastising myself for putting all my eggs in the Gentry basket when I flipped on the news.

> "Last night the remains of Flora Sanchez, of Riverside, was found a half-mile from her home. Preliminary reports point to her abductor being the same as Bobbi King. The Sanchez family is asking for privacy at this time and has not made a comment. The families of Lisa Henderson and Kelly Parker are asking the public to help in finding them. If anyone has any information, please call the hotline below."

I double-checked Gentry's tracker, not one trip to Riverside. Back to square one. I spent the morning reviewing security footage of Flora Sanchez's neighborhood. It was only from a small flash did I see a grainy image of a white Prius, but it also could have been silver or any other light color. I set up another alert for the autopsy report. It was a priority, so I expected it back within 48 hours. I wrote out the timeline.

On February 3, Bobbi King went missing. On February 8, Flora Sanchez went missing. On February 17, Lisa Henderson went missing. On February 18, Bobbi King's remains were found. On February 21, Kelly Parker went missing. On February 23, Flora Sanchez's remains were found.

I stared at it until my eyes felt like they were burned with bleach. The abductions seemed like they were randomly timed. But the remains left behind were planned. Approximately fifteen days after abduction they were found within a mile of their home. They were placed back with care to appear to be sleeping.

What does this mean? One, whoever this is has the room to store three women at a time. If the GPS tracker had not ruled out Gentry, this did. He went nowhere that could possibly house three individuals or that was secluded enough to drown out any screams. Two, it also meant if the killer did stay on his fifteen-day timeline, Lisa Henderson only had nine days left - eight if you include the torture before, which I do.

Three, a little over a week to find Lisa, and I was back to square one.

I decided to call the tip line and share the coincidence about the white Prius. If someone took it seriously, they could have twenty men going through the Prius registries. They could get through half the list before Lisa Henderson was found. At least it was something, maybe they would finish the list before Kelly Parker fell victim.

What I really needed was the connection. How does the abductor know them all? Did he happen upon them randomly and stalk them? I pretty much ruled out a delivery guy. What other industries could have someone living and working in multiple areas? Auditors, OSHA reps, health inspectors, even state government workers could be called into any of these cities with the right catalyst.

Grasping at more straws, I delved into the health inspectors' websites. I made a fresh matrix of restaurants and grocery stores that the state could have been called into. Not much came up, health inspections are mostly county. I checked Weights and Measures, same county ordinance. I checked OSHA and its auditors. A few keystrokes and I was able to find violations that had been investigated. Nothing connected to the victims was evident.

Nothing fit together to put these four women across the path of the same person. I was swimming laps when the thought came to me. Maybe there is a small business with only a few locations that match the victim's cities. What if there is a restaurant or bakery or manufacturer that would spread their enterprise across Southern California? I finished up, dried off, and began a new matrix.

My best lead was Frooty Tooty Smoothie's owner Scott Pickens. Three locations: Riverside, Dana Point, and Culver City. I almost knocked the chair backwards when I saw a silver Prius was registered in Pickens name. And I had to stop myself from running out the door when I saw his ex-wife lived in Yorba Linda. Scott Pickens himself lived in Claremont; I had another suspect. One that was connected to four of the cities. I made a plan and went to bed feeling a little bit smug and a lot relieved.

I rushed to my Monday morning meeting. Fortunately, it was shorter than usual. I left as soon as it was over, rescheduling two vendor meetings for later in the week. I was pulling into Scott Picken's neighborhood by 8:30am.

Scott Pickens lived in a cute historic home across from Claremont College's campus. The street was tree-lined and lovely. His silver Prius was sitting in the driveway. It appeared to be freshly washed without a smear of mud in sight. When I bent down to "tie my shoe" and braced myself against the bumper while adhering the little tracker on, my hand did not come away with the usual black grime. Gentry's truck and delivery vehicle, which I had just visited to relieve them of the devices, were filthy. It made me envious of the moms that always had baby wipes in their car. As it was, Leslie Mixon had nothing in her car, so I sacrificed the bottom of my black tank top to get the majority of the grime off.

I looped around campus a few times before Pickens finally left for work. From what I gathered he was to be working at his Riverside location today. I had plenty of time to wait for him to leave so I can check out his house and the overall health of his head before needing to go to my own appointment to check my head.

At 9:15, he pulled out of his driveway, and by 9:30 I was easing myself into a spare bedroom window. His model of security alarm was only tripped by the front door or the noise of breaking glass, but it's pretty simple to not break a window when it is left open.

The guest bedroom had a double-sized bed in the middle, a chest of drawers in the corner, and a small desk in the other corner. I flipped on the computer. It was older but I could tell it was where he did his business when he was at home. First, I checked his internet browser. It left me feeling like he could be gay and closeted. That does not fit the typical profile of rapists, but he could just hate women. Perhaps he has a bad relationship with his mom.

I carefully walked out into the living room. Every available surface was a picture with him and an older woman. One picture was not framed, I flipped it over, "Me and mom on her 88th birthday". Okay, so no mother issues. I flipped through his books. I checked his drawers one by one. I checked his attic space. I even opened his vents in hopes of finding some sort of trophy or keepsake from Bobbi and Flora. I heard it was a thing serial killers do. They take a token to help them relive the moment. I felt disappointed that I had not found a big red x on a box that said *guilty confession here.* Nothing in Scott Pickens' house said serial kidnapper, rapist, or murderer. But I did remind myself, his home was not big enough or secluded enough for torture. He had to own another property, one where he could store the victims, and keep his trophies.

I headed home with a new list of avenues to research. One, I needed to see if he owned any secluded property. Two, I needed to see if his smoothie shops had a basement that he could have sound proofed. Three, I needed to keep track of all of his movements. Surely, he would visit the women so he could at least give them water.

When I pulled out my laptop, I saw the autopsy report was ready in record time. Riverside Coroner's office and police departments must have felt the pressure to help solve this. They clearly prioritized Sanchez's body before everyone else waiting for their own closure in their loved one's death. I pulled it up. I grimaced when I noticed the details in death were the same as Bobbi King, down to the bleached organs. Whoever was doing this had a vulgar interest in human anatomy. Another thing to investigate from Scott Pickens, did he have medical aspirations as a child?

What did I know about Scott Pickens? He owns a semi-successful smoothie shop with three locations. The three locations match the cities for three of the four victims. The fourth victim shares the city with his ex-wife. I know he adores his mom. I am thinking he could be gay and in consideration of that, his sexuality was probably the cause of his divorce, but it was circumstantial at best. What I needed was proof that the victims had gone into one of his shops.

I started pulling up the bank statements of Bobbi King, Flora Sanchez, and Kelly Parker. It should have been harder to get into their bank, but all had emails that were obnoxiously easy to take over. Procuring their passwords to their banking institutions was a few steps after that.

According to King's bank statements, she never visited Frooty Tooty's. Sanchez and Parker did. Parker went most mornings before she would head to the beach. Sanchez went once, based on her bank statement, after a day of shopping. Lisa Henderson lived about a mile away from Pickens's ex. I still did not have any connection to Bobbi King. I scrunched my nose.

I thought about canceling my appointment with Nina Williams, but I had already rescheduled once to spend time with Thomas and after his bombshell, I had a lot to unpack. I checked the connection of the tracker to my cell signal and headed out to see Nina.

Chapter 9

February 24

"Did I ever tell you about the time a homeless man peed on me while I was sleeping in my own bed?" I had been staring out of Nina Williams' window. I turned my attention over to her to see how she would react. She had been writing notes, her reading glasses low on her nose. Her eyes grew wide with surprise and she pulled her readers off to better look into my eyes.

"No, I do not believe you have shared this with me." She knew I hadn't, she was being diplomatic.

"After my dad died," I started but decided to change course.

"When my mom was sober, she had a heart of gold. Anyone that she saw that needed help, she would do whatever she could to help them. If she saw a stray dog, she would bring it home, fleas and all. If she saw a homeless person, she would invite them to stay the night, get a hot shower and warm food in their bellies." I scrunched my face at the memories.

"She once let a woman and her three daughters live with us for six months after the woman left her abusive husband. There was no room to breathe, there were already six of us living in a three-bedroom house." The unfinished basement was where Thomas stayed. Lauren and I shared a room, Jennifer and Annie shared a room. "My mom slept on the couch while Ms. Tricia and her girls stayed in my mother's bedroom." I shook my head at the memories of bathroom rotation between the ten of us.

"Did one of the little girls urinate on you?" Nina asked. I looked at her confused, then realized I was confusing her with my meshing memories.

"No, I was just giving you an example of my mom letting strangers live with us." She nodded, trying to keep up, "Continue."

"Anyway, my mom met this guy outside of an AA meeting. He was drunk and she took pity on him. Don't ask me why my mom thought it would be safe to bring an unknown 40-year-old homeless man into her house with four daughters." I stopped, rolled my eyes at how obtuse my mother could be. I took a deep breath, "Fortunately, he was not a pervert, just a confused, drunk asshole who mistook my bed for a toilet."

Nina nodded and looked thoughtful for a moment, "Did you ever tell your mother you did not feel comfortable with strangers living in your house?"

I thought about the question for a minute. I never did tell her to stop. "No. I never did."

She narrowed her eyes and pursed her lips, thinking, "Would you venture the guess as to why you never told her?"

I did not need to venture a guess. I was fully aware as to why I never confronted her. She was too vulnerable, too weak. I did not want to say something to set her off on another bender, to make her feel like she was failing as a parent.

Or maybe, "I did not want to know which she would choose if I made her decide." I said finally. The thought had formed as the words flowed out, uncensored.

"And why would you think she would not have chosen you and your wishes? Surely she would want to make sure you felt safe after all you had experienced."

Because she never chose me. She chose to get drunk the majority of my childhood. She chose to ignore Lyle's abuse. Well, actually, according to Thomas, she did not know. But had she been sober, she would have known. I am sure of it. She chose to live a life of denial. She chose to stay with an abusive husband. She did not have room in her head to choose me or my siblings. I shrugged in response. Nina could see that I was editing my thoughts.

She sighed, "Let's change gears." She closed her notebook. Apparently, this is not something she had predetermined to talk to me about. Or maybe it was, and she had just caught up on her own notes.

"Do you believe your mother cares about you?"

"Of course, I know she cares about me." My tone may have been a smidge indignant.

"So, you know your mother cares, but you doubt whether she cared if you felt safe in your childhood home?" She was leaning forward looking excited, apparently, this was "psychologist going for the kill" mannerisms. I understood her eagerness. Of course, all of the things that are messed up in my brain is a direct response to my childhood. Mommy issues, daddy issues, abuse, neglect. It's not unique. Even an aunt saying an innocuous thing like, "I'm rubbing your belly for good luck," to a four-year-old is enough to give someone body dysmorphia. Which is exactly what happened to me. That's a problem for another day.

"I think my mother was sick and caring for five kids after burying a child and husband messed with the reasoning part of her brain." I did not want to look her in the eyes, so I pulled my gaze back out the window. It was raining. It never rains in LA.

In Charleston, rainstorms are a force of God. I remember sitting on our front porch, rocking in the rocking chair, watching the black-blue clouds roll in. I loved watching the lightning streak across the sky, illuminating the world in the dead of night. The rumble of thunder, the patter of rain that would grow into a steady pounding as the thunderclap finally matched the lightning. In LA if it rained the tiniest of sprinkles, people would call out of work citing dangerous driving conditions.

"Does that mean you forgive her?" Nina pulled me back into the present.

"Of course, I forgave her. She was sick and was dealt a rotten hand." I really meant it. Despite everything, I had forgiven her a long time ago. I had forgiven, but I had not forgotten. I was too stubborn to forget. I did not want her to pay for her transgressions by wallowing in her past. But too many times she had promised us that she was going to stop drinking, only to relapse a few days later. When you are eleven and cleaning up vomit from your mother's last binge for the umpteenth time after she said she was going to stop, it made forgetting all but impossible.

"Have you forgiven your father and brother as well?"

I should have been expecting that question, but the wind had just picked up. Spring flowers were swirling in the parking lot. It was a beautifully distracting sight like a real storm was picking up. I could just hear the pitter patter of rain on the roof of Nina's office.

I took a deep breath, "Grief is complicated." I repeated the words she had spoken to me a few weeks ago back to her.

"So, you forgave your mother because she could not help it due to illness, but you do not offer yourself the same release from your brother or father? Bipolar can be a very serious illness as well." Nina had replaced her readers and was jotting down notes quickly.

I sat in silence for a few seconds, trying to calmly breathe and collect my thoughts.

"Grief is complicated. Some days I think I can forgive them. Other days, not so much."

Other days, like when I have a flashback and my trauma responses overrides my rational brain. Other days, like when a person accidentally brushes up against me in a restaurant, I have to refrain from going in for the attack. Or like when someone tries to show me that they care but I won't allow myself to receive it because I am skeptical of its authenticity. Or days when I think I may actually like someone, but I keep them at an arm's length. Beck's face flashed before my eyes. Other days like never wanting to feel vulnerable again because you can only be hurt if you are vulnerable in the first place.

I took a deep breath to clear my head from the PTSD that my dad and brother's actions still reeked in my daily life. I wanted to blurt out to Nina, how can I possibly forgive someone who has damaged me so severely that even twenty years removed, I am still suffering? I changed the subject.

"Mom came to visit a few weeks ago. Right after our last appointment actually."

Nina nodded and made a few notes, "And how was the visit?"

I shrugged, "It was good. I was pretty busy, so I only saw her a few times, but the boys loved having their grandma around."

Nina narrowed her eyes at me, "Did you love having your mother around?"

No, it felt forced and obligatory. I settled for a shrug, "She looked good. She is excited because Jennifer is pregnant."

Nina gave me the not-so-fast-smile, "That's nice, but what about you? Did you enjoy her taking the time out of her schedule to visit with you?"

I took a deep breath and flared my nostrils, "She was not in town to visit me. She was here to see her grandchildren. Me living here is an afterthought of her coming into town. So, no, I didn't really make time for her."

She nodded knowingly, "Are you sure you have forgiven her?"

I pinched my face, "I thought I had. It wasn't until Thomas's visit that I realized there were some issues that were not resolved."

Nina looked taken back, "So your mother and your brother visited you? The brother that is a traveling doctor?" *No, the dead one.* I took a deep breath and refrained from using sarcasm towards one of the few women in Southern California that could see through my sass with ease.

I nodded, "But not at the same time. Thomas came out a few days after to see Lauren, the boys, and me."

"Okay, so what about Thomas's visit prompted you to revisit these unresolved issues?"

A knife wound and a spouting off brother that was taking advantage of my weakened state.

"He mentioned that he spoke with mom, Annie, and Jennifer. He said that they did not know about the abuse. He said that mom was pretty upset about it."

Nina narrowed her eyes as she adjusted her glasses. "Why had you never mentioned it to your mother or your sisters?"

Good question, "I was told to never speak ill of the dead." This was true, but honestly, I never told Annie because she hero-worshipped dad and Lyle. I had already physically taken them away; I did not want to take them away emotionally when she learned it was all a façade.

"Do you believe Thomas was acting in your best interest?"

"Yeah, he said he was sticking up for me because Annie was being, well, Annie. And he told them why I was such a pain in the ass growing up."

She nodded again, "Do you believe that with Annie, Jennifer, and your mom knowing your trauma, you can forgive them and release your pain?

I scoffed, "I am not in pain! Annie believed what she needed to believe to make sense of the deaths of her personal heroes. Mom was sick, and Jennifer was too young to understand."

"You don't find it painful that your relationships with half of your family have been incredibly strained? You avoid your mother, you have no relationship with Annie, and you talk to Jennifer once a month, at most. While your siblings, who endured the suffering with you, remain your closest friends and allies."

I think I was gaping like a fish out of water. I had never thought about that.

"Our time is up Caroline, but I want you to think about what you would gain by releasing this pain."

I took my dismissal with grace. I stepped out into the rain, face-up looking into the falling drops. My hair whipped around my face in the storm. The water dripping down my face calmed me down from my confrontational session. I headed home in a state of shell shock and ruminated on forgiveness.

I walked into my house in a catatonic state, but I was snapped out of it when I smelled food being prepared in my kitchen, "Thomas?" I called out, but it was unlikely. He was in Haiti, he texted me when he landed. But there were definitely sizzling noises coming from my kitchen. I grabbed my taser, the last thing I wanted was to rip open my stitches, my doctor was in another country after all. I took a deep breath and proceeded into the kitchen with caution.

Beck looked up from the stove, he smiled briefly and went back to his cooking. I checked my phone in annoyance that my security systems did not forewarn me of my visitor. I silently cursed at myself for having my phone turned off. I had turned it off so I would not be disturbed during my appointment. I switched it back on and was greeted by six notifications and one missed call, Annie. I frowned; I could not think of one time she had ever called me.

"What are you doing here?" I might have been a little breathless, the missed call from Annie threw me. I felt off-kilter to be looking at Beck. I had just mentally accepted that I would not see him again. I had not seen or heard from him in days and he left without the smallest trace as to when I may see him again. He looked better than I remembered, and he appeared to be making me dinner. But he did completely ghost me for... three days. Okay, maybe I was being dramatic, and I did not once call him. I just waited up nights hoping he would glide into my bedroom like a knight in shining armor. I pulled my hand out of my purse that was still holding tightly to the taser. I slipped my purse off my shoulder and dropped it into a vacant stool.

"Did you enjoy your walk in the rain?" He looked amused at me. I looked down to realize that I was dripping from my hair down to my squeaking shoes. I had enjoyed the rain for five minutes after my appointment until it had abruptly stopped like a faucet being turned off. I did not want to explain to Beck my weird attachment to the storm that had just passed. For those five minutes, I was free of my past burdens as they were being washed away into the nearest aqueduct. Now I looked like a half-drowned rat. I shook some water from my face and headed to the bedroom without another word.

I could not put my finger on what emotion I was feeling. After appointments with Nina, I emote in unpredictable ways. It's why I choose the end of the week, so I have a few days to myself to gather my thoughts and pull back my calm and cool façade. Unfortunately, because I had rescheduled, I did not have a few days to acclimate to my emotional climate. Annie's call was lingering on my mind. Maybe Thomas was right, and she was "coming around." And then there was Beck, the ghost ninja that I did not want to want.

I stripped off the wet clothes. The jeans bunched oddly as I tried to pull my pants down and I ended up hopping to the edge of the bed to fully kick off the wet jeans. I decided an oversized sweatshirt and comfortable running shorts was more than appropriate to wear in front of a man that has shown little preference for my physical appearance. I walked on my tiptoes to make my approach to the kitchen as silent as possible. Beck had plated dinner and was sitting at the island.

He watched me approach, and his eyebrows dropped in silent concern as he looked at my exposed thigh. I had forgotten about my bandage concealing the stitches from my knife wound. Thomas had assured me the stitches would dissolve on their own, but I needed to keep it covered for at least two weeks. It no longer hurt, and I was used to the cotton bandage that I replaced each morning. I only had a week left before I would be sans bandage. I had checked the wound this morning. It looked pretty well healed. The cut was an angry red-purple line about four inches long. Thomas had assured me the scar would fade and be minimally noticeable as it matched with a contour of muscle.

"What happened to your leg?" Beck sounded concerned and almost angry. I had no idea why he would be angry with me. I had no obligation to call him and say that I was almost mugged. Although, I am sure if I had told him I would not have had to wait days before he graced me with his presence. I shrugged.

"What's for dinner?" I sat down on the stool opposite of Beck and tucked my knees under the counter, cutting off his line of sight from the white bandage. He narrowed his eyes and set his jaw; his nostrils flared. I picked up my fork and kept my eyes down. I could tell Beck was frustrated by my intentional evasiveness regarding my knife wound.

I swirled my fork into a green and purple salad, it looked like cucumbers and radishes cut in ribbons with sesame seeds. I slurped up a bite. It was tangy and sweet. I looked up at him, meeting his eyes for the first time, "Is this cucumber kimchi?"

He did not relax his jaw, but his silver eyes softened the tiniest degree. I slurped another bit of the kimchi. It was refreshing and delicious. I moved on to the pan-fried scallops, tender and perfectly cooked. Dinner was a symphony of textures and flavors. We ate in silence. He was upset, I could feel the tension filling the kitchen. When I finished, he grabbed my plate and set them in the sink. He turned around with his arms crossed over his chest and faced me.

I finally built up the courage that had evaded me since I walked in and saw him cooking, "Are you upset with me?"

He narrowed his eyes, "I am waiting for you to answer my question." His tone was calm and quiet. It did not match the intensity of his eyes.

"Oh." I bit my lip and narrowed my eyes. I decided the truth would be the only thing that might loosen his tense jaw.

"I went out to celebrate a friend's birthday. Someone tried to mug me. I knocked the knife out of his hand, but my leg got in the way." He relaxed his arms and rolled his eyes at me.

He approached me in two quick strides, "Show me." He was looking down at my thigh.

I sighed and peeled back the bandage. The angry, red-purple line looked harsh in the light of the kitchen. You could see where some stitches had dissolved and where some still tied my skin together. He bent his head down for a closer look.

"The stitches look professional. I'm surprised, you seem too stubborn to actually go to the hospital and have doctors attend to your wounds."

I cringed; I was too stubborn to go. Thomas chastised me for it.

"Don't tell me you know how to stitch yourself up at such a precise degree." Beck looked dubious.

I shook my head, "No, Thomas stitched me up. He is a doctor."

He let the words settle, he snapped his head up and walked a few paces back. "Another stray?" His jaw was smiling but his eyes looked upset.

It took me a second to follow his train of thought, "No, Thomas is my brother. He was visiting from Haiti. He stays here when he visits." I stood up to close the distance between us, "Contrary to what you may believe, I do not have guys that are interested in me like that."

He shot one eyebrow up.

"Nathan is just a friend. He does not have feelings for me. It's just a pressure release." Oh my god, why was I sharing this? "And besides, I have ended it with Nathan." Kind of, not officially. Actually, I am not sure if Nathan was aware that I had ended it with him.

Beck's jaw relaxed. I wonder if he was relieved that I was "single", but his arms stayed tight across his chest. I decided to change the subject.

"Dinner was delicious, thank you." He gave me one stiff nod but did not relax his posture one iota. I sighed and tilted my head at him.

"Not that I mind that you are here. Actually, it is nice to see you considering you left without saying goodbye and I haven't heard from you in days. But why are you here?" I was wringing my hands together to keep them from running up and down Beck's muscly arms. I desperately wanted to unknot them and wrap them around my waist.

He took a deep breath, his nostrils flared as he exhaled, "I was wondering if you had made any progress with Rebecca Hamilton's case."

I was not expecting that. I was hoping he would say something closer to, "I could not wait a second longer, I needed to see you." Of course, it made sense for him to wonder. I had roped him into helping me stakeout Griffith Park.

I stepped away to grab my Hamilton case book and thumbed through where I had left off. I passed him my progress. He read for a second, eventually relaxing from his position against the counter and back to sitting at the island.

He passed the book back, "It's not a random attacker at Griffith Park."

I stared back confused, "How could you know that?"

"I have been visiting the park every day and watching out for anything suspicious. Not even the homeless were interested in the sunbathers. Hamilton was attacked by someone that knew her."

I thought about his assessment. I felt confident he was right, but all the people in Rebecca's life had been ruled out through DNA. I explained that I was on the friends-of-friends list and still coming up empty.

"I agree, it is someone that knew about her condition. Has anyone looked into the boys her brother sold her medication to? They would know she was out of medication and would have been able to follow her and wait for an opportunity."

"It is something to look into," I nodded, "And I am sure a person buying pharmies on the street would know someone who could get him ketamine."

Beck looked confused, "Pharmies?" One eyebrow was in a high arch.

I laughed, “Pharmaceuticals.” His face relaxed and smiled at the lingo.

“I also think you should look into her day-to-day life. You have ruled out Hamilton’s job and coworkers, and the police are collecting DNA from all the males at school. What about her horseback riding lessons?”

I shook my head, “Her instructor is a woman.”

He cut me off, “Surely there are men that use the stables.” My jaw dropped at my oversight, he continued, “It is also possible it was one of her father’s friends. They had a BBQ during that two-week time period.”

This time I made a noise in surprise. “How did you know that?”

He gave me a sly smile, “You are not the only one who can play detective.”

Chapter 10

February 26-28

Beck did not stay much longer after we had finished dinner. I went to bed feeling confused that he had driven thirty miles to make me dinner and ask me questions. I did not want to be hopeful that he liked me when all physical evidence said otherwise. It was entirely possible that he really was just interested in the case. I spent the next day milling around and trying to follow new leads.

I spent my spare time tracing down the new leads that Beck brought to my attention. I researched the two friends of Rebecca Hamilton's father. Larry Boker and Oscar Perez. Larry Boker was Hamilton's golf partner and Oscar Perez was Hamilton's neighbor.

Larry Boker was an avid golfer, partially retired from his security consulting business (home not cyber) and had been married for thirty years. They had three children, all grown and living on their own. His internet browsing was mostly about golf swing techniques and information on meat smokers. Apparently, Larry was thinking about becoming a pit master in his spare time. He commented on several internet boards regarding BBQ competitions and frequently flew to Memphis and Austin to attend festivals. He also dressed in his wife's lingerie when he was out of town. He hid the photos deep in a file on his phone that looked like a calculator. *Whatever floats your boat, buddy.*

I crossed him off the list when one of the BBQ pits contests in Memphis corresponded during the two-week missing time gap. In the other parts of the two weeks, he had well-documented pictures from golf courses, and he had visited his son in Nashville.

Oscar Perez was a bit harder to investigate. He had no

social media profiles. I was able to gather his information from sale registries at his home's address. He bought the home fifteen years ago and was married at that time. He refinanced five years ago as the only name on the deed. I found out that he took a million-dollar life insurance policy out on his wife, they were divorced one month after that then she died a month after the divorce. He was the sole inheritor. Her family was fighting the inheritance because of the divorce. The money was locked in a legal quagmire as it was in her will that she had updated a week before the divorce finalized.

No autopsy report was performed, per Oscar Perez's request. Did he kill his wife? It was starting to look like it. Why would a life insurance policy be taken out within a month of divorce and two months before her death? The timing felt too convenient.

He ran a convenience store with terrible quality security equipment. The man practically lived at work. He worked six days a week, only on Mondays did he take off. He had two other people working for him. From what I could gather, the security cameras were a closed circuit, meaning I could only have access to the footage physically on-site.

I checked the time. His store closed in one hour and it would take 45 minutes to get there. I grabbed my purse and headed out. I cursed myself for not having enough time to become Leslie Mixon, but I reminded myself I was just going there to get a lay of the land and buy something small.

I pulled up to 'Food and Things' as Oscar was pulling a menu sign in. He looked tired and more than prepared to lock up for the day.

"We are closing in ten minutes." His voice was gruff and annoyed. He was about 5'8" 180lbs with hair graying at the temples. He wore thick glasses. His shirt was tucked in and his pants were slightly wrinkled as if he had been sitting the majority of the day.

"I'll be just a minute," I promised. He narrowed his eyes at me and followed me in. I looped to the back wall first. It had a small hallway with a bathroom and an "Employees Only" sign that I assumed was the office. The video cameras were oversized and yellowing with age, but they all had red lights on - which meant they were all recording and working. I walked along the wall of glass door coolers and pulled one open. I grabbed a bottle of water.

Perez had settled himself back behind the counter. It was separated from the main shopping area by a thick plexiglass wall. Cigarettes, lotto tickets, and condoms were behind him. I walked along the wall away from the coolers to a display of fresh fruit. I grabbed a few green bananas. I had always been weird about how I liked my bananas. I only liked them with a green stem. If the stem had begun to brown, or god forbid the skin brown, they would be given to Lauren to make banana bread. I enjoyed the nearly tart taste of a green banana. Perez cleared his throat, pulling me back to the present. I looked at my watch, five minutes to close.

I walked up to the register and grabbed a pack of gum. I placed my items in the plexiglass box that he slid back to his side of the cash register. I looked around as he weighed my bananas and scanned my items. He had a security system panel next to the glass double doors. I recognized the system; it would be easy to override. The rolling gate that covered the doors on the other hand would not be easy to override, it was manual with a chain. In order to break in, I would have to disable the alarm, pick the padlock on the chain, roll the heavy door up, and pick the front door lock. It would be loud and take me too long under the bright security lights. And if someone came up to me while I was dealing with the heavy gate? *Don't mind me, I'm not going to steal anything.* Infiltrating Food and Things from the front door, was a no-go.

"$5.45" Oscar slid my items back to me from the plexiglass box. I slid $6 to him and grabbed my items.

"Keep the change." I smiled and headed back to my car. I made a wide loop out of the parking lot and went to the back of the buildings. I found his back door. It had a single lock, no handle. Armed with a plan, I headed over to Pasadena to change into Leslie Mixon and grab supplies.

Traffic had significantly died down, making my round trip fast. I stopped in to change into my black tactical pants, tank, and a leather jacket. I put my wig in place and filled my bag with a heavy magnet, a lock-key, and my night vision goggles. I logged into Perez's security company's website that I had read on the front door of Food and Things and scheduled a deactivation in a half hour. It was a fairly basic service; the rolling door provided the majority of the protection the shop needed. I headed back to Food and Things.

The parking lot of the shopping center had one car on cement blocks in the corner of the lot. Someone had been kind enough to remove the tires from the vehicle. I had not noticed it when I was there earlier, it just punctuated the fact the neighborhood was not the best.

I looped around the back of the building. It was deserted. There was a small area for trucks to unload their goods and a small strip of trees that separated it from the neighborhood behind it. I drove around until I made it to the neighborhood that backed into the Food and Things shopping center, parked, and slipped into the trees.

There was a half-moon, but the clouds had rolled in to cover its light. I was slowly moving through the sparse forest when I heard a twig snap behind me. I slunk behind a tree and held my breath hoping it was some nocturnal animal. I stood quietly with my back to a pine for a few minutes waiting for another noise. The bark scratched at my jacket; I could smell the fresh sticky sap.

I slowly crept from my hiding place. I had moved five feet from the tree when I felt a hand slap around my mouth, my left arm was pinned behind my back. I tried to rear my head back, but my attacker held my head firmly against their chest. I heard a low rumble, were they laughing or growling? My attacker adjusted their grip to where my ear was pressed tight against their chest, their heart was a slow even rhythm. My head was pinned with their long fingers barely covering my lips. My own heart was beating frantically. I assessed my situation. Only seconds had passed since I heard the initial hand slap. I couldn't try to flip them or else my arm would dislocate. I could not headbutt because my head was pinned. I had a free right arm and two free legs.

I needed to be careful of what movements I tried, if their grip tightened then my arm would break. I needed to do something that would make them drop one of the holds. I shifted my body towards my pinned arm creating a space and threw my elbow into my attacker's solar plexus. My arm was released, I swung it forward, but they adjusted their vice-tight grip across my chest, pinning both my arms to my side.

I planted my feet hard and jumped backward, knocking us both off our feet. I heard my attacker hit the ground; their breath whooshed from their lungs. The grip loosened just enough for me to scramble away. They got to their feet in an instant and lunged at me again. I kicked backward as hard as I could. My foot was grabbed before I could make contact and was twisted away. I was thrown back to the ground. I was crawling away, but I felt them on my back. I threw my head and it made contact with their chin. I heard it pop as they fell back on the ground with a thump. Instead of trying to escape, I had to be on the defensive.

I charged at the dark figure before they could get to their feet. I landed on top of the perpetrator. Again, an iron tight grip was around my chest. It was hard to breathe, I was kicking madly with my legs. I broke the grip and pushed them to the ground so I could straddle their stomach. I had pulled my lock-key from my pocket and held it to their throat. Their body relaxed as the low rumble I heard before started once more, *are they laughing?*

The clouds shifted and moonlight twinkled through the trees, it was enough to shed light on my attacker.

"Beck?" I was breathless. One, for surviving an attack, and two, to be straddling Beck.

Without answering he sat up and grabbed my face. He kissed me hard. His tongue felt cool in my mouth. My hormones kicked into high gear. I blame it on the adrenaline. I dropped the lock-key while I was grabbing at his shirt pulling him into me, scrambling to take it off. His hands were hot against my arms, his lips moved from my mouth and were kissing my neck. I shivered as he reached down between us. I felt something sharp poke my neck opposite of his lips. I stopped moving. He pulled away chuckling, my lock-key pressed firmly against my neck.

"You are easily distracted, Caroline." Anger and pissy hormones slapped his hand away. I retrieved my lock-key from his relaxed grip and jumped off of him. My bag was discarded a few feet away. I scooped that up. I was practically running to the edge of the trees moving towards the shopping center.

The back of the shopping center was not well lit, there was a small series of security lights that were placed 20 feet from any door in either direction. I ran into the shadow next to the back door. It took a few tries with the lock-key to pop the lock, my nerves from the attack still had not calmed down. I did not have the leverage to open it with only the edge of the door exposed. I pulled out my magnet to create a makeshift door handle and pulled the door open with a groan of tired metal hinges. I was pushing the back door shut when a foot and hand caught the edge and shoved it open. The force was too great for me to fight back. I really wanted to slam his hand and foot in the doorway. Beck slipped in and smiled.

"Did you follow me?" I hissed.

He shook his head, "I knew you would come back here. I was waiting."

"What do you mean you knew I would come back?" It dawned on me that I was not the only person that had scoped out Food and Things. Beck was probably in the parking lot when I pulled in.

"What if I was planning to come back another night?" I hissed feeling annoyed at my predictability.

He raised one eyebrow in response and walked up to the office door. It was locked, but Beck had his own tool to pick the lock. The door popped open with ease. His nerves seem to be just fine. The office was dingy but clutter-free. Boxes with daily totaling, receipts, and deposit paperwork lined the wall with every box clearly labeled. Another wall had an old tube-style television with the security system set up. It had an old school VHS recorder. He kept six months of videos at a time. It looked like he just kept re-recording over the old tapes. I wondered whether it was because it was cheaper or because VHS tapes were not easy to find. I selected the first day during the time gap. It took us 10 minutes to fast forward through the first tape to verify he had an alibi for the first of fourteen days.

"I can't believe you attacked me." My nerves had finally stopped my shaking hands, but I was still angry.

He chuckled again. I wanted to punch him, but the deep rumble did things to my insides.

"You did well. I can tell you are trained to get away from an attacker. You only turned to attack me as a last resort." He chuckled again. The combination of that low rumble and the compliment had me wanting to straddle him again.

"You almost beat me." I turned to glare at him. He was smiling at my profile. I let my hair fall between us, he reached up and slid it behind my ear. His finger lingered on my cheek. I stopped breathing, he leaned forward again. His lips were in my ear. I felt them brush against my lobe and glide down my cheek to my neck. I fumbled with the tape and dropped it. His lips were back at my ear, "Easily distracted." He whispered again. I flung my head sideways, making him back his face away before he could point out any more weaknesses. I narrowed my eyes and set my jaw to focus.

I reached down and picked up the tape and moved my position away from him.

Two hours later, I was appreciative of Beck being there for company. It was boring work, and having him there, no matter how irritating the attack was, was nice. He smelled good, he was sexy, and he kissed me. Yes, he kissed me to distract me, but he kissed me. We sat in silence as we watched the hours of security footage. I was able to replay the kiss, how he tasted, how he felt. I had to keep myself from biting my lip and moaning, or worse, attacking him and kissing him again. I fought my overwhelming desire to cast furtive glances at his handsome face every few seconds. The last tape clicked to its ending.

"It's not him," I whispered to myself but also, since he was here, Beck too.

He nodded in my assessment and motioned towards the door. We relocked the office door, slipped out the back, relocked that as well, and dashed into the trees. "Where are you parked?" I asked as we were approaching my black car. "Few streets down."

"Come on, I'll drive you." We got in together and closed our doors at the same time. The noise was jarring after being in relative silence for two hours. "He did not attack Rebecca, but he may have murdered his ex-wife." I glanced over to Beck as I pulled away, he was facing me. His eyes were wide, but he did not say anything. He took a few deep breaths before he broke the silence.

"I am parked up here." He pointed to a car at the corner of the next street. I could see the light veining in his muscular arms as he pointed. I pulled next to his car. He turned to me before he opened the door. "There is a 24-hour diner about ten minutes from here, follow me there." He shut the door and walked to his car. I admired his broad shoulders and the fluid movement of his narrow hips. He turned to look at me as he unlocked his door, and he slid into his vehicle.

If I were faster and pithier, I would have said something close to, "are you asking me on a date?" But as it stood, my nerves were shot from the attack, my hormones were protesting from the fake kiss, I was too confused by his lack of reaction, then his demand for a new location. It was hard to keep up with his emotional climate.

We reached Sal's Diner and parked next to each other. I pulled my wig off and stashed it in the glove compartment and fluffed my hair back. My head was sweaty, and it itched from being confined. It was a relief to let my hair fall to my shoulders. Beck was waiting for me behind my car. His eyes paused at my red waves, and I could just make out the smallest of lift from the corner of his lips.

"Tadashi Becken? I was wondering when you'd come visit me." An older Black woman came up and pinched his cheek, then pulled him in for a hug. She was about my height, white hair, a rounded figure with large hips. Her face was round and kind with deep-set dimples.

"Tabatha, it is good to see you. You look well."

"You are so handsome, always was." She turned to me and smiled, her teeth were gleaming against her dark lips, "Isn't he just the most handsome man?" I nodded politely, hoping Beck would not see my motion of agreement. It was pointless to hope, he turned his head and watched me agree. He smiled to himself, his eyes flitting towards the ground before he turned away from us. She winked at me.

"What does my sweet boy need tonight? Sal doesn't work anymore, but he stops most mornings for breakfast." She volunteered the information with more familiarity that made me curious about how close Beck was with these people. I made a mental note to look up Sal and Tabatha later. It is always a good idea to know as much as you can about a ninja assassin. If Marvel has taught me anything, origin stories matter.

"Just wanted to get some food and talk to my friend here." Beck motioned his hand towards me. I gave her a small wave.

"Aren't you going to introduce me to your girl, honey?" I was flattered that she implied that I could ever be his, but I knew the truth. He said it best, I am his friend, and nothing else.

I stuck out my hand, "I'm Caroline." She swatted my hand away and pulled me in for a hug. Tabatha was a woman that knew how to hug, it was warm and homey. She felt like a fluffy towel straight out of the dryer. She draped her arm around my shoulder and led the way to the empty corner of the diner.

"He is a special man, my Beck. I know he is tough as nails, but he is a good man. Don't mess with his heart girl, or you'll have me to deal with." She whispered in my ear.

I shook my head, "It's not like that." I murmured back.

She interrupted, "He brought you here, baby, it's *exactly* like that." She unwound her arm from around my shoulder as we all walked inside the diner. I slid into the booth; Beck slid on the bench opposite of me. He narrowed his eyes, "What did she say to you?"

I smiled, "She said that you were a good man." I wanted to feel warm and fuzzy that he brought me to a place that meant something to him. But the reality is, it was an old diner that was open during the time frame we needed a place to talk, and it happened to be near where we were. Tabatha may know how to hug, she may know Beck, but she did not know the situation.

He relaxed and passed me a menu, "Everything is good here." A ringing endorsement from an amazing chef, but that was not going to help me narrow it down. The menu was nine pages long.

"How do you know about this place?" I waved my hand around. It was an average looking diner. I could smell the maple syrup as if it were impregnated in the walls. The booths were all hunter green vinyl with cream piping, the tables were white and gold flecked.

"I worked here from the age of sixteen and straight through culinary school." He had set his menu down, his eyes laser-focused on me. I knew he could cook; I had no idea he was formally trained.

"Tabatha is like your family?" I asked, trying to gauge whether my assessment was correct.

He nodded, still looking at me with his silver eyes narrowed and focused.

"I think I will have an order of fries and a piece of apple pie," I said out loud, to no one in particular because Tabatha was back at the front counter and Beck was not interested in my midnight snack order.

"Stop stalling." He spoke with narrowed eyes. Hmmm, I wasn't stalling. I was dealing with interpreting why he took me to a place that actually meant something to him. And as much as I had dismissed what Tabatha told me, I wanted it to be true. My facial expression met his tone of annoyance. I scowled at him.

"Why do you think Oscar Perez killed his ex-wife?" He

had calmed his tone to a rumble of a whisper, but his face still looked annoyed.

"When I was researching him, I came across a few things that raised red flags. He took a million-dollar life insurance policy out on her a month before their divorce finalized. A month later she was dead, and no autopsy was performed."

His eyes narrowed and changed back to calm as Tabatha approached us. She brought water and took our order and left us again. "Who started the divorce proceedings?" He asked when Tabatha was out of earshot.

"She did, it was a non-contested divorce, she did not want anything."

His eyes narrowed again thinking, "So you think he was upset by the divorce and killed her in a fit of passion."

I nodded, "Stranger things have happened."

"Why no autopsy?" He asked after Tabatha placed our food on the table.

"I have not gotten that far in the research. I could not find anything on my first pass. I am planning on going into his home tomorrow, see what I can find." I grabbed a fry. It was golden brown with a crispy exterior, perfectly cooked interior, lightly seasoned. As far as fries went, they were pretty close to perfect.

Beck made a face. "What?" I asked innocently, dropping my next fry and wiping the leftover salt from my fingertips.

"Can you really afford to be distracted from the two other cases you are working on?" He picked up my discarded fry. I had not thought about that. I was normally more focused, but the dead ends were bogging me down. An easy win was something that I wanted to have on my plate. Then I decided, I had a decent handle on the missing women case, and I was still researching leads in the Rebecca Hamilton case.

I nodded, "Yes I can take time to check whether a man killed his ex-wife. It happened five years ago; at this point, he feels like he actually got away with murder. Besides, he is the next-door neighbor to Rebecca Hamilton. Who is to say that I will not see something while I am in the neighborhood?"

His nostrils flared. "Fine, but I do not think you should spend more than a day on this."

I felt like I was being chastised by a minister for being too loud during communion. Which I would know, it happened to me. One of the few sober Sundays my mother experienced, she forced all her children to attend church with her. I did not have time to eat breakfast as I was getting Jennifer ready. My stomach growled loudly as the plate of crackers passed under my nose. The minister shushed me loudly as if I could help my stomach from reacting to a plate of snacks passing by my hungry frame. I was too young and ill-versed in religion to know that the crackers represented anything other than a snack time in the center of the long speech given by the guy in a robe.

I narrowed my eyes and dug into my pie. Whoa. If I thought the fries were perfect...

"I told you it would be good." He smiled at my reaction but dropped his lips back to a flat line.

I swallowed my bite and nodded. "I have never had an apple pie like this." I pointed to it with my fork.

"Tabatha makes them fresh every day. She comes in around noon and starts making them for the lunch and dinner rush." I looked around to the dessert case, it was nearly empty. I frowned that I would not be able to test out another piece and take one for the road.

"What are you doing about the missing women?" He asked finally.

I chewed another warm, perfectly balanced bite, "I

have a tracker on a suspect's car, so far he has not strayed from his work schedule. I have checked his home. It's clean. I need to check his work locations and the buildings to rule them out." I took the last bite of pie, sad that it was gone. "I need to see if he is storing them there."

"What if it is not him?"

I had considered it; all my evidence did not fit completely. But I still had not found the link that brought all the victims together.

"Unfortunately, I can't do anything until I have more evidence. I have exhausted all the social media outlets looking for clues into the women's lives. I have watched hundreds of hours of security footage. The clue to break the case is literally just outside the camera's lens."

He looked grim, "So if it is not him, Lisa Henderson will be next."

"Yep." I looked down at my empty plates, ashamed that I could not help the women being tortured. I was trying to help Rebecca Hamilton, but everything kept coming back negative.

"Don't give up." Beck's tone was earnest. He grabbed my hand and squeezed it. The touch sent a zing through my nervous system. He continued, "Your deductive reasoning skills are better than most people I have met. You work from different angles. You are intelligent. And you are helping."

After his teasing rejection and the constant dead ends, I got to say if there was a moment that I needed a pep talk, this was it. His palm was still clasped around my hand. It was so warm; I did not want to move my cold fingers to remind him that he was touching me.

"Can I ask you something?" I said finally.

"You can ask me anything, I just may not answer it." He smiled coolly. I tried not to roll my eyes and scoff, I was already well aware of his evasive nature.

"Do you like me?" It was probably the most childish question I had ever asked in my adult years. I could not believe that I had voiced the whiney question out loud like we were fifth graders. I mean, I did want to know. I held my breath.

He chuckled, "Do you want me to like you?" Ugh, that is not an answer, it was an evasive question of a question, his specialty. I narrowed my eyes and pulled my hand away from his. I leaned forward with my hands in my lap.

"I'm serious, Beck! After all this time we have spent together I have no idea where we stand. Are we friends? Or... what are we?" Not eloquent, but it got to the point. I think.

He looked thoughtful and sighed, "Those are all very different questions, so I will answer to the best of my ability. Yes, I think we are friends." I felt disappointed to be in the friend category, but not surprised. He had introduced me as such to Tabatha. My stupid optimistic heart blurted out, "But do you *like* me?" Ugh, *kill me*. I'm so embarrassing.

"I believe it is socially acceptable to like your friends, I believe there is another word for people that you know but do not like." He smiled; his eyes were alight with the humor in his statement. I grimaced, that was not what I meant, and he knew it.

"It is getting late, and you have added many things to your itinerary tomorrow." He stood up and held his hand out to me, to help me up. I took his hand in mine. I did not need help getting up, but I was happy for an excuse to touch him again. His palm was still warm, his fingers entwined into mine.

I did not let go of him and he did not drop my hand until we made it up to Tabatha. She saw our clasped fingers and gave me the I-told-you-so look and gave Beck a hug goodbye. He dropped a twenty in the tip jar and we parted.

Chapter 11

February 29

Anxiety about entering Oscar Perez's house woke me at 4am and disallowed me from going back to sleep. I tapped into different home security cameras to see which one had the best view of Perez's front door. As luck would have it, his neighbor across the street had a doorbell camera. I was able to watch footage from the past few weeks to establish his movement patterns. He left most mornings around 6am and got home most evenings, at 9:30pm. On Mondays, he stayed home and cared for his lawn. On Wednesdays and Saturdays, he came home at 5pm. He would leave his house again at 5:30pm and would return at 7pm every Saturday. I checked back as far as the camera would go, he did not falter from his schedule.

I stretched, ran, ate breakfast, and waited until 8am to leave. By 9:15 I was pulling into the street behind Perez's house. I checked my wig and slung my fanny-pack on. It was not a fashionable choice, but no one questioned a jogger with a bum-bag. A backpack on the other hand looked suspicious.

The houses were all separated with four-foot concrete walls in the back that attached to the sides of the house. I jogged onto Perez's street to verify no one was home and looped back to the street behind. The tricky part was hopping the fence that led to his backyard. I was just building up my courage to run and jump over his back-neighbor's fence when their garage door opened. I dropped to my knee and tied my shoes. One at a time, slowly. The neighbor looked down at me on the sidewalk as they were exiting their property, but the glance was so dismissive, I was sure they were just making sure they were not going to run me over. They pulled away, I stood up and stretched my legs, waiting for them to be out of sight. Their car turned, I waited, took a deep breath, and launched myself over their fence, and ran full out to the fence that separated their domain from Perez's. I catapulted myself over the wall and landed in a roll. I stayed still for a few breaths listening for anything that might hint that I was seen.

After an eternity, or 3 minutes, it all feels the same when you are being reckless, I popped his lock and slid into his back door. Nothing jumped out and screamed, so far so good. In fact, nothing moved at all. His house was completely quiet.

I walked silently into his bedroom. One side of the bed was in a small heap, the other side of the bed was neatly made with covers tucked under the mattress. There was a large gold framed wedding picture on the unkempt side's bed table. I delicately picked up the frame, it was an old photo. The clothing and hairstyles were dated, but his wife was lovely, the adoration in his eyes was unmistakable. I replaced the frame and opened the drawer. Nothing of significance rattled in the drawer. I opened the closet. Three-quarters was filled with women's clothes. They smelled dusty with a small hint of perfume. I backed out. Why would he leave everything of hers as she left it? Maybe his guilt would not allow him to move on. Maybe he was in a psychosis where he does not believe she is gone and is waiting for her to return?

The hallway was lined in hundreds of pictures, each featuring the couple. Smiling, happy, in love. I walked into the office. The desk had piles of bills, his day planner, and an old computer. I rifled through the bills, a past due note from USC Norris addressed to his wife laid on the top. It was not open. The file cabinet was locked. I rocked it back to release the lock pin and opened the drawers one at a time. I found their marriage certificate, their divorce certificate, and her death certificate.

Under the medical file, I found an old bill from five years prior, for $20,000 from the USC Norris Comprehensive Cancer Center. I found another bill from two months later for

$5000 in her name. I stared at the two statements. The exact procedures had been done on both bills. The top corner gave me my answer. Emma Perez had changed insurance providers after the divorce and the new insurance covered more. I was staring out the window, contemplating why someone would divorce after they were diagnosed with something, cancer I assume, and then never move. She divorced him but continued to live with him. It made no sense.

I slid the bills back in place. I opened his daily planner. It was brown leather and old, but it looked like he used it frequently. I checked today's date for any clue as to what he did every Saturday. A small note was circled, "Bartlett Foothill Center, 6:00pm."

A flash of white caught my eye from the window. I looked over and ducked down, crawling towards the window to make sure no one had seen me. A young man was shimming down a tree. A young woman was in the window watching his descent. I chanced a second look and noticed the young woman was Rebecca Hamilton. The pregnant narcoleptic virgin had a gentleman caller in her bedroom. The young man was still working his way down the tree. I grabbed my things and ran out the backdoor to follow my new lead.

I was hopping mad when I was sure she had made the whole thing up so she would not get in trouble with her parents. He left through their backyard. I mirrored his movements in Perez's backyard. He was jogging a few steps ahead of me when we reached the sidewalk he stopped and turned around. I took my opportunity and ran into him hard, knocking us both to the ground.

"Oh gosh, I did not see you there!" I put on my southern accent. He had scraped his palms on the concrete, they were bleeding from two surface scratches. Perfect.

He sat on his butt for a second and scowled at me. I frowned at him with all the innocence a Southern woman possesses and helped him off the ground, wiping the dirt from my knees with my free hand. My act of kindness made the boy release his scowl as he darted his eyes around the street nervously.

"Oh no! It was my fault ma'am. I should not have stopped without looking around." He was looking at his palms frowning. I unzipped my pack and pulled out a tissue, passing it to him.

"Here you go, sugar, sorry about your hand." He wadded the tissue into the small cuts and started to brush his backside off. He looked around nervously at the cars passing by. He turned to leave, I panicked. I needed the tissue to prove Rebecca Hamilton was a lying twit.

"Hold on, let me get you a Band-Aid. I am sure I have one in here somewhere." I chuckled to myself, shaking the pack. Where the hell are my freaking band-aids?

"It's not a problem, it's hardly bleeding." He was walking backwards with his eyes on me. He showed me his palm. "See it's already done." He was looking around nervously again as another car passed by, he spotted a trash can and tossed the used bloody tissue aside. As another car drove towards the intersection, he turned on his heel and jogged briskly to his car parked twenty feet from mine. I memorized his plates and turned to watch the car at the intersection proceed through. The nervous boy left the street, going a little faster than street legal. It's safe to assume he was not supposed to be in her room, on this street, or in this neighborhood. I fished out the used tissue, wrapped it in another tissue, and walked over to my car.

I was speeding East on the 210 freeway and pulling into the condo parking deck within the hour. I ran inside and started writing down everything I could remember. The license plate, the description of the boy. Then I switched gears, wrote down Perez's wife, medical facility, bill numbers, and his 6pm appointment tonight.

I decided first I needed to identify the nervous boy. I pulled the registry of his car based on its plates. It was registered in his dad's name. Bless social media, I found the nervous boy in question within an hour. Brian Landers, age 16, former employee of Java, attends the rival high school of Rebecca Hamilton. HA! I filled out a DNA profile and gathered the kit that allowed blood as its specimen. I paid online for expedited processing and expedited the postage. Within 48 hours I would know for sure whether or not Rebecca Hamilton was a nervous girl too afraid of her parent's wrath to tell the truth. Satisfied with a crack in the case, I turned to the Perez information.

Emma Perez was a certified medical coder and had been for twenty years. She married Perez at the age of thirty. Three years into their marriage they bought their house where Oscar lives today. Emma took out a life insurance policy on herself in October of 2015, was diagnosed with stage 4 breast cancer in November. She divorced Perez in December of 2015. Merry Christmas Oscar. She changed her medical insurance the day after the divorce was finalized, but no records indicated she moved out of their shared home. By January of 2016 she died, presumably from her breast cancer that had metastasized.

I tried to make sense of it. The timing was too perfect. His adoration of his wife was too evident to make the pieces fit together. It made no sense why she would divorce him when she would want to have a solid support system in place. Frustrated, I gave Lauren a call, hoping to glean insight from the trauma of a cancer diagnosis.

"Ro, what's wrong?" She sounded tense.

"Nothing is wrong, I just had a quick question for you." I heard her sigh in relief. "Why would something need to be wrong for me to call you?"

She snorted, "Because you only call on the Sundays to confirm dinner, and never in the middle of a Saturday." I thought about that. I was pretty regimented in my calling schedule.

"Well, sorry about that. I will try to stick to my scheduled chat time in the future." Even I could hear the eye roll in my voice.

Another sigh, "It's fine, what's up?"

I had almost forgotten about the reason for my call, but my jotted shorthand caught my brain up to my mouth. "In your professional opinion, why would a woman divorce her husband a month after a serious cancer diagnosis but continue to live with him? If she wanted the support system, why divorce him?"

"Insurance." She said it as if I were dumb to be asking, as if it were the most obvious answer in the world.

"Pardon my ignorance on the intricate nuances of the insurance industry, but do you care to expound upon your cursory response?" I had my uppity persona dialed in.

She laughed, "Ro! Calm down, I was not implying you were ignorant. I was giving you the short answer. The long answer is insurance is complicated and tiered. Depending on your company and what they pay versus what you pay as the employee varies greatly. Not all insurances are created equal, even companies have their own rules that you would need an advanced degree to understand."

I was starting to possibly, maybe, make sense out of what she was saying, "what if the primary insurance provider was a business owner? Wouldn't he be able to change his insurance to better insurance?"

Another laugh, "Wouldn't that be nice! But no, and if he is a business owner the rules are even more complicated. Depending on income of the business, the number of insured, and the time of year would all have to work out perfectly in order to make any changes. Sometimes married couples will divorce so the sick partner will qualify for a different insurance that is based on income and will cover more. Sometimes it is recommended to patients as a way to circumvent heavy hospital bills that would incur with the lesser than insurance." I blinked at the wall taking in what she was saying.

"The divorce just becomes a business transaction to qualify for better insurance?" I asked, feeling a little breathless.

"Yeah, basically, but listen Ro, I am super busy. Drinks tomorrow night? David bought a margarita mixer and wants to test it out!" Lauren sounded excited.

"Sure, yeah, I will see you tomorrow night around 8." I hung up and added the notes to the other Perez information. I still could not piece together the life insurance policy. The timing was still too perfect. I checked the clock. I had two hours before Oscar's appointment at Bartlett Foothill Center. I pulled up the website. It was a community center a few miles from his house. They had adult learning classes, gym classes, and different social groups. I pulled up the community center's schedule for 6pm. Two classes listed, a grief group and a Lamaze class. I was hedging my bets towards the grief group.

An hour later I was heading back West, Leslie Mixon firmly in place, wearing a charcoal wrap dress and chunky, black-framed glasses. I hated grief groups. My school counselor forced me to attend a grief group. It was uncomfortable watching the pitbull-mean basketball coach that headed the group bawling like a spanked baby. I shook off the memory and reminded myself that I was here to figure Oscar Perez out.

I walked into a smaller classroom. A small table with coffee and stale donuts sat under the chalkboard. There was a circle of chairs in the middle of the classroom, desks were pushed along the wall. There were a few people milling around the coffee. Oscar Perez was talking with an older woman by the circle of chairs. A few people looked up as I approached the chairs and took a seat. One by one people joined me in the circle and at exactly 6pm the older woman, that Perez was talking to, started.

"Welcome to Surviving Loss, most of you know me, but I see a few new faces." She looked over to me, I squirmed, she moved her gaze to three other people and continued. "For those of you who do not know me, I am Karen Childs. I am a certified grief counselor, and I have been volunteering here for five years." She looked back around the circle with a gentle smile.

"Would any of our newcomers like to introduce themselves?" She made another pointed look towards me, a few eyes followed hers. *Shit.* I cleared my throat, "I am Leslie Mixon." I gave a small wave. Karen was still looking at me, "Who did you lose dear?" Shit. Shit. Shit. I knew there was a possibility of being asked, but I never fully decided what to say. If I mentioned John's death it would be pretty easy to track if anyone was looking to do just that. Only ten firefighters died during that fire. I settled on an old memory that would be hard to trace from another state twenty years ago.

"My father and brother died in a car accident where I was also a passenger." I was looking down at my hands, praying that they would not ask any more details.

Karen made a small noise in her throat, "Survivors guilt along with the loss of a father and sibling must be a difficult cross to bear. Thank you for sharing Leslie." Like I had a choice. A few people murmured in my direction. "Anyone else that would like to introduce themselves?"

Two other people introduced themselves before Karen spoke back to the group.

"Many of you know Oscar Perez. He has been attending for a few years now. He would like to share his experience with the group." She turned to Perez, "Oscar, you have the floor."

All eyes turned to Perez. Silent tears gathered in the crinkle of his eyes. He wiped them away harshly and coughed to clear his throat.

"My wife was the best thing in my world. I was lucky to spend over twenty-five years with her. We met in school, she was funny and smart. It took me a month to talk to her. When I finally did, she asked me what took so long." He chuckled at the memory.

"She took care of me, she made me eat vegetables and take vitamins. She made me walk with her in our neighborhood every night. She'd tell me, 'You only get the one body Oscar, better take care of it!'" He wagged his finger at his impersonation of her. "She was always taking care of me. I should have been taking care of her, but she did not tell me she was sick. See, she was a medical coder. She spent her life writing down conditions and the diagnosis. She was smart, she knew she was sick before the doctors did." He bent down and took a sip of his water. "She must have known it was bad because she took out a life insurance policy and did not tell me anything about it. I found out when her lawyer gave me her will. She waited until the policy was valid before she went in to get her diagnosis confirmed. It was worse than she feared. She died within a few months." He wiped his eyes and took another sip of water. "Now it has been years and I cannot help but wonder if she had just this once, taken care of herself first, if she would have gone in three months before she did. Would she be with me today?" His voice cracked in the end.

I heard a few sniffles, a few murmurs. Karen was talking, but I was not listening. I had my answer. Perez was innocent. I was deep in thought when Karen dismissed the group. Chairs grinding across the linoleum brought me out of my reverie. I looked up, she was standing in front me, looking down at my seated figure. I nodded and rose from my seat, "How long ago did your father and brother die, Leslie?"

I took a breath, not expecting to give any more details into my life, "Twenty years ago."

She smiled sweetly and patted my shoulder, "Grief never fully goes away, does it? I hope to see you next week Leslie."

Chapter 12

March 1

I fully anticipated Beck to greet me in the morning for an update, but nothing. I followed through with my normal routine and delved back into Scott Pickens. I felt guilty for neglecting the case. I should not have spent the day prior looking into Oscar Perez. I wasted a day that I could have dedicated to looking for Lisa Henderson and Kelly Parker.

Pickens had not strayed one minute from his schedule. Every day he went to the planned locations, every day he went back to his small home. I had one day before Lisa Henderson's body would be dumped somewhere near her Yorba Linda home. I checked Pickens's GPS and schedule. He would be in Dana Point all day. I forewent changing my persona and headed to Riverside to check out his location as myself in my fuel-efficient car.

An hour and a half later, I was pulling into the small shopping center. Frooty-Tooty was between a Vons grocery store and Great Clips. There was a Mexican restaurant at the end of the center. A Bank of the West was in the center of the parking lot. Considering the time of day, the parking lot was fairly full. I watched a few people walk into the smoothie shop. I stepped in and found myself last in a four-person line. One peppy girl with long black hair was taking orders and making smoothies, a loud whirring of the blenders punctuating the end of each order. Everything smelled like vanilla, banana, and strawberries. I looked around for the security system. One camera was trained on the register. One camera was trained on the front door. A small hallway with a single person bathroom sat at the end of the hall next to the emergency exit. The office sat on the opposite side. Based on the dimension of the smoothie shop, the office was no more than 5' feet wide and about 8 feet deep, same as the bathroom.

"What can I make you today?" The peppy girl asked me. I glanced at the menu. I had been too busy scoping out the place, I forgot to look. "Peach Surprise, no sugar, please." The loud whirring of the blender filled the small space again. The peppy girl passed the freshly made smoothies to patrons that were waiting in front of me. They left quickly, slurping their drinks as the door chimed to notify us of their exit.

"$4.50 is your total for the Peach Surprise, no sugar." Her smile was bright. Her black hair was pulled in a tight ponytail, it was shiny and looked silky as she swung it back and forth between the blenders and the register. I gave her a five-dollar bill and motioned towards the bathroom. She nodded and continued with the next order.

The bathroom was small and clean. I pushed the toilet lid down and stood on it. I slid a ceiling tile to the side and poked my head in it. It was a clear shot to the office. I hoisted myself up and pulled myself against the plenum space above, careful not to put too much weight on the ceiling panels. I carefully crawled over the hallway and dropped myself into the office. Nothing, no trap doors, just a metal safe, boxes of cups, a few cases of bananas, and a filing cabinet. It was less of an office and more of a food storage room with a safe. I pulled myself back through the ceiling and was crossing the hallway as someone knocked on the bathroom door.

"Just a minute," I called; it was a reflex. I was hoping whoever was knocking did not notice the voice coming from above them instead of in front of them. I shimmied down unto the toilet and did a cursory flush. I had to wash the dust off my hands and pat my clothing off before I walked out of the bathroom. A mother and a wiggling toddler were waiting for me to free up the space. I stepped around them and back into the main shop. I spotted my smoothie sitting on the counter. I grabbed it quickly, nodded to the peppy girl, and headed back to my car.

The smoothie was good, but the drive there was a waste. There was no place for Scott Pickens to store anything more than a few cases of bananas.

I had to mentally prepare myself for the hike across town to Culver City.

Two hours later, the smoothie cup rattled in my console and I was still a half-hour away. Traffic was backing up for an unknown reason. Most of the time traffic slows in the middle of the day is from a driver not paying attention to the road and going twenty miles per hour less than the speed limit, a phone is always involved. I once asked Manny how a sprawling city with highways to spare could have so many people in no hurry to get anywhere? "What's the point in speeding up, when you know you have to slow back down in a mile?" That was the mentality of the born and bred Angelinos. It was the transplants like me that would speed around and flip fingers at the slowpokes.

Finally, after an eon in the car, I parked in front of the Culver City location. My legs felt stiff, my fingers ached from gripping the steering wheel in frustration. I stretched my legs, flexed my fingers, took a deep breath, and walked into Frooty-Tooty. The shop was empty, I heard the door ding as I walked in, but no one was behind the counter. It was laid out similarly to the Riverside location, but the hallway had a bend at the end with an additional door. I opened the door to let it ding again, hoping the noise would make whoever was supposed to be working think someone had left. I quickly walked to the back hall. The bathroom was occupied. I heard the water running and slipped into the bend of the hallway. The hallway ended abruptly at a door. I opened it, it was a mop closet with electrical boxes and a sink. I slunk in as I heard the bathroom door open.

I heard another ding of the door and whatever patron

that walked in was greeted. I stacked some boxes that contained cleaning chemicals up and hoisted myself into the drop ceiling. The path to the office was a little longer with the ducting making it difficult to maneuver without hitting the floating tiles. My foot slipped once and shifted a tile. I had a quick glimpse into the hallway. I held my breath as I slipped the tile back in place. I shimmied into the back room. It was larger than the Riverside location. There was a row of shelves dividing the computers from the stored goods. A row of refrigerators lined the wall opposite the office. Cases of bananas, syrups, and protein powders filled the shelves. I heard the door click and rushed to the opposite side of a tall banana pile. The person was quick, grabbing something from a fridge and dashing back out.

I took a deep breath and looked around the office. Sitting below the office chair was a metal trap door. It was about 3 feet by 3 feet with a rusted padlock on it. My heart started racing, *why would there be a trapdoor? Why would it be locked?* I crawled beneath the desk to get a better view of the padlock. I rifled through my bag and pulled out a nail file and bobby pin. The bobby pin snapped within one minute, the nail file was too broad to fit. I looked around frantically for the key. There was a lockbox hanging on the wall above the computers. That lock was easy to pop with the nail file. Inside the lockbox was at least a hundred keys. I rolled my head back in frustration.

I grabbed a handful of keys and dove back under the desk and began trying them one by one. The door opened another two times, fortunately, both times were quick, and they left before the door fully shut. Forty-five keys later the padlock clicked open. My heart stopped and started again; I held my breath as I slid the office chair away. The old metal trap door groaned loudly. I gasped and dropped myself in and shut the lid hastily above me. I heard the office door open again, and someone walked around. I stood in the pitch darkness holding my breath waiting for the footfalls to retreat. Finally, the office door opened again, and I was alone. I took a steadying breath. It smelled dank and musty like a basement. There was no lighting. I grabbed my phone and used it as a flashlight. The room was small, approximately 10 by 10 feet, conduit piping lead away from the room. There was a series of boxes on one wall, the bottom row was waterlogged. I looked around for any signs of life, just my stuttering breath, and spiders. I hate spiders.

I made my way back to the trap door, careful not to push it open more than necessary. It emitted only a small groan as I slipped out of the dank storage room. I was just at the office door when it sprung open. A young boy with chin acne and hair draped over his eyes walked in and halted at the sight of me. I resisted the urge to hit and run or scream. I just stood there mute.

"Bro, you can't be in here." He flicked his bangs out of his eyes with the flick of his head.

I shrugged with my hands facing up, and put on a confused apologetic face, "Got, lost, where's the bathroom?"

He seemed to buy my lie, "Cross the hall, dude." He pointed behind him, I slid past him and into the bathroom. I splashed cool water on my cheeks and gulped in calming breaths. My hair had cobwebs stuck to the left side above my ear. My shirt had dirt and rust on it. I cringed as I worked the cobwebs out of my hair and wiped away the dirt and rust off madly.

I high stepped it to the door. "Dude, the bathrooms are for customers only." I stopped with my hand on the cold metal handle, turned around, tossed a five in the tip jar with a wink, and dashed out.

Another wasted trip. I checked the clock; I was two hours from home with traffic building every minute. I rationalized a trip to Dana Point would be pointless. The location was on the second story of a busy mall, there were no storage units allowed on the mall property and it looked like Culver City was all the storage Pickens' small operation needed.

I chastised myself for wasting another day. Lisa Henderson was one more day closer to death and I was nowhere near being able to help her. I should have listened to the little voice that was rationalizing about Pickens not being the guy. It was all circumstantial. Had I been less stubborn and less sure of myself, maybe I would have found the real culprit.

I pulled into my driveway feeling angsty and worn. I almost felt responsible for Lisa Henderson's impending death. I had time, hours, but I had no leads. I still could not find the link. Frustrated, I pulled out of my driveway before I turned the car off. I needed to get my mind off the case. I pulled into the Krav Maga Studio and grabbed my gym bag as I plowed through the door.

Excess energy from sitting in a car most of the day moved through my system, tensing my muscles in anticipation of release. I had not sparred with anyone since Beck attacked me in the woods outside of Food and Things. I was still reeling from him beating me. Distracted, I bumped into Nathan on my way out of the locker room. His smile was beautiful. I stuttered to a stop, "You don't teach tonight." My tone may have been closer to accusatory. I was not mentally prepared to see him.

He chuckled, "Can't teach what you don't know." I stared back confused, blinking silently.

"I am here to practice." Duh, makes sense. "Be my partner tonight?" He tilted his head down, his brown eyes looked like melted chocolate, his stubble was the perfect balance between rugged and sexy. I shrugged, "If you feel like getting your ass kicked, sure." He smiled again and followed me to the mats.

We circled once, "don't hold back." Nathan chortled. I think I growled in response. He was stronger, but I was faster.

He came in for a strike, attempting to punch me, I grabbed his arm. With his fist in my hands, I shoved it down and used it as a stepping point, jumping up and wrapping my legs around the back of his neck. I rolled my weight forward, making him lose balance and I flung him in an armbar.

He tapped, laughing.

We circled again, he faked a right and dodged to my left, grabbing me from behind. I pulled my body down, moving the center of gravity to my advantage, I punched my arm backward hard, looking for his groin. He was wearing a cup. I kicked my foot back trying to get his knee, he moved it quickly out of the way. I faked my left elbow back. He dodged, and I threw my right elbow back hitting his head. He released me at the pop. I turned around. He was rubbing his jaw, "Damn, Caroline, who pissed you off today?"

I dropped my hands, "You told me not to hold back!" I bit back defiantly.

He laughed, "Okay, hold back a little. Black eyes and busted lips are bad for business."

We circled again, "Okay, you attack me now." I did not like being the attacker as much. There was something about being the victim that made me quicker, most resourceful. Purposely attacking someone went against all my extensive training. I shrugged and lunged at him. He had me on my back within thirty seconds.

"Again!" I hated being bested. Thirty minutes later and we were just about even in taps and submission holds. A small group was watching from the benches along the wall. A few women were whispering to each other, they looked at me in awe. I felt pride that they saw a woman half the size of her partner and holding her own.

Nathan was waiting for me outside of the locker room. Apparently, we both decided to shower at home versus the communal showers provided. "That was fun."

I nodded, "It was a good workout." My arms felt shaky and weak, my legs felt like noodles.

"You were more feisty tonight. I was serious when I asked if someone pissed you off." His hair was slicked back with sweat, but he had changed into a dry cotton t-shirt and loose drawstring shorts. A hand towel hung around his neck.

"No one in particular. Just stressed." I opened the exit door. He walked me to my car, such a gentleman.

"What's stressing you out, beautiful?" I made a face at the pet name. I doubt he saw it; I was facing my car door when he said it. I shrugged. "Work and stuff. I have not been sleeping well."

A low rumble of a chuckle came from his chest. He leaned against my door, keeping me from opening it. "Sex is a pretty good stress reliever. And I always sleep like a baby after." His arms were crossed over his chest, he looked at me through his lashes. He was a handsome man. I smiled sweetly to him, "Funny, last time you came by I was not very *relieved* at the end."

He chuckled and bounced out of his leaning posture.

"What are you doing tonight?" He had moved in front of me. My back was pressed against the door frame.

"Drinks with my sister." I sounded a little breathless, most likely from the rigorous workout. Or maybe because he was propositioning me, and he was the only one interested in me like *that*. Despite my wild fantasies about Beck, he had never shown any interest in sex. Maybe he was a monk in a past life and was having a hard time adjusting.

"What about after?" His eyebrows arched in a look of hope. He shifted closer to me, his chest against mine, I could feel something hard and hot next to my belly. It was nice to know that I had that effect on someone at least. I playfully pushed him back, "Going to sleep. I have been up since four. I will not be good company."

He leaned forward and kissed my cheek. It was sweet but did nothing to make my stomach erupt in hot fire like when Beck did the same thing. "Caroline, even when you are beating the shit out of someone, you are good company."

It was a weird compliment. I rolled my eyes, "Good night, Nathan." I pulled the door open and slid in. He stopped the door before I was able to close it.

"You're still into the other guy, huh? Beck?" His face looked soft, slightly wounded, although it could be the swelling on his jaw.

"Nothing is going on with anyone. Beck is just a friend." It hurt to say the words out loud, like putting them into the ether made them absolutely true. I swallowed the lump that formed.

"I get it, you want something more than a quick roll in the hay." He tapped my door frame with his fingers a few times and nodded to himself. He ducked his head in for another kiss on the cheek and gently closed my door.

I did not know what I wanted. Did I want something more than a quick roll in the hay, as Nathan so eloquently put it? In my fantasies, there was nothing quick about Beck, and funny, no hay involved.

Chapter 13

March 1

"Sister!" Lauren met me on her walkway. She had a margarita in each hand. She was doing a weird shimmy dance towards me. She already was a few margaritas in, no doubt. I relieved her of the full drink and followed her to the backyard. She shushed me as we walked through the house. As if I was going to start marching and yelling to wake up Lennon and Taylor.

"What took you so long?" her words were slurred.

I took a sip, it was a fruity frozen margarita, "I walked here."

"Good call, Ro. You are always thinking ahead." She attempted to poke my nose but missed and stuck her finger in my drink. "Oops." She giggled.

"How many of these have you had?" I handed her a rogue napkin. She dried a finger off and shrugged.

"David wanted to try a mango recipe, it's good huh?" She took a gulp, I mimicked. It was good, refreshing, with a solid kick.

"Where is David?" I looked around but could not find him anywhere.

"You are late, missy! He went to bed; he has a conference call with some Japanese company at some ungodly hour." She wagged her finger at me and hiccupped.

"Lo, it is 8:30, I am a half hour late."

She giggled, "I started at 7:30, it's been a rough few days." She sighed and took another sip. "David insisted, and he put the boys and himself to bed at 8."

"What's going on? Something with work?" I pried. I

wanted to be her sounding board. I also wanted to hear of someone else's problems that would overshadow my own.

"Some good, some bad, some ugly." She hiccupped again and topped her glass off.

"Let's start with the good, Lo."

She rolled her head back and yawned an exaggerated yawn.

"You know that girl with narcolepsy I was telling you about?" My attention was immediately undivided on Lauren's slurred words. I nodded, "The pregnant one?"

"Yaaaasssss, ugh, it is a mess. So, she comes in and tells me that she has a boyfriend. She said that she did not want her parents to find out because they said she can't have a boyfriend until she is eighteen." She rolled her eyes, "Anyway, she tells me that she has a boyfriend, but she did not have sex with him." The image of the nervous boy clouded my vision. I doubted sneaking out of a window was to hide their scrabble addiction.

"What if she is lying?" She raised her eyebrows and shrugged.

"Could be, but she promised me she only did hand and mouth stuff. Remind me to have you have that talk with the boys. I cringe at the idea of hand and mouth stuff talk." She shuttered and took another sip.

"Anyway, she seemed pretty honest. I can tell when someone is lying to me, and she was earnest. She said she told me because she did not want it to get out and he gets in trouble." She shook her head, "The mind of a sixteen-year-old!" She threw a hand in the air to emphasize how preposterous a sixteen-year old's reasoning could be.

"She came to the hospital, to your office to tell you about a hand job?" I sounded amused. She snorted.

"Nah, she was in the area. Visiting her brother." My head jerked up.

"The drug-dealer? Did he get arrested?" My mind was clicking along, I had forgotten about the drug-dealing brother and the possible suspects that bought her narcolepsy medicine off of him.

She took another deep drink, "Turns out, he did not sell her drugs. He was taking them for himself, apparently, he is less of a dealer and more of a user. He took her pregnancy pretty hard. He blamed himself. He overdosed a few days after her initial visit." She shook her head, "Poor kid, has his whole life in front of him."

"Did he… die?" I cringed with guilt at the whole scenario.

She stared at me with wide eyes, "No, he is in rehab. Rock bottom has its pros and cons depending on whether you are at the top or at the bottom."

I took a drink, so that ruled out the drug dealer brother's friends. It possibly ruled out the boyfriend. I had another day before that report would confirm anything. I felt bogged down as another avenue to a lead shut tightly in my face.

"That doesn't sound so bad. It sounds like he is getting the help that he needs." I sounded earnest. Lauren was too good for her own good.

"That was the good!" She made a sad chuckle, it dawned on me that there was more than one patient that was bothering her.

"So, tell me the bad."

She slurped the last dregs down, "I got called in for a consult. Cute girl, seventeen. Her boyfriend was mad she was breaking up with him. Beat the shit out of her, literally. Broken ribs, raped her, and left her with a bleeding rectum."

She sniffed and rubbed her face.

"Her mother comes in as we are trying to get the paperwork together to fill out a police report. She snatched the papers from me and stuffed them into her brand-new Louis Vuitton purse. She said that her daughter was not pressing charges, and it was all a misunderstanding. We couldn't really challenge much. Girl was still a minor and she had not told us who her ex-boyfriend was."

"It was confusing because what mother would say that if she knew the extent of her daughter's injuries. The other sticky thing, the insurance the girl was using was income qualified. No one at that income level could afford a purse like that!" She frowned at her empty cup and grabbed mine and took a sip.

"It was the real deal too. I know designer when I see it. You could smell the leather from the moment she stormed in." She sighed, "Anyway, a few days later the girl comes back for her follow-ups. She comes to my office saying she wants to file a police report."

"What about her mom?" I asked curiously and still contemplating how terrible of a mother this poor girl had.

"She came in on her eighteenth birthday." She gave me a full grin, "Gives me the kid's full name. Turns out this kid's family is rich. Like really rich. Like political-pull rich. Turns out the kid told his dad what he did, and his dad paid the mother off!"

I gasped. What an awful bitch. Lauren shook her head. "Ro, poor people believe that money can fix every problem. And this girl's family is poor. I don't want to make an excuse for the mother. It is just something that I have to come to grips with."

I found my voice again.

"That's awful. What are the police doing?"

She laughed and shook her head, "That's the ugly part. Rich dad reached out to all his powerful buddies. No judge in the area will sign a subpoena for the kid's DNA. We can't confirm he did anything to her. We have her 'attacker's' DNA on file, but nothing to compare it to. Judges have kiboshed any sort of collecting of DNA, even through discarded trash." She tossed the rest of my margarita back.

It took me a minute to collect my thoughts, "What if the kid slipped up and his DNA ended up at the police precinct?" I asked eagerly. She snorted.

"No cop will risk his career to do that. The girl's family is poor. The kid's family is rich. And short of him walking into the police precinct holding a cup of his specimen, they can't do anything."

I was thinking hard, trying to find a solution. "What about a private detective?"

She chortled, "Her family is poor and happily accepting payola. They are not going to hire a private detective and lose their cash cow."

"There has to be something. What could work to get this kid's DNA on file without someone losing their job?"

She shrugged, "I told you it was ugly. The kid would literally have to turn himself in."

I bit my lip considering it.

My entire walk home I was going back and forth as to whether or not to get myself involved. It felt pretty cut and dry. Do what I normally do, get the DNA, submit it online under his name and information and let the dominoes fall into place. The judges refusing the sign any subpoena was disturbing. The mother being bought off made me angry. The girl just wanted justice. She wanted him arrested so he would not hurt anyone else.

I had already spread myself thin. All my suspects have

ruled themselves out. Scott Pickens did not have the time or the place to hold anyone hostage. He had not varied from his schedule once. Surely, he would have needed to stop by and fill up water. No autopsy report said they were dehydrated, they were starved, but not dehydrated.

According to Lauren, Brian Landers was only accepting handies and blowjobs from Rebecca Hamilton. It did seem like an odd admission, why would Rebecca bring it up at all? There were no leads with the drug-buying kids because no kid bought them. At this point, all-male employees at her school and Java have been ruled out. Her classmates were still being asked to submit a cheek swab, and from what I read, no parent had objected. My last avenue was where she took riding lessons. I was doubtful, her instructor is a woman.

I thought about Rebecca Hamilton's parents and compared them to Lauren's new client. Rebecca's parents were moving heaven and earth to get their daughter justice. Hundreds of people had to submit their DNA, and the police were working overtime. Even Rebecca's brother cared enough to go to rehab. Lauren's new client had no one. Everyone's hands were tied by some kid's rich daddy.

My hands were not tied, and it did not feel right that some rich prick could get away because of who his father was. I made up my mind and pulled up Lauren's work files after a few minutes.

Morgan Butler, eighteen and three days old. I read through her patient file. I grimaced while reading through her injuries. Lauren had omitted the busted lip. Pictures of her bruised face made me want to cry. She looked so hopeless. The end of the report listed her ex-boyfriend, Chad Westfield.

I poured into Morgan Butler's life first. Her parents were of lower income. Her dad was in and out of jail for petty crimes. He seemed closer to a grifter than anything violent. Her mother looked like she was once beautiful, but bad decisions had taken a lot of her beauty. Her face was prematurely lined, and she had a hungry look in her eyes, like someone wanting more from life. Like someone who got pissed when someone else succeeded.

Morgan Butler was adorable. In all her images, her makeup was perfectly applied, hair perfectly curled. A sweet but alluring smile was the primary feature, always accompanied by a hand on her hip, posing. She had green eyes and shiny light brown hair. During the summer her light brown hair had shimmers of gold. She was always at the beach, laughing, enjoying life. My heart squeezed for her.

I looked up Chad Westfield. He was a grade-A entitled rich boy. He was very attractive but carried himself with an air of arrogance that was off-putting. He posted several videos with his friends, most of which were pranking each other. The pranks were getting more serious and less funny the longer I watched his antics. He was constantly posing with expensive cars or posting videos of him illegally racing down residential streets. His social media friends consisted of busty girls and his comments on their pictures were degrading and misogynistic. He made one comment on how a girl needed to lose a few pounds, she didn't. He was twenty-two, which technically meant all his relations with Morgan could be deemed as statutory rape as she was under the age of eighteen, not that that clearly meant a thing in the present situation.

I looked into Chad's father since he was so prone to getting his son out of any scrape Chad found himself in. Desmond Westfield was a developer. Not just any developer, the fastest-growing developer in the Southwest. He was a major contributor to the current Congressman. He went to high school with the congressman and stayed close all the way to the House of Representatives. I shook my head, political ties indeed.

The more I learned the more I wanted justice for the sweet innocent Morgan Butler. The more I wanted to wipe the smirk off Chad Westfield's overly tanned face. Fortunately, Chad was the type that let the world know when he was breathing and where to find him at any given moment in his over-privileged world. I glanced at the clock, 11pm.

I desperately wanted to sleep, but I knew that sleep would evade me until more evidence presented itself in any of the cases. I also knew that Chad was at a bar that he normally frequented and would be there until closer to 2am when the bar closed down. I rubbed the sleep from my eyes and walked over to my closet.

I was a well preserved thirty-something-year-old woman. I dressed age-appropriately, if I dressed a little younger, I could pass for twenty-five at the youngest. Chad Westfield was twenty-two. I was not sure what my plan was, but I was going to go and see what I could find out. I was still waffling between finding a way to steal his DNA or straight up decking him in the face and collecting a blood sample. My boxing coach had commented my right hook was getting dangerously effective.

I selected a mini pleated skirt I had bought as a Halloween costume a few years prior. It was a Quentin Tarantino theme night, and I went as GoGo from Kill Bill. This particular skirt was lined in charcoal satin, I flipped it satin side out. I added a cream silky top, tucked in, and finished off the look with a black belt cinched at the waist and black peep-toe stilettos. I fluffed my hair out and added red lip gloss, it was more youthful than lipstick. I added a garter up high and attached a pocketknife. He was a proven abusive rapist, after all. My outfit definitely gave me a youthful look. I grabbed my clutch, and I was out the door.

Chapter 14

March 1-2

There was a line at Standing Room Only, but apparently, my skirt was short enough to avoid the que. I was waved in without even a cursory glance at my license.

It was loud and busy, apparently, it was Ladies Night. Tables scattered around the perimeter of the club; in the center was a huge rectangular bar that had at least 6 bartenders working. The space between the tables and the bar was all dance space. Large men dressed in all black, sporting earpieces posted up in every corner and at every exit. Even the bathrooms had a bouncer looking for trouble.

I casually walked around the perimeter tables looking for Chad. He had just posted on his online profile that he was at SRO, and it looked like he was at a table. I got buffeted a few times as I made my way through the tables. The patrons were all young, tipsy, and bearing a lot of skin.

"Caroline?!" I heard a familiar squeal coming from behind me. My hand was pulled back and I was spun around into a hug. Whoever she was, she had long blonde hair and smelled like sunshine. She pulled away, "Jessica?" My tone was shocked at seeing my employee. Mostly I was feeling squirmy for being dressed like a twenty-year-old, showing more thigh than I do in my swimsuit, and in a bar that I aged out of at least five years ago. Jessica did not seem to mind, she seemed drunk and giddy.

She tugged at my arm, "Oh my God! You have to come meet my friends! I talk about you all the time. They are never going to believe you are here!" She was shouting in my ear; the music had just picked up and the bass was making my brain rattle. She pulled me to a table I had passed a few minutes before.

The table had three other people at it, one girl, and two guys. The girl was as equally as beautiful as Jessica with her darker features. The boys were holding each other's hands. One was a cute-as-a-button skinny Black gentleman in his early twenties with thick-framed glasses, making him look hipster. His boyfriend, I presume, was a tall and handsome Asian guy who looked like he modeled for H&M in his spare time.

"Guys! This is the coolest boss in the world! My Caroline!" I sheepishly waved as Jessica hopped up and down in place while clapping. The boys looked up in interest, "Like Infinity, Caroline?"

I smiled, "Guilty."

"Love the vibe of your shop. I got my mom her birthday presents there. My sister only buys makeup from there." The cute Asian guy said. I nodded, it felt weird to yell "thanks for your patronage" when Post Malone was making the beat drop.

"Oh my God! I love this song!" Jessica was grabbing the hand of the other girl at the table, motioning her to stand up.

"It was great running into you, Jessica!" I yelled, I shook the hands that were extended out to me and walked into the crowd surrounding the bar. Bodies were swaying, jumping, and grinding to the music. Being hyper-aware of my body I can say my butt was grabbed three times and a few too many arms found themselves brushing into my boobs to call it an accident. I spotted an empty chair at the bar and went for it.

"What can I get ya?" An absurdly attractive bartender screamed at me. Her hair was pulled into a messy bun. One arm was completely covered in tattoos. Her makeup made her look like a pinup. Her lilac hair faded to blue with a few pieces framing her face. She was thin and at least 5'9". Her jeans were tight, and she was wearing a simple black tank. Even without trying, she was the most attractive woman within at least a crowded twenty feet. "Bud Light," I yelled back. She nodded, pulled her hand under the bar, and popped the top within 15 seconds. "Want to start a tab?" I nodded and passed her a card.

I nursed my beer and looked around carefully for Chad. I spotted him a few minutes later. He was surrounded by his posse of guys. He was in the center and they were all laughing. I motioned to my bartender. She made her way over to me as fast as she could. She stopped three times, popping beers on her way.

I passed her a twenty, "What do you know about that guy down there?" I nodded to Chad. She shook her head, "Dip-shit, decent tipper if you've got tits. The male bartenders won't go near him. He's some rich, influencer-want-to-be." She took another order from my right but kept her head turned towards me.

"I need to talk to him," I shouted. Her eyes narrowed, "His drink is crown." I nodded, understanding.

"Send him one on me." She smiled and disappeared to the other side of the bar. I saw her motion towards me. I sipped my beer waiting. A few minutes had gone by. I was just beginning to doubt my plan when someone was talking directly in my ear.

"You may be the hottest red-head I have ever seen in my life."

I plastered on a coy smile and swiveled in my seat. It was not Chad talking to me, it was some unknown guy. A guy who was scaring off Chad from approaching me. I glanced around. Chad was still talking to his friends. I turned back to the unknown guy. He was tall, brown hair, green eyes, and a smile that lit up half of the bar, in that boy next door sort of way. I stuck out my hand, "I'm Caroline." He took it and instead of shaking my hand, he kissed my knuckles.

I shook my head and laughed, "That was corny, right?" he chuckled to himself. "Call me Hank. My buddies," He pointed to his left, "dared me to kiss your hand. That's not normally my style." He smiled again.

I don't know what my face was saying, but it must have been closer to offended.

"You are talking to me on a dare?" Maybe I was feeling self-conscious for only out aging the owner of the club's youthful clientele, but in my experience, boys being dared to do something to me was normally out of cruelty.

His face looked shocked and sorry at the same time, "No, I mean, yes, but not because anything is wrong with you. I was serious, you are the most beautiful red-head I have ever seen in my life. My buddies just goaded me because they didn't think I'd have the balls on my own."

I turned around and took another sip of beer. He elbowed forward onto the bar and got my bartender's attention, "Put her tab on mine." He turned to me, "I'm sorry if I offended you." He actually did look sorry, and he was definitely cute, maybe even hot. I grabbed his hand.

"Hank, is it?" I said with the coy smile back in place.

He turned slowly, looking uncertain but hopeful. Maybe he was worried I was going to throw a drink in his face but hoping I wouldn't. "Yeah?"

"Sit with me while I finish the beer you just bought," I said while taking another small sip. He looked around hopefully, but there was no place for him to sit.

"I have a table over there, come join me." He yelled in my ear. I looked over to where he was pointing. It was next to the bathroom. It had potential for "running into Chad" I could definitely keep an eye on him from the table. I grabbed my beer and nodded to my bartender and followed Hank to his table. He guided me, with one hand on my mid-back. It was a little possessive, but it was four inches north of being offensive. One of his friends saw us approaching, grinned at

Hank, and excused himself a moment later. It was significantly quieter in the corner, instead of yelling, we just needed to speak loudly, or directly in each other's ear. Hank took the opportunity to put his arm around my shoulder in the pretense of easier discussion making.

"What are you going to school for, Hank?" My lips were practically in his ear. He smelled good, like fabric softener and woodsy cologne.

He turned his face towards my ear, "I'm a second-year resident at UCLA Medical." Well color-me-surprised.

"How old are you, Hank?" He had smooth skin, a freshly shaven face. He had a nice jawline and a deep voice. There could have been a worse way to spend an evening.

"Twenty-eight. I know, I'm too old for this place, but I am here for my brother." He pointed to a shorter version of himself. The resemblance was uncanny, except his brother was sporting a beard.

"What are you studying?" He licked his lips and grinned at me.

The curves of your lips, Hank. Which were broad and pink. I shook my head to clear the smutty thoughts.

"I'm not a student at UCLA, I was supposed to meet someone here, but she canceled after I got here. I was just about to leave when you came by." The lie came easily, I was clearly too old for this crowd, might as well explain my presence.

"My luck then! If you are not a student, what do you do?" He had a small bump in his nose, it was enough to give it character. I wonder if it was an old sport's injury or a little rambunctious fight with his brother.

"I own a small business in Pasadena." Maybe it was the beer that was causing me to tell him the truth, or maybe it was because he was as cute as a teddy bear. A handsome, green-eyed teddy bear with a strong jaw, and clean clothes.

I saw Chad making his way towards the bathroom. I excused myself and walked into the hallway thirty feet before Chad. I walked to the women's doorway and waited for him to come my way. The men's bathroom was one door down, he would have to pass me. When he turned the corner into the hallway, I started to stumble in his direction, feigning intoxication.

He weaved one way trying to avoid me, I went the same way giggling. In an attempt to be cute, I threw my arms around his neck and spun myself around like we were dancing.

"If you wanted to dance, handsome, you'd just have to ask." I threw in another giggle. He settled his hands around my lower back on the top of my butt.

"Damn girl, you're drunk. I was looking for you. Thanks for the drink, by the way." I giggled again, I ran my fingers through his hair and yanked a small clump out. "Ouch!"

"Oops, I'm sorry, my watch got you." I dropped my arms and looked at the watch like I was chastising it. On my other hand, I was tightly holding on to the hairs I had pulled. I started to turn and looked at him over my shoulder, "See you around, handsome." And I shimmied my hips like a supermodel down the hallway and back into the club.

Hank was looking towards the bathroom hall anxiously, his face lit up when he saw me.

"Sorry, there was a long wait." I grabbed a napkin and folded the hairs in it and stashed it in my clutch. Hank watched the motion with suspicion but said nothing.

"Do you want to find a quieter place to talk?" He spoke in my ear loudly, but he did not drape his arm over my shoulder. I gave him a suspicious look. A 'quieter place' normally meant someone's house. I didn't even know Hank's last name. It's bad form to go to a man's house if you do not know their last name. It's a weird rule, but I am still alive and kicking, so my rules work apparently.

"There is a Denny's near here. I'm starving." He said hopefully.

I gave a noncommittal shrug. To be honest, I was kind of hungry too, and Hank seemed normal and kind, and into me. What the hell, a late-night snack with a doctor seemed right up my alley.

"Okay, yeah, that sounds good." He grinned and helped me stand up. I looked around, Chad was back at the bar, looking around. I ducked my head, worrying he was looking for me. Hank leaned into me, "I need to close out my tab. Can you meet me outside?"

I nodded, "Oh! The bartender has my card, can you get it for me?"

He smiled even bigger, "What's your last name?" Well shit Caroline, if he is a stalker, you are just giving him all your details! "Henry."

He laughed, "You're kidding! That's my last name too!"

I watched Hank walk up to the bar. When the bartender looked over at me, I gave her the thumbs up, she nodded and passed my card to Hank. I kept my head down, as I walked to the exit of the club. The bouncers were still sitting on their perch, looking for trouble, and opened the door for me to leave.

The night had cooled down dramatically, the wind off the ocean was cold and strong. It made me shiver and I cursed myself for wearing a thimble as a skirt. Thankfully, Hank was fast to exit the club.

"Do you want me to walk you to your car?" He asked as he swiveled his head around. It was late, so there were only a few people milling around the club entrance smoking. Such a gentleman.

"I'm right over there, I'll be fine." He narrowed his eyes but did not follow me. He did not move either, he kept his eyes on me until I got into my car and he jogged over to his car in the opposite direction. I waited for him to pull his car out, and I followed him. As promised, Denny's was less than ten minutes away.

It was empty except for a few students drinking coffee with the tables covered in books. Hank frowned at them as we were ushered past them. "I don't envy them at all." He said as we slid into the booth.

The waitress was quick to take our orders.

"So, Hank, what was the occasion to take your brother out and then ditch him?" I was leaning on my elbows, with my hands under my chin. Lauren called it my cherub pose.

He laughed, "I didn't ditch him. One of my buddies is going to drop him off at my place when they are ready to go." He took a sip of water, "He is visiting me from out of town. Still lives near where we grew up. It's my first night out in weeks."

"Where did you grow up?"

He shifted in his seat. I realized my blouse was a little low cut and my arms were squeezing a good amount of cleavage. He was trying not to look. I eased myself back casually.

"Atlanta." He said with a grin. No wonder why he was such a gentleman. Southern boys have manners, no matter how far away they travel, those manners follow.

"You're kidding! I'm from the South, too. Charleston, born and bred." I smiled at him and took a sip of my own water. The food arrived. I picked up a slice of toast and started buttering it.

"I thought I heard a small accent coming from you! Hey, our last names are the same, I hope we aren't related or something. Since we both grew up in the same part of the world, you know, like third cousins." He cringed at the end of the statement. I grimaced.

"No, um..." I broke off a piece of crust "Henry is not my maiden name." I shoved the piece of crust in my mouth. I hated having awkward conversations and if there is one way to make it awkward, it's to make your date think you are married.

His eyes grew wide and his jaw dropped, "Wow! Okay, so. Okay." He started looking around. I reached out and grabbed his hand. "I'm not married, I'm a widow." He relaxed his position and his eyes narrowed into an uncomfortable squint.

"The point is, we," I pointed my finger between the both of us, "are not related." I tried to smile at him sweetly. He looked down at his food.

He broke the silence after a minute, "I'm sorry, that is awful, you're so young."

I smiled in response, "It's fine. He was a volunteer firefighter. He died in a forest fire a few years ago."

He nodded and looked awkwardly back at his food. I shoveled some eggs onto my fork.

"Topic change, so Hank, I assume your name is not Henry Henry, so what is your first name?"

His shoulders dropped in relief; the awkward moment was passing. "It's Graham."

I nodded as I swallowed another bite of eggs, "I like the name Graham. Why do you go by Hank?"

He lifted his shoulder, "I played a lot of baseball growing up, coaches called me by last name. It just morphed. Even now as a doctor, people call me Dr. Hank. Only my parents and brother call me Graham. It's funny how nicknames stick."

"Well, Graham, don't be offended when I call you by

your proper name. I like it better." I added with a sly grin.

We talked until late. The students all left one by one and soon it was just us left in the Denny's. He asked about my work. I asked about being a doctor. He was very pleasant company and a really nice guy.

"I have to ask you something awkward." Hank squinted his green eyes at me when he made the statement.

I tilted my head, I thought we were past awkward, "Shoot."

He took a deep breath through his nose and scrunched his face. "Why did you put a piece of hair in a napkin and put it in your purse?"

Shit. I wanted to laugh. Or run. Hell, run away laughing. I had to give him credit, it was an awkward thing for me to do without context and he took it in stride. I decided to give him as close to the truth as possible.

"A friend of mine was raped by a guy." He winced, I continued, "He won't submit his DNA, and no one can make him."

He sat straight up and pushed his plate away and took a long sip of water, "You were not there to meet a friend, were you?" He asked with a tilted head.

I shook my head. He chortled and sighed, "Well, if you ever need a DNA sample, just call me."

My eyes grew wide and I looked down awkwardly. He caught on to the double entendre and immediately blushed.

"That's not what I meant." He rubbed his face, it made his cheeks pinker, "Oh God, this is awkward. I meant, since I am a doctor, I have access to people and can assist you in procuring DNA samples in a way that would not put you in any danger. Not like, I would give you some of... mine." His voice trailed off at the end.

I laughed at his blushing, "Thank you, Graham, that is

very kind of you." And helpful. I looked at my watch, 2:00am.

"This has been great, but I need to go to bed." I yawned right on cue.

He walked me to my car, I did not object this time. He leaned over and kissed me. It was a nice kiss, not too firm or soft, just the right amount of pressure. He even cupped one cheek like they do in movies. He pulled away with a sigh. "Can I get your number at least?"

I smiled, "I think you know enough about me, that if you need to get in contact with me, you can."

He smiled and rolled his eyes, "What if you want to call me? I am a catch." I leaned forward to kiss his cheek. "I can find you online in five minutes."

He smiled and looked hopeful, "so are you going to call me?" He asked.

I shook my head, "Ball's in your court Graham. But it was a pleasure all the same."

I slid in my car and was home within thirty minutes, go figure, traffic was light after 2am.

I sent a quick email to Manny and Rani to cancel our Monday meeting, and went to bed.

Chapter 15

March 2

Funny thing is when you go to bed when you normally get up, your whole day goes helter-skelter.

I woke up to my doorbell ringing at 9am. I checked my security systems and moaned. It was Nathan.

I rolled out ofbed and opened the front door. He looked confused by my entire demeanor. At this point, any other day I had stretched, run, showered, and dressed. Today, I was still wearing a tank and boy shorts. My hair was in a messy bun, I had slippers on. I yawned and waved him in.

“I was going to go running with you this morning, but you did not run your normal route.” He handed me a hot tea from a local coffee shop. I took it eagerly. “Now, I see why.” He leaned forward and kissed my cheek. I could feel his stubble, and I immediately felt self-conscious. I hoped I didn’t smell like college nightlife and woodsy cologne.

“Late night?” He asked as I shuffled over to the kitchen counter, I turned around and nodded. Maybe I was being so laconic because I had morning breath, maybe I had nothing to say. Either way, I stayed silent, looking like a shell-shocked lost cat. I assume a shell-shocked lost cat looked wild and grumpy. Nathan took a seat at the counter and stared up at me. I squirmed.

“Did you have fun with Lauren?” I felt bad for him, conversing with me was like pulling teeth today. I looked at him confused. *Oh yeah,* I had margaritas with Lauren before going to Standing Room Only. It felt like that happened days ago, not relative hours ago. I recomposed my face. I nodded again.

“Is there a reason why you are not talking?” Nathan started to get annoyed. His eyes were narrowed on me and his jaw was flexing back and forth.

I shrugged and finished off the tea he brought. He heavily sighed. I held up one finger and left the kitchen. I went straight to my bathroom and brushed my teeth. Mascara had smudged down one eye. I washed my face thoroughly. I pulled on a sweatshirt and a pair of drawstring shorts and walked back into the kitchen where Nathan was waiting.

"You look better." He smiled. I scowled. He scowled back, "Are you going to say anything this morning?"

I threw my hands in the air, "It was a really late night. I went to bed after three. I am still trying to get my head wrapped around the time." I waved my hand towards the nearby clock. Nathan chuckled.

"Are you hungover?"

"No, Lauren just had a lot on her mind. She has a hard job; it takes its toll mentally."

Nathan nodded thoughtfully, "Listen, the reason why I wanted to see you this morning was because I was thinking about asking you out on a proper date."

I narrowed my eyes but said nothing. He continued, "I have taken you for granted and I want to change that. I want to take you to dinner. Get to know you. Let you get to know me."

"I don't know, Nathan." I began, but he interrupted.

"Don't answer right now, just think about it." He leaned forward and kissed my cheek and left.

I did not know what I wanted. I wasn't sure if jeopardizing my superb pool service and pretty equally superb sparring partner was worth a date. Okay, that was bitchy, but of all the time I knew him, he never made me want to want him. Or even want to get to know him past my cursory background check to make sure he did not harbor illegal intentions. Maybe he was right. I did not know him. Maybe if I got to know him better, my mind would change. I was skeptical. He had months to decide to do this. He was only reacting like a Cro-Magnon man protecting his prized kill because he felt threatened by another. Who would have thought moaning another guy's name during coitus would have that effect?

I rubbed my burning eyes and opted to go for a run to help clear my mind.

I was sluggish during the first few miles. I figured six hours of sleep over the course of 48-hours is bound to mess up running times. I pushed through the wall of exhaustion and loped into my driveway a little over an hour later. Sweating like a pig, and smelling like... well, a pig.

I was starving, I reflected on how grateful I was to eat eggs and toast at 2am. Then I realized, had I not, I probably would not be starving because my schedule would be normal. I would not have gone out, I would not have met Graham, and I would not have enjoyed the rarified air of a Denny's at 2am. It still smelled like bacon, go figure. I shrugged to myself, it was worth it. Graham was a nice guy and good company. And a pretty good kisser. My brain lagged behind trying to remember why I went to Standing Room Only. It seemed like a separate evening all together.

The thought hit me like a thunderclap. I scrambled around looking for my clutch. I found it wedged between my toilet and my vanity. I had my priorities straight when I got home, pee and brush my teeth, and crash. I carefully pulled out the wadded napkin and placed the hairs in a specimen bag.

I rushed to my computer and waited impatiently for it to boot up. Finally, after it updated its drivers... is there ever a convenient time for a computer to update? I typed furiously to my favorite DNA website. I filled out the online profile for Chad Westfield. By the time I was finished I had practically marked it with a big red X and told the police how to find the buried treasure.

I checked the movements of Scott Pickens, nothing new. My doubts were mounting that he was the culprit. I re-watched security footage looking for anything that stood out. I came up with nothing.

I decided to learn what I could about Graham Henry. I was right, within five minutes I had his cell and work phone written down. He had been honest about everything he told me.

He grew up in Atlanta. He played baseball for a big junior club, the type that recruits. They did not allow kids to walk on to the team, you had to try out. His team went to the junior world series and won. He had a younger brother. His parents were still happily married, living in Woodstock, Georgia.

He attended Emery for both his undergrad and doctorate. He moved to LA two years ago when he was assigned his residency. His last real relationship was three years ago to a girl who is now married with one on the way. Graham was a good guy. Ambitious, good looking, and kind. I mentally shook my head. My man-plate was already full. I decided to keep Graham in the friend zone until further notice. I still had Nathan and Beck things to work through.

A night at the club, followed by running six miles, made me smell like the monkey exhibit at the LA Zoo, so I opted for a shower. I almost felt like a new person when I got out. I was still exhausted beyond words, but at least I did not smell funky.

While I was combing my hair, I had a realization that Brian Lander's DNA profile should be completely loaded and ready. I logged into his account and read through it.

I slumped in my seat and let my head hit the counter. It was genetically impossible for him to be the father. Rebecca's blood type was O. The fetus's blood type was AB. Brian Lander's blood type was O.

I chastised myself for putting all my eggs in the Pickens/Landers basket. The only silver lining was that I did not make any hasty decisions and ruin these men's lives. I let my cheek rest on the cold granite, wallowing. I should give up, right?

Surely, my efforts and skills could be used for things more in my league. My league, which consisted of pulling a rich boy's hair and deciding a grieving man didn't kill his wife. I groaned. I am not a quitter, but it was tempting. Quitting meant I could... sleep. The thought comforted me; sleep sounded nice.

I woke up to an odd chirping noise next to my head. I felt disoriented and my face felt cold. I lifted my head to take stock of my surroundings. I had fallen asleep on the counter and woken up in a puddle of drool. I assume mine. My computer was issuing warning beeps of low battery. Or maybe my computer and I had bonded over years of pouring over it, and it was gently reminding me to wake up. It beeped again, an impatient little thing. I fumbled around to close it when I noticed the time.

I sat bolt upright. I slept all day. My cheek felt oddly numb and my neck was stiff. I had thirty minutes before I had to go to Nina Williams's office, and it was her only appointment time available this week as she would be on vacation during our normal scheduled time. My stomach growled to further enforce my need to get moving.

I shuffled to the fridge, all things required a lot of effort to make, I settled for an apple. I rubbed the sleep out of my eyes as I crunched into my apple and eyed my wardrobe. I was tempted to go looking like I had just rolled out of bed, or in my case, off the counter. I decided that Nina would have too many questions if I showed up looking like a poorly dressed prepubescent boy.

I pulled off my sweatshirt and tugged down my drawstring shorts. I settled for a calf-length pleated floral skirt and a plain cotton tank top and shuffled out the door.

Chapter 16

March 2-3

"Did you reach out to your mother or sisters as we discussed?"

I shook my head. I was feeling guilty, "Annie called, but I missed it." I had just remembered about my missed call.

"That seems promising. Did you call her back?" Nina was looking down at her notes, but she looked at me for her question.

"No, honestly I forgot she called until this moment."

Nina narrowed her eyes to me and took a breath through her nose, "Caroline, I am not sure if I can help you if you do not try to take my advice or at least follow through on promises you make me."

I did not remember making her any such promise. I remember it was raining during the last appointment. I remember talking about a homeless man, but I do not remember talking about promising to talk to my sisters or mom. While I was annoyed at the vague threat, I was also afraid of her follow-through.

"Nina, I have made progress. I have shared things with you that I thought I would never tell anyone." I was fiddling with the hem of my skirt, not looking up at her. I could still feel her eyes on me. I could see her twirling her readers in the air in front of me. "But you are asking me to put aside twenty years of anger and pain in a week. I have lived with the guilt that my relationship strain with Annie was my fault and my fault alone. I could have told her a long time ago, but I chose not to. Now that she knows I don't want to rush her." I squinted my eyes.

Nina took advantage of my pause, "Do you want to heal

your relationship with Annie?"

I thought about that, "Of course, I do. But it can't just be me fixing it. She has spent twenty years hating me. I want to give her time to sort things out for herself."

Nina interrupted, "But she called you."

I nodded. Nina continued, "Has she ever called you?" I shook my head. She set her glasses down and leaned forward, "Why do you think she called you?"

I shrugged and bit my lip, "Probably to confirm what Thomas told her. I just am not ready to talk about it with her. There is too much... too many walls that need to come down first."

Nina started to push on the subject, but I interrupted.

"Nina, with all due respect. I don't want to talk about Annie today. I don't want to talk about my family at all."

She nodded with a resigned sigh, "Okay, Caroline, what do you want to discuss today?"

"I want to talk about John."

I saw Nina slump slightly in her chair. We had discussed John for the first few months, every session was about the loss. Only recently had I dropped the bombshell of my youth. I am sure as a psychologist main goals go, problems that stemmed from childhood are like catnip.

"Are you feeling grief that is causing introspection?" She had picked up her glasses again and slid them on the tip of her nose. She was making notes in my file.

"Months before John died, he and I had a random hypothetical conversation about what life would be like for the other if one of us passed." I squinted to the memory.

"I had asked him if he would remarry. He joked and said he would not have time to remarry because he would be following close behind." I shook my head smiling, "His sense of humor was so dark. I pressed the subject and asked what he thought I should do if he went first. He laughed at me. He said that there was no way that he would die before me because I was so competitive that I would beat him in death too." I took a few breaths to calm myself. "I told him that if he remarried, I would haunt him and scare off his new wife, he laughed at me."

Nina was looking at me, giving me her full attention. I had never shared this memory before.

"I told him to be serious, and he told me that it was all a moot point because we were going to grow old together and die at the age of a hundred holding hands." I wiped a tear that was gathering in my eye.

"The thing is, he never told me what he wanted. I am a widow in my thirties, and I have no idea if he would be okay with me moving on." I wiped another tear.

"Do you want to move on?" Nina's tone was soft, not the usual ultra-professional emotionless prattle.

"I don't know. I have been numb to the idea of it. I have not even considered the idea of being serious with someone else."

"Do you have anyone in mind?"

"I don't know, maybe. I was perfectly content being alone, being a spinster. But recently, it feels like it may be a waste. Like, I thought my heart was in complete disrepair but maybe it's not. I have just been hiding it from the world, not letting anyone in."

She nodded; her hands were steepled together. She looked sincere, in the ultra-professional shrink way. "I think you should allow yourself to open up. Surely there are men in your life that have shown interest. Perhaps it is time to reconsider being numb around them and let them in. See what it feels like to want someone in your life again."

"There is a guy, he keeps asking me out." I was speaking

of Nathan. I was not ready to even discuss the complexities of my emotional climate when it came to Beck. And Graham and I had just met.

"That sounds positive. How do you know him?" Nina was smiling, she had leaned back in her chair.

"Actually, he is kind of like a zero-strings-attached sexual partner that I met a few months ago."

Apparently, that was not something Nina was expecting me to say because she dropped her jaw slightly and tried to recover by rubbing her chin. I decided to clarify.

"I do not feel anything for him. For me, it is just a pressure release. Recently he has made mention that he would like to get to know me better. I just don't know what to do."

She nodded, "You do not feel as if your sexual congress would upset John beyond the grave?"

I shook my head, "No, it's just sex. You and I both know an emotional affair is far more damaging."

She smiled, but her eyes were tight, she narrowed them, "But you cannot have an affair if someone has passed away. Even marriage vows include, 'til death do us part' so the mere fact that you have been purposely holding this man at an arm's length is based on faulty logic."

"You think I should date him?" I was confused, probably because it felt weird and wrong to date Nathan. Maybe had I not met Beck, but since I had...

"I think you should allow this guy to show you who he is and decide if that is someone you want to let into your life."

I left her office feeling slightly better, slightly confused. If I started dating Nathan, what do I do with my Beck feelings? Or would the mere fact that I even have "Beck feelings" negated me from even dating Nathan? Then again, Nathan had shown me verifiable interest, asked me out even. Beck on the other hand... maybe all the Beck emotions were one-sided. I could not remember a single instance where he was interested in me more than my hobbies.

I checked the time. If I hurried, I would be able to get to the Krav Maga studio before Nathan left. I made my way up and parked with five minutes to spare before his juniors' class would let out. I fiddled with my radio looking for something to listen to, but I got restless and turned it off. Maybe I was nervous. Why would I be nervous? I was simply answering his question on if I would consider going to dinner with him. I saw the studio doors open and children accompanied by their parents ushering them to their individual cars. I opened the door to the Prius and walked to my trunk, leaning on it casually.

Nathan appeared a few minutes later. He was talking to a father holding a young girl's hand. Nathan did a double take when he saw me and smiled. I could tell he was making a polite excuse to leave the conversation and he made his way over to me. The father looked annoyed by his abrupt dismissal and stared after Nathan for a second then gathered his daughter's hand in a huff.

Nathan was sweaty at the brow, but his shirt looked clean and dry. I could still see the fold lines cutting across his abdomen. "Hey, pretty lady." He came in and kissed my cheek but backed away. I was right about the fresh shirt; I could smell laundry detergent. "Have you reconsidered my offer for dinner?" He smiled and looked hopeful. Hmmm, perhaps he did like me more than I was giving him credit for.

"Actually, yes, I have reconsidered it. I decided it couldn't hurt to get to know you better... as a friend." I was trying my diplomatic tone, but by the end, it sounded like I was scolding Lennon for taking his brother's toy.

Nathan ignored my tonal change and smiled back, "Great! Because once you get to know me, maybe you will like me as a friend." His smile widened, "or maybe more."

I doubted it, but I was going to get to know him. At least so I would not have to lie to Nina at my next appointment. Lying to your therapist is completely pointless.

"Are you free tomorrow night at 7:30? There is a great little place in San Dimas, outdoor dining, good food. I think you would like it." He looked hopeful. I considered it.

"Sounds good, but I will meet you there. I don't want you to get the wrong impression."

He chortled, "Caroline, we have been banging for months, I don't know what impression I could possibly have." Ugh, I hated that term, his impish grin made me want to reconsider. I settled for a haughty sigh and I left.

I got home and checked for progress on any of the cases I was working on, nothing was new, nothing had changed. No one had heard a word from Lisa Henderson. I checked the date. We only had a few more days before I was sure her body would show up. I groaned in my failure, but I was at a loss. No new evidence, no new leads. It was frustrating to deal with. I could only imagine the mounting pressure if I were working for any law enforcement agency working the case. I flipped on the news.

> "The family of Lisa Henderson is pleading with the public for their assistance. They are offering a $10,000 reward for anything that would lead to the identity of her abductor. The following was pre-recorded earlier today."

It was a video of the Henderson family offering the $10,000 and the caveats to earn such a sum. The family was lined up. Their faces were ranging from sullen to outright crying. I winced at their pain, but I cursed the reward. Did they not realize a bounty that size would bring out the crazies? The tip line would be inundated with false promises. Even if there was a real tip in there it would take weeks to weed through all the bullshit to find it. Shit. The police must be desperate to find anything. I had been keeping tabs on their investigation closely. I knew they had nothing, but I was hopeful that they had a rogue agent that was able to work some magic that was not recorded in the official computer files.

I felt like beating my head into a wall, or against the counter again. I decided concussing myself was a bad decision and opted for a swim. Steam was rising off the water, it looked inviting.

The water was as warm as it looked. Instead of a full-bore training session I grabbed my kickboard to move across the pool in silence. It was amazing what I was normally able to pontificate while listening to the silent evening. A dog barking a few streets away, rustling of leaves, the occasional dropping of fruit to the earth, the water lapping the sides of the pool walls.

All the noises were soothing, but no new thoughts came to me. I was completely stuck in both cases. I felt guilty for not putting more effort into Rebecca Hamilton's case, but as the days got closer to the end of Lisa Henderson's life, it was harder for me to concentrate on a healthy, non-abducted teen, who I presumed was safe in her bed. She had been brutalized, but she did not have a ticking time bomb over her head like Henderson. I dried off roughly and went to bed mad at myself for not procuring an epiphany to save the day.

I woke up early, stretched, ran, and headed to work. It felt awkward only helping customers while my brain was fully playing out who had Lisa Henderson. I was only half cognizant of my surroundings for a good portion of my shift. I was working with Jessica.

"It was fun the other night!" She was smiling at me from the cosmetics table.

I was confused, she could be talking about her birthday or she could be talking about the other night when I ran into her at a bar that was way too young for me to frequent.

She laughed, "Not my birthday, at Standing Room Only. I really don't remember my birthday." She ended with a blush across her cheeks and a pout. "I think I threw up in Manny's car."

I laughed, "No, he opened the door right before you did. I think you may have gotten his shoes though."

She cringed her face, her blush deepening, "I am so sorry if I seemed unprofessional." I waved my hand and shook my head, "It was your birthday, your twenty-first birthday, there is no need to feel the tiniest bit ashamed for letting loose on such an occasion."

She smiled looking relieved and continued, "I was surprised to see you at SRO. It's mostly drunk college kids." I couldn't agree more. I felt like a grandma trying to be hip with the youths the moment I walked in. "You're right, it is not really my scene."

"If you don't mind me asking, why were you there?"

To stalk a rich-boy rapist to get his DNA that a series of judges refused to distribute a subpoena for.

"I was meeting a friend there."

Her eyes grew wide, "Not Chad Westfield I hope!" God, everyone knew this jackass.

"You know Chad?" I said the words before I could deny I knew who she was talking about. I was starting to get anxious that Chad had treated Jessica with the same treatment as poor Morgan Butler.

She shook her head, "Only by reputation. He went to a competing high school. His parents are rich. He is a grade-A asshole." She dropped her face, "Pardon my French." I laughed, I did not know *asshole* was French, hmmm.

"No, I was not there to meet Chad, but he introduced himself to me." Not really, I was hitting on him, in the flirtatious way. I wanted to be hitting him with my car. I shivered to play up my dislike in front of Jessica, "He did seem like a jerk though."

Jessica's face looked relieved and I was relieved that she knew to stay away from punks such as Chad Westfield.

We continued the rest of our respective shifts chatting occasionally about guys and customers. She had a propensity to date guys that shared DNA with cannibalistic gorillas or dumb meatheads that would cheat on her. I wanted to bring her under my wing like mother hen and protect her from her terrible taste in men. Alas, it was not my place. All I could offer was a safe space to vent her relationship woes and be prepared to take out the first dick that hurt her physically in any way. *Call me sentimental.*

I got home and realized I had about an hour to get ready for my pending date with Nathan.

I checked for directions to the restaurant. It was twenty minutes away, and not in San Dimas, but in La Verne. Shit, now I have only forty minutes. I decided that I should not rush, and it would be okay if I strolled in ten minutes late. He had told me the wrong city after all.

I took a shower and pondered what I should wear.

Chapter 17

March 3

I decided on a long cotton dress that hugged my curves without being constricting. I paired it with flat leather sandals with braided straps. I looked casual but put together. I decided to wear my hair down in red waves. I hated putting on a full face of makeup just for an evening out, so I put on a few coats of mascara and lined my lips with a tinted balm that made them look pouty and cute. It was an understated look between cute and sexy, my sweet spot.

I was heading towards my garage when the front doorbell rang. I was not expecting company, I assumed it was a Jehovah's Witness, no one but the witnesses rang my doorbell after 4pm. I was tempted to ignore it, but I figured if I were a little late, it would be no big deal. I opened the door to see Nathan standing on the front stoop. I stepped back surprised. He smiled his beautiful smile. He looked good.

His brown hair was combed instead of its normal unkempt mess of curls. He was wearing khaki shorts and a long-sleeve button-up shirt with the sleeves rolled up. He was wearing nice casual loafers that set the tone of his outfit to a casual beach dinner vibe. It was jarring seeing him in shorts that had more than just an elastic band. I was more taken aback to see actual shoes on his feet, he normally wore sandals or was barefoot.

"I thought I was meeting you there." My tone sounded skeptical, I tried to keep the accusation from my face. He leaned over and kissed my cheek.

"I decided that this was a proper date, which meant I was going to pick you up."

And drop me off and hope for a happy ending. "Nathan,

I don't want you to get the wrong impression."

He cut me off. "I am hedging my bets that you will like me as a friend so much that things may progress." He wagged his eyebrows at me.

I shook my head and pushed him. "Give me a minute." I shut the door in his face and walked into my kitchen.

He was optimistic and pushy, but he had a sense of humor and he did look good. What if the evening progressed as he hoped? I was not getting any other offers and it had been weeks since the last bit of action. I grabbed my purse and checked to see if my taser was in it. I smiled to myself. I did not want to tase him, but it would be pretty funny if he did try something and I whipped it out. I gave myself one more look in the mirror, satisfied that it was as good as it was going to get. I opened the door and locked it behind me. Nathan was still on the stoop waiting patiently.

"After you." He waved behind him towards his SUV. He high stepped it in front of me to grab my door and hold it open, "It's a date, remember?" He winked at the end.

I had to admit he was being a bit charming. Far better than the bang and bolt that I was accustomed to. Although, I had trained him to leave as soon as I was finished with him. I wonder if he is actually someone that likes to cuddle after. I had never given him the option. Truth be told, I always enjoyed being held by John. But that kind of cuddle always seemed more intimate than the actual act of fornication.

The drive was a fast twenty minutes through neighborhoods and historic streets. The establishment only had street parking, but it was small and quaint. The majority of the restaurant was a bar with a large patio. We were brought to our table near the outdoor fireplace. It was merrily crackling. I sat facing it, allowing it to warm my cheeks and bare shoulders. California may have perfect weather nine months of the year, but in the evening in early spring, it gets chilly.

I ordered the duck burger with parsnip fries; Nathan ordered the steak. We shared the hummus.

"What do you think of this place?" Nathan sipped on his gin and tonic. I had opted for a beer, more calories, but the hangover was more manageable.

I looked around, "It's nice. The atmosphere is... pleasant." He smiled and nodded. The twinkling lights glimmered with the overhead night sky. We sat in silence. I was enjoying the warm fire on my face.

"Aren't you supposed to be trying to get to know me?" Nathan asked. I guess it was not public knowledge that I frequently did thorough research into people before I engage in any type of relationship, friend, lover, or professional.

"Okay," I was thumbing the lip of my bottle, "Tell me about your childhood."

He squinted his eyes at the basic question, shrugged, and delved in, "I was born and raised in Corona. I am the oldest of three. I have two sisters, one has kids, one is 'never getting married'. My parents are still married, still live in Corona." I already knew all of that. I knew his shoe size and what kind of porn he surfed, I let him continue.

"My first and only real job was working for my dad's pool company. When business started picking up West, dad and I decided to open a second location where I was in charge of the western part of the IE."

When I first moved to California, everyone talked about the IE. It took me a few months to build the courage to ask what the heck people were talking about. Inland Empire, fancy name that basically says, not the coast of California, not the deserts of Palm Springs.

I sipped my beer, ate a carrot, and nodded for him to go on. "I started taking Krav Maga in elementary school after some bully stole my backpack. I have been taking it ever since.

I started teaching it part-time about a year ago. I love it. I thought about a career change, but my dad got sick. Now I am in charge of the entire IE. My younger sister manages the eastern part, but I am in charge of the big picture business decisions."

I looked around while taking in what he was saying. It was lovely out. The sky was lilac changing to deep purple with a full moon. Stars were just starting to shimmer when our entrees arrived. My parsnips were cut in ribbons and the dipping sauce was tangy but sweet. I crunched quietly to myself as he dug into his steak, "What about you?" He asked thickly between bites.

I had just taken a bite of my burger. It was a bit messy, juice and sauce dripped down my palm. I had to remember to keep my eyes from rolling into my head from the first bite. It was salty and tender with a hint of spice. The cabbage on top crunched, the bread was slightly toasted and chewy. I swallowed, "What about me?"

He snagged one of my parsnips and popped it in his mouth, "What about your childhood?" Crap. I should have guessed he would want to know. There are few modifications that don't sound tragic and sad. I took another orgasmic bite to stall. The waitress appeared to refresh our drinks, I opted for one more, I was not driving after all. Nathan switched to water.

I shrugged acting nonchalant, "I grew up in Charleston, moved out here with my husband, John. He died in the Bayside fire a few years ago." It was as vague as I could get, and even that was sad and tragic. A widow at thirty was never something anyone liked to talk about. Lots of pity, followed by awkward silences.

Nathan's face looked tense, but his eyes looked tender. It must be hard to navigate this conversation for all parties involved. "Sorry about that. I heard about it, but I am sorry all the same."

I took another bite, although my appetite was waning from the awkward conversation. It was too good to waste.

"What about your childhood? I know your sister lives here and I met Thomas a few weeks ago. Is it just you three?" He dug back into his own steak. Fresh beer and water hit the table. We bid our thanks and I continued, "No, I am the middle of 6, but my oldest brother died when I was fourteen."

"Damn, that sucks." His face looked pained like he was sorry he asked. Here comes the pity that I always got at this point in the questionnaire.

I tried to be dismissive to make him feel better, "It was a long time ago. I am over it." He nodded gratefully.

"What about your parents, what do they do?" *Well, this is just going to be an awkward evening, isn't it?*

"My mom basically was a homemaker, she got a job working at a bank when we were older, but she is retired now." I was crossing my fingers that my omittance on my father would be a clue to drop it. It was a tactic that normally worked with women from work that wanted to get to know me or make small talk.

"What about your dad?" Shit. Well, I never thought it was a fool-proof tactic anyway.

"Uh. He actually died in the same car accident that my brother died in." I winced at his reaction. It was that awkward mix of pity and why-can't-I-shut-up.

"Shit. I'm sorry."

Another dismissive hand, "It was a long time ago."

He looked awkward, "Do you want to keep talking about your family?" Now he asks.

I squinted one eye and shook my head. "No, I don't, but you can tell me about your sisters."

He looked grateful for the subject change and regaled me with stories of his youth. Turns out, his sisters were hilarious. We spent the rest of the evening laughing at the different pranks and bets he lost and their ramifications. The waitress had cleared away our plates. Nathan was chewing his ice and I had just finished my fourth beer. To say I was a cheap drunk is an understatement. By two I am buzzed, by three I am drunk, by four I am looking around for the nearest secluded spot to hump whoever crossed my path. The waitress dropped the check.

"You lost the bet and your sister dressed you up as a girl?"

He nodded and chuckled, "The straightened my hair to make it longer. It looked like a bowl cut from the eighties. They found a blue sailor dress. I had to endure an hour of them laughing while they applied my makeup. They even used that thing on your eyelashes to make them curl."

I wiped a tear away. I was laughing hard enough to emit tears, "An eyelash curler." I supplied.

"Yeah, that thing. I thought they were going to rip out all my lashes, they were laughing so hard." He chuckled a few times, I wiped away another tear. "I had to parade around the house singing 'I'm a Little Teapot'. My mom almost had a heart attack, my dad said I was the ugliest girl he had ever seen."

He passed his card to the waitress. She was quick to return it. I looked around. The restaurant was almost empty; only two other people were sitting at the bar inside.

"What do you want to do, Caroline?" Nathan smiled at me. I don't know why I ever thought of him as a brute, he was funny and handsome. I knew I was not into him in a romantic way. I knew that my true feelings were lying closer to the mysterious Beck. The Beck who I had not seen in days.

My drunk horny persona answered, "I think you should take me home." I added a wink at the end.

The ride back was interesting. At one point he leaned across to kiss me. I almost attacked him; I was letting my sex-deprived part of my brain take the lead. We stopped groping each other when someone honked their horns at us, the light was green. He pulled away chuckling and drove to my street.

He leaned over and kissed me again, "I think you should invite me in." Ugh, my slutty hormones started to nod, but I caught movement at my front door. Nathan followed my confused gaze. I opened the car door and launched myself towards the moving figure. Beck was standing on my stoop. I thought his face looked disappointed, but by the time I reached him, he looked bored and impassive.

"You look well, Caroline." He leaned forward to kiss my cheek. Even the heavy make-out session in the car with Nathan did not compare to the spontaneous combustion that occurred in my stomach when his lips touched my cheek. I heard a car door shut but was too involved in calming my erratic nerves.

"What are you doing here, Beck?" My voice sounded far away, warbled. Or maybe I was slurring my words. I guess it will remain a mystery.

"I wanted to discuss some things with you." He jerked his attention behind me. I realized the closing car door was Nathan and he was right behind me. I watched Beck's eyes narrow and nostrils flare for the briefest of moments.

"You must be the famous Beck." Nathan reached out his hand. Beck looked at me amused by the moniker that I had nothing to do with. Mysterious, sexy, ninja, assassin, yes. Famous, no. I watched the handshake in slow motion. Their tendons were a little bit more corded than necessary; the shake lasted a little longer than normal. It was a pissing contest in palm strength.

"I am sorry, I do not believe Caroline has ever mentioned *you.*" He emphasized the last word to imply that Nathan was not worth mentioning. It was not lost by Nathan. I wanted to roll my eyes. I knew that I had mentioned Nathan. Hell, Beck had asked about him.

Nathan released Beck's hand and wrapped his free arm around my waist, "Is there something we can help you with this evening?" Nathan was looking expectantly at Beck. Beck was only looking at me. I shook free from Nathan's grasp.

"I need to speak with Beck." I looked meaningfully at Nathan, "thank you for dinner."

Nathan smoothed his face from the disappointment that flickered across it but turned on his heel and walked to his SUV without more than a nod at me.

I turned to Beck. He still looked amused, "famous?"

I pushed past him and unlocked the door. The key missed once, but I was determined to get it open without assistance. I marched into the kitchen to deposit my purse, my taser spilled out. Beck picked it up laughing, "If you needed protection, you could have just asked me to escort you."

I grabbed it from him and shoved it back in my purse. I tried to act pissy, I put one hand on my hip and tried to stare him down. Funny thing about being drunk in a staring contest, it makes you lose balance pretty easily. Even standing still I swayed slightly, Beck was quick to grab at me before I hit the floor.

"How much did you drink?" He sounded annoyed with a hint of amusement.

"Enough to know what I want." Even to my drunk ears, it sounded slurred. He was still holding on to me, his hips were pressed into my butt. I slid my body around; his hips were against my stomach. My butt was against the counter. I reached back to lift myself up. He looked confused but helped me with my assent. I started pulling the long skirt of my dress up, I shimmied it to my knees. Beck was watching me, but he did not appear to be breathing. When my dress made it to mid-thigh, he looked up at me. His silver eyes flashed something I had never fully seen before. I took the opportunity of our faces being inches apart.

I thrust my arms around his neck and pulled him in to kiss him. My lips crushed against his. I forced his lips open and tasted him. He tasted sweet. I wrapped my newly freed legs around his waist. He tried to pull away, I pulled closer. I lifted myself up with my legs wrapped firmly around him. He was finally kissing me back. He was leaning forward to deposit me back on the counter. I was hoping for more, so I let him dip me back. His palms felt hot against my face. I moved my arms, trying to redirect his hands to other parts of my body. He took his opportunity and gently pushed my face away. I was gasping and squeezing him between my thighs. I did not want to let him get any more space between us.

"Caroline." His voice was quiet but commanding.

"You are drunk, you do not know what you are doing. I do not want to hurt you." His hands were reaching back at my calves, he was gently prying them away from his back.

The weight of his rejection hit me in the chest and my legs dropped in response. I pushed myself away scooting to the other side of the counter. I spun around and dropped to the floor. I could not turn around to face him. My chest was heaving in drunken disappointment and rejection.

"I did not come here to ruin your evening, but I do want to discuss some things with you."

I still could not turn around, I just nodded in understanding, "I will give you some time to collect yourself." He walked past me and through the back door. He did not look at me as he slid the door shut. I watched him sit down in front of the pool, cross-legged and calm.

I whimpered and wiped a tear away. It was difficult to decide whether the pain of rejection was worth the time to be with him. Unrequited love is a bitch, but then I remembered that I don't love him. I don't know him enough to love him. Was this unrequited lust? An unrequited crush? It seemed more of an appropriate verb versus a noun because I was definitely crushed. I went to the bathroom to check myself in the mirror. A small smudge of mascara had escaped my lashes, I rubbed it away. I fluffed my hair and pushed my boobs up. If I was going to talk to him, I was going to look damn sexy while doing it. I hiccupped in the mirror.

I walked outside as silently as possible. It is amazing how much embarrassment and supreme rejection can sober one up. I sat across the pool from him. His eyes were closed. I hiked my dress up to my thighs and placed my legs in the water. He opened his eyes at the light lapping noises the water made as it hit the wall.

"I apologize for before. I should not have..."

I interrupted, "I don't want to talk about it."

He nodded and stared at the water. My leg's movements were forming endless ripples.

"The reward for Lisa Henderson is making things difficult." He started.

"Yeah, I figured it would. They must be desperate to allow the riffraff to come out of the woodwork."

He narrowed his eyes to me, "We do not have much time if you want to save her."

"I know, one day." I watched a bee struggle to get out of the pool. I scooped my hand in to save it.

"I thought I had a suspect, but nothing adds up. I have checked everything. His home, his work, his mom's house. I have checked any real estate that they may hold. Nothing. He follows his schedule and has not gone anywhere that could house the victims." I threw my hands in the air, sprinkling my face with water droplets. "She is probably dead at this point. I'm basically waiting for Henderson's body to appear to confirm it is not him." I shook my head in frustration. "I have nothing on it."

He nodded, "What about Rebecca Hamilton?"

"I'm stuck there too." I chuckled, "Maybe it *is* an immaculate conception."

Beck did not find my joke nearly as funny as I did. "I checked into her dad's friends. They are not involved. One has an affinity for women's lingerie, but not drugging young girls." He arched his brow at me.

"Have you been investigating on your own?" I asked Beck hopefully.

"I have been busy with work. The restaurant is growing in popularity." He was watching me kick my legs in circles in the water.

"Why did you come tonight?" It was the question I wanted to ask since the second he rejected me. Before that moment I was convinced he came because he wanted to see me.

He stopped watching my legs move and looked me in the eye. I was glad there were fifteen feet separating us otherwise I would have forced myself on him again.

"Why do you think I came by?" He asked, the seriousness was out of place for such a mundane question. To ruin a perfectly good date? To chastise me for having fun?

I threw my head back and snorted, "Well, clearly, it was not because you missed me, or wanted to see me. You have made that clear. It's a mystery to me why you keep coming back here." Drunken anger was thinly controlled as I spit out the words.

He rose fluidly, "Do not make such assumptions about my intentions." My brain was scrambling to understand what he was saying. I rose to follow him, tracking slippery water through my kitchen. I caught his hand before he opened the front door. He turned around slowly, looking at his grasped hand first and following the path up my arm to finally make it to my face. "Why did you come by tonight?" My voice was barely above a whisper.

He shook his hand free of mine, "I was worried you had given up on the women you are trying to help." His jaw was tense, and his eyes were narrow focused on mine. I was holding my breath. Was he psychic too?

"Then you don't know me at all. I can't give up." His jaw loosened but his eyes were still narrow with anger. I took a deep breath, "Are you sure you did not come for any other reason?" Stupid optimistic heart. I wanted to hear something that made me feel like our friendship was not one-sided. I wanted him to kiss me like he did in the woods, but this time without the motivation to distract me.

He leaned forward very slowly. I closed my eyes in anticipation. A very soft kiss landed on my cheek. I opened my eyes disappointed, his eyes were burning with an unknown emotion, "You are drunk, Caroline, nothing I say or do tonight would be right." He turned and left, leaving me confused and frustrated, and *frustrated.*

Chapter 18

March 4-5

I was restless most of the night. Once again, Beck had confounded my emotions into a snarl. Nathan caught up with me halfway through my morning run.

"Is this why you are in such good shape?" He huffed at me while walking up to my driveway. I wiped the sweat from my brow and shrugged, "You're in good shape, you know what it takes to stay fit." He chuckled and flung his head back and forth showering the ground with sweat. Droplets hit the concrete and my thigh. *Gross.*

"You look tired." He said as he slicked his tendrils back. "Late night?"

I laughed at his thinly veiled attempt at seeing if Beck stayed, "feeling jealous?"

He leaned against the wall of the house, "No, I told you, we were not exclusive. I was just amped up last night. Thought we had fun." He was trying to look casual, but his eyes were sad puppy eyes.

"It was not a late-night last night, I just did not sleep well. And I *did* have fun last night."

He grinned, "Up all-night thinking of me?" I rolled my eyes at him and pushed my key in the door.

"Goodbye Nathan." He stopped the door as I was closing it. He leaned forward and kissed my lips quickly.

"Call me if you want *anything*." He let go of the door and walked away.

In my sober-slightly-hungover state, the kiss felt a little lackluster. It was nothing compared to the kiss from Beck last night. But I was drunk last night, so I could not really hold anything too true to heart.

I hurried to get ready for work. I placed my hair in a high bun. I dressed in a navy pencil skirt with a white button-up. With crimson lips and black lashes, I dashed out the door to attend my manager meeting.

Manny and Rani were waiting for me as I tottered in holding donuts and coffee. They forgave me for being a few minutes late for our rescheduled meeting and accepted their sustenance. Business was doing well. The newest cosmetic line, we signed an exclusivity contract for distribution, was doing great. Our cosmetic sales were up 75% compared to the previous year. Manny and Rani discussed possibly hiring someone specifically for cosmetics. Manny was looking into a new company that has a great online following. It was cruelty-free, vegan, non-comedogenic, and paraben-free. It was perfect for our clientele and with an additional line, it would bring us to carrying five lines. We all agreed, if we were able to sign the new company on, we would have to hire a new person.

Manny decided to start scouting make-up online influencers to see if we could work out a deal to have them work for us as our make-up consultant. He was practically bouncing out of his seat when Rani mentioned the new hire handle our online presence on social media. I agreed on all fronts.

The rest of the day Manny was practically giddy with showing me influencer's profiles. I too was excited at the prospect of building our business and growing our online presence. Rani kept coming up and asking about building an online store for when we hired the influencer. It was a lot to plan, but computer-wise, I knew I would be able to build the website. Logistically speaking, I had full confidence in Rani's ability to keep up with online fulfillment.

We both agreed to leave the hiring to Manny with a second interview with Rani and myself. I did have to be the buzz kill and remind them that the contract for the newest cosmetic company could take weeks. The website would be a minimum of a month before it was functional. And hiring always takes closer to a month before we find the right fit.

As I was gathering my belongings, Manny popped his head in my office. "Caroline, there is a tall and handsome guy here, asking to see you." My brows dropped in confusion. "Did he say what he needed?"

Manny laughed, "Not with words, girl, but it looked like he needed a little time with a beautiful red-head." He smiled and wagged his eyebrows at me. I grabbed my purse and followed him with caution onto the sales floor.

Graham Henry was standing awkwardly next to the face creams. His face lit up when he saw me. He started to blush; his ears glowed against the backlit sunshine.

"It was not as easy to find you, as you promised." He said as he leaned in to kiss my cheek. I heard Manny chuckle and walk away. I looked over as he winked at me and tended to another customer.

I adjusted my purse on my shoulder, "I was just leaving for the day. You can walk me to my car."

I led the way out, he chuckled, "Let me get this straight. At 5:30 on a Wednesday evening, on a busy street, in a good neighborhood, I can walk you to your car. But in a seedy part of town in the early hours of the day outside of a nightclub, you insist on going at it alone." I could see the irony, I shrugged.

"I was not sure if you were a psychopath the other night. I decided that you are not. And walking me to my car seemed like a good segue way to leave work."

I heard him chuckle behind me, "Can I get you a coffee?" I stopped and stared at him. I was trying to decide if he was desperate or just nice. Nice made me feel better. I nodded once. He led the way to a coffee shop that was a few storefronts away.

I ordered a tea and sat down at an available table outside. The business on the street was starting to pick up from evening commuters. Graham sat across from me, holding his own coffee, taking a sip.

"You found me, bought me a tea. What can I do for you, Graham?" I leaned forward and tucked my crossed ankles under my seat.

He looked sheepishly at me, "You challenged me to find you. Do I get anything for being the victor?"

I wouldn't say I challenged him, and I was not sure what victory he had in mind. I tilted my face and narrowed my eyes at him, giving him my best, I-don't-know-what-you're-talking-about face. He nervously laughed, "Okay, that was lame. I just wanted to see if you gave me the real information on you or if you made it up."

That was an honest answer. I smiled back at him, "Well, what do I get for being honest?" I asked.

"Dinner?" He asked hopefully. I made another face, "Tea?" I smiled.

He continued, "My number?"

I laughed. "I told you I could get your number within five minutes."

It was his turn to look confused, "I don't think you found it. You would have called." He was confident in his resolve. I chuckled, "I told you I wouldn't call." I reached into my bag and pulled out the scrap of paper I had jotted his information on, his phone number, not the personal history. I passed it to him.

I watched his eyes grow wide and blush. "Can I take you to dinner sometime?" His green eyes looked hopeful. I felt bad. I did not want to lead him on.

"Graham, at this point in my life, I am only looking for a friend. If you think you can have dinner with a friend without pushing for anything, then yes I will go to dinner with you sometime."

He looked disappointed, but covered it with a shrug, "You're right, a friend could be good. At this point in my residency, I would be crazy to pursue anything serious. I actually have to get back to the hospital soon." He looked down at his watch. I smiled back and nodded, wondering if he really needed to get back to work or if he was trying to end our awkward encounter gracefully.

He walked me to my car and kissed my cheek. "Always a pleasure Graham." He nodded. "If I start feeling peck-ish I will give you a call." I tried to smile sweetly back to him as I passed off my brush-off line. "Thanks for the tea."

I got home and felt happy but tired. I convinced myself it was the right thing to do to let Graham down gently. He was handsome, smart, and kind. Ugh, what was I thinking? Oh yeah, I was thinking I am involved in two dead-end cases, waiting for a body to show up. My work life just got hectic with the mounting pressure to sign the new cosmetic company, build and relaunch our website. My love life, if I could even call what I was feeling as love, was a weird love trio with Nathan liking me more than him, and me liking Beck more than he liked me. I shook my head. It didn't help clear the thoughts away.

I changed my clothes and headed to a boxing club. After Beck and Nathan's comments about my attack being weak, I decided it was a good idea to work on my form and strength behind throwing punches. I wondered which of the two would be unsuspecting guinea pigs when they challenged me again. I smiled at the thought of punching either.

I was not a beginner at boxing, but it was my weakest self-defense. I had started seeing a new coach. He reminded me that I projected too early making my punches easy to block. He reminded me that my size and strength worked against me and all I could do to make a difference was work on less projection and faster jabs in more sensitive areas. My back and arms felt like lead weights when I pulled into my home.

I made dinner in silence, longing to hear Beck's soft footfalls in my hall. I felt restless, I checked the date. I swallowed my defeat. Lisa Henderson was surely already dead as I sat there eating my chicken stir fry. When did she give up hope? Was there any hope for Kelly Parker? I swallowed the lump in my throat.

Scott Pickens was parked in his driveway at home, some maniac was parked somewhere else, violating Henderson's body. I shuttered. My failure felt like a solid mass in my stomach. I checked my calendar again. Kelly Parker had four days before I failed her too. The Triple S Killer (Steal, Stash, Slash as dubbed by the media) had not abducted anyone since Parker. It seemed suspicious. Maybe he got scared, maybe he died in a car accident. I cringed; it happens all the time. It would seal Parker's fate, but no one else would go missing.

I did not want to be alone. I was tempted to call Nathan or even Graham. Surely either of them would be happy to spend the night, distracting me. But if I were honest with myself, I only wanted one person to distract me or at the very least, spend the night, and he had walked out of my life.

I slunk into my bed when I imagined the disappointed look on Beck's face when he realized I gave up. I could not help the Triple S victims. But maybe, just maybe, I could redouble my efforts and get justice for Rebecca Hamilton.

The news the next morning was as grim as I worried it would be. They had found Lisa Henderson's body a mile from her home around dinner time. She was lying in a garden of roses at a flower nursery. Her hands were folded across her belly, her hair was neatly splayed out behind her head. Her body looked gaunt and frail. I crossed Scott Pickens off the list.

The nursery's security footage gave no further clues. Only one small clip of a white Prius on a nearby street gave anything. The license plate was obscured again. I followed the progress of the white car through several traffic cameras, but eventually lost him after he went into a neighborhood. I called the tip line and shared the neighborhood. I only hoped that someone would take my tip seriously. I pulled up the 400-page list of registered white Prius owners in Southern California. I narrowed the search to the zip code; it was still 25 pages long. I narrowed to the neighborhood and nothing came back. I scowled. I checked the maps. That particular neighborhood was used as a cut through. It was a labyrinth of turns; it was easy to lose a tail.

I felt worn and restless. There was still no obvious link between the victims. I shoved the Triple S notes aside and picked up my notes on Rebecca Hamilton. I reread each line with scrutiny. I had a thought, it was on the tip of my tongue, but I could not formulate the words.

Whoever was responsible knew her. Knew of her condition. I felt like I was close to a break when my phone rang. I was pissed that my brain had almost made the connection I had been begging it to make for weeks. It was Jennifer. Guilt swarmed me. I told Lauren and mom that I would call Jennifer. I never did.

Chapter 19

March 5

"Hey, Jennifer. I am sorry I have not called you. I have been very busy." I started with my excuses.

"It's not Jennifer."

I almost dropped the phone. I had not heard Annie's voice in almost twelve years, since my wedding. It's a strange thing to think you had forgotten something completely, but as soon as I heard her voice, I knew it was her. The recesses of my brain knew her tone, inflection, and cadence without second-guessing.

"Annie?"

"Well, I guess I know you were screening your calls now." Her tone was angry and hurt, but when she was talking to me it was always angry. Hurt, on the other hand, was a new aspect of her tenor. My brain clipped into gear.

"I was not screening your calls. I was at my therapist's office when you called. Things have been crazy, I forgot that you called."

Silence stretched on for a few minutes. I thought she had hung up when she finally spoke again.

"Is it true?"

Leave it to Annie to cut right to the chase. I squeezed my eyes shut.

"Is what true?" I knew what she was talking about, but I did not want to assume and fracture our relationship further.

"Thomas told us some fucked up shit about dad and Lyle. I did not want to believe it, but I talked to Lauren. She said it was all true."

I took a deep breath, and gave her statement some thought, "Why are you asking if it is true, when you were told by two people that it was?"

She sighed; silent seconds ticked on. "Why didn't *you* tell me?" Her voice cracked, but she cleared her throat.

She asked the one question that was the hardest to admit and explain. I had nothing to lose.

"You already lost them physically and blamed me. I did not want to take the image you had of them. You worshipped them. I did not want to be blamed for ruining that too."

She laughed a humorless laugh, "So you took away twenty years of our relationship because you did not want to hurt me?"

I had not fully thought about her side of wanting to have me in her life, "You made it pretty clear you wanted nothing to do with me, Annie. You have openly hated me for years. What was the point in telling you? I did not think you would listen or believe me." I was angry for her trying to blame me for all of it. I shouldered the blame for their deaths, but the broken relationship was equally shared.

"You could have told me. You should have told me!" She was speaking through her teeth into the phone. It was a habit she and I both had shared when we were extremely mad and frustrated.

"I don't know what you want me to say?" I said as calmly as my voice would allow.

Another silent few seconds, "Why did you try to kick Lyle?"

I chanted to myself that I had nothing to lose and took another deep breath, "He told me he was tired of me protecting you. He told me he was going to kill you. I was trying to provoke him so he would turn his aggression towards me. My foot slipped and hit dad."

"You went that day to protect me." She murmured into the phone, it was not a question, it was a realization.

"Jennifer wants to talk to you." Annie's voice was void of all emotion. I let out the breath I did not know I was holding. I heard the phone exchange hands.

"Mama said you were going to call me!" Jennifer's voice appeared on the other line. She was the one in the family that had preserved her Southern draw to sweet perfection.

"I'm sorry Jen, I have been really busy at work. We are expanding our lines and updating the website. I should have called you a week ago, I am sorry."

"Uh-huh. It's a good thing Lauren lives there, otherwise, we would have no idea whether you were dead or alive." As well-mannered as Southerners are, they are equally as adept at laying on guilt.

"I'm sorry Jen."

She sighed. I heard her moving and she whispered into the phone, "Are you okay?"

I assume she was walking away from Annie and wanted to get to the heart of her reason for wanting to talk to me. "I am okay. How long has Annie been in town?"

"'Bout three days, she's gonna stay another two, I think. Mama is happy to see her." She hissed into the phone.

"Did you know she was going to call me on your phone, or did you plan it?"

Silence, "She said she thought you were screening her calls, but she did not say she was going to use my phone to call you. I had left it in the kitchen to charge."

"I was not screening her calls. I was busy when she called, and I forgot to call her back."

"Uh-huh."

I decided to change the subject, "Jennifer, is there something you need to tell me?" Like you're pregnant.

"Why didn't you say anything? You and Lauren have always been thick as thieves, and now I just know you survived something together. Something big and terrible and ya'll kept it a secret from us all, Ro. That's messed up!" Jennifer's voice grew a little louder, just above a whisper.

"You were eight, Jennifer. Eight-years-old. No one in their right mind would ever share the horrors we experienced to an eight-year-old!" I was hoping the sincerity in my tone was enough to calm the anger I could feel cross-continental.

"I'm not eight anymore. I haven't been eight for a long time, Ro. You should have said something."

I sighed, "There was no point in dredging up the past and destroying your perspective on dad and Lyle. I don't want to talk about this anymore. Please, can we get to the point in the conversation where you tell me you are pregnant!"

She snorted, "Crap it, did mama tell ya?"

"Yes, weeks ago, and congratulations. I am very happy for you."

"Mama is the worst at keeping secrets. Well, anyway, yes, I am pregnant, but it's still really early. Mama and Annie are throwing me a baby shower in a few months. You and Lauren are required to attend."

Required, huh? "What about Thomas?"

She laughed, "Boys don't care about baby showers. Besides, it has been ages since you came to visit."

She was right. I could not even think of the last time I had been to Charleston. I moved away and never went back. "Okay, just tell me when it is, and I will do my best to work you into my busy schedule."

"You are still allergic to horses?"

Now I was confused, "I thought you were having a human baby, was I wrong?"

She cackled into the phone, "No, dum-dum, mama and Annie want to do the shower at a cute plantation. They have horses to ride. There is this beautiful lake with a horse trail. But it'll be hell if anyone is allergic to the horsehair."

My brain made the connection that I was willing it to make.

"Jennifer, I need to call you back." I hung up before she responded.

Rebecca Hamilton took horseback riding lessons. I dismissed it because her instructor was a woman. Even Beck mentioned it while discussing Hamilton's neighbor and her father's golfing buddy. I focused too quickly on one and forgot about the other. He even mentioned that just because her instructor was a female it did not mean that everyone on staff was a woman. It did not mean every patron was a woman. It was the last stone unturned. Every other place in Rebecca Hamilton's world was being swabbed and tested. I felt mad at myself for the oversight.

I launched back into the personal profiles of Rebecca Hamilton. I found pictures of her with her horse. I cross-referenced other pictures to find her riding facility. Serenity Aces in Santa Barbara. Ooof, it was far away.

I looked into the owners of Serenity, Joan and Michael Bentley. I found their business ledger pretty easily and found that they had a few veterinary transactions without a specific horse attached to it. Another hour later and I found the transactions through the vet's paperwork.

Serenity Acres had a vet on staff that would order ketamine on the regular. Which would not raise any red flags considering ketamine is used largely as a horse tranquilizer. I cursed at myself for not making the connection earlier.

I spent the rest of the morning gathering all the information on Serenity the internet had to offer. When it came down to it, I had to visit the place to check things out on my own.

Chapter 20

March 5

I checked the stable's website looking for information on adult beginner lessons. Hamilton took lessons once a week in Santa Barbara. It was practically on the other side of California and traffic would be brutal. I conceded to myself that the long and frustrating commute was the last stone in the investigation to turn.

I threw a few fingers and yelled at drivers who forgot to use their blinkers. I calmed myself down when I realized no one could see me through the BMWs tint. At least in the Prius, I have the satisfaction of watching someone try to ignore my waving finger. After three hours and a stroke from high blood pressure later, I was pulling into Serenity Acres.

It was a beautiful piece of property. A white fence lined the way, and the large arched gate was bearing its name in a metal curve. The road to the main stables was surrounded by green rolling hills. I rolled down the window to let the wind hit my face, but quickly changed my mind when the smell of manure hit my nose. The driveway up to the stable was long, finally, ten minutes after driving through the metal arch, I was parking in front of a large white house with large columns. It had a two-story wrap around porch with rocking chairs every 5 feet along the deck.

I felt like I was transported back to Charleston looking at a plantation home. I had no doubt a home like this was where mom and Annie had planned to throw Jennifer's baby shower. To the left of the house, large rows of green stables lined the vista, and to the right, rows of vineyard hedges. Their website said they used the main house for events, and they made their own wine. Just past the hedges, I could see another crop of buildings, I assume, the winery.

A place this size would easily have fifty people to maintain. I got out of my BMW, straightened my light brown wig, and headed towards the stables. The smell increased with each step, by the time I was walking through the open barn doors I was exclusively breathing from my mouth.

"You must be Leslie Mixon." An older woman, close to sixty, stuck out her wide hand. She was about 5'6" with short white hair pulled back in a small bun at the nape of her neck. She had broad shoulders and the appropriate belly with age. She was wearing faded jeans and a matching button-up shirt with snaps on the chest. She looked weather-worn from days in the sun, her skin looked like supple leather. I took her hand in mine. It was heavily calloused in the palm. Her grip was firm, but she released after one pump and squinted down at me.

"Yes, I am Leslie. And you are?" I spoke with a slight Southern twang I had fought years to wrestle out of my vernacular.

"I'm Lilli Ann Brown, the manager of Serenity's stables. Bette Little will be the one giving you your first lesson. Have you ever ridden before Ms. Mixon?" Lilli was walking in front of me, leading me away from the stable and towards a smaller fenced-in area. She walked with a slight bow-legged limp, like a female John Wayne. Another older woman was waiting in the paddock with a shiny brown horse. She was brushing the horse's side. A saddle hung across the top of the fence.

"I went when I was a kid, I loved it, always wanted to properly learn though." I thought back to the summer days when my dad would take us to a local horse farm. We would ride in circles for hours. Once, he arranged for us to take the horses down a trail for about an hour ride. I remembered the horsehair itching my legs. When I got home, I was covered in hives. Mom made me sit in the tub with Dreft and oatmeal for three nights straight until the hives went away. It was the last time we went horseback riding. I thanked myself for wearing loose-fitting jeans.

We had made it to the paddock, "This is Bette Little, Bette, this is Leslie Mixon." Bette's hands were smaller and not as rough, but she definitely had calluses in a few spots. Bette Little was slight with salt and pepper hair. She wore it shoulder length and down. She had a kind face and square jaw.

"Nice to meet you, Leslie." Her voice was low and gruff, like she had a serious smoking problem in her youth. The light lines around her mouth confirmed my suspicions. Lilli Ann had already turned around and was limping her way back to the stables. I turned back to Bette and motioned to the shiny brown horse, "Who is this?"

Bette gave the beast a few pats on the side, "This is Semi-Sweet Chocolate, we call her Cocoa. She is older, but she is a patient girl. First, I am going to show you how to properly set a saddle."

She was a woman of a few words. I felt uneasy at first when within 5 minutes Bette was showing me how to mount. It was very different attempting to mount on my own. In my youth, my father would pluck me from the ground and place me on the waiting horse. It took me a few tries, but I got the hang of it. She got Cocoa up to a gallop before calling the lesson. It was liberating. More childhood memories flooded in, happy memories. I had to remind myself that I was actually at Serenity to investigate a rapist.

"Do you mind showing me around the property?" I asked Bette hopefully.

She gave me a brief smile, "Got another lesson and stalls to muck, but I can have Josh Bentley show you around. He works the stalls and cares for the horses. He is basically our errand boy." We were walking back up to the main green stable, "Bentley, give Ms. Mixon the tour." Bette tipped her head to me as a goodbye and walked back to Cocoa.

"Hello, I'm Leslie Mixon." I stuck out my hand.

"Call me Josh." His hand was blistering hot and the calluses felt like sandpaper to my skin. He was in his early twenties, about 5'10", skinny but muscular with brown hair and brown eyes. He was cute and polite. I had to remind myself that most psychopaths are able to conceal their true identity behind cute and polite. Skepticism back in place, I followed Josh to a souped-up golf cart, "We will take the gator around, it's going to get bumpy, so hold on."

He took me around the whole property. As predicted, it was bumpy, I nearly bounced out as we were passing through a vineyard hedge. He was spitting his tobacco dip in a discarded coke bottle. I cringed but recognized a good opportunity to get DNA. Just because Josh Bentley appeared cute and polite, I did not rule him out.

"What do you do around here, Josh?" It was hard to talk through the bumping, but I needed information. We had finally stopped at the outcrop of buildings. It was the winery. Josh stopped by a trashcan and tossed out his coke bottle. I cursed at myself for not grabbing it, but honestly, no one could ever justify wanting to keep someone's spit cup, even if I tried the recycle line. Josh popped a piece of gum in his mouth.

"Odds and ends. I am here for the horses mostly. My aunt and uncle own Serenity. My parents thought it would be a good job to learn discipline." He ended with a smile in my direction. His teeth looked white against his browned skin.

"You a problem child?" My southern accent was coming back in full force.

He laughed and popped his gum, "Not as bad as my brother, but I skipped a few too many classes in school. Mom and dad were mad I failed the semester. Apparently, USC is too expensive to blow off." He chuckled again and blew another bubble. USC is a difficult school to get into. Josh must be smarter than I gave him credit for. And what about his brother? We looped back around to the stables. I followed him to a few stalls as he was showing me the different horses and telling me of their illustrious owners.

We were at a solid white horse's stall when a man dressed impeccably in riding gear walked out. He gave me a curious up and down that gave me the creeps. Josh quickly spat the gum into his hand. Apparently, whoever we were approaching was not a fan of gum.

"Hey Mr. Regions, how is Snowfall today?" I watched Josh very casually stick the gum on the side of the stall.

"Josh, so glad you approached. I just finished my weekly ride with Snowfall, and I noticed her oats looked a little damp. Can you make sure you discard these and replace them with fresh oats at once?" Josh nodded and entered the stall.

Mr. Regions turned to me, "And you are?" He was already grabbing my hand in both of his, "Leslie Mixon. I am here for beginner riding lessons."

He chuckled, "Riding lessons indeed. I am sure a woman of your caliber knows her way around a saddle." I didn't even know what that double entendre could mean. I simply smiled in response. He squeezed my hands again, "I am Clinton Regions, perhaps you have heard of me?" I had not.

"My family owns a series of hotels. You must have heard of The Regions Resorts." I had. The Regions were upscale resort hotels on exotic beaches. Celebrities and the rich enjoyed the resorts for their commitment to privacy.

"Wow, what a pleasure to meet you, Mr. Regions." I smiled sweetly at him.

"Call me Clint." He finally released my hands. They felt damp. I stifled a grimace and discreetly wiped my hands on my jeans. "Leslie, your accent is intoxicating, where are you from?"

"Oh!" I put my hand to my chest, with my best 'why-little-ole-me' impersonation, "I am from Charleston."

"Charleston is lovely, we are acquiring a hotel there this summer."

I was trying to find the right way to grab the discarded gum. Josh's back was to us, he was bent down. The white horse's head stuck over the edge of the stall. I leaned forward to pat her head.

"She is a beautiful horse, Snowfall is it?" I was frantically patting the side of the stall, trying to act casual, while the other hand continued to pet the beast's head.

"Oh yes, Snowfall. She is a Camarillo; her coloring is incredibly rare. When I saw her, I spared no expense, her lineage is a direct descendant of Adolpho Camarillo."

I had no idea who or what he was talking about. I smiled and nodded and batted my lashes at the appropriate pauses. Say what you will about the South, but we know how to fake interest in a conversation. He was starting to talk about the State Fair when I found the slightly wet discarded piece of gum, I balled it in my hand and casually shoved it in my pocket.

"What brought you to California, Ms. Mixon?"

I batted my lashes, "Call me Leslie, please. The wind blew me from Charleston." He chortled.

"Well, perhaps the wind can blow you towards Breakers tomorrow night." Breakers was a five star, Michelin rated restaurant in Santa Monica. I typically avoided Santa Monica, the traffic to and from was enough to drive anyone crazy. However, the Breakers was a restaurant I did want to try. I also considered it an opportunity to get more information about Serenity and possibly more information on Mr. Regions.

I smiled coyly, "Perhaps the wind will blow me in around 7:30."

He chuckled and kissed my hand. "I'm looking forward to it."

I fought the grimace from the spit left on my fist and bid Clint goodbye and thanked Josh for the tour.

I casually walked to the car, trying to sway my hips as I was pretty sure Regions was staring hard at my derriere. The BMW's maps were telling me it would be over two hours to get to Pasadena, and another hour after that. God loves rush hour. Considering my long commute and my rumbling stomach, I decided to make a small detour.

I pulled into Banjo a little over an hour and a half later. At that point, I was starved and was hoping Beck was working. There was a small wait, but I was in no hurry to get back in the car just to sit and inhale exhaust.

I was shown to my table by a cute brunette with pigtails and a cutoff gingham shirt. Her apron covered more than her shorts. I had to remind myself that she lived off gratuity, and skin gets you pretty good tips. I also reminded myself that it was good for her to feel so confident in so little.

"My name is Dory; I will be your server tonight. The specials are smoked wings with an Asian BBQ sauce, the duck bok choy, and the BBQ pork dim sum. I will give you a few minutes to get settled."

I looked around; it was an interesting ambience. The last time I had been in his restaurant, I had sat on the other side of the building. I was sitting at the wall of old battered license plates. The opposite wall had oversize Japanese characters written on it like a word cloud. The tables were corrugated metal with glass on top to make a servable surface. Seating ranged from metal naval chairs to benches with individual cushions. The center table was on a dais where the patrons would sit on tatami mats.

Dory was back before I had a chance to look at the

menu. "Compliments of the chef." She winked and placed a plate with rose-shaped cucumbers and carrots with a peanut dipping sauce on the table. I looked around, but Beck was not within my sight. I smiled to myself, perhaps this was his version of giving a girl flowers? One could hope.

I ate the delicate vegetables and ordered a green tea with the duck bok choy. Dory was enthused, "I have never seen Chef Tadashi send a special before." I smiled and shrugged, trying to act casual.

"You his girl?" Dory took a seat across from me. Apparently, he was just as mysterious at work as he was with me.

"Does he have a girl?" Now I was just prying, but she seemed more than happy to gossip.

She sat forward like she was telling a secret, "He does not talk about his personal life, but in the past month or so he has been much nicer." She bent further forward and whispered, "Richard thinks he's got a lady that is chilling him out or heating him up if you know what I mean." She threw another wink in my direction and excused herself to put in my order. I ate another cucumber rose; the peanut sauce had a little spice to it. Thankfully Dory had deposited ice water before getting her fill of gossip.

I looked around and several waiters were staring at me. When I caught their gaze, they all scattered. I felt my ears blushing beneath my wig. It was starting to get hot. I could not look around anymore. I was just starting to feel like it was a mistake for coming when Beck sat down across from me. He passed me my green tea. I felt eyes back on me, instinct had me look towards the source. The whole wait staff was staring at my table with mouths open, some craning to get a better look. I ducked my head and grabbed the tea.

Beck looked amused, he turned his head towards the gossip mill and they all scattered like wild geese.

"I guess you don't get a lot of visitors," I mumbled to myself. I was still trying to get my coloring back in order and I could not meet his eyes. Of course, this is Beck we are talking about. He lifted his finger to my chin and directed my face to his. I heard a glass break, I felt like an actor on the stage.

"No, I do not. What brings you in tonight?" I don't know how he was not distracted by the increasing number of waiters that happen to pass the table. I was keeping count; we were on the fifth person in two minutes. I tried to act casual, "I heard good things about the duck bok choy."

He gave me a brief smile and returned to his serious smolder, "What is it you need of me?"

I tried to break his eye contact, but I was already deep in the silver depths, "Maybe I just wanted to see you." My voice was a squeaky attempt at a whisper.

"I should be so lucky." He dropped my chin and began to stand up. I was stuck on the lucky comment.

"Wait," I made a motion to grab at his hand. He canted his head and relaxed his position back into sitting.

"I have a date tomorrow night." His face was unreadable, but his eyes narrowed and possibly looked upset.

"Considering it is not with me, I am not sure why you are telling me this." His jaw tightened.

I shook my head to break the eye contact, I needed to think and explain otherwise he was going to think I was a petty woman rubbing another date in his face.

"No, it's a fake date, but the guy does not know it. He is a possible suspect in the Rebecca Hamilton case." He relaxed his jaw and raised one eyebrow.

I continued, "It's at Breakers tomorrow night at 7:30. I am concerned that if he is responsible for Rebecca's condition..." I let the sentence hang. He nodded in understanding.

"It's with Clint Regions."

He cut me off, "Of the hotel empire?"

I nodded.

"I did not have time to research him before I agreed to go, so could be a perfectly nice guy. I just don't want to risk it." I started to ring my hands together, feeling anxious that he was going to tell me no.

"And if he doses you with ketamine, you will be a sitting…"

"Duck bok choy!" Beck was interrupted by another server that had not walked past my table yet. He was delivering my food, "Chef Tadashi, is this your girl?" Popular question tonight. Beck stood up without addressing the curious server.

"I will see you tomorrow night, enjoy your meal, Leslie."

I finished the meal as quickly as I could. I wanted to savor it. It was perfectly seasoned, and the duck was tender and delicious, but the highway of goose-necking waitstaff made me eat a little faster and get the hell out of dodge.

"Check has been covered." Another person stopped by the table. If I was not mistaken, Clark. He was not quite as tall as his giant brother, Richard, but still at least 6'4". I had met him briefly a month before, though I was not dressed in disguise then, so he did not recognize me. If I was not so embarrassed by all the attention it would have been comical.

"That is not necessary." I began. Clark shook his head, "Nah, anyone who is responsible for that personality shift can eat free." I blushed again, threw a twenty on the table, and rushed out.

I knew Beck was prickly, but seriously he is not that bad. Mysterious and brooding, but sexy and kind. He was considerate and quite honestly insistent that I eat dinners when he thinks I am stressed. Of course, I did know his background. I imagine the perma-scowl of an assassin ninja turned chef could be intimidating. I wanted to take credit for the possible change, but honestly, how could I take credit for that? He could have a girl. A girl that was not me. I mean, I know I already tried to figure that out and came up empty. But wasn't the entire staff at his place of work insistent that he in fact had a girl.

I scowled out the windshield as I made my way home.

Chapter 21

March 6

The next morning, my computer informed me that the autopsy of Lisa Henderson was ready. She died the same way as the other two. I paused at one detail that seemed odd. Lisa Henderson weighed 115lbs at her death. I double checked the reports from Bobbi King and Flora Sanchez. They also weighed 115lbs at the time of their death. I pondered what that could possibly mean. Perhaps the fifteen days was circumstantial based on how quickly the women lost weight.

Bobbi King and Flora Sanchez were both around the same height and build. Lisa Henderson was taller, but slimmer. Kelly Parker was the most muscular out of all the victims. I would venture the guess that the abduction weight of the first three was around 125lbs. A ten-pound weight loss in two weeks is significant, but not unheard of considering the basal metabolic rate would have them shed at least half a pound day, it was not a stretch. Kelly Parker's abduction weight was probably closer to 135-140lbs based on her height and musculature. If the Triple S was determining when to kill based on the weight of his victims, then... I had more time. Instead of one day, I had another week at least. It was a circumstantial hope and possibly simply a coincidence, but I crossed my fingers that Parker had more time.

I breathed a heavy sigh and started working through the information I had collected for Rebecca Hamilton's case.

I dug the wadded gum out of my jeans pocket and began creating a profile for Josh Bentley. I congratulated myself for killing two birds with one stone. If Rebecca's attacker was Josh's brother, then the DNA match would suggest his sibling as the attacker.

I completed my twenty-minute yoga and ran full

strength for my six miles. It felt good to use my muscles again after getting off schedule from my late-night adventure with Graham. I spent my morning researching Clint Regions. He was a public figure with a very good cybersecurity system. It took an hour to get through his firewalls. The man was obsessed with his horses. From what I could tell, he owned 6 horses, but Snowfall was his pride and joy.

Based on his internet history, he did lean towards the younger girls. But again, he asked me out and no matter how much expensive cream I slather on my face daily, it will never be as wrinkle-free as a sixteen-year-old. I checked his Amazon account and any other place where ketamine could be purchased. He had no transactional history of it. I felt myself easing slightly.

I switched gears and looked into Josh Bentley. He was a typical rich California boy. He enjoyed surfing and smoking pot. His aunt and uncle did in fact own Serenity. His brother, Jackson, was a first-rate dipshit. It looked like he was a minor drug dealer and had a few DUIs under his belt. I pondered on the drug dealer brother to be the source of the ketamine. There was no way I could trace that. If he did get it from his brother, the likelihood of small-time dealers using their computer to keep track of their clients was slim.

I thought about the on-site vet. I would see what I could find out about him, but he was looking like another likely suspect. Maybe I would slip in a few questions to Clint about the vet and any other male that he knew of that traipsed through Serenity.

I was feeling more comfortable with the date. At that point, I had another good lead, the on-staff vet at Serenity, and I was going to eat dinner at a five-star restaurant. Not to mention, I was hopeful to see Beck afterward for a debriefing. I would take both double entendre, but he would stick to the play-by-play of dinner.

I carefully selected my clothing for the night. A well-fit black bandage-style dress with a visible gold zipper that went from the low-slung back, over the caboose, until the end of the dress. It was sexy, but not overstated. I paired it with red patent pumps and cute little lacey lingerie. I felt good, and if things went well, I might be able to seduce Beck to stay the night and get the second debriefing. I rolled my own eyes at my ridiculous joke, but I was hopeful, and I felt sexy. I pulled on my wig and secured it tightly in place, donned my brown contacts, and wiggled in front of the mirror.

I arrived at Breakers at 7:25pm and left my car with the valet. Clint was waiting at the bar sipping on a whiskey as I approached, "You look amazing. I had no idea what you were hiding under your jeans." Outwardly I bat my lashes and did a small spin, inwardly I cringed and growled. Every conversation with this guy kept going back to my body.

We were ushered to our table. He ordered a bold red wine, his words not mine, and escargot with our house salads for starters. He ordered my meal for me as well. Playing as the sweet Southern bell was already wearing on my feminist heart, but I played my part with grace.

"How long have you owned Snowfall?" I wanted to lull him into security and from everything I knew about him he loved Snowfall and tight-fitting black dresses.

"A few years, she is the pride of my collection." His eyes looked far off.

"How long have you been riding?"

"Oh, my entire life. My father bought me my first horse when I was five. They are beautiful beasts." His gaze settled back to my face. I took a sip of the wine. The waitress set the salads in front of us. They were divine. I cut the lettuce into smaller pieces so I could continue to pry into Clint's life.

"How long have you been with Serenity Acres?" I took a

dainty bite oflettuce.

"Five years at least. My family has been friends with the Bentley's for years. They are like a second family." A family that would cover the tracks of a rapist?

"You must know everyone there then? Tell me, who should I trust my horse to when I decide to get one?"

He chuckled a few times and passed his empty salad plate to the server and spooned the escargot through a garlic aioli. "Bette is a superb teacher, Josh can be talented, he is just a little lazy." He scowled at his statement. "Any horse is in good hands with Lilly, I daresay as big as they are, most mammals would be." He laughed at his own joke.

"Is there an onsite vet or do they contract with someone near?" Finally, the question I wanted an answer to.

He smiled briefly, "They have an on-site vet of excellent caliber. Look him up, Dr. Carl Littleton. He and I have been known to golf together from time to time. He is the man to ask any questions about the Equus family." Bingo!

I excused myself to the restroom after the salad. I wanted an excuse to sneer without being watched. I also was hoping to get a glimpse of Beck. I had yet to see him and was getting worried that he was not going to show. I got into the restroom and realized the wine was having an effect on my bladder, too. As I was leaving the stall, I heard a small metallic click and glanced up to the door.

"You look stunning." Beck was smiling letting his eyes rove up and down my figure. He was wearing a black suit that was cut to perfection. His hair was pulled back, his tie was thin, his jaw could cut diamonds. He looked sexy as hell.

"You're not so bad yourself." I walked over to the sink to wash my hands. Dang, I am casual. He followed my movements closely. He passed me a paper towel and stroked my cheek with his finger. I nearly combusted. It was hard not to shove him into the wall and have my way with him.

I resisted, "I should get back. I would hate for Clint to think I drowned." He chuckled and moved to kiss my cheek. He smelled like the love child of Calvin Klein and Georgio Armani, I shivered. My cheek blazed under his kiss. He pulled away and opened the door. However, brief the encounter, my heart was racing, and my stomach felt hot. I tried to convince myself it was just the wine, but my inner dialog was pretty vocal that it was not.

My entree was waiting when I arrived at the table. A waiter was also waiting to put my napkin back in my lap. It was a very fancy place. Clint droned on about the hotel industry and different supermodel ex-girlfriends he had. I would occasionally look around to see where Beck was sitting. Once I thought I saw him at the bar, but I could not get a better view to confirm. I took small careful bites of my sea bass. Clint was masticating his aged beef medallions.

By the time dessert arrived, I was well fairly full. He insisted on a chocolate raspberry volcano cake. It sounded lovely. I took a few bites to be polite. It was like nothing like I had ever tasted, but I set my fork down resolutely. I may be fit as a fiddle, but my bandage dress only had so much give. He ate the majority of the cake without apologies.

"It was a lovely evening Clint, thank you so much for asking me to join you." We were walking to the valet stand. "Oh, the pleasure was all mine, please I'll give the ticket to the valet." He plucked my ticket I had waiting out of my hand. I ground my teeth but remembered I was still a Southern Belle. He passed our tickets over to the valet, whispered something, and passed a hundred. We were left alone to wait.

The parking lot was not well lit, there was only one true light above the valet stand. I was starting to feel uneasy. I shivered at the thought of a dark parking lot, reminding me of my own almost mugging. Clint turned to me, "Are you cold?

You look freezing. The wind off the ocean at this time of night will chill you to the bone." Clint reached around me to rub my arms. The movement looked awkward; his wrist was bent at an odd angle. I felt a pinch on the back of my arm and jerked my head back to look at Clint's face. He was smiling coolly down to me; his arms went from chaffing my arms to secured around my naked back. It felt wrong, off.

I saw the valet show back up, but the car was not mine, it was Clint's, "Oh look at you, darling, it appears the wine was a little strong tonight." Darling? I tried to back away, but my legs felt like lead. I felt my body slump into Clint's arms. "Can you get the door, sir? It appears my lovely has over imbibed tonight." I wanted to yell, but it was taking all of my strength to keep my eyes open. My mouth was limp with my lips slightly parted. I was sure I looked three-sheets to the wind to the poor valet attendant.

I was starting to panic. I tried to move my head, but it felt like it weighed a hundred pounds. I felt a second set of hands on me, I assume the valet was earning his $100 tip. I slumped in the front seat of the Mercedes. My eyes were sliding shut, "Oh darling, you forgot to fasten your seat belt." I heard the buckle click. I could not open my eyes. The lids were held down with boulders of drug-induced weights.

I was cognizant enough to understand that I had been drugged and the pinch I felt was the injection. I started panicking when I gathered, I had been drugged with ketamine. My warbled brain slid the narrative in order. Clint Regions had access to the vet's stores. He ordered enough people around that they just let him have a run of Serenity when he was there. He had seen Rebecca. He knew she was narcoleptic. Even hotel moguls would think that bit of gossip was interesting. Maybe he dosed Rebecca at Serenity and he was so precise at getting her back she was not aware she lost time. Maybe he stalked her and waited for his opportunity at Griffith Park.

I tried to open my eyes, lead weights, unmovable flaps of skin. The only reason why I was even the smidgen of conscious was because of my damn red-headed genetics. The car was purring beneath me. Clint was in a hurry. He had probably done this so many times he knew exactly how long he would have. Would he have his way with me and deposit me back into my BMW where I would wake up none the wiser? It seemed like the likely end.

I wondered how much time had passed. Did Beck see what was happening? How long would Clint need before he deposited me back? Would I be able to fight or just be conscious enough to be scarred for life? I tried to move my finger, nothing. My toe, nothing. My body was completely unresponsive. Even my heart was beating slowly as if it was unaware of our danger. I had no adrenaline to save me, just enough will-power to stay aware with no means of preventing my pending attack.

The car stopped. Clint was whistling. I felt his hand slip up my thigh, his pinky grazed the folds past my lacey underwear. He pulled it away, I heard a quiet sucking noise. "You taste as good as you look, Leslie." Fuck. Did he know I was awake, or did he always have one-way conversations with his conquests? Did he just taste his finger? This was a sick shithead. Tasting me as if I were a sample of wine before committing to the whole bottle. I felt angry but my body remained unresponsive to the emotional climate. I heard his door open and close. I was alone in the car. *Do something, move, anything, fight!*

My car door opened, and I could smell Clint's cologne close to my face, "Darling, you must unbuckle before we go inside. As tempting as it is to pleasure you out here. I must insist we go to my bedchamber." *What kind of twisted fantasy was he playing out?*

I was going to be sick, but my stomach was as responsive as the rest of me. He unclicked my seat belt and hoisted me up. He was carrying me in his arms. I heard another door open and the temperature changed. The sounds of the ocean were gone, and it was warmer. We were inside. I heard his feet click against tile flooring. I heard another click of metal and his footfalls were softened. He was walking on carpet.

"So nice of you to wear this lovely frock tonight." I felt him unzipping my dress. I was trying to let the ketamine take my mind away. I did not want to remember this. He set me down and pulled my dress off.

"Did you wear your sexy black lingerie for me my darling? You know exactly how to get me in the mood." *Go to sleep or wake up and kill him. This limbo is not going to work.* I tried to will my brain into submission, nothing.

I felt him tug my bra aside and pull my nipple into his mouth. *Go to sleep or wake up.*

I heard a grunt and his body fell on mine. He was heavy and not moving, it was getting hard to breathe with the extra weight on my chest. Then the weight was gone. Could I be so lucky that he finished before he could start? I felt his hands on my body, my breast was tucked into my bra, but gently. Something warm was wrapped around me. My body lifted from the bed. Clint smelled different, he smelled like... Beck!

"Caroline, I have you, you are safe." He whispered in my ear. He was carrying me through the house, the air shifted, and I heard the ocean. He placed me in a car. It smelled like my BMW. He gently buckled me in, "I have not forgotten the mission." He kissed my cheek and shut the door. I was alone for what seemed like hours but was probably closer to five minutes. He returned and grabbed my hand as he drove off. It was then that the ketamine took its hold on me.

I woke up still feeling groggy. My limbs were heavy, but I was able to move them. I looked up to the wood-paneled ceiling. I felt around my body and blinked reality back. I was safe. I was in Beck's loft. I recognized the ceiling, but it was dark in the room. It felt like the early hours of the day. I looked around to find a clock, but I saw nothing. I sat up slowly, my head ached. I squinted my eyes to the pain.

"Shhh, rest, Caroline. The ketamine will take time to leave your system." I felt Beck's warm hand on my cheek. My eyes found his. He was sitting next to me on the edge of the bed. I sat up and reached for him.

I clasped my arms around him, "Beck! You saved me. How did you..." I was not sure exactly what I wanted to ask him, "get to me?"

"He drugged you." I nodded, "I know."

"He took you into his car." I nodded again, "I know."

"How do you know this?" His eyes were soft like melting silver.

"I never react to sedatives correctly; I always have to be dosed higher." I reached up and pointed to my red hair. "I could not move, but I was awake for all of it."

His face looked pained, "I am sorry I was not faster to get to you. His front door was locked, I had to find another way in." His eyes turned to ice, his jaw was tight, anger had replaced the relief that was on his face when I woke up.

"You saved me." I reached up to cup his cheek, but he pulled away and stood up. "I was nearly too late. You asked me to protect you, and I nearly failed you." He was standing next to his dresser with his arms crossed against his chest. He looked ashamed and angry. But he was here, he had saved me from the weird fantasy I was forced to play out with Clint.

I tried to get up to go to him, but black fleurettes took over my vision at the sudden movement. I shook my head to clear the darkness, "You saved me, you came for me." I wanted my words to absolve Beck of his emotions, but he stood stubbornly away. I tried not to focus on the veins on his arms or the tendons that were tight at his neck. The tension on his body was palpable. I took a few fortifying breaths and tried again. "Thank you." I had started but my brain finally caught up with the implications of Beck saving me.

"I have to go." I pushed myself to my feet and moved quickly forward. I was looking for my clothes, anything to get ready to leave. My movements were too quick, and the floor pitched towards my face. It was a strange way for gravity to react. I was just looking for my shoes. I felt Beck's arms around my waist as I stared at his concrete floor and a geometric rug. It was a pretty rug, but I was uncertain why Beck was holding me over it. As quickly as the floor came to my face, my world was righted again. Beck was holding me upright and steadying me by the shoulders. I realized that I had fallen forward, and he caught me before I smashed my face into his hard concrete or fancy rug.

"You need to rest, Caroline."

I focused my eyes back on him. I felt a little drunk, a little giddy, a little belligerent, "I need to go." I may have stuck my lower lip out pouting. His nostrils flared as he gently let me down on the bed. I tried to swat at his caring hands, but my own hands were covered in black fabric. I looked down and saw I was in his suit jacket, the arms were too long, but I was definitely wearing the jacket he wore last night. I spotted my dress hanging on the back of a reading chair in the corner of the room. Of course, he had covered me up, when he found me, I was stripped down to my black lacy lingerie. Seconds ticked by as I was slowly connecting the fuzzy dots.

"Where is it you feel so eager to go to at this very moment?" His tone was patient, but like the tone your parent has after asking you to do something twice and the third time would not be as polite. I shook my head; the movement was slow. The walls did not move at the same pace as my head. I blinked and waited for the walls to become still again. Why did I need to go anywhere? The thought escaped me. I was pretty content in Beck's warm jacket, sitting on his comfortable bed, with his warm hands gripped around my arms. Actually, the grasp was a little tight. I wriggled my arms to ease his hold, he relaxed immediately, "Sorry." His tone was gruff and low.

I smiled back at him, feeling a little loopy, "What are you sorry for?" My words sounded a little slurred. I tried to lean back and prop myself on one elbow. I could feel the heat radiating off his body. He looked good enough to eat. He was here, I was here. And I could not remember what was so important before I stood up. I let the jacket open with the movement, exposing my lacy bra. I tried to bat my lashes at him, but they were too slow to be sexy. He noticed the exposed flesh, but instead of leaning into me, he closed his eyes. I watched him shake his head a few times and his nostrils flared. He opened his eyes and slowly reached forward to close the jacket.

"The ketamine is still in your system, rest now." He stood up, I watched him walk away through the bedroom door. I slumped back in frustration. I wanted to fly the coop, but the sudden movement of me dropping my head back was enough to slip me back into unconsciousness.

I woke up again. The light had shifted in the room, it was like the morning glow just before the full sunrise. I was alone in the room. My limbs no longer felt like lead weights. I moved gingerly hoping to avoid falling on my face again. Beck was not here to protect my teeth from hitting the concrete, after all. I was still wearing his jacket, but I noticed he had buttoned all three buttons. I cringed at my poor attempts at seduction. I could always claim ignorance, I *was* drugged on a powerful horse sedative.

I walked slowly and carefully out of his bedroom. Beck was sleeping on his couch. I was not sure which I felt worse about; the fact that he had slept on the couch because he did not want to sleep near me or the ketamine hangover. I walked over to the kitchen to get a glass of water. My throat felt like the Sahara on a hot July afternoon.

Beck sat up slowly, "you look better." He murmured to me, rising from the couch. He was shirtless and wearing a pair of gray sweatpants. I don't know what it is about men in gray sweatpants. Maybe it is the fact that the cotton held little to the imagination or maybe it was how easily accessible everything was. I took a gulp of water to put out the fire that had erupted with the sight of the perfect bulge in the gray sweatpants. I looked up and found the view was even better. His abs were beautiful, still hard, still perfect. He was walking over to me like a tiger stalking its prey. His movements were fast and fluid. I took another deep drink of the cool water remembering he slept on the couch for a reason.

He moved around the kitchen, making some kind of drink. I sat on an available stool, nursing my water, and my headache. He passed me a green concoction, "Drink. It will help with the headache." I sniffed at it. Disgusting. I took a small sip. Worse than the smell. "Drink it all." I plugged my nose and tipped it back. It felt like sludge moving down my throat. I gulped down water to chase the gooey mixture.

My head did feel better. I felt like I could think clearly for the first time in a day. I looked into the empty miracle glass as if it would answer my silent questions. "Secret recipe." Beck chuckled and took the glass away to rinse it out.

"What do you remember?" He said turning back to me.

"I remember everything until I was in my car, after that it is fuzzy." He nodded. I hoped I was convincing enough. It was bad enough I had propositioned him, worse was that I looked like a tornado victim with dry mouth and morning breath. I cringed again at my drug-addled attempt at sexy. With my brain working at full speed again, I remembered my foolhardy attempts to leave hours ago by saying, "I have to go!" and standing up to leave even with ketamine still in my system. I went to the bedroom. He was walking behind me. I am not sure whether it was his own amusement that made him follow me, or if he was concerned, I would collapse again.

I started unbuttoning the jacket and collecting my dress and shoes. My wig was placed across his dresser, next to my purse. I shoved the hair in my bag and started shaking the jacket off.

"Where is it exactly you must attend at five-thirty in the morning?"

Dang, I lost the whole night! "I need to go back to Clint's house. I need proof that he is the man who impregnated Rebecca." I was shrugging into my dress, struggling with the zipper. Beck was slow to approach, but he slowly slid the zipper up my back. It slowed ever so slightly around the curve of my butt. I was tempted to turn around, but my brain was fully set on taking Clint down.

"It is unnecessary for you to take such risk."

I turned around and glared at him.

"He raped a girl; he was going to rape me. He has done this to countless women. I need to do my part in this!" I was flushing with anger that he seemed to forget the whole reason for the fiasco last night. I was risking myself for the greater good. He stroked my cheek and smiled gently.

"What is it you wish to accomplish by re-entering the home of a rapist?" His tone was patient, but there was an edge of smugness that I could not identify the reason.

I threw my hands in the air, "To get proof! To get his DNA! To get him put behind bars!"

He chuckled, I sneered. I hated to be laughed at. Beck walked a few steps away and opened the drawer to one of his nightstands, the one that is normally empty. He pulled out a plastic zip-top bag. It had a wadded tissue, a used condom, and a toothbrush. I cringed at the toothbrush's proximity to the used condom, but I stared back with questions in my eyes. "I assume these samples will be sufficient for your specific research and, therefore, does not require you to go back into the lion's den?"

My air escaped my lips in a hiss as I gently took the bag in my hands, looking at it as if to verify it was real.

"Yeah, this will work," I said finally.

"Then, come eat breakfast."

Chapter 22

March 10

"Police arrested 42-year-old hotel heir, Clint Region, today. He is suspected of drugging, kidnapping, and raping a 16-year-old girl. Police have been following leads into the victim's rape for weeks and were able to finally bring the victim closure after an anonymous tip, along with a DNA match on a popular genetic website. Police used similar technology that was used to catch The Golden State Killer in opening its case against Region. His family has no comments about the allegations at this time."

I smiled to myself as I flipped the tv off. It had been a few days since I had submitted Region's DNA and his profile. Beck insisted on calling with the anonymous tip. He used the public phone at his restaurant to call the tip in. I felt relieved, smug, tired. I tried not to let my mind stray to what would have happened had Beck not saved me. We had not seen each other since I left his loft. We had both been busy with work. I had to finish up my case notes on Rebecca Hamilton and I was still digging into the Triple S cases. I was no closer to finding the killer than the police.

I stretched and went for a run. I was still getting my stamina back after the knife wound, and I would get waves of dizziness from the ketamine. The days were starting to heat up. A heatwave in March had the temperatures reaching a hundred during the day but at night it was dropping to sixty degrees. I got home, checked my work email, and gave Lauren a call.

"Did you see the news?" was Lauren's greeting to me.

"I did! That's why I am calling you. Was Region responsible for Rebecca's situation?" I was trying to act curious but surprised at my own assumptions.

“He was! The bastard keeps his horses at the same stables Rebecca rides. The stables have an on-site vet clinic. Region was getting his ketamine from there.”

I cursed, playing along in the shock.

“Yeah, so far, he has not confessed to anything, but the police and the DA are pretty happy they have Region’s DNA, his access to the ketamine, and how he managed to do it. The Hamilton’s are thinking about suing for damages. They could get a couple mil.”

“Wow!” Was all I managed to say. It seemed a little too early to sue the Regions.

“Have lunch with me today!” Lauren sounded excited. I could hear the teenage whining of desperation if I did not comply waiting for me at the other end. Since we were children, any time I would tell Lauren no, and did not have a good reason, she would whine and beg until I changed my mind.

“Sure.” I did want to see her. I had not seen Lauren since we last spoke about Morgan Butler and subsequently procured Chad Westfield’s DNA that no judge would permit.

“Meet me at work around one. We can go to the sushi place you like.” I smiled. I loved that place. It had all-you-could-eat sushi specials for lunch. It was not one of those places where it was on a buffet. In this place, you can order three rolls at a time and keep going until you could no longer stuff another piece of sticky rice in your gullet.

“Deal, I will see you then!” I hung up satisfied with my day’s plans. I took a shower and lounged the rest of the morning. I occasionally checked my computer for any updates on the Triple S case or hopeful brainwaves as to the identity of the guilty party. None.

I was feeling culpable, Kelly Parker had approximately five days, according to my rudimentary knowledge on weight loss and the metabolic rate while starving, before she would show up somewhere around her home. My hunch about the death weight seemed to be holding true because on March 8 her body was not found. Police were scratching their heads when the Triple S bypassed his predicted schedule. I was unable to share my hunch with the authorities because all the autopsies I had read were not public knowledge and would have implicated me.

I wanted to stop her death, but I had no leads. I was scratching my head in befuddlement, too. I tried to ease my guilt by reminding myself that I was not responsible for her safe return. It pained me to believe that, but it was the truth. I was just a hobbyist with good intentions and deductive reasoning skills. The unseen connection between women was still tugging at me. I flipped off my computer and changed into jeans with a slight stretch to prepare for my sushi fest and headed to Lauren's work.

I parked in the visitor's lot. It was across campus from Lauren's office near the ER. It was a tree-lined walk. The day was hot, and I skirted to the 85-degree shadows. Lauren had directed me to meet her in her office as she had some paperwork she was trying to finish before lunch.

I walked into the main ER doors, as it was the closest entrance to her office. There were two people at the reception desk. I recognized Gayle. She normally worked the front desk. A younger man was sitting on the other side of the curved work space, typing away at his computer.

"Hey, Gayle! How are you today?"

Gayle smiled; her round face pulled back producing a small double chin. Her eyes crinkled behind her glasses. "Ms. Caroline, it's been awhile since you came to visit." She patted the folder she was working on shut.

"What have you been up to, missy?" She sat back with her hands on her hips as if she was scolding me. I laughed, "Work, running, the usual. How are your kids?" Gayle had three children, all in their late teens to early twenties. "Same, staying out, giving me heart attacks, but they are keeping their grades up." I knew one child was still in high school, the other two were attending college. "You know Trevor transferred from Fullerton College and now he is at the Cal State Fullerton campus." There was pride in her voice.

"I did not know that that's great!" She nodded and made a face as if understanding my reason for coming was not to talk about her children's educational accomplishments.

"You remember where Lauren's office is, right?"

I nodded as she buzzed me in, "It was good seeing you, Gayle!" I walked past the other occupant of the desk. He had not interrupted our conversation, he only stopped typing when Gayle buzzed me in, he glanced up as I was passing. He looked like a young forty or late thirties. His hair was brown. He sported a little stubble but was a nice-enough looking guy. He wore nurse scrubs; I assume he was helping Gayle with admittance to the ER. It gets crazy around spring break. I walked through the buzzing door and into the brightly lit corridor.

Lauren's office was located a few halls down away from the main nursing station and patient rooms. I leaned into her door frame. Her desk had a small pile of files to the left of the phone. She was typing quickly as I leaned. She glanced up and pointed to a guest chair, "Give me three minutes." And continue her fury of typing.

She had her hair pulled back in a twist. Her shirt was cleanly pressed, but she had folded her sleeves up to help with the heatwave. Her office was small. There were a few plants sitting in her window, a wall of files, and framed pictures of Lennon and Taylor on her desk. Her degrees and clinical certifications were neatly lined in a grid on the wall. Despite it being a sterile white concrete block wall room, her small touches warmed it up.

"Okay, are you ready?" She was already standing up and

grabbing her purse. She flipped her screen off and the light as we were leaving, she locked her door and led the way. We were walking away from the ER to the staff parking deck. She was chattering on about work and apologizing for making me wait. We made our way to the restaurant chatting about work and the boys.

"Taylor is actually making really good progress on the potty training!" We had already ordered our first three rolls.

"That's great, I assume he is no longer pooping on the floor." I smiled at the memory from a few weeks ago.

"That was one time, and had Lennon not called you, you would be none the wiser! David and I think he might be ready for big boy underwear in the next few weeks. At least during the day, bless him, so far he has no bladder control at night." Our rolls arrived. I took a few bites and continued our conversation thickly.

"So, what's going on with you? Are you still seeing that Nathan guy? Thomas said he was nice." I had forgotten Thomas met Nathan. I shook my head. "No, Nathan and I are just friends."

"Uh-huh. Thomas said he acted like there may be something more going on." I rolled my eyes.

"Thomas was high on anti-malarial medication. Nathan is just a sparring partner."

"I think he wants to be more than that." Lauren was eyeing me suspiciously.

I shrugged, "He can want all he wants, I am not interested in a relationship with him."

Her face softened, her forehead creased, "It's okay to date someone else, you know. John would want you to move on."

Ugh, I hated this talk, "I am moving on. I stopped lighting a candle at his shrine weeks ago."

She scoffed and rolled her eyes, "I'm serious Ro, it has been three years. When are you going to allow yourself to live again?" Her face looked absolutely sincere. I tried not to focus on the anger that was giving me indigestion from the conversation that I did not want to have. Or it could be the nine sushi rolls.

I sighed, "Listen, I appreciate your concern, and I have really started to move on." Her eyes narrowed again, "Really, I have. I went out on a date with Nathan, so I can tell you honestly, we are just friends. I understand for the past few years I have been practically asexual, but I *may* have met someone." I gushed the last part.

"I knew you had something going on with Nathan." She looked triumphant and she pumped her fist. I rolled my eyes again and shook my head, "It's *not* Nathan. It's someone else, it is kind of new. He gets me. He understands me. I just don't want to talk about it because..." I stopped and crinkled my nose, "I don't think he likes me like that."

"But you like *him*, like that." It should have been a question, but Lauren knew me too well.

"How did you meet?" I cringed and shook my head, "Too long of a story." She flared her nostrils but accepted that I did not want to discuss how Beck was introduced into my life.

"I think you are wrong." She said finally. I was forcing another piece of sushi down my protesting throat, "About what?" My mouth was full and sounded closer to "baaa whhaaa"

"I think he does like you like that because he would be crazy, blind, and stupid if he did not. And my Ro does not put up with crazy, blind, and stupid." I smiled to myself.

"He's pretty cryptic, Lo." I started.

"Cryptic is the new mysterious. He likes you. You just

need to figure out what you are going to do about it."

I bit my lip. I was trying to stop myself from adding another piece down my stuffed throat. I nodded in response. It was probably the safest thing to do.

"Listen, David wants to have a low country boil this weekend. Invite your guy! Let me get a read on him. I am sure I am right!" It was tempting to have someone attempt to decipher the cryptic comments and controlled motions.

"I will think about it," I said finally.

"Fine, I will accept that for now." Lauren looked at her watch, "I need to get back, are you done, or should I brush up on my knowledge of the Heimlich?" Ha. Ha.

"I am ready," I said as I pushed my nearly empty plate away. There was only one lonely piece left.

The ride back was quiet. My stomach ached from eating too much. She dropped me off at the visitor's parking deck. I waved goodbye and huffed up the flights of stairs that led to my car.

Traffic was light, between the rushes, my sweet spot. I stopped by work for a little bit to catch up on a few more emails.

I checked my surroundings before I made my way over to Leslie's condo. It was overlooking Infinity, so I did not want any prying eyes seeing me go into my secret lair. I needed to deposit my wig and select a fresh look-alike wig, a fresh pair of contacts, and charge up the taser that I had not used. I realized my go-bag needed a refresh. I grabbed a few pairs of black tactical pants, a knife, a few tanks. I slid the new wig and contacts on the top. I checked a few more things and headed back to Glendora.

I felt restless when I got home. I still had the nagging feeling that I was forgetting something. I felt like the link between the Triple S victims was right at the cusp of my brain, but it was too stubborn to fall into place.

I stared at my case notes. I reviewed my failed suspect attempts. Gentry Jackson was a tired bakery worker working ungodly hours with no downtime to do anything but rest. His delivery route matched the victim's cities, but nothing else.

Scott Pickens had so much promise. He had the means, the connection to two of the victims, and was in the proximity of all the abductions. Problem was, he was nowhere near Yorba Linda when Lisa Henderson's body was discovered. He also did not have one building secluded enough that could house up to three women and muffled any cries for help.

I stared at my matrixes of industries that overlapped the cities. Nothing made sense. I could not draw one connection that linked all the women. I slammed my laptop shut and pushed away the composition book.

I paced the house for something to do. I was still restless. My indigestion and the pacing were making me queasy. I fished through my cabinet for some antacids, chewed their chalky exterior, and ruminated on the possibilities. Nothing came to mind. Since my mind was already empty of any useful thought, I decided maybe to rid my mind of the rest of the thoughts that were hoping for inspiration in the quiet.

I selected my favorite Zen music and tried to meditate. Or at least practice mindfulness. Hadn't Beck implied I needed to meditate more? I was hoping for a miracle. Breathing deeply trying to "focus my breath". In and out, allowing my mind to empty. It was stubborn. It kept reminding me that Kelly Parker was running out of time. I gave up and slumped backwards. I slid my elbow to cover my eyes from the afternoon light that was streaming into my house.

I woke up to a blaring noise to my left. I felt groggy and confused. I was still slumped on the floor with my arm draped over my face, but the light had shifted from afternoon bright to early evening warm glow. The blaring noise happened again. I realized it was my phone. I looked down at it. David was calling. I mentally sighed, Lauren was sending the big guns to convince me to invite Beck for dinner. I ignored it and stood up. I was almost in the kitchen when he called again. Lauren had probably told him to keep calling. I ignored it. I really did not want to talk about Beck and the thought of asking him over to my sister's for dinner felt odd. Juvenile even. He called again.

"Tell Lauren I have not decided about inviting him over for your low country boil!"

"Caroline?" David's voice sounded tense. It snapped me out of my snooty mood.

"David, what's wrong?"

"When was the last time you talked to Lauren?" His voice sounded desperate, like he had been crying.

"I had lunch with her today."

"When?!" He interrupted with a plea in his voice.

"She dropped me off at my car around 2:15pm, Why?"

"Shit, oh fuck."

Anxiety and dread started to fill me, "What is going on David?"

"She did not go back to work." His voice was a forced whisper. He was holding back emotions, trying to stay focused on the conversation.

"What are you talking about? David, she dropped me off at my car at 2:15pm. It's a three-minute drive to the staff parking lot. Why wouldn't she go back to work?"

"She parked; her car is there. She is not."

I was trying to catch up, processing what he was saying. "What do you mean, 'she is not there'? She has to be there!"

His voice cracked and he sobbed, but reigned his emotions back, "No, security footage shows her parking and walking to the hospital, but she disappears between camera feeds."

I was clutching my phone so hard my knuckles had turned white and were protesting at my grip.

"What are you saying, David?" I was taking calming breaths.

He sobbed, "She missed her 2:30 appointment with her boss. She missed another appointment at 4pm. Her boss got worried and started asking around. You know Lauren, she would never miss an appointment, let alone two. Gayle, the receptionist, said you stopped by. Lauren's boss pulled the video feed to verify. They saw her drop you off, but she's.... she's..." He started sobbing.

"David, what are you saying?" My mind was spinning, I knew what he was saying. I did not want my brain to be right.

"The police think he took her." He said between sobs.

"Who took her, David?" I was desperate, I may have been yelling into the phone.

"The Triple S." He gasped.

Chapter 23

March 10

I could not process what David was saying, my head was filled with a buzzing noise. What did he mean "gone"? Why Lauren? I did not want to accept that she had been abducted like so many before her. The circumstances were the same as the Snatch, Stash, and Slash killer. The police even confirmed it.

Guilt overtook me. I had just seen her. I was the last person to see her. She was perfect and well hours ago. It seemed impossible that this could be happening, but it was. I had tapped into the hospital security footage. I watched frame by frame. In one, gone the next. I watched it over and over again. Nothing stood out. I pulled out the matrix and tried to fit Lauren's work into the grids. Nothing made sense, if anything, it further skewed connections I had made with Gentry and Scott.

I was speeding West on the 210 freeway passing slow-moving drivers on the shoulder. I prayed I would not be pulled over, but I needed to rush to the other side of town. Time was ticking by and all the women were abducted, starved until they weighed 115lbs, and finally, when they were too weak to fight, they were brutalized and cast out. I could not allow that fate for my sister. She was too good to be snuffed out in such a horrifying way, and what of David, Taylor, and Lennon? I needed to find Lauren.

I screeched my tires to a stop in front of the Banjo and ran inside. The giant proprietor blocked the entryway. He was easily 6'7, outweighed me by at least 140lbs. I had seen him before. The first time with Chris Cunningham. He had nearly pulled my arm out of the socket, pulling me into him to shake his hand. The second time was only a week ago, and I had been wearing my wig and donning my alter ego.

"Hey, Ginger Dumpling, what are you in a hurry for?" He asked while his thumbs were stuck in his belt loops. I went to move past, but he grabbed my arm. His hand was large, his thumb easily wrapped around my upper arm, and was resting on his knuckles, holding firmly.

"I know our food is good ginger, but you gotta wait your turn." He nodded towards the 15 people waiting for a table. I shook my arm out of his iron tight grasp, "I'm not here to eat, I need your Chef."

"We are pretty busy now, pretty lady, why don't you leave him a message, and I will get it to him." He went behind the hostess stand to grab something to write with, I took the opportunity and rushed past him. I pushed the kitchen door open and swung my head wildly around trying to find my bearings.

The kitchen was immaculate, line cooks chopping wildly, a din of pans clinging together, and orders being barked out. A few line cooks glanced up confused in my direction. The back door was propped open, I could see the outline of a commercial-grade meat smoker. The air smelled of hickory. Before I could step further into the kitchen a bang came from behind. Before I could turn around an ironclad grip around my rib cage threatened to suffocate me, "Little lady you can't be back here." The proprietor had picked me off the ground and was carrying me out.

I thrashed around wildly, "I need him, I need to talk to Beck." I threw my head back and clipped him in the jaw. I felt him tighten his grip, further restraining my breathing. I reached back and searched blindly for his eye. I did not want to hurt him, I just wanted him to let me go. I found what I was looking for and poked him hard. He dropped me almost instantly. He howled with pain, "Dang girl, why did you do that?"

"Caroline, what brings you here this evening?" The ridiculously handsome and stoic Beck appeared five feet in front of me. Had I not been dropped on the ground and straight to my butt, I would have run into his arms. I rose unsteadily to my feet, hastily brushing my backside as I stood.

"He took her! He took Lauren! Help me!" I pleaded with my eyes.

"This your girl, Beck?" The beefy proprietor let out a loud laugh, "She's feisty."

Oh God, not this again. I had barely made it through dinner without the workers of Banjo parading past my table with curious glances and smiles, and I did not make one iota of a spectacle. This time, however, I was bucking people like a wild Bronco looking like a crazed lune. Beck remained immobile as if he had not heard a word.

"Why didn't you tell me you were his girl?" The proprietor, Richard, turned to me and pat some rogue dust off my back. *Give it a rest with the "girl" comments.* The line cooks had stopped chopping. A few waiters were standing in the doorway to the kitchen with their mouths slightly agape.

"I need your help, Beck! You owe me!" I yelled and lunged at him. I don't know why I said that he owed me. He did not owe me anything. Actually, the scales of saving each other were even. They were possibly tipped in his direction because he never truly needed saving.

Before I could do anything, he reached out and grabbed both of my arms, pinning them to my sides. His grip was firm, but he was not trying to restrain me. "Calm down." He was not yelling, he was asking me politely, quietly. It reminded me of my audience that was forming in salivating circles around my exit points. He stared into my eyes for silent seconds. He chaffed my arms a few times, I watched his nostrils flare as he thought. He released me and passed me his keys, "Go to my house, I will be there in an hour."

I took my dismissal by stumbling out of the kitchen and running through the restaurant and back into the safe haven of my car. Silent faces turned in my direction as I rushed past them and away from the kitchen. I could feel hot tears burning in my eyes as I drove away. I slowed down to a safer pace and made my way into Beck's loft. It was exactly as I had remembered it from the last time I was here, at least this time I was an invited guest. I cringed; actually, last time I had been here he had saved me from Clint Region. I shook my head, trying to focus on what I was going to do next.

I paced from his kitchen to his low sofa until my legs felt like lead weights. I sat at the edge of the couch, breathing fast shallow breaths, my hands were shaking uncontrollably. I had to calm down. My hysterics were not helping Lauren. My mind felt hazy and erratic. I forced a deep breath into my lungs, it cleared my head for a moment. I forced another lung full of air. *Calm down.* I slid off the sofa on the floor and forced myself to sit quietly taking deep breaths. I closed my eyes and tried to empty my mind. Where I was unsuccessful hours before, I was finally able to focus on my breathing.

I am not sure how long I sat there, but I became aware I was not alone when I felt the air shift next to me. I looked over to see Beck sitting quietly, his face looked serene and calm. His eyes, on the other hand, were smoldering mercury at me, a burning in the pit of my stomach erupted.

"What is it you need me to do?" His voice was soft. I shook my head to release myself from the trance of his sex appeal. *Bed me and help me save my sister.* It was possibly the worst timing ever for my hormones to be reminding me constantly about my intense attraction to Beck.

"Lauren has been taken. It's him I know it." My voice was calm, but a tear breached and slid down my face.

He reached over and palmed my cheek, thumbing away the rogue tear, "Who took Lauren?" His tone was equally as calming.

"What's the stupid moniker the media gave him? The Triple S." Another tear slid down. He wiped it again. I could not help myself, I turned into his palm feeling secure. His palm was hot against my cheek, light calluses rubbed against my skin.

"How can I help?" His eyes were soft but pleading.

I shrugged and he dropped his hand. He pulled me off the floor and sat me on the sofa. "I'm stuck. I have been coming up empty for weeks. The evidence is practically non-existent. I chased down a few leads, nothing but innocent bystanders." I took another breath to steady myself.

"Show me what you have so far."

I blindly reached into my bag that had fallen off the sofa. I pulled the composition book out and handed it to him. He thumbed the volume in silence. I grabbed my laptop and started to stare at my own digital trail trying to make sense of it.

"Interesting theory about the timing of their deaths tied to weight. I was wondering what your thoughts were since he appeared to be off his schedule." He narrowed his eyes at the notes again before flipping to the last page.

"Are you certain these are all the victims?" I gaped at him, "My research is thorough." I almost felt offended.

He just shook his head, "I do not mean your local victims. It seems unlikely this is the first series of its kind. They are too closely spaced together. Serial killers start slower than this."

I think I stopped breathing as I realized my short-sighted findings. Of course, they started slowly. They normally did it once and waited a while for the next. Allowing himself to relive the moments until he wanted to recreate new memories. Typically, serials would increase their crimes over years.

I typed out the gruesome details into a browser. The current victims were the first nine pages of results. Finally, on page ten I found more small mentions of similar disappearances and injuries. Dottie Manard from Dallas, Texas abducted, held for 19 days and her body was discarded in the woods behind her home. She was starved, raped, and disemboweled. At the time of her death, she weighed 115lbs. Her death has been unsolved for two years. My heart quickened. Page twelve gave me another victim, Kendra Lewis, Atlanta, Georgia, same details in torture and death, crime left unsolved for three years.

I grabbed the composition book from Beck and began creating profiles for the new victims. I feverishly typed to find out about their short lives. Beck went into the kitchen and made tea. He passed me the hot beverage and left me quietly working while he went into his bedroom. He emerged a few minutes later carrying his own laptop and sat next to me. He glanced over at my computer. I had pulled up Dottie Manard's social media pages, making notes on her life.

Beck pulled up Kendra Lewis's profiles and quietly took notes on his own loose sheet of paper. After fifteen minutes we exchanged notes and reread the findings, grasping at straws to find any common thread.

"Hospitals," I murmured to myself, one eyebrow arched, and a smile played in one corner of Beck's face.

"Three of the victims worked at a hospital." I spread out the information and circled the three separate profiles. "Lauren works at Cedars Sinai, Kendra Lewis was a paramedic for Grady Memorial, Dottie Manard was a NICU nurse at Medical City in Dallas."

I shuffled through more papers looking for my confirmed hunch. I pulled out the autopsy report for Bobbi King.

"Look, she broke her arm approximately two years ago." I checked the closest emergency room from King's address and noted Southern California Hospital.

"We need to see if any of the other victims have been in the hospital over the past three years," Beck murmured to himself and began typing with renewed fervor. He passed me the local hospitals to each of the victims, "Here, confirm our theory." He stood up and walked back into the kitchen.

"What are you doing?"

"Making you food, concentrate."

I began breaking into the first hospital's patient portal. It took me 15 minutes to discover Flora Sanchez had visited Riverside Community six months prior with the flu. I marked it down.

Beck passed me a bowl with rice and chicken, "Eat." It smelled delicious. I felt guilty stopping when I was actually onto something. I balanced the bowl next to the laptop, shoveling bites in as I continued to work on my computer. Beck looked over my shoulder and made notes of his own.

"Lisa Henderson was hospitalized at Placentia Linda a year ago for a severe allergic reaction to shellfish."

"Kelly Parker was in a car accident three months ago; she went to Saddleback Memorial." Beck showed me his laptop screen.

We stared at each other in the understanding we had found a commonality in all the victims.

"He's a traveling doctor, like Doctors Without Borders." I contemplated calling Thomas, but he was in Haiti. It was past midnight in his time zone.

Beck shook his head, "Don't doctors have contracts longer than three months?" He had a point, Doctors without Borders had no reason to stop in Dana Point, Dallas, or Atlanta.

"Then what?" I threw my hands in the air and began pacing.

The thought struck me like a lightning strike, "Don't hospitals employ traveling nurses?"

"We need staff rosters for each hospital during each victim's visit. Check the staff roster for the employees around the time of their abduction or injuries. If there is anyone on the list that makes three hits, it's the miscreant." Beck was not looking at me but was staring off at the wall housing his books, his eyes squinted in concentration.

It was past midnight when we found one name that was employed at each hospital over the past three years, Eric Manly. He was 38 years old, had been a traveling nurse for eight years. He was orphaned at seven and lived in foster homes until he aged out of the system at 18. He had one vehicle registered in his name, a white Prius. I stared at the Cedars photo of his employee badge.

"He was there," I murmured.

Beck leaned over to get in front of me, "Who was where?"

I pointed at Manly's picture, "He was at the registration desk when I visited Lauren. He was there." I felt like the last bit of oxygen in the world had escaped my lungs. He was three feet away from me. I was completely unaware of his intentions for Lauren. I was completely unaware of how closely I had come to the murderer I had been searching for. Anger pulsed through me.

"Let's get the fucker." I stood up and went for the door.

Beck grabbed my hand and pulled me back to the sofa, "Sorumeito, you must stop and think."

I jerked my head in his direction and tugged my hand from his grasp.

"What did you call me?" I stared at him trying to interpret his new nickname for me.

"It means stubborn woman." He almost smiled at me.

I scoffed. I was not being stubborn. I was right, we needed to get him. We needed to stop him. We needed to... I wanted to kill him.

"I'm not being stubborn; we do not have *time*!" I was trying to breathe calmly and shake my mind away from killing him.

"We have two days before the next victim is brutalized and fourteen days before your sister is touched according to your theory. If we storm in there and make one mistake, he could kill them all. If we plan this, if we are careful, we can save more than just your sister."

"I have a plan! I'm going to stab him in the femur and watch him bleed to death." My chest was heaving in anger now. My vision was blurred in red at Beck trying to stop me. Why had I come to him in the first place? I thought he was going to help me, not hold me back.

"That action would make no sense. You do not know where these women are being held. Even if you did manage to kill him, you would seal their fates to starve and die of hypovolemic shock. Surely you wish better for your sister?" His voice was gentle but seeking reason. He had a point. I had no idea where he could be stashing the women. I had no idea if there were devices that triggered if someone besides him approached. I shivered at the thought of my sister being strapped down with explosives. Of course, that was a dramatic train of thought, and I could not put anything past this guy. He was a certifiable psychopath.

"Then what do you suggest?" I bit back bitterly.

"We plan."

I rolled my eyes. It was always his suggestion. I doubted there was any action he took that he had not premeditated a hundred times before finally pulling the trigger. I took a deep breath and pulled my computer back into my lap.

We found his apartment, his work schedule, and his bank statements. I checked for properties in his name. Nothing came up. He was a kid that came from nothing, graduated on a full-ride scholarship to UCLA. He had been a nurse since he was 24. He became a traveling nurse when he turned 30. He had been traveling to different cities for eight years. I was tempted to check the other cities for missing persons, but I needed to stay present at our goal.

He had Lauren. He had been torturing Kelly Parker, starving her, for eighteen days. Surely, she was aware of Lisa Henderson and Flora Sanchez being tortured and eventually snuffed out. I imagined this poor woman, whose eyes had been so light with wonder, dimmed with the understanding that she was going to die in a few days.

We made a plan. We needed to get a tracker on Eric's car. We needed to get into his apartment. I felt obligated to prove it was him. I had traveled down the rabbit hole twice already convinced I had found the Triple S but came back empty. I was going to find proof before Kelly Parker appeared. I was going to save them both. I had to.

Chapter 24

March 11

At some point, around 2am, I fell asleep laying my head on Beck's shoulder. I was barely disturbed in my sleep when he lifted me and brought me to the bed. I vaguely remember nestling my head into his warm chest as he carried me. I woke up at 8am, both of my arms were extended, and I was clinging to his muscly arm. He was laying on his back, staring at the wood-lined ceiling, probably waiting for me to release my death grip. I was relieved that he had not shunned himself to his couch again. Although, my death grip may have been the reason.

"Sorry." I released his arm, embarrassed by my neediness. Even my subconscious had given up on not wanting him in my life. I think I clung to him in hopes that he would not disappear like he always seemed to do. He would disappear for days at a time. If there was any time in my whole life, I needed someone, it was now. And here was someone that was everything I wanted, and I knew he did not want me like that. I ignored the pity that was growing in my stomach from the constant rejection.

He turned his head, his silver eyes looked amused, something burned deeply in my gut. "Why did you apologize?"

I rolled onto my back, breaking the eye contact, shrugging, "I was emotional last night. I am sorry I yelled at you. And I'm sorry I clung to your arm; it must have been uncomfortable for you."

He rolled onto his side, looking over at my profile, "Do you want me to feel uncomfortable around you?" He smoothed hair from my eyes and tucked it behind my ear. I did not have room in my brain to try to figure out this man. He had basically rejected me so many times before, and now when my sister's life lays in the balance; when we finally broke the case; when we finally had a plan; was he coming on to me? No, it was wishful thinking. I was always wishful thinking when it came to Beck.

I sat up and cleared my throat to break the silence, "I need to change my clothes, take a shower." He looked thoughtfully at me. "I have a go-bag in my car, just give me a minute." I stood up, stretched, and walked briskly out of his loft. The cool morning air was refreshing, clearing my mind from the guttural desires. I needed to get my head together. Lauren needed me to focus.

When I reached my car, I resisted the urge to drive off, but the reality was, I needed help and his loft was only 20 minutes from Cedars. It made his home the ideal place to wait until Eric Manly would get off work. His shift started two hours ago. He worked three 12-hour shifts and had four days off. Today was day two of his scheduled block. I grabbed my go-bag from the trunk and proceeded back into the loft.

I walked straight into the bedroom to drop my bag in the closet, out of the way. As I walked into the bedroom, the bathroom door opened. I looked over to the movement and was greeted by Beck, naked drying his face with a towel. His abs were perfectly planed, sharp definition separating each muscle. My eyes followed the path of water dripping down his v-cut to see his well-proportioned plum-colored member listing to the left. I jerked my eyes up as he dropped the towel down to wrap around his waist.

"S-sorry." I turned on my heel and went into the kitchen. Panicked and embarrassed I grabbed his kettle and started making tea. He came out less than two minutes later wearing loose linen drawstring pants. His hair was pulled up in a knot, his abs were still damp.

"I'll just..." I pointed to the bathroom, but I could not

meet his eyes. I was too embarrassed to look at him. And it's not like I had not seen him naked; I accidently saw him naked through the security footage in my condo. The security footage was nothing to seeing him live and in person. And the image of his perfect body was bringing my guttural desires back to the forefront.

I turned the cold water on, trying to wake up and douse the fire in my belly. We had a long day of waiting. I still needed to try to research any possible places Manly was renting short term. I needed to stay distraction-free. And Beck's well-proportioned body was definitely a distraction. I stood under the cold water until my teeth chattered. I stepped out of the bathroom to the smell of breakfast being made. I pulled on my black tank and black boy shorts. I finger-combed my hair and pulled it up in a messy wet bun. I did not bother putting on a stitch of makeup, he had made it clear he was not attracted to me.

When I had stalled long enough, I silently walked into the kitchen. He was pouring eggs into the center of a plate. Sliced tomatoes with a pesto dressing were on the right, a piece of sourdough toast was on the left. He had turned away from me to put the pan into the sink and washed his knife. His bare back emphasized his broad shoulders and narrow waist. His drawstring pants hung low. The contours of his butt made me feel like I was on fire despite the goosebumps my arms sported. I grabbed my plate and sat on one of the stools.

I focused on the food. Everything was delicious. I kept my eyes down when he sat next to me.

We sat in silence. I did not want to look at him while he wore only a drawstring pair of pants, it was too tempting to embarrass myself. I could feel the heat of his bare arm near mine.

"Are you cold?" His body was still facing the counter, but I could see from the corner of my eye he had canted his head in my direction. He was looking at my arms; they were still covered in goosebumps from my cold shower. I shivered as I pulled my arm down to rest in my lap, out of his eye's line of sight. He watched my arm stop and rest on my legs with an almost tender look in his eye before he gently pulled my arm from my lap and into his warm hands. He rubbed my arm from shoulder to elbow warming my skin with each pass.

"Thank you," I shrugged my arm out of his grasp, still unable to look him in the eye. He gently spun my stool towards him, my legs were tucked between his. I watched him lift one hand gently as he pointed my chin up to look at him.

"Have I upset you?" His eyes looked like melting ice as he stared into mine. I tried to turn my head back, but he cupped my cheeks in each hand. He thumbed my bottom lip, "I did not mean to upset you."

I licked my lips hopeful to taste the empty trail his thumb left behind. He watched me intently, "You did not upset me. I'm embarrassed. I feel like I can't control my emotions around you." I shrugged and averted my eyes.

"Anger is normal under these circumstances, there is nothing to be embarrassed about." He leaned in a little closer. My eyes drifted back to his, I bit my lip. "Unless you feel something other than anger, then I would say that is normal as well." *What does that mean?*

Oh God, he was so close, his lips only two inches from mine. I needed to resist the urge to taste him. I doubted he would think it was normal for me to want to experience every sizable inch of him. I shouldn't be feeling this when my sister was being held by a psychotic killer. Guilt swarmed my eyes, but the realization that I wanted him in a way I did not think possible again made a tear drop. I hated feeling vulnerable, I had shut off that part of me for so long. And it's just my luck I am feeling this carnal desire, this gratitude that he is good, this emotion squeezing my heart, and it's wasted on a man who had shown no signs of reciprocation. *Unrequited love is a bitch.*

I took a steadying breath, but it quivered and swallowed back my desire.

"What would be normal?" My voice was barely more than a whisper, but I could still hear the tremble. I heard a soft chuckle that sent a thrill through me. He thumbed my bottom lip two more passes and released my face. His hands dropped as his eyes released their hold on me. I sighed in frustration at his non-verbal answer. I swung my legs around knocking his as I went and walked briskly away. I needed to be alone to deal with my own thoughts and squash this desire to be around him for good.

He caught my hand before I reached the doorway. He spun me towards him before my reflexes could react, I blame it on my saturated hormones. His hands found my waist as my hips settled against his thighs. I looked up to him as he bent his face down to be level with mine. "What are *you* feeling, Caroline?"

I bit my lip and looked away. He moved my face back to his, "what are you feeling?" His tone was softer now. His Zen resolve was doing voodoo to my normally controlled responses, "rejected." I winced as I heard my own words breach my ears. Blush flooded my cheeks.

"How have I rejected you?" His eyes and tone were clear, I think I snorted.

"How can I reject you when no invitation has been presented." He tilted his head to me.

My jaw dropped.

My mind reeled at his statement for a split second. Who would have thought a ninja assassin would be concerned with sober consent. I blinked up at him. His face was unreadable, but he released his hold on my waist and pulled away. The distance created felt painful and empty. I reached out to him to close the gap; his expression almost looked hopeful. He strode forward and wrapped his hand around my neck and pulled me in to kiss him.

My stomach burst into fireworks as I kissed the man I desired. His bare chest felt hot against my chest. Despite the heat, my nipples budded. My arms wrapped around his neck as my legs wrapped around his waist bringing myself level with his face. One hand was holding my head, the other was gripping my butt. He was pulling me into him. I felt him walk and he gently sat me on the stainless-steel counter. It was cold against my skin; I stifled a shiver as I tasted his tongue.

A strap of my tank fell off my shoulder. He tipped his head to kiss my bare shoulder. I knotted my hands into his silky hair. He kissed a trail to my neck and slipped the other strap down. He continued to kiss my other bare shoulder. My chest was heaving as I was gasping, breathing in each pleasurable scent of him against me. He had moved his lips back to my clavicle, working his way to my chest. When he reached the crest of my breast my whole body was vibrating.

At least at first, I thought I was vibrating. It took me a few seconds to realize the vibrating was my phone that was clattering next to me on the counter. I looked down; it was David calling. I think I growled and threw my head back in frustration. Beck looked up confused and saw my phone in hand. He raised an eyebrow, "Are you going to get that?"

I took a deep breath and nodded as I answered the phone.

"David, what's going on?"

I could hear the tired emotion in his voice, "Police just left."

I held my breath fearing the worst, "They think it's the Triple S that has her." He broke down in sobs.

"David, you have to calm down. You have to be strong for Taylor and Lennon. Take a breath. We will figure this out." I tried to be calming, but we had shared fears.

"How can you say that? You read the news more than anyone I know. I know Lauren confides in you over the horrors of her job." His sobs made the last part hard to understand. I felt helpless in his sorrow. "Sick and twisted people share our world, Ro! A sick and twisted man took our Lauren."

"David, you have to trust me. She will be fine." I forced my tone to stay positive. His response was a loud moan like an injured animal.

"David, listen. I have a plan. I'm going to find her. I'm going to bring her home."

He gulped air, "Whatever your plan is, take it to the police Caroline. If Lauren does not come back the boys will need you."

"David, please trust me that if I involve the police, I will have to answer too many questions. Trust me, nothing will happen to me." He began to protest, but I cut him off again. "David, I need to go. Keep your phone on you. The next time I call you, I will need you to drop what you are doing." I hung up before he could protest.

Beck had walked away and was sitting on the sofa looking through his laptop. Although I felt frustration for the interruption, it was a godsend. I needed to focus.

"I need to get a GPS tracker on Manly's car."

He nodded in understanding. I walked to the bedroom to get dressed. I slipped on my black tactical pants. They were form-fitting but had stretch that allowed movements freely. Beck joined me in the bedroom a few minutes later to select a shirt for himself.

I slipped my light brown wig on and donned the muddy brown contacts; chunky glasses finished the look. Beck shook his head smiling, but he did not say anything. "I need you to drive me there. I don't have Leslie's car." He nodded silently as he buttoned his shirt closed.

I pulled up the garage security footage to verify what floor in the parking deck Eric Manly had parked his car. Fortunately, he was on time for work, so it did not take long to find him in the footage and follow his progress through the floors. "He's parked on the fourth floor next to the stairs."

Twenty minutes later we were parking in the visitor lot. The ride had been silent. I was collecting my thoughts. It went back and forth between my desire to bring Lauren home safely, my main concern. But I also kept thinking about the kiss, what it could possibly mean.

He turned off his car and turned towards me, breaking the silence, "I want you to stay in the car. I will go and install the GPS tracker."

I shook my head emphatically. "I can't ask you to do that."

He cupped my cheek with his hand tenderly, "It was worth asking, but I am coming with you." I nodded once as I unbuckled. To be honest, I was hoping he would go with me. I did not want to chance that Eric would take a lunch break away from the hospital. If he happened to be walking to his car while I was near... I shuttered. I would surely kill him, and Beck was right, we needed him alive to show us where he kept his victims.

The walk to the other side of the hospital campus seemed to take forever. Beck held my hand. I assume it was so we would blend in with anyone paying attention to random hospital patrons.

We reached the fourth floor, "Go up to the fifth floor, head across to the elevators. I will meet you in the elevator." Beck said as he let go of my hand. I tried to protest, but he slid the small tracker out of my pocket and slipped through the door. I took the steps to the fifth floor two at a time. I rushed across the deck and mashed the down button. It felt like an eternity, but it was probably 30 seconds. The elevator was empty. I jammed the 4th-floor button and "door close" button.

Soothing jazz played lightly in the background. It was odd listening to something so smooth when my heart was beating frantically off its rhythm. The elevator door slid open, Beck was smiling and walked into the opposite corner. He stole a couple glances at me but said nothing. The elevator lurched and settled on the ground floor. We had already queued next to each other. The door slid open and Eric Manly was waiting to get in. Beck threw his arm around me and kissed my mouth as we passed Eric. Another diversion tactic. Or maybe he worried I would do something, like kill Eric. Eric selected his floor and the door binged close before Beck released me.

"Be patient. The tracker is on his car, if you confront him, there will be consequences." I tried to protest, but he firmly pulled me along. We made it back to his car in record time. He kept tugging at my arm to slow me down. "If you start running through a medical campus it will bring undue attention, calm down Sorumeito."

Stubborn woman, I rolled my eyes. He clicked his fob and I launched myself into the passenger seat. "We have to hurry. I have not synced the tracker on my phone!" Huge stupid oversight on my part, I began berating myself internally. Twenty-five minutes later Beck was unlocking his door. My hands were shaking in anticipation, worry, anxiety, anger.

I logged into the tracker to see Eric leaving a location about a mile away from the hospital. I pulled up the address he was leaving, In and Out. I sighed in frustration. He was just going to lunch. My own stomach rumbled. Beck might be a mind reader because it was about then that he handed me a sandwich. I ate quickly and kept my eyes on the tracker notification.

"We have five hours before he gets off work, maybe you should rest." Beck was sitting next to me; his tone was gentle.

I shook my head, "No, we have five hours. I am going to go to his home." He shook his head, I interrupted, "They could be there! This can all be over in an hour!"

He sat silently waiting for me to finish my tirade, "I do not think they will be there, Caroline. Think about it, his apartment is small and surrounded on all sides with neighbors. I doubt he would be able to bring his victims in undetected and then torture them without his neighbors hearing a noise." His reasoning was sound.

I stood up, "I have to check it off my list. I have to verify it is him. We don't have time to be chasing the wrong guy." I tapped my watch, "If you do not want to come, that's fine. I have been doing this a long time without any help." I was feeling defiant.

He took a deep breath through his nose and closed his eyes, "Of course, I understand. Your judgment is clouded by the love you have for your sister. Where does he live?" When he opened his eyes, they looked like liquid mercury, but his expression was unreadable.

Thirty-five minutes later we were idling in front of a series of apartment buildings off of Hollywood Boulevard. They all had an entry gate and an underground parking deck. Street parking was available, but I imagine at night it would be extremely limited. We waited until we saw someone go in. "Two-Four-Nine-Zero" I mumbled to myself. I rechecked the fire escape plan I found online for Eric Manly's apartment and nodded to myself as Beck cut the engine. "Check his tracker," Beck suggested. "He's still at work," I said after a few minutes.

We closed our doors in unison, proceeded to the gate, punched the numbers in, and were thankfully granted access. We walked into an entry area where the tenant's mailboxes lined one wall. Straight ahead there was a large courtyard with a fountain in the center, seating areas around it. The apartments lined the courtyard, the sun was shining into the fountain's water casting glares all around.

We walked up the two flights and walked past his apartment. Like all the apartments, it had a large window facing the courtyard. Old vertical blinds were shut across the opening leaving nothing to be seen from the outside. We did a loop around the floor, waiting for a young woman to lock up her own apartment and proceed towards the mailboxes. When all was clear we walked over to the door, Beck was ready with a small silver tool. He was so fast it was like he was unlocking the door with a key. We slipped in and latched the lock behind us.

The apartment was hot and stuffy. No air conditioning. It was a small space. A living room and dining room attached to a kitchen the size of a hallway. The bathroom was four foot by five feet. The bedroom was about ten by ten feet. A pile of dirty clothes was in the closet, but the rest of the apartment was clean. There was no place for him to keep anyone there, Beck was right. The desire to find proof it was Manly pushed me to keep going.

I walked back out to the living room, Beck was on his knees looking through the small assortment of books and DVDs. He was carefully pulling each off the shelf and replacing it. I noticed he had put gloves on while I was in the bedroom. He turned to me, "Did you touch anything in there?" I shook my head as he passed me a pair of gloves for me to don. "Have you found anything?" I whispered to him.

He shook his head. I went back into the bedroom, carefully pulling the mattress up from the frame to see if he kept anything hidden there. Nothing. I opened the small bedside table. It was full of condoms, tissue, and lotion. *Yuck.* I walked back over to the closet. It looked like hiking clothes, dark in color, a little mud on the edge of the cuff of the jeans. A muddy pair of hiking boots were tucked under the bed.

My mind began ticking along, he is keeping them in a secluded place he has to hike to, I concluded. I walked over to his dresser and opened the bottom drawer first. I heard that burglars start at the bottom of a set of drawers and proceed up, saving time from having to close each one. I did not want to throw his items about, I gently pushed aside neatly folded pants. Nothing. The next drawer up was color-coded folded t-shirts. The next drawer up was socks and underwear, all folded in the Kondo Mari method. The top drawer was similar to the rest but held medical scrubs. The top of his dresser held a small wooden cross. I carefully closed each drawer one by one until I slid the bottom drawer shut. Something ever so quietly rattled. I opened and reclosed it a little harder. Another rattle.

Beck was standing in the doorway, apparently, he had heard the rattle too. I took a picture of the drawer so I would be able to replace everything exactly. One neat stack at a time, I pulled everything out. I felt around the bottom. In the back-right corner, there was a small hole. I tugged at the corner to reveal the false bottom. A small cigar box sat in the center. I slowly pulled open the hinged lid. It was a series of microfilm, and five small USB memory sticks. Beck disappeared and re-appeared holding my laptop passing it to me. As I booted up, Beck was gently holding the microfilm up to the light.

"If it is not him, he is still very disturbed." He passed me the microfilm he had just looked at. I held it up towards the window, an image of a disemboweled cat, an image of a disem-boweled dog. I handed it back before I felt my stomach lurch.

I slid the first memory stick in. It was a video file. I clicked on it and held my breath. The naked image of Dottie

Manard from Dallas tied to a bed was the first frame. I gasped and clutched my mouth. Beck removed the USB, pushed it back into the cigar box. I sat back in shock. It was him. He had Lauren. He had killed these women. And Lauren was tied to some bed, naked and tortured.

I fought the temptation to make a copy of everything in case Eric was tipped off and left, but I knew too much about those particular types of memory sticks. It would not take a talented coder to see that the images were saved to a different computer, and recently at that. It would bring too much undue attention and possibly lead the authorities to believe Eric was not acting alone. And I did not want to give the tiniest chance of a jury of his peers seeing a shadow of a doubt that he was a murdering rapist.

Item by item Beck replaced in perfect order, replacing the false bottom, and then each pair of pants. He slid the drawer shut and helped me off the floor. I felt catatonic with worry.

We were back at his loft before I said anything. "We need supplies."

Chapter 25

March 11

Beck was staring out of my Pasadena condo's window. The view was nice, looking down on the busy Colorado Blvd. It was bustling with shoppers. "Is that the famous Infinity Apothecary?" He pointed to the corner of the window. I walked over to him and looked to where he was pointing. Of course, I knew that it was, I think I was making up an excuse to be near him again. Stupid hormones. Or maybe I just felt safe around him. He did know all my secrets. Knew them and did not question or judge me.

"I don't know about famous, but it's my business, yes." I was standing next to him, my shoulder resting against his arm. He took a step away from the closeness and walked around. It was a decent size living space that was opened up to a large kitchen. A center island separated the spaces. It had two bedrooms, one by the front door, one at the rear of the condo, the "roommate plan". The room closest to the door was my office with top-of-the-line computers, surveillance equipment, disguises, and different types of weapons. The other room was set up as an actual bedroom.

"Why not live here? It is so much closer to your work?" He asked as he took a seat on the overstuffed cream sofa. I shrugged. "I like being close to my sister and nephews."

A small smile played in the corners of his lips, "But this place is so much closer to mine." I think I laughed and rolled my eyes, "Sorry you have to drive the extra fifteen miles to sneak into my home at all hours of the night."

"Let's go over the plan again," I said to change the subject. I did not want to linger on what he could mean about me wanting to live closer to him. My nerves were already destroyed, I did not need to bring my heart into the discussion about Beck.

"We wait for movement past his work and his home." Beck started.

"We can assume he is keeping them somewhere remote that he has to hike to, at least a short distance." I supplied, he nodded in agreement.

"When he gets wherever that is, we swoop in and get the girls. We take them to safety and call the police." I finished.

"You see the holes in your plan?" Beck had one eyebrow raised. Yeah, it was practically swiss cheese, but we could not go, observe, come back, and plan without action. We did not have time. At this point, we only have approximately two to three days before he touches his Kelly Parker. I nodded. Silence.

"We need food," he said finally, "call me if anything changes." He was standing in the doorway, "Don't leave without me." He stepped out and left me to my thoughts. I felt restless. I did not realize the effect Beck's presence was having on me. I felt lonely and anxious. I walked into the bedroom and pulled the treadmill out from under the bed. I figured running would at least give me something to do.

Forty-five minutes later I was running at a 30% incline, sweat cascading down when I heard someone set bags down on the counter. Considering no one but Beck knew about this place, it was safe to assume he had returned with food.

"I appreciate your dedication to fitness," Beck spoke gently behind me. "But it is also acceptable to allow your body days to rest."

I increased the incline and speed. He chuckled and left. Fifteen minutes later I was done. My hair was completely saturated, and my tank clung to me with uncomfortable suction. I stepped into the bath and turned the shower on, but at the last moment decided a bath would be better. If I could not swim tonight, at least I would take a bath and ruminate in a different type of water.

I heard a gentle knock on the door after thirty minutes of soaking. "Caroline, I have made you something to eat." I opened my eyes and stared at the door. I finally said, "I am not hungry." Ten minutes later he knocked gently again, "come in." I was resigned to the fact that he was going to make me eat, but he was going to have to tell me face to face.

He did not look surprised that I was still in the tub and definitely not surprised that I was naked. It would have been a smidge eccentric to be soaking in my own tub wearing a bathing suit. His eyes did not stray from my face. He sat down on the edge of the tub, "You must eat. You need your strength." His silver eyes were burning into mine.

"I'm plenty strong." But my tone was a little weak.

He stood up and retrieved a towel, he unfolded it. He held up the terrycloth, spanning from one hand to the other. I accepted defeat. I stood up slowly and stepped out of the tub, maintaining intense eye contact. I was trying to look seductive, but I probably looked like a half-drowned puppy. He wrapped the towel around my shoulders and held me in an embrace. His muscles were hard as he pressed against me. I could feel him rest his chin on my head. I could hear him breathing quietly. I could hear and feel everything, including the fact that he was as limp as a windsock. I stifled a sigh; doesn't that pretty much confirm it? If he isn't aroused by me naked in a tub, then he just does not find me attractive. *Perhaps he realizes this is a bad time to try anything. Or what if he is impotent?* That would be unfortunate. Another mental sigh. But he did kiss me, right? I had not imagined it. Or maybe he kissed me to distract me. Did I need to be distracted? I don't remember yelling at him. In fact, I thought we were eating breakfast. Was I remembering it wrong? No, I was frustrated with him at the time. Perhaps it was all a distraction from my clear terror that I would lose my sister.

Just because he does not want to be my boyfriend, ugh I hate that term, doesn't mean he can't be my good friend. I mean, clearly, we are good friends. He's here after all.

He released me from his embrace. I stepped into the bedroom and got dressed.

We ate in silence. He truly was an amazing chef. If I was not so full of self-loathing, I would have appreciated it more, but as it was, I was pretty deep in the pity pit.

"Have I upset you again?" He murmured. I guess he knew how to read my emotions better than I realized.

"Not really, I just keep..." He kissed my lips gently. Hmmm, that is nice, but I don't think he is trying to distract me.

"You keep what?" My head felt dizzy. It's hard going back and forth as to whether or not a guy is into you for real or just a really good friend. That kiss felt friendly, but I don't kiss my friends, so....

I licked my lips, "I just keep mismanaging my expectations." I said finally. He narrowed his eyes at me into silver slits. His mouth puckered thinking. "You *have* been trying to seduce me." It was a statement, not a question. I blushed and tried to refute.

"It's hard to seduce anything when it's not... hard." God kill me, why would I say that. He could be impotent, and I am making light of a serious medical condition.

He chuckled, "Surely, you do not value my attraction to you based on my level of arousal." I could hear the scoff in his tone like I had offended him. I looked down sheepishly.

"I have immense self-control, and now is not the time." He nodded to my vibrating phone. Eric was leaving work.

First, Eric went home. He was there for an hour. Then he

headed out. He stopped at a grocery store, but instead of heading home, he headed east. "Get ready *Leslie*, it's time." I put on a fresh pair of tactical pants. Filled a small backpack with water, apples, a taser, a knife, a few shirts, sandals, and sweatpants. He was still traveling east and approaching Pasadena. He was on the 210 freeway; we made our way to the black BMW. The sun was setting fast over the horizon. We pulled on the freeway about a mile before he was to pass us. We were going slowly in the far-right lane.

"He'll be approaching us in about 30 seconds. You'll want to let him pass and get a good distance ahead. We don't want him to figure out he is being followed." He looked up from the GPS and over to me. I nodded as we drove into the night.

Traffic was light, we had been on the 210 freeway for 45 minutes. "He is getting on the 15 North," Beck said as he was watching Eric's progress. I could no longer see him. It was too dark, and I was too far back. We drove another 40 minutes, he passed Victorville, turning onto route 66 going North on National Trails Highway. Jesus, we were far out. This had to be where he was keeping them. The highway was deserted. I could see the pinpricks of his lights a few miles ahead of me. It was dark now and we were the only two cars on the road. "He can see us." I shook my head and pulled over. Beck looked confused. I stepped to the trunk and pulled out a set of goggles. I slid back into the front.

Beck looked amused, "Are those night vision goggles?"

I did not answer. I turned the car back on and turned the headlights off. I turned back onto the highway. Beck tightened his grip on the door but kept his eyes on the GPS. I can only imagine how odd, possibly unnerving it would be for a passenger traveling in a car going 80 mph with no headlights on when there is no moon to even illuminate the sky.

"He is stopping. It looks like he is about one mile off the

highway, on an unmarked road. I do not see any buildings in the area." Then this is it.

I pulled off a mile before Eric's parked car. "We need to hike over." He nodded and opened the door. "Take those off and let your eyes get used to the darkness. It will be a disadvantage if you lose those before you can adjust."

I slipped them off and was greeted by pitch darkness. I heard him chuckled as I rubbed my eyes and fumbled to stash the goggles in my backpack. He grabbed my hand and led me while my eyes lagged behind in adjusting. It took about ten minutes before I was able to see definition around me. I was still being led by Beck; his hand was gently interlaced in my fingers. The only noise I could hear was my own feet crunching into the parched vegetation. Beck moved silently, missing all the twigs that I apparently could not see to miss.

"His car is just above this ridge. Can you see yet?" Beck whispered.

I nodded; he released my hand. It felt cold and empty, but it was not practical to ambush someone while holding hands like some love-bird cartoon characters. "Can you track?" Tracking was my weakness when it came to rescuing. John had only given me a few lessons before he died. I was always a little dubious because, for the most part, I was looking for city-dwelling dickheads. Reading broken twigs seemed unimportant to master. Another oversight on my part.

I gave him a face that looked a little iffy. He understood. "Stay close behind me and don't make a sound. If you need to get my attention, touch my shoulder."

We approached the white Prius; it was still warm. Eric was nowhere in sight. Beck looked around and proceeded down a small goat path. We walked slowly for another fifteen minutes before we saw a pinprick of light ahead, like a candle in a window or a single flashlight. My palms were sweating. I went to touch his shoulder, but he had already turned around, motioning for me to follow him off the trail. We maintained our distance from the light and walked a circle around it. There was a small stream to the north.

The cabin looked tiny, no bigger than a large single room. We approached from the rear of the property. My heart was beating frantically. The windows were dingy, there was a single camping lamp on the windowsill. There was a rocking chair, a table, and a camp bed. I felt numb. They were not here. We made a mistake somewhere along the way. I was staving off my panic and frustration when Beck tapped my shoulder and pointed to the corner of the cabin. A small line of light lit up the corner from a split in the floorboards. There was a bunker hidden below the cabin.

Beck leaned into me, quieter than breathing, "If we go in now, we will be at a disadvantage. We must wait until he leaves." Always so practical, but I was so worried. What if the reports were all wrong and he was abusing them every night? What if my theory was completely off and tonight was the night that Kelly Parker would die?

He was reading my expression, "If we hear any signs of distress, we will go in." By signs of distress, I guess he meant raping, murdering, disemboweling. I shuttered. I nodded at him trying to hide my anxiety for my sister's safety.

It was the longest night of my life. Beck and I took turns looking out. We had repositioned ourselves to the north of the cabin, we could just make out the slit of gold light emitting from the corner. Beck calmed my hands when I started fidgeting. He was content staying perfectly still. The silence was pounding in my ears. Finally, past midnight the golden slit splashed the wall with a soft glow and as quickly as the light was there, it was gone. We watched in silence as the camping lantern bobbled out of the cabin. I held my breath and waited until we heard the crackling of dead vegetation fade.

Beck motioned for me to stay. I was going to protest,

but he did not go into the cabin, he looped away checking the perimeter for Eric. Beck came back within 3 minutes; he was silent and startled me as he popped up behind me. I stifled a gasp. "You must be more vigilant in times of stress." I rolled my eyes. Now was not the time for a lesson.

We crouched and walked our way into the cabin. It smelled like death, decay, and dust. I gagged. Beck pulled the trap door, but no light flooded the cabin. A small ladder led down ten feet into a concrete chamber. I could just make out an area where three small beds lined a wall. There was a series of metal bars separating the room down the middle: A prison cell. I walked up and gripped the bars looking through to the beds. One bed was empty, the other two had motionless bodies. The figures had both arms chained on the wall. A weird tube hung over their heads. Against the wall, I could barely make out a digital reading for a scale. Kelly Parker's scale read 118lbs. I winced at our near miss. Both were completely naked.

"Lauren?" I whispered. There was no movement. The room filled with light, I looked around to find Beck standing on the opposite wall next to a light switch. His finger looped around a ring of keys. On our side of the bars was a platform with adjustable light. Under the platform was a drain. His operating table. I felt faint. Next to the platform was a medical table with scalpels, a saw, and needles, all laid out uniformly. A small pile of white cylinders was on a cabinet near the light switch.

I walked over and opened the cabinet. It was full of IV fluid and equipment. The small cylinders were smelling salts. I grabbed one and turned around to Beck, my mouth was open aghast. He was trying a different key in the cell door, trying to find the right one to release the two prisoners. He worked silently and patiently. Had it been my job to open the cell, I was sure I would have dropped the keys a dozen times from my hands shaking.

A quiet click of metal and the groan of cell doors opening was the only noise that was made. I walked over to Lauren. I tried shaking her awake. She did not stir. I checked her pulse, felt her breathing. I sighed at the signs of life but jerked my attention to Beck silently begging him for help. He was going through the keys trying to find the correct one to release the cuffs at Kelly Parker's feet. I looked around and realized Lauren was being sedated. I carefully unhooked her IV bag. I tried to wake her again, still no luck. I rushed over to the cabinet and grabbed a smelling salt capsule. Beck stopped me before I could crack it open.

"Let me free her first. It will be more difficult to release her if she is disoriented." I nodded feeling anxious for Lauren to be free. I moved over to Kelly Parker's newly released form. I snapped the salts under her nose. Her eyes flickered, but she passed back out. I had forgotten to remove the IV. I carefully removed the drips and needles. I snapped a new salt. Her eyes fluttered again, but she was weak. She tried to focus on my face, "Help me." Her voice was feeble and scratchy. She slid out of consciousness before I could respond.

I turned back to Beck, "I can't keep her awake." I whispered. He switched beds with me. Lauren was free from her binds. I snapped another salt. Her eyes flickered a few times and lazily focused on my face. I started crying in earnest when I saw she was alive and whole. "How?" Lauren whispered. I shook my head, "I will explain later. Can you walk?" She slowly sat up. I pulled my backpack around and handed her a pair of sweatpants, an oversize shirt, and sandals. I passed a similar set of clothes to Beck. He made quick work of dressing Kelly Parker in the oversized coverings.

Beck was holding Parker on his shoulder like a sack of potatoes, "She's too weak to walk." Lauren whispered solemnly. I pushed Lauren to follow Beck up the ladder. I lead the rear, the musty smell greeting me as I emerged from the underground prison. We left the cabin silently. The cool air was refreshing to my senses. Lauren was crying quiet tears but following Beck closely. Occasionally she would stumble as her sandal would get caught on a twig. I heard a snap behind me just in time to whirl around as Eric Manly was swinging a blunt weapon towards the back of my head. He hit me in the shoulder. I gasped in pain, "Run Lauren!"

My scream pierced through the night. My shoulder was throbbing, but adrenaline was keeping me efficiently immune to the pain. I saw his weapon was a thick and short branch. I lunged forward to knock him off balance. He dodged my initial lunge. He swung the branch and barely missed my chest as I slid past him. I took a running leap, flipping my body in the air. I crooked my knee around the back of his neck, allowing my body to swing around. My body acted like a pendulum and it was enough to swing him around. I felt my eyeglasses go flying as he hit the ground hard, twigs crackling, as air whooshed from his lungs. I proceeded over to kick him in the face. I straddled his chest and punched his face repeatedly. Blood dripped down his unconscious face. Beck pulled me off him gently, "We need to go, I need your help getting them to safety."

I looked murderously towards him, "His death is not the priority, Sorumeito." He spoke in a calm whisper.

I was not being stubborn. I looked at Lauren. Her eyes were wide, staring at me in disbelief. She had watched the entire attack. She had watched my murderous intentions. Her shocked expression was enough to snap me back to reality. I picked up my broken eyeglasses. Beck moved back to the still form of Kelly Parker, slung her back over his shoulder, and began jogging through the brush. I grabbed Lauren's hand and pulled her along. She resisted, pulling her hand out of mine.

She looked scared, "How... who... what's going on?" She started to cry again.

"I will explain everything in the car, but we have to move now!" Manly's form was still behind us, but I did not want to take any chances. She reluctantly followed behind. We were back at the hidden BMW fifteen minutes later. I helped Beck secure Kelly Parker; she was beginning to stir but was too weak from lack of food for weeks. I slid behind the wheel and donned the night vision goggles. I whipped the car around and we were heading south. A short mile later I saw a small convenience store that was closed. A phone booth was lit under a streetlamp. I slammed on my breaks and pulled over to the side of the road.

"Lauren, I know you want answers, but now is not the time. I need you to do something for me. Number one, I need you to tell the police that you escaped on your own. You carried Kelly Parker here and called 911. Do not under any circumstances tell the police that Beck or I was here. Do you understand?" She nodded. "Good, can you carry Kelly to the phone booth?" She looked determined, "Yes, I think I can."

"I know you can, Lauren. First call 911, then call David. I will call him first with your coordinates. He may get here around the same time as the police. We are in the middle of nowhere."

"You can't leave me." Lauren was pleading her hands were shaking.

"Shhhhh, Lauren, we are not going to let you out of our sights. We just can't be right here. Beck is going to stay with you. I am going to drive a mile up the road and park. We will be in the woods; we will not leave until the police get here."

Her sobs quieted. She turned to Beck, "Are you Beck?" He nodded. She looked over to me with a million questions. Beck removed Kelly Parker from the backseat and set her down on the dry earth. He and I shared a silent exchange, "Give me eight minutes and I will be back."

I sped down the road another mile, found a secluded spot behind a copse, and ran full tilt back to my sister.

"You made good timing." Beck was smiling and holding Lauren who was holding Kelly. I was breathing heavily; I just nodded my response. Between exhales, "Okay Lauren, you know what to do."

Lauren looked numb but determined. Beck placed Kelly over Lauren's shoulder. She sagged slightly and stumbled before she caught her footing. She made slow progress across the street before making it to the phone booth and shrugging Kelly to the ground. Beck and I moved into the shadows watching the surroundings. I pulled my phone out at 2:35am.

"David."

"Wh-what's going on?" David's voice was gruff with sleep.

"I found her, tell no one. She is going to call you in a minute."

"What? How?" He sounded breathless.

"David, that does not matter. I never called you, do you understand?"

"Is she okay?"

"Yes. David, tell no one about this call, please tell me you understand."

He hesitated a minute, "I understand."

I gave him the coordinates and hung up.

My breathing was finally returning to normal. It felt like hours before the police arrived. It was only sixty minutes. David got there 4 minutes after. I could just make out Lennon and Taylor in the back seat. Beck stood up first and I followed quickly after him. We made it to the BMW in record time. He slid into the driver's seat.

"You need to rest." It was a command I was happy to follow.

Chapter 26

March 12

Beck brought me back to my Pasadena condo. He carried me upstairs. I was awake enough to walk when he clicked the door open. He set me down. "Go shower."

I walked into the bathroom. I was a mess. I pulled my wig off. My hair was plastered down with sweat. Mud was streaked across my face. My knuckles were covered in blood.

I scrubbed aggressively until the water ran clear. All the blood on my arms and fists was Manly's. I sighed in relief that I left no DNA behind. My body felt like it had been hit with a battering ram. The water was hot and kneading into the knots stress had formed. My eyes swelled with relief that Lauren was safe.

I stepped into the living room as Beck was leaving, "Where are you going?" I felt hurt. I did not want him to go, but I had no right to ask him to stay. I had already forced him to put his life on hold for two days, going on three.

"It seems like the right thing to do." I walked over to him and closed the distance before he could turn and leave. "I don't want you to go." He reached out and stroked my cheek, and slowly bent down to kiss my lips, gently at first, but building. I pulled myself into him. He slowed the kiss down and gently pulled away.

"I do not want to go either, but the timing does not feel right. I may have incredible self-control, but I am a man with normal inclinations."

What? What do normal inclinations even mean? What does he mean by timing? Okay, I knew what he meant by timing. We had just rescued two women from torture and death, one of which was my sister.

"Come with me to my home." I pleaded. He looked around.

"Not this one, my real home." I grabbed at his hand. He sighed at me, "Not tonight."

Before I could protest, he pulled away and walked out the door.

After his departure, I was quick to follow. I did not want to be in my fake home anymore. I gathered my belongings and snuck out to my Prius. Exhaustion tugged at my eyelids, but I safely pulled into my Glendora garage 15 minutes later, watching the sunrise. I reset all my alarms and crawled into bed, falling asleep instantly.

The sun streaming in woke me up: 12:00pm

I had not slept in until noon since I was a child recovering from chickenpox. I stretched my stiff limbs. My stomach grumbled loudly forcing me to find sustenance in the kitchen. I was too hungry to make anything. I drank a protein shake and stared numbly at the pool. Lauren had not called, but I was expecting it soon. I was not ready to share with her my duplicity. I strapped on my shoes and went for a run.

It was hot. I normally run before the sun heats up the asphalt. I ran and I thought about the night's events. Surely the police found Eric's unconscious body in the woods and arrested him. I smiled smugly as I thought about him being held without bail. I thought about the relief Kelly Parker's family must feel. I thought about how grateful I was for Beck. I thought about the torture chamber and shivered. The police would be searching his apartment off Hollywood Boulevard. Would they find the false bottom drawer? I loped into my driveway, mentally preparing myself for the inevitable conversation with Lauren.

"Hello?" David's voice sounded tired.

"Hey David, how is she?"

"They are keeping her at the hospital for a few more hours." I nodded into the phone. It made sense as to why she has not called me.

He continued, "The boys won't leave her side, but she needs her rest. Lauren won't tell me anything about your involvement. She keeps maintaining that she does not understand and won't make assumptions until she talks to you." Good girl, I mentally sighed in relief that she had listened.

"I'm sorry David, but I cannot discuss anything right now. When will you be home?"

"It's hard to say, the doctors don't want to release her yet, social services need to talk to her, the police still have questions."

"Ok, just keep me posted. Is there anything else I can do to help?" I kept my tone gentle, but I was fighting exhaustion.

"Caroline, I think saving her life is enough for today."

Shortly after that, we ended the conversation.

The house felt empty. I pulled out my composition book and filled out the missing details and slid it next to soldier the other solved cases. I looked around my study and decided to tidy up the neglected surfaces. I dusted, vacuumed, mopped. I moved room by room until the entire house was dust free and shining. I still felt restless, I checked my work email, still running a successful business.

I was surprised by my hunger, but then I saw it was 6pm. I flipped on the news as I began preparing dinner. I decided a pasta salad would be easy and the kind of comfort food that would nourish my soul and maybe make my empty house feel less so.

> "A statewide manhunt is underway for Eric Manly. Police have reason to believe he is the infamous Triple S killer that claimed the lives of Bobbi King, Flora Sanchez, and Lisa Henderson. Early this morning, Kelly Parker and Lau-

ren Kemp escaped from Manly's Victorville area cabin. Kemp was able to carry Parker to a safe place and notify the authorities. Police found Manly's cabin where his victims were held, but there is no sign of Manly."

Shit. That fucker got away. Well, at least the whole state will be looking for him. I finished my pasta, added tomatoes, cucumbers, and feta cheese. I turned off the news and turned on the stereo. I selected my favorite Queen album and turned it low. I grabbed a bottle of wine and poured myself a celebratory glass. I considered being concerned about Eric Manly, but the whole of Southern California's finest were looking for him. There was an APB on his vehicle. And there was relatively no reason for him to associate me with the brown-haired, brown-eyed woman that attacked him last night. I finished my dinner and listened to the end of the album. I cleaned up and decided a pleasant evening swim would cap off my day nicely.

The water was warm, there was a cool breeze that made me submerge faster. I started my laps slowly at first. I sped up gradually, I swam until I felt my legs turning to lead. I grabbed my kickboard to swim the last twenty minutes, collecting my thoughts, enjoying the warm water on my skin. I felt a ripple of water hit me. Maybe Beck had decided now was the right time. I smiled and turned around in anticipation.

It was not Beck that was wading towards me, it was Eric Manly. There was a cut above his eye and his jaw was bruised, but I could not mistake that face.

"What are you doing here?" My voice caught in my throat. My smile slid to a grimace.

"Followed you from Pasadena." I was treading water holding onto my board. He kept wading towards me. He was still 10 feet away.

"Imagine my surprise when I followed some bitch that attacked me all the way to Pasadena, and when I was waiting for her to leave again, I see you crossing Colorado Blvd." I was trying to catch up. He did not realize I was the same woman from last night. I was just careless.

"Why did you follow me?" I tried to make my voice clear, but it trembled.

"You are Lauren's sister. I recognized you from the other day. I saw you going to her office. I considered making you my new target, but I had put so much work into Lauren." He chuckled and moved closer, I swam backwards to maintain our distance, but I was still eight feet in any direction to the pool's side.

"It was a sign from God when I saw you this morning. It took a little time finding new wheels and your address, but I could not resist. When God shows you signs, you listen." He smiled at me. I shivered.

I swam hard towards the wall, but he had the advantage of a solid surface to kick off from. He snagged my foot and dragged me back to him. My board went flying. I took a deep breath; he shoved my head down. I thrashed trying to get away, but he was stronger and had the upper hand of using me as a float. He pushed me down harder. He released me slightly, my head bobbed to the surface. I took another gasp of air and he shoved me back down. I wriggled free again by kicking him in the groin. Another gasp of air before he regained his grip. He pushed my head down and mounted my back. He was holding my head with his hands and my body was being squeezed by his thighs.

I stopped thrashing; I was wasting my energy. I thought back to when John and I had moved here. He was excited about the pool. I was already a fair swimmer. He insisted that if I could increase my lung capacity, then I would be able to run further faster and swim more efficiently. I remembered John's encouraging words as he challenged me.

"I think if you really worked on your lung capacity, it

would help you train for a marathon. I know you mentioned running the Boston Marathon as a joke, but I know you can do it, baby."

It took a few more years to convince me, but I did eventually run the Boston Marathon. He was so proud of me. His next challenge was for me to swim the English Channel, but I never accomplished that.

We would have contests on who could hold their breath longer. The longest I had ever held my breath was just short of two minutes. I had wasted precious energy fighting, I only had about a minute before my lungs would give way. I decided to fake the end of a drowning.

Drowning victims convulse as their lungs fill with water. I began jerking spastically trying to mimic the symptoms. Lights burst in my eyes fading to black as I was running out of air. I misjudged my time, but he loosened his grip. Then he was completely pulled from my back. My head breached the surface as I gasped for air before my lungs gave in and reflexed in a lung of water.

I coughed spastically clawing towards the pool's wall. Eric was not attacking me yet; I chanced a glance backward to the thrashing I heard behind me. I feared it was Eric coming back for me. I braced for another plunge into the water, but Eric was scrambling to the stairs. A dark figure was quick to follow his retreat. With weak oxygen-deprived arms, I pulled myself out of the pool, collapsing on the pool deck, coughing and retching water from my lungs. *Get up, there is a killer on the loose.*

I slowly pushed myself to my feet stumbling as I caught my bearings. I realized the dark figure in the pool was Beck. Eric had a scalpel and was slashing wildly at Beck. He was dodging each slash, a grimace of rage on his face. He looked determined. At that moment, I saw the assassin killer that I found weeks ago. He was not intimidated by Eric's feeble attempts to cut him. Beck made a lightning kick movement, and Eric's leg collapsed backwards, he howled in pain. The scalpel cluttered to the ground. Beck made another cobra strike and Eric's arm hung limply to his side. I ran forward to kick the scalpel away from the fight. Beck took no notice of my contribution. Another lightning-quick movement and Eric crumpled to the ground.

Beck pulled up from his stance and looked over at me. I was five feet away, looking back and forth between Beck and Eric. "Are you okay?" He asked me, his face was full of concern. I nodded a few shaky nods, but my legs were stuck. "I will not hurt you; you do not have to be afraid." He reached his hand out towards me.

Confusion from his statement made me find my voice, "Is he dead?"

He dropped his arm, his face was deadpan, "Do you want him to be?"

I shivered, "No." It was a shaky murmur without much feeling behind it because I did want him dead.

"Good, a dead body of a wanted man will be a complicated discussion to have with the police."

My legs still could not move, in fact, my knees started to give out. I sagged to the ground. Beck squatted down and brushed the hair from my face, "Do you have anything that can restrain him?"

I looked into his eyes, they were simmering, "there is towing rope in the garage." He stood up and left me staring into the pool. The surface was calm. The light illuminated the pool like a topaz stone.

Beck was back before I was able to dissolve in tears. He passed me my phone and a robe. I realized that I was still naked from swimming. I shrugged my robe on as he started tying Eric's unconscious form. Within minutes he was hog-tied. Beck looked over at me. "Call the police, Sorumeito."

"I don't know what to say." My brain had finally clicked into gear. "Are you here right now?"

He looked confused, "Do you want me to go?"

"No!" My response was a little louder and more desperate than I had intended. "Please don't leave. I just meant, what am I supposed to tell the police?"

Understanding dawned on him. We both valued our privacy. I did not want him to leave, but I did not want to force him into a long complicated legal matter. My life was going to be flipped because of this attempt on my life, but his life did not need to be. Additionally, how was I supposed to explain the battered and hog-tied murderer that was out cold in my backyard? He snapped me out of my reverie.

"Tell them he attacked you because you are Lauren's sister. And tell the truth of the attack." He was pulling me to my feet.

"Including you being here?" I blinked appreciative tears from my eyes. He chuckled, "You are well-skilled, but surviving an attempted drowning then breaking his leg, arm, and jaw seems unlikely." He sighed and rubbed my arms, goosebumps followed his hand's path, "Call the police."

The police sent a swat team of officers into my home. Beck sat next to me on the sofa while the police came and went. Apparently, Eric had stolen a car from Colorado Blvd and parked it in my driveway. A tow truck came to remove the stolen vehicle. Beck and I both gave our statements as close to the truth as possible. We left our part in Lauren and Kelly's rescue out of our story. My ears perked up when he was asked about the nature of our relationship. He said something along the lines of "friends but why does that matter". When the circus left, we sat in silence. I slouched back on the couch, closing my eyes.

"I should let you rest." I felt the couch move as Beck stood up. My eyes shot open and I stood to stop him. I swayed from the sudden movement. He steadied me and kissed my forehead. "You are exhausted. You suffered a trauma today. You need your rest." He turned away. I grasped at his hand and pulled it to my face. I wanted him to stay tonight and every night, but I had already once again disrupted his night, his week, hell, even his month.

"If you do not have anywhere you need to be, I would appreciate it if you stayed tonight." I wanted to give him the option. Too many times I had demanded his time without asking. It may be why I could not get a grasp on what he wanted from me, of me. I was forcing him to be at my side. He kissed my forehead again, then rested his chin on my head. "Is that what you want?" I nodded silently "But it does not matter what I want, it matters what you want in this instance. I have hijacked your week, forced you to help me. I feel… bad."

He chuckled, "Sorumeito, you could never force me to do anything. You are no match for my strength or speed." I felt my face drop into annoyance at the challenge. My arms tensed to push him away. He felt me flex and rubbed my arms in response. "Do not be offended. You are more than a match for the average man. I am just not an average man." He could say that again. I had seen him in action, and I had seen him naked, either instance was nowhere near average.

"I will stay if you want me to stay." It was back to my decision. I just wanted to hear him say that he wanted to be around me, with me. Although, he had just told me that I could not force him into anything. *Stop trying to analyze this, he is interested.*

"I want you to stay." My voice was barely above a whisper. He kissed my forehead again and pulled away. His jaw was tense, he looked angry. I saw a flash of emotion in his eyes.

"What's wrong?" I reached up to smooth the muscles

around his chiseled jaw.

"I wanted to kill him. When I saw you in the pool, I thought you were dead. I wanted to rip him from limb to limb. I have worked very hard to keep the assassin separated from who I want to be. I am trained in a way that you could not imagine. When I broke that miscreant's jaw and saw your face." He closed his eyes and breathed slowly through his nose, his nostrils flaring slightly, "I thought I lost you in a different way. No one should associate with a killer. No one should want a killer." I smoothed my hand up to his cheek.

I swallowed back the words; I do want you. I don't care that you beat the shit out of a killer without breaking a sweat. I don't care that you had a challenging upbringing. I want you. I want you in a way I did not think possible. Instead, I said, "You saw me stab a man in a leg. You saw me intentionally cause a man to bleed to death."

He slowly opened his eyes and tilted his face towards mine. "He was going to kill you. It is very different from defending yourself compared to someone paying you to take a life away." That was a fair point. I could not argue, but if it meant he was going to leave I was going to fight back.

"You are not that person anymore. You stopped, you could have killed Eric and you stopped. You saved my sister and Kelly Parker. You helped me get Rebecca Hamilton justice. You are a good person." He scoffed, but he did not rebut. "You *are* a good person. I want you to stay. I just want you to... I want you."

His jaw remained tight, but his eyes were soft. "Do you want to shower?" My hormones zinged into attention. Hell, yes! I want to shower. Then I realized there was a possibility he meant alone. I clarified, "Are you going to join me?"

He chuckled, "I think you have pushed my self-control to its limits." I pouted but I was going to respect his limits. My shower was brief. I wanted to get back to my company. Hot tea was waiting on the kitchen counter. Beck was meditating by the pool. He looked peaceful in the gem-like glow. I did not want to disturb him. I took a sip of tea and quietly approached the pool to get a better look at his beautiful face. I shivered at the memory of the attack a few hours before.

His eyes opened and followed my approach, "Sorry, I did not mean to disturb you." I murmured but I sat next to him. "Thank you for the tea."

He did not move. He looked tired. I grabbed his hand, "Come to bed." One eyebrow moved the slightest degree, "You can't sleep on the couch. You need rest too, not a backache." He did not look convinced. "Okay, I will not try to seduce you. It's done nothing but embarrass me. I just want you to be near me tonight. I need to feel safe, and... you make me feel safe." I was trying to manipulate him, I knew it, he knew it. He had closed his eyes again, but his nostrils seemed to flare at exhale.

"You should not feel safe around me. You do not know me. Allowing you to care about me is wrong." I scoffed and snorted and made any other dismissive noise I could make. My non-verbal noises made no difference, he was still sitting there, still with his eyes closed.

"If I knew you, if you let me know you..." I reached out to stroke his cheek. He did not move; it was as if I was touching a statue.

"If you knew me, then you would wish you did not."

"So that's it? I get no say in this? You are not going to let me decide whether or not that is true?" My temper was flaring, my heart was beating hard as I was taking in what he was saying. "You decided that you know me so well that I could not *handle* things you have done in your past?"

"Do not be angry, Sorumeito, I am trying to protect you."

I interrupted, "Protect me or you?"

He opened his eyes as one eyebrow arched.

I continued, "Do you think I have not gathered who you are, who you were? Do you think I would...? Do you think I could not accept a few childhood stories? Or is it the fact you already know I am emotionally broken, and I could not possibly..." My chest was heaving now as I was trying to control my tear ducts from betraying me. I learned a long time ago, don't let people who are going to hurt you, see your tears. I was stopping myself from saying 'let me love you the way you deserve,' but instead, I said, "Tell me who you are, let me decide for myself." I had calmed down enough to say the last bit a little more pleading than intended.

He closed his eyes again, but the serenity in his face was gone. His expression was tense, "Not tonight, Caroline." I let the silence permeate for a few minutes. My anger was abating. Not tonight did not mean never. I still had a chance. I started to internally chastise myself for even arguing with someone who was pushing me away. I knew better. Why kick and scream into someone's life when they don't want you to be there? *Not tonight.*

"Can you at least stay?" I hugged my knees into my chest, I had not realized how cold I had become. "I don't want to be alone," I repeated, barely above a whisper. I gave my knees one more squeeze and silently walked back into the house. I crawled into bed feeling the weight of rejection and heartache pushing down in suffocating blows. I was breaths away from succumbing to tears when the bed shifted, and Beck wrapped his arms around me. I slept peacefully as he held me all night.

Chapter 27

March 13

I woke up to an empty bed. I sat up slowly, searching with my eyes. I did not want to jump out of bed if he was merely sitting on the bedside chair. That would make me look like a love-sick desperate lune. No one was in the room. The house was silent. I slipped out of bed.

"Beck?" I knew he was gone. I did not want to accept it. He had been saying goodbye in his own way last night. I walked into the kitchen, "Beck?" Still no answer.

I did not want to spiral into self-pity, and I did not want to be home alone surrounded by screaming silence. I pulled on my running shorts and shoes. I was frantic to leave the empty house and clear my mind.

I made my way up my street and confirmed my house was indeed void of Beck. His car was gone from the spot he normally parks. I tried to focus on something else. Something that did not have me feeling *things*. Someone who was not saying goodbye. Someone who I did not feel numb around. I had been numb for so long, and now... I wanted to allow the numbness to settle around me again. I needed to distract myself. It was a beautiful day. The sky was Carolina blue, not a cloud to disrupt its expanse. The mountains were green and inviting. I should hike the GMR trail soon. It's beautiful and secluded... like me. I shook my head at the thought. I was not secluded. I had my sister and nephews. My sister who was whole and safe because of me and... Beck. Ugh, my nephews who were loud and funny and erratic. My nephews whose mom was safe and home because of... ugh.

I ran through a murder of crows, fifty black birds scattered at my approach and repositioned over the power lines and nearby rooftops. The murder of... women was solved because. Ugh. I looped down another street. The wind in my face was cool and coming from the Pacific with the assist of the Santa Ana winds. My ponytail whipped behind me as I breathed in the fresh cold air. I could hear macaws screeching on nearby power lines, sprinklers oscillating to revive the lawns. God, it is beautiful here.

I proceeded down another street. I saw a flock of peacocks pecking their way lazily down the middle of the street. The males were blue and beautiful, the females were brown and following the male's lead. Wild but domesticated. No longer bothered by runners or cars approaching. The last time I had seen the peacocks was when I was with Taylor and Lennon upon first meeting Chris. Chris, who almost hit the proud blue male peacock with her car. Chris, who roped me into looking for...

I crossed another street. I focused on the sounds of my feet hitting the pavement in a satisfying rhythm. I focused on my breathing. I listened to the birds chirping, children giggling in their front yards. I tried to quiet my mind, but it kept going back to Beck. He had somehow woven himself into the tapestry of my life over the past few months. And now after he was pretty well established as someone I viewed as an equal, now he wants to pull his thread out. Unweave the tapestry, ruin the design. Ha! Nope, I am a stubborn woman, he reminds me of that all the time. I was not going to allow him to dictate our friendship. I would follow the pace that he was comfortable with, but whether he wanted to admit it or not; we were in each other's life.

In my last mile, I was resolved. I was going to get to know him. He knew some of my childhood. Not every story or detail, but enough and I wanted to know the same. I would ask him first. If he did not want to share, I would have to take a deeper dive than I had when Chris wanted me to investigate his disappearance. I would have to get my hands dirty. I had already exhausted my internet sources into his life, but I had a few leads to follow up on. But, of course, I would give him the opportunity to tell me himself.

I jogged onto my street with a clearer head than when I left. I was not going to be self-loathing. I was resourceful. I always get my man. *Okay, that was ridiculous.* But when I put my mind to something, I am able to make it happen with hard work and determination. I stuttered to a stop at the mouth of my driveway.

"Baby I was so worried!" Nathan was jogging towards me with his arms open. "Baby" was new. He is not the pet-name kind of guy. I internally cringed but remembered that he did care about me and I should be grateful for a man that was able to do that openly. I accepted his hug. He pulled me out at an arm's length to look at me.

"I saw the news this morning, I recognized your house right away. Are you okay?" I nodded numbly and he released my arms. "What happened?" He asked as he followed me inside. It was still empty. I shrugged. "I was picking up something from work and he saw me, followed me home. He attacked me while I was swimming." I was going for nonchalant but by the end, I was wincing at the memory. He pulled me into another hug and kissed my forehead. "I guess all that training paid off." I just stared at him and bit my lip. He narrowed his eyes, "The news made it sound like you were not alone." I looked down and made a non-committal face. "Ahhh the famous mysterious Beck." Nathan may be a lot of things, but slow was not one of them.

"Yep, the mysterious Beck." I finally agreed.

"Well, I want to thank him, and size up my competition."

I scoffed, "I think you have the wrong impression of Beck." Or completely the right impression. He is a mystery, but Nathan was implying that Beck was a competition. Beck was pulling himself from the race, or at least trying to.

"What impression should I have then?"

"Beck is just a friend. He is not interested in me like that." I kept my tone from betraying my longing for it to not be true.

"Caroline, I think you may have the wrong impression of his intentions then." His expression was soft.

I looked at him confused. Beck had been pretty clear last night and so many times of his intentions. My impression was pretty clear.

"There is no way he only wants your friendship." He chuckled and patted my head. Like a short puppy, I growled internally. "Okay, I'll let you go on with your day. Call me if you need anything."

He thumped the doorway with his thumb a few times and left.

Alone again.

I called the hospital. Lauren had been released last night. She had probably not seen the news yet. I got changed and went over to see her before she would worry about me and my close call with Eric Manly.

"Auntie Ro!" Lennon and Taylor were playing in the sprinklers in the front yard running towards me. I bent down to receive their wet happy hugs.

"How are my boys doing?" I kissed them each on their foreheads.

"Mama was sick, but the hospital said she is alllll better." I looked up to see Lauren sitting on the stairs of her stoop. "I know buddy!" I patted Lennon on the head and stood up. Lauren moved off the steps, emotions playing in the corners of her eyes. I walked up to hug her, "Don't cry, Lo!"

She sobbed on my shoulder, "I just saw the news, I tried to call you. You did not answer." She started to hiccup. I had forgotten to remove "Do not disturb" from my phone. I looked down at it, twenty-five missed calls. Whoops. I needed to call Infinity and the five other people that called me multiple times to verify my safety.

"Sorry," I held up my phone as I slid off "Do not disturb."

"How did he get to you?" Lauren had calmed down now. David replaced Lauren at the front stoop, and we were now sitting at the patio table. I cupped my warm beverage and told her the practiced version of the story I had shared with the police. She chewed on her lip.

"I still don't know how you found me." Her eyes were imploring. I nodded but did not say anything.

She narrowed her imploring eyes and set her jaw, "You said that you would explain everything later." She looked around and checked her watch, "It's later!" Gone was the typical patient Lauren. This was the "you have been keeping serious shit from me for years and I'm pissed as hell you did not tell me." It was a very specific mood.

"Okay! Jeez, calm down. I will tell you." I took a sip to rehydrate my mouth that had gone dry in anxiety.

"But first," I continued, "You need to promise me that what I tell you will not leave this table." I pointed my finger at the wood top. Lauren rolled her eyes and swatted her hands, "Fine!"

"After the accident and everything we survived, I started taking self-defense."

She rolled her eyes, "Yeah I am aware of that, get to the part where you turned yourself into Black Widow with a brown wig!"

I chuckled. I had always loved Black Widow. "Okay. Very long story short, John taught me how to investigate cases methodically. I am pretty good at it. He would give me solved cases and show me how to work them out. When the solved cases ran out, he started bringing home cold cases. When John died, I did not stop investigating cases. I just changed how I got them." Her shoulders dropped and she pursed her lips. "My clients?"

I nodded sheepishly, "At no point would I actually talk to them or make them rehash their experiences. I just worked the cases from a different angle from the police. And you and I both know that the rape victims rarely see justice." She took a deep breath. "How do you do it?"

"I find the guys, get their DNA, and submit it anonymously." She snorted and threw her head back in a full laugh. "And guys just what, jerk off in a cup?" Gross. I snorted.

"No, sometimes the DNA is from a discarded coffee cup. Sometimes if it comes to a physical altercation, I get a lock of hair. I try to stay in the periphery. I work really hard to stay in the shadows. I just want these guys to go to jail. I don't want anything else."

She smiled, "Like the Golden State Killer." I nodded back, exactly. "Caught through DNA tracing and a rogue discarded piece of trash. It has only become possible to really do this over the past three years."

"One thing I do not understand, how do you get the details? I never tell you the victim's name or anything that could lead you to find their identity."

Another sheepish grin, "Lauren, did you really think your password on a post-it under your keyboard was the safest place?"

She rolled her eyes, "You can't do that! It's an invasion of privacy and you are breaking like a thousand HIIPA laws. Now I have to change my password and you know how hard it is to remember that kind of thing!"

"Lauren, even if you change your password. I would just get it again." I was smiling at her. It seemed the worst of her annoyance and anger was over.

She laughed, "Well now that I know you will be looking for a post-it, I will find a new way of saving my password."

I smiled at her like she was missing out on the joke. She stopped yammering on and paused with her eyes narrowed. "What else did John teach you?" She finally resigned to the fact that she already knew the changed password would be a minor annoyance but would not actually stop me.

"Cybersecurity and its flaws."

She let out an exasperated sigh and motioned for me to continue.

"I had been following the disappearances for a few weeks, following my own leads, doing my own investigation in tandem with the police. I could see what they were working on, I would work down a different path." I paused to collect my thoughts.

"You hacked police files?!" Lauren's voice grew louder, tenser. "That's a serious crime! What if you were caught?" I shook my head.

"I look into files through police usernames and I use an IP scrambler. Even if someone was looking for me, they would be pinged to the Virgin Islands then to China then to Australia then to England before they could trace it back to me. Local police do not have the wherewithal to do such an investigation. I leave no trace behind and disturb no evidence. No one is even looking."

Her mouth was open, and she was wide-eyed blinking at me.

"Anyway, I followed a few leads to dead ends. It was not until you were abducted until Beck helped me make the connection."

Lauren waved her hands for me to pause, "And Beck is

the guy that rescued us. The sexy anime character?" I laughed; he did look like a real-life anime ninja. "Is he the guy you did not want to tell me about?" Confusion flitted across my face. "At sushi? Before… everything?"

Oh! God, that seemed like ages ago. My brain caught up with the memory, I nodded in confirmation. Lauren smiled back. "He likes you. You seemed unsure, called him cryptic. But he really likes you."

I shook my head, "I know where you are going with this. He came along because he was invested in catching Eric Manly and I asked him to. He has a history with… things that I thought would be beneficial in rescuing you."

She laughed and patted my hand, "I am sure that is why you invited him. That is not why he agreed. He likes you, trust me." I narrowed my eyes wishing the words were true.

"How can you be so sure?" I asked skeptically.

She smiled at me again and lifted her hand to her own mug, "Something he said to you while you were… when Eric attacked you in the woods."

It was my turn to motion for her to go on, "He said something like, 'His death is not the priority, Sorumeito' or something along those lines."

I scoffed. That was what she was talking about? "Lauren, he did not want me to kill him, he was trying to keep my hands clean. He did not want me to deal with the ramifications of you witnessing me… do that." I was certain that is why he stopped me. I saw Lauren's face in the woods, I had scared her. He had to have seen it too. He knew my relationship was too precious for me to destroy by my anger and lack of restraint.

Lauren's face looked somber at the memory, "You are right, I did not want to see you like that, but that is not what I meant." Her lips raised slightly in a small smile.

"He calls you "Sorumeito"." She was smiling now, l like I was missing out on the joke.

I rolled my eyes, "It's not a cute pet name, Lo, it means stubborn woman."

She laughed and shook her head, "Is that what he told you?" She laughed again, "David is learning Japanese for work. We decided to learn it together so we can take a trip. Stubborn woman is gankona on'na."

I blinked at her. "Well, what does it mean then?" I set my jaw and crossed my arms settling in for a real pissing contest.

"You have two choices: you can ask him yourself, or you can invite him for dinner."

I looked around confused, she smiled back.

"David and I want to meet him, thank him."

I shook my head, "No, you want to Spanish Inquisition him." Panicked thoughts on the questions of how we met flowed through my brain.

"We are not going to embarrass you, I promise!"

I considered it, "I'll ask him, but I doubt if he will come. He is a very private person."

Her face was skeptical, "Uh-huh, just tell him I want to thank him, which I do."

"Okay, I will ask. When shall I tell him of your fortuitous dinner?"

"Ro, I told you the other day! David wants to do a low country boil on Saturday."

I was shocked, "That's still going to happen? After everything that happened, you still want to do your boil?" I think I cursed or snorted, probably both.

She shrugged and smiled, "I will not allow my past to

poison my future Ro. I have been telling you this for years."

"Okay, I will see you Saturday, but please do not be disappointed if I am alone." I stood up to leave. Lauren followed me to the front yard. I gave the boys a hug and kiss. David pulled me for a rib-cracking hug, Lauren followed behind with a gentler embrace.

"Saturday."

Chapter 28

March 14

I nervously fiddled with the hem of my shirt as Beck and I walked up to Lauren's front stoop. Beck noticed my twitchy fingers and pulled my hand into his and gave it a squeeze.

"Why are you nervous?" He asked while looking at me from his sideways glance. Maybe because my sister had promised to evaluate all your movements and report back what they mean. Maybe because I'm worried, she is going to confirm that you only like me as a friend. Or maybe because I was terrified that Lauren would not like him and it would leave me in a bad position. I shrugged. He squeezed my fingers one more time before dropping my hand and ringing the doorbell.

Lennon pulled the door open and looked up and down at Beck, "Who are you?" He asked with narrowed eyes. I bent down and gave Lennon a hug. Beck bent to his knee and stuck out his hand, "My friends call me Beck."

Lennon looked back and forth between me and Beck and whispered loud enough for Beck to hear, "Is that my new uncle?" Oh, from the mouths of babes.

"No, honey, he is my friend." I stood up and ruffled his hair.

"Auntie Wo!" I heard the telltale pitter-patter of quickly moving bare toddler feet on the hardwood. I scooped up Taylor and held him on my hip. "Hey, sweet boy!" I gave him a kiss on the cheek. Lennon grabbed my hand and pulled me away from the door. Beck followed behind. I threw a quick apologetic look back, but he looked amused. "Mama said to go outside," Lennon informed me as he tugged me through the back door.

Lauren greeted us wearing oven mitts. She hugged me with Taylor still resting on my hip. Taylor squirmed and I set him down. She turned quickly to Beck and without the slightest hesitation she pulled him into a hug, oven mitts patting him on his back in a muffled thump.

"You must be Beck!" She pulled away to look at his face for confirmation and pulled him back into another hug. She finally released him and turned to the boys, shaking off her oven mitts, and passed them off. "Give these to dad." She pointed towards the edge of the patio where David was tending to a large boiling pot on top of a portable propane stove.

David looked up as Lennon approached and gave us a wave and tended back to the boiling pot, adding shrimp.

"Dinner will be ready in about 6 minutes." Lauren watched the addition to the pot as a confirmation of time. David stood up and jogged over towards us. He pulled me in for a quick hug and turned to Beck, "You are Beck, right?" and threw out his hand. I noticed the handshake was a lot tamer than the one that Beck shared with Nathan. His tendons did not strain, and it lasted the appropriate amount of time. I was trying to ignore the familiarity Lauren and David had towards Beck. I was too distracted by the way Beck's shirt hugged his chest and by how comfortable he seemed to be.

Dinner was a delicious mess of flavors, textures, and discarded seafood shells. David kept the beer flowing, but Beck abstained. It was a pleasant evening and at no point did David or Lauren ask or say anything that made me want to cringe.

"Where are your parents from, Beck?" Lauren had cleared the table of the soggy newspapers that held the boil from dripping everywhere. Beck wiped his hand on a wet paper towel.

"My mother is Japanese; my father was in the Norwegian armed forces when they met." He answered, Lauren looked impressed. I was impressed, I did not know about his father's profession, and Lauren seemed to get the information with extreme ease.

"What brought you to the US?" Lauren continued. My ears perked up. I thought I knew the answer, but his familial roots were not well documented.

"My mother sent me to live with my uncle when I was fourteen. I have been here ever since." Lauren made a face, but David spoke up, "So you are a Japanese citizen? I am actually going to Japan in a few weeks for work."

Beck smiled, "No, I had to drop my Japanese citizenship when I moved here. It was easier to become an American citizen with my origins shared with Norway. I am a dual citizen." My brain tucked the new information away for further investigation.

The evening was pleasant. Lauren put the boys to bed before the conversations turned serious.

"Beck, I want to thank you for being so brave and rescuing Lauren. We are forever indebted to you." David was holding Lauren's hand. Her eyes had moisture gathering at the corners. David continued, "I wanted to thank you the minute you walked in, but the boys have no idea what happened. We told them that Lauren was sick in the hospital."

Beck tipped his head, "My role was a small part, Caroline is the true hero." I felt myself blushing, or maybe it was the free-flowing beers that were causing a flushing response. Beck grabbed my hand, his fingers felt warm. I decided I was definitely blushing. Lauren watched the movement with rapt attention, smiling at me.

The evening ended shortly after the boys went to bed. Beck walked me home, holding my hand. It felt good, comfortable.

"Do you want to come in?" I asked Beck, hopefully

looking at him through my lashes. We were standing in front of my door. He smiled and gave me the quickest peck on the cheek. Beer confidence overtook me. I wrapped my arms around his neck and drew him in for a real kiss. I put all the unsaid things I was feeling behind the kiss, but he pulled away with a chuckle. "Not until you can make an informed decision."

We were back to this. Back to his past. Back to him not sharing diddly with me and holding me at an arm's length, literally. I was breathing in to begin my verbal protest when it was his turn to kiss me. It was slow, his tongue dipped slowly into my mouth. His hands were slowly moving down my back. He pulled away too soon with a chuckle, "So easily distracted."

My phone inside rang and stopped my rebuttal. "You are my friend, Sorumeito. Please do not be upset by my desire to protect you." He kissed my cheek, "You should answer your phone."

He pushed me through the door as he walked out into the night.

I ran to the phone before it could ring again.

"Hello?"

"Ro, I figured you would have been home a few minutes ago, but you did not call!" Lauren was chastising me for not letting her know I was home safe.

"Lo, you know Beck was walking me home." I started, she interrupted. "Is he still there? Did I interrupt anything?" Her tone sounded hopeful.

"No, he just left, and no you did not interrupt anything." Not anything, really.

"You know I want you to be happy. And I know that you like him. I was watching your body language all night." She said, I slumped my shoulders. Of course, she had been watching me too.

"Are you in love with him?" Yes, probably.

I made a few indiscernible noises, "It does not matter. We are just friends. In fact, he just reminded me of that before he left.

"He likes you too. I wanted to see it for myself. Ro, I don't care if he is telling you that you are just friends. David and I agree he really likes you, maybe more."

"Uhhh, no, he just told me we were friends. Like, just now, said we are just friends."

Lauren interrupted, "I know he is cryptic. I was listening to him all night. But sometimes, you have to ignore what is being said and look at how he is saying it. He really likes you, Ro."

I did not want to fill myself with false hope. As much as I wanted to believe what Lauren was saying, I had too many instances that proved his intentions for me were purely friendly.

"I'd love to believe that, Lo, really I would, but..."

She interrupted again, "He calls you his soulmate!"

I almost dropped the phone, I stopped breathing, "What?"

Lauren laughed, "He calls you 'Sorumeito' right? It means soul mate."

Blue fleurettes overtook my vision as I held my breath until the blue turned to black and I was no longer conscious.

SNEAK PEEK INTO BROAD DAY GONE

Chapter 1

April 17-18

The wind whipped around my hair. I dug my crampons into the Solheimajokull Glacier in Iceland and checked my ropes attaching to Thomas. He looked back at me, I could barely make out his smile through his glasses and scarf he had wrapped around his face, I could just discern the tiniest uptick in his cheek.

"This is the most beautiful place I have ever been." Thomas, my younger brother yelled over the wind.

We tried to travel together at least once a year. He is a doctor with Doctors Without Borders, and we would meet somewhere during his breaks. This vacation we were checking out Iceland and we were planning a few days in Norway. Having Norwegian heritage made us want to "see our motherland."

My size, blue eyes, and red hair made the locals speak to us in Icelandic. It was odd fitting into a place physically. Gingers normally stick out like a sore thumb, but here in Iceland, I was mistaken for a local.

I nodded and turned towards a small, but popular fissure to the right of where we were hiking. We made slow progress; the wind kept lifting my foot with each step, making me dig harder in with the crampons. We slipped into the silvery-blue nature-made shelter. It was protecting us from the wind, giving us a break from yelling and fighting the elements. Despite being in shape, my legs were screaming from the near-vertical hike up the glacier against the wind. When I am not climbing ice mountains, I run six miles daily, swim, and have been practicing different forms of self-defense since I was fourteen.

"That's better, I could barely hear you." Thomas's muffled words shouted over to me. We had been attempting to talk to each other over the howling wind for nearly thirty minutes.

Thomas was still talking loudly as he unraveled his scarf from his face. He shook the snow out of his light brown hair and blinked it out of his light blue eyes. I pulled out my phone to check the weather, "It says the wind advisory is in place for another 30 minutes. We might as well explore a little and wait it out." We stepped cautiously through the ice hallway when my phone beeped.

I stopped, the rope attaching me and Thomas lurched as he stopped his progress, his crampons skidded.

"What's going on?" He asked cautiously.

I could tell he was worried about the weather. Icelandic springs were unpredictable at best. The saying is, "If you don't like the weather, just wait ten minutes."

But it was not the weather, someone was at my house at 3am in California, my security system had just informed me. No one was breaking in, technically you would need to break something. I have two security systems in place, one that is monitored and will send police if something is broken, and one that I monitor in case someone makes it past the standard security.

I heard Thomas sigh in annoyance. "Nothing with the weather, just give me a minute."

I opened my security camera feed to see who had entered my domain without my permission. I scowled at my phone. Tadashi Becken, or Beck as I called him, was making tea in my kitchen.

Beck is tall, muscular, silver-eyed, and a ridiculously attractive mix of Japanese and Norwegian. He was also at one point a hired hitman with the skills of a ninja, but most recently he was a chef. He had helped me out of a few scraps from my weird hobby. I investigate the crimes that police give up on, mostly rapes where the evidence is not substantial enough to find the attacker. I get most of my information from my sister, Lauren. She is a social worker at Cedars Sinai, so her caseload is always filled with victims with limited ability to get justice. I honed my investigation skills from my husband, John Henry. He was military police specializing in cybersecurity, but he died in a forest fire as a volunteer firefighter nearly three years ago. He taught me how to work through a case and how to hack computers. That, combined with my self-defense skills and my small stature, allowed me to procure information and more often than not, DNA to prove the guilt of the rapist.

I had not seen Beck in over a month. I had thought that maybe I was finally getting over John's death, opening up to the ability to actually care for someone else, maybe even... eventually... love them. Beck made my thoughts superfluous and I thought that he might even feel the same for me. According to Lauren, he had called me his soul mate (in Japanese) on more than one occasion. About a month ago I braved the subject and told him, in not so many words, that I could eventually see myself falling for him. If I was being honest, I would have said it was too late for "eventually" because it was already here. It was then that he informed me, in not so many words, that I was an idiot for thinking that. His actual words were, "You think that you may love me one day? I think that you do not know me well enough to love me. My own mother found out who I was and discarded me when I was fourteen. No one can love a monster."

And despite my stellar investigative skills, I had not been able to corroborate his childhood abandonment story. Nor had I been able to find out what had happened at 14 that preempted his exile from Japan to California. He did not exist in any system until he was fourteen. And his uncle, whom he lived with, died when he was 18. I had a few diner patrons (a job from his youth) to follow up with, but Beck was incredibly protective of his past. His past was like a ghost, nothing solid to edify. He was interviewed about his restaurant and mentioned once that he grew up with his mother and grandfather in Japan. That was all I knew, and it was nothing because I had no idea what his mother or grandfather's name was.

After a month of silence, there he was, making tea in my kitchen while I am 4,300 miles away hiking on a glacier. I tucked my phone back into my green snow jacket and pulled my gloves back on. Thomas was shuffling his feet back and forth; I am not sure whether it was impatience or just the temperature that was threatening the survival of all ten toes.

"The fissure curves in about fifty feet, we should get a pretty solid look down a crevasse."

Thomas was double-checking the map before tucking it back in and securing his own gloves. The brilliant displays of blue and teal were almost, *almost* enough of a distraction from Beck's presence in my home. Why was he there? I was too hopeful to assume he decided he was being an ass. He was a lot of things, but apologetic was not one of them.

"I think I hear the wind dying out," I said as I turned around to make our way out of the fissure.

We still had quite a way to go to reach the top of the glacier and I wanted to be back in the car to rest my screaming hip flexors. I also wanted to rest a little before dinner and for the night of chasing the northern lights that we had scheduled... Thomas nodded to me as we made our way out into the sunshine, and sure enough, the wind had died down to a gentle breeze. By the time we made it back to the car my hip flexors were burning, and my blisters had blisters from where the crampons pushed on the heel of my boots, but the view was absolutely stunning. I only wished I could have appreciated the view more; my own thoughts were feeling less appreciative and more angsty. Beck had stayed at my house for more than two hours. He checked all the rooms, including my bedroom, and eventually settled into my study to review the cases I had just finished working on.

The trip back to Reykjavik was longer than expected. The weather changed again, and the wind blew in a massive snowstorm making visibility through the windshield near impossible and the wind kicked up and buffeted the car for a nail-biting forty-five minutes. We limped into our rented apartment to rest and pack before our dinner at an award-winning restaurant. We had been driving around Iceland for five days, and we were flying to Oslo the next day. I stripped out of my six layers of clothing and took a quick shower before getting ready for dinner.

It was a quiet affair as both Thomas, and I were exhausted from the hike. All the food was locally sourced. All fruits and vegetables were grown in greenhouses, watered with glacier water, and heated by the natural seismic activities of the tectonic plates. Even the ice cream was made fresh from a local dairy. I did not know what to expect from the culinary delights of a country known for fermenting shark, but every meal I had was better and more delicious than the last. I thought of Beck as I patted my well-fettered stomach. Not because I cared about him. No, that was taboo. But because I thought as a chef, he would appreciate the culinary delights.

"Hey, so I want to go back to the Secret Lagoon before our flight tomorrow. I think my muscles need it." Thomas took a swig of his $20 beer (2500ISK).

I nodded, "Yeah, my hips are a smidge sore."

Secret Lagoon was a natural hot spring and, if the stories were true, the water had healing properties. We had already gone when we landed from Los Angeles, and perhaps we were being overly optimistic, but it made our jetlag practically non-existent. Thomas pulled out his phone as I paid for dinner.

"There is no cloud cover at Skogafalls and the solar activity looks promising." Thomas nodded to himself.

"Sounds promising." I grabbed my bag and started shrugging into my snow coat and slipping the knitted cap over my red waves.

As promised, the night was clear and the solar flares lit up the sky in green, blue, and red. Streaks of light danced across the velvety black sky. I would be lying if I did not get emotional as a tear gathered in my eye. Thomas howled like a wolf bringing me out of my reverie of appreciation. We watched God's light show until 3am when we finally called it a night as the sun started to rise again.

The weather was drizzly and about 35 degrees when I walked outside in my bathing suit and into the naturally heated water. Steam rose from the surface like an inviting siren, welcoming me from the cold rain. My muscles ached from the glacier hike and days of exploring the land of fire and ice. I was grateful to Thomas for the lagoon suggestion. It did make the screaming pain I was feeling in my hips disappear to a mild whimper.

The flight into Oslo was uneventful. Thomas slept, slightly snoring with his mouth slightly agape for the majority of the flight. I could not sleep. I was feeling unnerved by Beck's visit into my domicile. I had convinced Thomas to add Oslo to our itinerary so we could become in touch with our roots, but I had ulterior motives. After Beck's proclamation that I did not know him, I made it a hobby to learn everything about his past from birth to fourteen. All I knew was his father was in some form of military-based out of Norway. All the archives were housed in the National Library in Oslo. The military archives were only available on microfilm and was not a priority to transcribe online.

We checked into our hotel. Our stay was to last another three days before we would fly transatlantic back to California. Well, I was going back to California. Thomas had not disclosed where he was going next. He told me he was waiting on confirmation of his next assignment.

"I need to sack out for a few hours, but I want to explore downtown tonight," Thomas said while mashing the elevator button in our small hotel.

We were checking out in the morning and heading to Stavanger to take in fjords. I had a few hours to head to the National Library, but I knew if I told him where I was going, he would forgo his nap and join. That was not ideal as I doubted, he would be patient as I went through hours of microfilm.

"It's cool. I need to polish off the new website for Infinity before Manny and Rani kill me." I said as we got off the elevator and separated our ways in the hotel hallway.

Infinity Apothecary was my small business in Pasadena that specializes in local artisan goods and high-quality face and body care. We had recently taken on another cosmetic line which was making our makeup business skyrocket. So much so that Manny, my sales manager, had insisted on hiring a makeup micro-influencer to promote our products. Rani, my operations manager, insisted we upped our website traffic by allowing purchases, so I had to overhaul the whole thing. Truth be told, I finished the website before we left for Iceland, but Thomas did not need to know that detail.

I heard his room door close with a click. I shoved my bag into the closet, washed my face, and headed back out to get to the Library. I figured I would have about two hours to find what I was looking for, three if I told him I was still napping and promised to meet him somewhere.

It was a balmy 30 degrees outside, but not a cloud was in the sky. It was a crisp sort of cold that made you appreciate spring in the tundra. The brightly colored brick buildings lined the route to the library; it was picturesque. I followed the directions towards the military archives. They were alphabetical, so I had a decent starting place.

Becken, as it turns out, is a pretty common last name. I was able to narrow down service dates for Beck's father within a twenty-year range. I was able to google the names and see if they corresponded to anything that related to Japan. I had no idea how Beck's parents met, nor their names. Only Beck's surname to hope to find his father. I was an hour into my search when my security system alerted me of Beck's arrival back into my house. This time at 5am.

I scowled at the phone. Two days in a row after radio silence. I doubted it was because he needed me. He had my cell phone number; he could easily call. Although he did love entering into my home at all hours of the night and perusing my house knowing full well I was watching him. I stepped away from my archives station and headed to the stairwell. My legs were stiff from the hike, the flight, and now sitting still hunching over the microfilm. It felt nice to stretch a little. I made up my mind with a deep breath. His phone rang four times before he answered. I watched him staring at his screen for all four rings before answering.

"Did you leave something in my house?" I asked.

I tried to keep the emotion out of my voice because had I let them creep out, they surely would have sounded a little wounded, a little mad, and a lot frustrated.

"Nothing physical, no." His low timber sent shock waves through my system. How had I forgotten the way his voice made me feel?

"Is there a reason you are trespassing into my home?" Maybe I let a little frustration seep out. At least I kept the wounded mad sneer out of my voice.

He sighed. I was watching him through the app and talking through my phone. He smiled and shook his head, "I was hoping to talk to you."

My breath caught, I swallowed the lump that had formed, "You could have called." I whispered to not betray the new rush of emotions, hope being one of them.

"In-person, where are you? I was hoping to catch you before you left for your day." He had wandered back into my bedroom. I saw him frown at my room looking the exact same as the day before.

“I’m not at a commutable distance currently.” I held my breath.

If he knew I was in Norway, it was possible he would guess what I am up to. Lying was out of the question because he could just as easily track my phone to determine where I am AND determine what I am doing AND be pissed that I lied about it.

He walked out of my bedroom and back into the kitchen to retrieve the kettle, “You would be surprised where I would be willing to go.”

I smiled. It was stupid to smile. Despite my abusive and neglectful childhood; and my general bad luck with love due to being a widow at thirty; I was still optimistic. I took a deep breath and closed my eyes, “I’m in Norway with Thomas. He wanted to see the fjords; reconnect with our heritage before he takes his next assignment. We just got in. I was in Iceland yesterday.”

His expression was unfathomable. Even from 5000 miles away I could feel the tension peeling off of him. I heard him breathe through his nose in frustration.

“What city?” His voice was deadpan, void of emotion.

“We flew into Oslo a few hours ago, but we are heading to Stavanger in the morning.”

I watched him close his eyes and roll his head back and forth, rubbing the back of his neck. I had seen him do that a few times. It normally meant he was beyond words frustrated and was trying to collect his thoughts before he spoke. It was clear he had an idea of what I was doing. I winced, but what choice did I have?

"Listen, Beck, you don't own the rights to visiting Oslo. I have ancestors here too. I heard you loud and clear, and the month of silence was even clearer."

He dropped his head back and his shoulders slumped. What did that mean?

"I will be back in a few days. Do you want me to call you when I get back in town?"

He shrugged; it was the first time I had ever seen his face look sad. He normally looked bored or mildly amused, but never sad.

"It's unimportant. Enjoy your trip." He hung up before I could respond. The butterflies he normally gave me turned sour in my stomach.

I walked back to my archives station with a little less wind beneath my wings. I was just convincing myself that snooping into his familial background was wrong when I hit pay dirt.

Leif Becken was a part of the Norwegian military from 1973-1983. He joined Interpol in 1984. He worked with a Japanese sect to help with drug trafficking that was starting in Japan and ending in Norway. He was reassigned in 1989. I found no other agent that was in Japan during the late eighties that had the last name, Becken. I printed out the information for further investigation. I was just leaving the library when a stroke of genius hit. I was being redirected to the newspaper archives when Thomas called. I ignored it, but he texted me.

Ro, I am going to be ready to go in about 30 minutes. I want to check out Karl Johans gate and the Royal Palace before we grab some lunch.

It gave me just enough time to check into my hunch and head back over to our hotel before he would know I was ever gone. I agreed as I pulled up newspaper microfilms from 1986. I was looking specifically for birthing announcements.

July 11, 1986, Leif Becken, welcomed a baby boy, Bekku Kazuo in Okinawa, Japan.

I blinked and rubbed my eyes. That was all the birth announcements said. It was entirely possible that Tadashi Becken was not his given name. I printed it out anyway and stashed it with the rest of the Leif Becken research. The only nugget of truth I held onto was the fact that he preferred to be called Beck, which could mean his given name was Bekku. I checked my watch. Shit. I had ten minutes to get across town. I hastily shoved all the research into my bag and headed back out to grab a taxi.

Thomas's nap had rejuvenated him to a point I wish I could have joined in his jubilation. I was tired from traveling; my emotions were frayed from Beck's unannounced visits, and the information I was sure was correct began to feel less accurate the more I thought about it.

Downtown Oslo was lovely. The crisp air and cloudless sky were an ideal backdrop to walk around the shopping areas. Lunch was a standard fare of lefse and fish. Thomas insisted we indulge in Krumkakes. He asked for clotted cream and strawberries, I ate mine plain. Thomas was the ideal traveling companion. We had similar temperaments and we were both willing to try local delicacies. Not all were great. We were both equally active in trying to experience the natural wonders of where we traveled to. The only drawback was the fact that at restaurants waiters assumed he was my husband. And Thomas tended to flirt heavily with any pretty waitress, so it always was uncomfortable to experience their apologetic expressions. A few times I had to blurt out that he was my brother. When the ladies found out about our familial bonds and that he was a doctor, it made me glad to have the foresight to have separate rooms. And glad he had access to antibiotics.

The drive to Stavanger was just as picturesque as the rest of the Nordic lands. Farmlands dotted the landscapes with ocean backgrounds taking up the other vistas. I had Thomas drive so I could do a little more research into Leif Becken's life.

Thomas complained, but I explained I was still getting the website running, so he was a little more understanding as I set up the hotspot.

ABOUT THE AUTHOR

Db Jacobson

DB is an American author that started writing as a hobby during the Covid-19 pandemic. The hobby quickly turned into a passion, writing eleven books in a feverish three months. DB uses her knowledge of the South, where she grew up, with the newfound knowledge of Southern California, where she moved in 2015. She is also a part of a large family, where she uses her experiences in navigating the different personalities that one family tends to have in her writing.

“I don’t know whether anyone will actually read these books, but I at least enjoyed writing them!” DB Jacobson

Connect with DB: on Instagram or TikTok @ dbjacobson-writes
Email: dbjacobsonwrites@gmail.com
Website: www.dbjacobson.com

BOOKS BY THIS AUTHOR

Finding Light

A human trafficking ring is terrorizing the young women of LA. In the meantime, Caroline gets roped into helping a new friend find a missing person, who just might be the key to figuring out the trafficking ring.

Catching Dark

A serial killer is on the loose in Southern California. Caroline works tirelessly to figure out who is guilty, so another woman does not fall victim to the SSS. While balancing her usual life with her nighttime investigations, her mysterious friend, Beck, keeps showing up when she least expects it. There is nothing like being attracted to a mystery man knowing there is no way for reciprocation.

Made in the USA
Columbia, SC
18 May 2022